Geraru s

Fortune

Robert Liebertz

I had lots of encouragement from friends and family when I started writing, but two people really helped me get to where I needed to be.

My wife Margaret Liebertz was patient, supportive and understanding when this book ate up so much of our time together. She let me ramble about my other universe, and helped me brainstorm ideas. Thank you for letting me sail away when the wind was blowing.

Rob Greisen has been helping me find trouble for over three decades now. As a coworker he sucked, as a friend he is terrific, but as my editor he has been exceptional. I handed him a thunderegg and he handed me back a cut crystal geode. Thank you for bringing out the inner beauty for the world to see.

Cover art by Nikole Beck

www.nilolorart.com

1

The dead elk emerged from the tree line and stepped into the clearing. It's watchful eye took in the meadow covered in snow: the pond, the clusters of bushes scattered here and there. The elk's breath was heavy in the still morning air, giant puffs of condensation blowing out in front of him. The technical name was European Red Deer, but the locals just called them elk. He was a good-sized male either seven or eight years old. It stood six feet at the shoulders and probably weighed 600 pounds. The antlers were five feet from tip to tip. The hunter could care less about the elk's antlers; it was the meat he was thinking about, food.

The hunter had been sitting in this spot for nearly three hours and was cold and stiff right down to his bones. His breath was slow and measured, to keep sound and condensation to a minimum. He had chosen this spot hours earlier after careful consideration. His hidden blind had been set up at a right angle to the game trail that emerged from the woods. He plotted out where the animal would most likely be, and then where he needed to be. His waiting spot had been cleared of anything that could make noise: leaves, twigs, and branches. His bow and arrows were placed where they could be picked up and nocked without the movement being seen by the prey.

The hunter crafted the arrows himself and tested them for accuracy, the shafts cut from a local ash tree that produced straight heavy wood, the flint tips painstakingly knapped and notched to fit each shaft. The fletching was made from White Tail Eagle feathers the hunter had collected while walking in the Kielder Forest. His bow was cut and carved from an old solid elm. The bowstring was a woven hemp rope he braided himself. Thin but strong, it could knock down larger animals... like the dead elk he was looking at today.

The elk was very much alive at the moment but that was not how the hunter thought of it once it entered the trap. In this clearing it had already been killed. The hunter had chosen the time and place. In his mind the elk had walked forward to where it was supposed to be. The hunter had taken aim, picked his spot, and softly released the arrow. The arrow was true and hit its mark. The elk fell, and the meat was harvested. Food.

The hunter picked up his bow and nocked an arrow but didn't move his head or stand up. The elk took more steps towards the pond and stopped again, looking and listening. The hunter waited patiently. Patience was hard, but rewarded. The animal moved forward again to the edge of the pond. It's feet broke through the thin ice there. It took one more look around, sniffed the air, then bowed its head to drink. The hunter was about to draw and aim when the elk's head snapped back up after only one quick sip. Taking one more look around, it then lowered its head again to drink fully.

William the Wolf drew the arrow back and slowly rose from his hidden blind. He was slightly behind the animal and out of its field of vision. He took careful aim, thinking about the anatomy of the elk. The soft 'twing' of the bowstring was the only sound he made. The shot landed exactly where he wanted it to be. The elk startled, bolting for the safety of the woods behind it.

William blew out a breath, stood and stretched. He gathered his gear and secured the bow over his shoulders. He walked forward to the spot where the elk had been drinking. Blood. He reached down and took the safety loop off his belt knife, but left it there for now. He followed the blood trail back into the woods. His shot was perfect so his quarry should be less than five hundred feet away.

He found the elk lying on its side in three hundred feet. It had already passed and didn't need the quick work of his knife to end any suffering. He took off his pack and looked at the trees around them. This is where the real work started.

It was early afternoon before William felt ready to head back home. The hide was hung tight between two trees with some cordage. He had packed up eighty pounds of meat to carry in a bag over his shoulder. The rest of the meat had been cut free, wrapped in another canvas bag, and hauled up into a tree. It would take him another two trips to bring everything home unless he could get a sled back out here.

With his gear packed up, William fitted his backpack on and then slung the bag of meat onto his shoulders. It was heavy but it also felt good. A reward, and a heavy reminder of a successful hunt and a good day's work. His hands and feet were cold, but he knew that once he started walking carrying all that weight, he would warm up fast.

Kathleen decided today was the day she would tell him. William left early for a hunt so she had time to make the day special. She cleaned the cabin and then spent some time on her appearance. A friend had given her some new purple ribbon that she braided into her hair and then put on one of her better dresses. Kathleen cut up vegetables for a stew and got them warming in a kettle hanging on an arm above the fireplace. She had traded for half a loaf of bread yesterday; she cut it thinly and spread a little of their precious butter between each slice. This was put into another kettle hung higher over the fire, it only needed to be warmed, not cooked. Now all she had to do was wait.

Lady Kathleen was originally from Montpelier Ireland. She came to England with her older sister Judith when the latter decided a change of scenery was needed. They fell in love with the town of Falstone England and both made fast friends. They preferred the small town feel of this hidden village to their former home. The two women talked from time to time about returning home to cold and foggy Ireland, but never seriously. Now Kathleen was married; and her heart was tied to the region. Their marriage was still new to both of them and they were learning to get along together. William the Wolf was the head gamekeeper for Dally Castle less than a mile away. The two of them met last spring at the open market where she was trading homemade wax candles. They smiled and talked and found they liked each other's company. They made it a point to seek each other out each week at the market and spend some time together. One of her friends told her he was called "the wolf" because of his temper but she had seen no evidence of it. Another friend told her it was because of his cunning and hunting ability. He was supposed to be one of the best. Regardless Kathleen was falling in love and by the fall they had made promises to each other.

It was afternoon before she heard his boots on the stairs of the porch. She put aside her sewing and went to the door to greet him. He was a mess as usual, covered with branches and leaves, but looked happy and exhausted. He lifted the heavy bag off his shoulder and dropped it onto a workbench outside the door with a heavy thud. She knew what that meant immediately.

"You got one?" Kathleen asked.

"Yes, a big one," William said and smiled his wolf smile, "I could only carry out some of it. I had to put the rest up in a tree until I got back."

Kathleen jumped into his arms and he swung her around twice. "I am so happy for you!"

"I need to get back out there with the sled and see if I can get it all back in one trip tonight," William said while removing the rest of his gear.

"But I have dinner ready for you, and you must be cold," Kathleen said, holding onto him.

"Let's share a quick dinner, but I need to get back out there. The faster I get that meat home, the less chance of scavengers getting to it. Wait until you see the hide. We could cover the whole floor with it once it's finished."

They moved inside and shut the door behind them. He had brought in some of the meat to be fried up in a skillet and he got to work cutting it up now. William was talking about drying some of the meat in the smoke shack and rubbing the rest down with salt to draw out the moisture. When the meat was ready they added it to the stew and stirred it for a few minutes before it was served into bowls. The two sat at the small table in the cabin. William wondered aloud if he could get their neighbor to go with him and help bring back the rest of the animal.

"We're having a baby," Kathleen said.

"What?" William said, spoon paused half way to his mouth.

"I'm pregnant. We're going to have a baby," she repeated.

Kathleen watched his face as it went through several changes. Surprise, happy, worried, happy, worried, happy.

"When?" He asked.

"Before summer I think, April or May."

"That's great news for us," William stated evenly.

"Are you happy?" Kathleen asked and held her breath.

He seemed to think about it for a few seconds before answering.

"Yes, I'm happy. Are you happy?" He asked back.

"Very much so," Kathleen said, "Our child can stay home with me, or go hunting with you. Either way, son or daughter, it matters not to me."

2

Gerard was born on May 13th, just after the couple moved into their new larger home. The home was a gift from their employer Edward the Black, Lord of Falstone, and his wife Lady Joan of Kent. The two couples were good friends despite the difference in social status. When Joan learned the couple was expecting she started a campaign with her husband to get William and Kathleen into a larger house. The house was completed just in time for the growing family, they couldn't be happier. Edward and Joan had been named Godparents and visited the couple often. They were trying to have children of their own but had no luck so far. The Lord and Lady had a rare marriage based on love; it was a good match. They were good people, kind to each other, and that compassion overflowed to the staff, servants, and citizens of the realm.

Dally Castle was located in Falstone England, eight miles south of the Scottish border. Falstone was a small village located in Northumberland just inside the Kielder Forest. The region received significant rainfall during the year, with snow throughout the winter months. Conversely, they enjoyed mostly clear and sunny days from May to September. Falstone was a gem of a town set in a lush and untamed landscape. The area was full of lakes, streams, and abundant game. It was a hunting destination town for hunters, sportsmen, and royalty.

Gerard started following his father on hunts as soon as he could walk. He watched, listened, and learned. He picked up tracking like it was second nature and soon he tracked better than most adults. He started using a small bow at three years old. He would become frustrated when his shots would not group the way he wanted, and would stay out and practice until he improved, his mom made him come inside, or it got too dark to see. He begged his parents to shoot muskets at age four, but they made him wait until his sixth birthday before they gave in. Even then William and Edward made him practice dry firing for a month until he could disassemble and reassemble the musket properly. Once he had the proper mechanics down, they finally let him shoot actual balls with powder. Of course, he loved it. He practiced as often as he was allowed. He'd shot wild boar and fallow deer at four years old with his bow. When he was five, he was allowed to hunt small black bears and chamois. The summer he turned six he shot his first elk with a musket. It was a great haul of meat for his family and the castle, but it felt less sporting than his bow did. He still practiced with the musket often, but preferred his bow and arrows on big hunts.

Gerard's life was split into two different worlds. On one side there was the time he spent hunting with his father. He listened to the advice, learned the tricks and practiced the skills. The other side was the time he spent learning with his mother. Kathleen taught him to read and write at the table in their home. She taught him math so he could keep accurate accounts and be in charge of his own money one day. She taught him games of skill, games of chance, and games of strategy. Cards, dice, checkers and chess. The two would spend hours playing a game and then hours more breaking down the victory, learning from the mistakes, and planning for the next game. She made sure he understood that you can lose a game and still learn from the lesson. You could lose now to win later. His favorite games were those of strategy and trying to outwit an opponent. She also kept him well supplied with books of adventures from all over the world. His favorites were books of ships sailing on the sea.

3

The summer he was seven years old Gerard was asked to lead a hunt for a visiting member of a royal house. James, Marquis of Lennox was passing through and had stopped to visit Edward the Black. The Marquis had six 'yes' men in his entourage whose only purpose was to listen to him tell stories. Over dinner the subject of hunting came up; and Edward invited them to go hunting with him sometime. Intrigued by the idea, the Marquis decided to delay his trip another day and announced they should go hunting the following day.

A messenger from the castle showed up at Gerard's home, stating that a guide was needed for a hunt the following morning. His father William had gone north to Glasgow two days prior and would be gone another four days. Gerard had been guiding hunts on his own for over a year now, but nobody more important than locals. He got his gear together and laid everything out to be ready to go first thing.

The next morning Gerard rose early, and headed to the castle before the sun was up. He waited in the common room until Lord Edward made his appearance. The Lord asked where William was and Gerard explained that he was in Scotland for a few days. Edward paused and seemed to be thinking about this when Gerard spoke up.

"I can guide your group, Sir Edward. I have been leading hunts on my own for nearly a year now. I will make sure your guest gets a good prize," Gerard said.

Edward nodded and said no more. He asked if Gerard had eaten and Gerard said he had been fed and his mom had packed him food for the hunt.

The early morning start turned into a late morning start by the time the Marquis of Lennox and his men were ready. The Marquis was already making comments about the young guide and the probability of them coming home empty handed. Gerard had been taught by his father to keep his mouth shut and said nothing. After the first barb, Edward the Black told the Marquis that Gerard was one of the best hunting guides in the region. The Marquis brushed this aside and the cutting remarks and jokes kept coming. Gerard was good natured and tried to let them all just roll off his back. The Marquis had four of his guests accompany him, while Edward had two guards with him. The group of nine collected horses from the livery and Gerard led them south into the Kielder Forest.

They rode for less than an hour to an area where the elk had been gathering for the past few weeks. Gerard had them stop and tie off the horses before cresting the last ridge on foot. The Marquis and his men struggled up the hill complaining while Gerard, Edward and his soldiers climbed up quickly. From the treeline on top of the hill they could see the herd moving down a valley that would come around the corner to their right. Gerard led the group down the side of the hill and located the game trail that the herd would come walking down. Gerard pointed out the spot where the Marquis should crouch and wait, then started to place the other men. The Marquis of Lennox interrupted him talking loud enough to scare away the elk on the next ridge.

"I think I can handle it from here, boy. Why don't you get out of the way so you don't get hurt."

The Marquis was standing in what Gerard figured was the bolt hole where the elk would run when startled.

Gerard tried one more time. "But sir, I think that you. . ."

The Marquis of Lennox cuffed him on the side of the head hard enough to knock him over.

"Shut up you street urchin, and stay out of my way," The Marquis said.

Gerard picked himself up and moved as far away from the Marquis as possible. He saw Edward watching him but he was too embarrassed to look back. Once everyone settled into their waiting spots, they got quiet and waited for the elk. Gerard quietly drifted over to where one of Edwards' soldiers was waiting. The soldier named Whitehead had been fair to Gerard in the past. Gerard got as close as he could and whispered to the soldier out of the side of his mouth.

"The Marquis is in the bolt hole, he is going to get trampled."

"You sure?" Whitehead asked with a smile.

"Pretty sure, I was trying to warn him," Gerard said.

"Yes, I heard you try. Well there is no use for it now, so better keep quiet," Whitehead said, and then walked over to where the other guard Collins was standing to whisper in his ear. Whatever he said made the other guard cheer up significantly.

A short time later the leading edge of the herd came around the corner down the trail. Two big males in front, with a large group of cows between them. The animals moved slowly and leisurely despite their large size, eating grasses as they walked. The group waited in silence for the guest of honor, the Marquis, to take his shot. The Marquis's musket had been made ready and the hammer cocked above the pan. The Marquis of Lennox tracked the lead male from his spot, when it was even with his position he fired and shot the elk in the neck.

The crack of the shot broke the calm of the herd and they scattered. The hunting guide knew the herd would go right, left, and backwards. The ones in the back turned and ran. The ones in the middle scattered. The ones in the front had a hillside on their right, and an open trail to the left. They all ran left. The Marquis stood to claim his prize and was promptly knocked down and trampled by one bull and three cows. Lord Edward and the entourage ran to where the Marquis was yelling, while Gerard stayed exactly where he was. He took a look at Edward's soldiers. They were laughing now, but he knew they would be stone faced once the Marquis was upright. Whitehead looked at Gerard and saluted him before getting his professional mask back on.

The Marquis of Lennox had taken a blow to the chest, and got stepped on twice: once in the thigh, and once in the abdomen. He was helped to his feet as his friends pulled grasses off him and tried to wipe some of the dirt off. He was limping and crouched over in pain as they led him back to the horses. Gerard put his guide face on showing no emotion, and not making eye contact with anyone. He untied the Marquis's horse and brought it forward so the Marquis didn't have to walk as far. When the Marquis was close enough, he slapped Gerard hard in the face and knocked him down again. Gerard was stunned and his ears were ringing but he saw Edward step in front of him.

"You had no cause to do that," Edward the Black said.

"That little shit didn't do his job. He should have warned me," the Marquis said furious.

"He tried to, twice, and you told him to shut up and knocked him down."

"What is he to you? Why do you defend the boy?" the Marquis asked.

Edward moved fast and closed the distance between them until he was face to face with the Marquis. He was much closer than normal talking distance but not quite nose to nose distance. Edward dropped his voice and spoke in a growl that Gerard had never heard before.

"He has pledged to serve me and my kingdom; and those who serve me are under my protection. Nobody fucks with my people. Not even you."

The group helped the Marquis back onto his horse, and everyone else climbed up onto their horses except Gerard. He stood quietly off to the side. The Marquis noticed him and yelled.

"We are leaving, what are you waiting for?"

Gerard stared silently at his feet.

"Gerard?" Edward said.

"He shot him in the neck, sir. It's out there bleeding and suffering. I need to find him and help him on his way. It's not right that we leave him, sire. It's not right," Gerard said, on the verge of tears.

Edward slid off his horse and tied it back up.

"You men head back and help the Marquis get settled. I'll catch up with you later," Edward said.

"I request permission to stay, sir," Whitehead said.

"Fine, the rest of you go. Collins will lead you back."

The Marquis turned his horse and started back the way they had come. Collins and the rest of the men kicked their horses to catch up.

Edward motioned for Gerard to proceed; he and Whitehead walked behind him. Gerard quickly found the blood trail and followed it, while Edward walked next to him.

"I'm sorry Gerard, I should have warned you to stay away from him after he was ran down," Whitehead said.

Edward the Black looked at his soldier above Gerard's head and made eye contact.

"He knew the Marquis was going to get trampled and came over and told me. I could have spoken up but I wanted to see that arrogant bollocks knocked on his arse," Whitehead said.

"He had no courage when I got in his truth range." Edward said.

"What's a truth range?" Gerard asked.

"When you move forward and put your face in somebody else's face, close enough to make them uncomfortable. That is what I call the truth range. They may still try to lie to you with their words, but their eyes cannot lie. You can see everything you're looking for in the truth range: fear, lies, courage, truth, and honor." Edward said.

"Your voice changed too, like the sound of a sword being pulled out of a scabbard," Gerard said.

Edward smiled. "I had never heard it put like that before Gerard but that is exactly what I was doing. Your voice is a weapon. It is much more powerful than your knife; and changing it is like putting your hand on the handle of your sword. You are warning someone without using words, but your meaning is clear."

They walked in silence for a time while Edward the Black tried to think of how to describe to Gerard what happened earlier with the Marquis and why it happened. It was obvious to him and Whitehead being adults, but not to Gerard who had almost no court experience.

"Gerard, you need to learn how to talk to people older than you, especially those of upper classes," Edward said.

"I don't understand what I did wrong sir. I tried to warn him."

"Yes you did, but you didn't do it in the right way," Edward said and thought about how to explain this.

"You are an expert hunter and guide, but most people don't see that; they see a small boy. They won't take suggestions from you, and they definitely won't take orders from you. You have to find a way to make them think your idea was their idea. You are just there to point out the obvious," Edward said.

"I don't understand why," Gerard said.

"People older than you, and those with higher status, need to feel superior to you, even if they are not. You have to pretend they are smart, or they get mad, like the Marquis did. It's a game all of us adults play. It's full of hundreds of secret rules and clues that everyone must follow, even me," Edward said.

"If the rules are secrets, how am I supposed to learn them?"

"I guess somebody who understands the game very well will have to teach you," Edward said, smiling and putting his hand on Gerard's shoulder.

They tracked the elk nearly a mile before they found him panting hard in a thicket under a tree. Blood ran down his neck and stained the side of his hide while he ran. Its eyes were wild with fright and pain.

Gerard stepped in front of Edward and Whitehead, drawing his knife while speaking softly to the elk in front of him.

"It's okay my friend, I am here to help you. Do not be afraid." Gerard crept towards the wounded animal.

4

When Gerard was nine years old something clicked in his head and his two worlds merged into one. He realized that the skills from one side of his life could be applied to the other side of his life. Hunting games in the woods were like strategy games at the table. Setting traps and using misdirection were skills he could use in all areas of his life. Being patient, waiting for your opponent to make a mistake, worked in both worlds. Using bait or setting an ambush could be used anywhere. Once Gerard started looking at every challenge as a game, he started winning. He became more successful on his hunts. He became a better winner and a better loser. He figured out that in order to know what your opponent will most likely do, you need to know what he should do, what he could do, and what he might do. If you were prepared for any possibility, you were never playing catch up. If you had a plan for every move your opponent could make, your chances of winning improved. Outsmarting animals was challenging and fun. Outsmarting people was more challenging, but more fun.

His ongoing practice with bows and muskets kept his skills up and by the time he was ten years old he was being hired to lead hunts on a regular basis. He started to get a reputation as the lucky guide. He always found the herd. He put shooters in the right spots. His tips were always spot on. By the time Gerard was eleven, he was being hired out as often as his father as a hunting guide. Gerard even had a better success rate, not that he was keeping track of course.

5

Lady Sophie of Falstone was born two years after Gerard and the children grew up together. Sophie was a bright child but wanted nothing to do with the court and girly things. She snuck out regularly and ran the half mile to the new house where Gerard lived. The two of them would play in the woods or she would tag along with Gerard while he went on hunts. At first she was a nuisance scaring off most of the animals and complaining about the cold. Gerard ended up making a second set of hunting clothes for her complete with fur lined boots and soft winter gloves they kept hidden at his house.

They were walking back from an unsuccessful hunt one day when everything changed for Gerard. The prey had gotten away and Gerard was upset. Seven-year-old Sophie kept pestering him as to why he was angry until finally Gerard lashed out and told her it was all her fault.

"You sat up too quickly and made a noise. Either one of those would have been enough to scare off the deer, but together you may as well have yelled a warning to the animal. If I was alone today, I would have brought home a deer, but because of you we go home empty handed," Gerard said.

Sophie had wanted to see the deer and had stood up as it approached. It had not occurred to her that this would make it run away. She was also unaware that she had made any noise. They walked in silence for a time before Sophie spoke to Gerard. "Why didn't you tell me not to move? I would have sat still had you asked me. How was I supposed to know?"

Gerard thought about this and realized he had just expected her to know. He started thinking about all the teaching his father had done for him and wondered if anyone was teaching Sophie anything.

As they walked Gerard thought about where to place the blame. Sophie didn't know how to hunt because nobody had ever taught her. She tagged along often enough but now he realized that he had tolerated her instead of teaching her. Sophie was smart, but not a mind reader. Gerard also understood that nobody in the castle was going to teach Lady Sophie about hunting, it was just not something girls did. There was only one person in the world to teach Sophie about hunting, and that was him.

"I'm sorry Sophie, I thought you knew that part already. I guess I have done a poor job of teaching you so far. How about from now on I tell you what I am doing and why, and you ask me questions about things you don't understand? That way both of us will get smarter at the same time."

"I would like that Gerard, thank you for not being mad at me. I will not make that mistake again I promise," Sophie said, looking hopeful.

"I am not mad at you Sophie, you're my best friend."

Sophie smiled.

"As your best friend," Gerard continued, "I need to do a better job teaching you about hunting. Father says that everyone in the game of life is either a hunter or the hunted. I need to make sure you are prepared for the game." Gerard looped his arm in hers.

Once he explained to her what she was doing wrong, she never repeated the same mistake. He taught her some of the tricks he knew, and then taught her to shoot a bow and arrow. She was rough at first and lacked the arm strength to pull the smaller bow he had used when he was younger. With practice she grew stronger and more confident, and her aim improved. She was coming over more often now and practicing her archery whenever she could. Gerard insisted she spend some time each day shooting left-handed as well.

Sophie told Gerard she wanted to hunt something on her own. Gerard said he would be her guide and help her, but her aim needed to get better before they shot at live animals. When she asked why he told her about missed shots on animals, animals suffering, and bad hunters putting them in unnecessary pain. Sophie realized she had not thought about this part of hunting, and promised to work to get better. Another two weeks went by; her aim improved with practice.

The two of them snuck out early one morning and headed into a dense section of the forest where Gerard had seen wild turkeys in the past. They walked quietly though the area, looking and listening. They heard the turkey call in the distance and worked their way towards the sound. Sophie had learned to watch her feet and not make noise when she walked. They came to a small rise and stopped behind it to peek over the top. Three turkeys were scratching and feeding in the clearing in front of them. Two medium sized birds and one larger bird. They ducked back down below the hillside and took their bows off their shoulders. Gerard talked her through the process again step-by-step: remember, the turkey is already dead, watch it until it turns away, rise up slowly and quietly, draw and hold on target. Imagine your shot, imagine it going into the spot you choose. Let your breath out slow and quiet, release the arrow while you exhale. Sophie nodded and nocked her arrow. She looked over the top of the mound again and watched the turkeys. They were moving from right to left, slightly away from her. One of them always seemed to be facing her direction. She was getting frustrated and Gerard, lying next to her, put his lips next to her ear. "Patience," he whispered. The birds had moved further left now and were soon going to be out of her range. The turkeys found a good spot and all three put their heads down at once. Sophie took a quiet breath and sat up slowly while drawing. She aimed, held, pictured the shot, and released with her exhale.

Her shot was true; the large turkey flapped twice and was still. The two smaller turkeys fled into the underbrush and were gone in seconds. Sophie and Gerard walked forward to check on their prey. Gerard normally retrieved her arrows, but told her she needed to do this one on her own. He showed her how to pull the arrow out without damaging the meat. She cleaned the arrow off and put it back in her quiver. Gerard put the turkey in a bag and told her she did well. Sophie hugged him and thanked him for his help. She had tears in her eyes and he asked if she was upset over the killing.

"No," she said. "I'm just so happy. Nobody lets me do anything important except you. This is real! I did this! We can eat turkey tomorrow because of me." She began to cry. Gerard didn't know much about girls yet, but he knew about his friend. He hugged her until she was done.

They walked back to the house in a great mood with Gerard carrying the turkey. Sophie talked about what she wanted to go after next. She wanted to try bigger game. Gerard explained that her smaller bow had limitations with weight and knock down power. She would need to work up to a bigger bow to go after bigger game.

When they got back to Gerard's house their four parents were standing on the porch waiting for them. Sophie's parents were furious. She had missed an important event this morning that she had been expected to attend. She had never mentioned it to Gerard. Her mother scolded her first and then her father took over. He was upset that she had disregarded her duties of the court. He told her she had no business following Gerard into the woods while he hunted. For the first time he looked at Gerard and noticed the big turkey in a bag.

"That's a fine turkey Gerard, good hunting," Lord Edward the Black said.

"Yes it's a fine turkey, but the credit belongs to Sophie. She tracked it and she shot it herself. I was just along as her guide," Gerard said.

For the first time Edward noticed the bow across his daughter's shoulders. He held his hand out for it and she reluctantly handed it over. He studied it for a few moments and then asked Gerard if it was his.

"Yes sir, one of my older bows. Sophie needs a bigger bow before she goes after bigger game. We started out small with a turkey," Gerard said.

Edward now really looked at Sophie standing next to Gerard. She had a defiant look on her face. She was dressed in clothing he didn't recognize, hunter's clothing that matched Gerard's.

"And this?" Edward said, pointing to her boots and clothing.

"I didn't want her to be cold so we made her clothing from some of my furs and hides. I made the poncho and boots, and Sophie made the gloves and the hat," Gerard said.

"I see," Edward said.

"She is a good hunter sir, and has good instincts. Never makes the same mistake twice," Gerard said.

"Let's go home Sophie. Bring your turkey. I'll show you how to feather it and dress it," Lord Edward the Black said. He walked away towards the castle. His wife followed. Gerard handed the sack over to Sophie who took it and then hugged Gerard once more before following her parents.

"You can't keep taking Lady Sophie of Dally Castle out hunting the woods, Gerard!" His father said. "It's not proper for a lady like her. If we make Lord Edward mad, he is going to sack us. You need to straighten up, and know your role."

6

He didn't see Sophie for the next two weeks. He wasn't worried about her, but he did miss his friend. He was walking along a cart path when Lord Edward came up riding horseback with three other men. They reined in the horses when they saw him. The group of men stopped but didn't dismount.

"Good morning Lord Edward," Gerard said. "How fare thee?"

"I am well, Gerard. How are you today?" The Lord asked.

"I am doing well, thank you. How is Lady Sophie?" Gerard asked.

Lord Edward told his fellow riders to go ahead and he would catch up with them. The three other men kicked the horses and they moved forward.

"I wanted to apologize if I did something wrong, sir. I didn't know Sophie had an important engagement that day," Gerard said.

"Yes, she told us you didn't know," Edward replied. "You didn't do anything wrong, Gerard. Sophie must learn to be a Lady, not a hunter. She has obligations and responsibilities to attend to."

"I understand, sir. It's just that. . ." Gerard trailed off.

"Just what?" Edward said.

"Why can't she be both?" Gerard said. "Couldn't hunting skills help her be a better Lady? She has already learned when to be patient and when to attack. She knows when to be quiet and when to make noise to flush out the game. I still need to teach her about concealment, ambushing, bait, and misdirection. I just think the more she knows, the smarter Lady she will be."

Edward looked at him for a long time. So long that Gerard felt he should say something else.

"I am sorry if I have misspoke sir. My father told me I need to stay within my role."

"And what is your role, Gerard?" Edward asked.

"I am a hunting guide. I would like to teach my friend Sophie to be a hunter in the world, instead of being hunted."

"You have given me much to think about Gerard, thank you. You speak without fear, which is something I look for in my advisors," Edward said. He kicked his horse forward and moved off to catch up with the others.

Another ten days passed by with no contact from his friend. Then one morning Sophie was at his door. She had a new bow but the same boots, hat and gloves.

"Come on, we need to go practice," Sophie said. "I need to break in this new bow if I am ever going to take down an elk."

"Are you . . . allowed to be here?" Gerard asked tentatively.

"Yes I am allowed to be here, as long as I keep up with my studies and don't miss any more formal functions. Father said in this world you are either a hunter or the hunted. He wants me to be prepared for whatever the future holds for me. So are we going to break in this new bow or what?"

7

Gerard and Sophie left before dawn. The mountain ridge they were hiking to was just under five miles away, and of course it was mostly uphill. A group of white rams had been seen on the rocky cliffs. That was their prize if they were lucky. They were traveling south and west mostly by foot trails, as there were no carts or roads in this direction. They had just crossed a ridge and stopped for a short break and a drink of water. Gerard excused himself to use the privy and walked a short distance away to a cluster of trees. He had just started back when he heard Sophie give a surprised yell. He started running but slowed down and got quiet when he heard multiple male voices talking.

"Don't fight like that dearie, we only mean you a little harm," one man said. Gerard crept close and looked around some trees. Two men were holding Sophie and two more men were standing in front of them. Four grown adults. Gerard was two weeks past his thirteenth birthday.

Sophie yelled for them to let her go, she was Lady Sophie of Dally Castle and her father was Lord Edward the Black. The men laughed and said she was a long way from home, and they were going to have a little bit of fun first. Gerard crept closer and reached through the trees for his new bow and quiver. It was a gift from Edward for his birthday. He belted the quiver around his waist and pulled three arrows putting two between his teeth. He allowed himself one deep breath to center himself. Then he stepped out from behind the trees and faced the four dead men.

The biggest man was holding Sophie by the hair and he shot that man in the neck. It was an easy shot at this distance, and he wanted maximum blood for effect. Gerard nocked the second arrow and drew before the other three even turned around to look at him. The second man holding Sophie's arm he shot in the chest right in the heart. The man grabbed the arrow as he slumped to the ground. The third man pulled a knife and ran towards him as Gerard took the third arrow from his mouth, nocked it fast and fired at the charging man. The gut shot hit the man low and stopped his charge, he slumped to the ground saying, "No no no no!"

The fourth man had stepped behind Sophie and pulled a knife which was now across her neck. Gerard took his time now and pulled two more arrows. He put one in his mouth and nocked the second one. He took careful aim at the man standing behind Sophie, who ducked behind her. He pivoted to the wounded man sitting on the ground and shot him in the heart. He was less than ten feet away and the shot knocked the man flat, stopping his crying almost immediately. Gerard took the other arrow out of his mouth and nocked it. He walked forward until he was thirty feet from Sophie and the man behind her. Thirty feet was the distance they started shooting practice with every session.

"I will give you one chance to walk away from here alive," Gerard said. "Let her go and you have my word I will let you live."

"You're just a kid!" The man screamed. "I don't take orders from kids."

"Neither did your friends. Last chance, let her go." Gerard said. He drew and held, and sighted on Sophie's right ear.

The man was right-handed and kept peeking out the right side of her head. Sophie was talking to him now, trying another route. She said she had some money in her bag and the man was welcome to it if he let her go. He asked how much money and Sophie rattled off a ridiculously high number. The man behind her was asking where the money was in her backpack and had leaned out to show less than two inches of his face. Gerard could see his eye though, and it would have to be enough. Gerard took a breath and let it out slowly. Sophie saw the breath and closed her eyes and stood rock still.

When he let the arrow go, he thought it was too close. His cry would never reach her in time but he opened his mouth to yell her name anyway. The arrow disappeared into her hair just above her right ear. He heard the familiar crack of an arrow on bone and his heart stopped. He thought he hit her, had cut it too close. The man behind her crumpled to the ground with the arrow sticking out of his cheek. His eyes were open and blinking but he was not moving or speaking. Sophie still had her eyes shut and had not moved. Gerard rushed forward and pulled her into a hug. She went panicky for half a second and then hugged him back once she realized who it was. They held each other for a few seconds before he stepped back and touched the side of her head. Just a hint of blood here. The arrow had nicked her. He pulled her back into the hug.

"I'm sorry, I'm sorry, it was too close!" Gerard said.

"It's okay, I'm fine," Sophie said. "I knew you wouldn't hurt me."

He held her for a while until they both stopped shaking. He looked down at the last man on the ground and saw that he was still alive and his eyes were moving all around. He moved back a step and asked if she wanted to take a short walk while he dispatched the last man.

"No, I'll do it." she said.

"Your father told me once that killing a man affects you differently than killing an animal. It's much different than putting down a deer or a boar, it weighs heavier on your mind. I would not put that burden on you if I could help it," Gerard said, tapping her forehead.

"You can take a walk if you want, but I'm doing it," she said, already back to her usual self.

"No, I'll be right here with you," Gerard said and pulled his knife.

Gerard took a knee next to the man on the ground.

"You should have taken orders from a kid," he said, handing the knife to Sophie.

"Tell me the best way to do it," she said, looking at Gerard.

"Picture where the heart is. Start from just below it between the ribs, up and in, nice and quick," Gerard explained.

Sophie took a breath, and then did it. The man's eyes went wide for a second and then relaxed and went flat. She seemed frozen for a moment so Gerard put his hand around hers and helped her pull the knife back out. He took it from Sophie, cleaned it off, and put it back into his belt.

"I'm sorry, Sophie," he said.

"What for?"

"Sorry this happened, sorry it ruined our day." He got up and started collecting arrows from the men. He cleaned each one and put them back in his quiver. Sophie gathered her gear back up that had been kicked around in the struggle.

"What should we do with them?" Sophie asked.

"Let me move them off the trail."

He worked quickly, dragging the bodies off the trail and over a log off to the side. The bodies were out of sight, and would probably not be found. Gerard and Sophie shouldered their packs and started for home.

"Father is going to freak out," Sophie said. She checked the side of her head again, it had already stopped bleeding. "I'm missing some hair right there. That was a very close shave," she said, and started giggling. What started small grew until she was snorting and honking.

Eventually Gerard joined in too and they laughed together on the trail. When she had wound down like a clock and got herself under control, he took her hand and they started the long walk home.

Gerard walked her up to the front door of the castle, past the outside guards but still outside the front door.

"Do you want me to come in and help you tell it? It might be easier," Gerard said.

"No, I am doing this on my own. I want my father to see how strong I can be before he gets angry. I am Lady Sophie of Dally Castle, killer of men who would do me harm," she said. "Thank you for saving me, Gerard. I was afraid until I saw you step out with your bow. You had the wolf face on, and I knew they were all dead already." She hugged him again and walked inside, back straight and head up.

Gerard turned and headed for home. He found the house empty and sat down at the table to eat a small lunch. He was just finishing up when he heard the horses out front. He walked outside to find Lord Edward the Black, six guards, and an empty horse. Lord Edward looked as angry as he had ever seen him. He was boiling. "Get on," he said. Gerard ducked back inside and grabbed his backpack and put his knife belt back on. He also grabbed his bow and quiver because it was his habit to be prepared for anything. He hurried back outside and jumped on the horse. Edward motioned for him to lead and he set off towards the trail in what he thought was a good pace. Edward urged him to ride faster and they trotted for a few seconds. Edward said faster and they cantered, Edward said faster and they galloped. Edward yelled faster and Gerard leaned down and got a fistful of mane and held on for life. They covered three plus miles in seven minutes by his estimate. The horses were blowing air but had not lathered up just yet. Gerard's horse was doing the best because he was the lightest rider. He slowed it down as the area they'd been attacked came into view, and slowed down again a hundred yards out. He took the horse down to a walk as they entered the clearing and brought his horse to a stop. He dismounted and was going to hold the reins for Edwards' horse, but he slid off the side and landed on his feet. The guards dismounted and gathered in the reins to hold for the group.

"Show me," Lord Edward the Black said. Gerard led him over to the edge of the clearing and the fallen log that marked the edge of the drop off. Gerard hopped over the log with Edward close behind. The dead men were right where he left them, lined up in a row. Edward checked each man, and examined the locations of every arrow hole. The six guards had lined up on the edge of the drop off, watching and listening to them.

"Tell me everything, leave nothing out," Edward said in a growl.

Gerard told him the whole tale starting with them leaving his house. Him walking away to go to the bathroom, hearing the men, grabbing his bow and arrows. Putting them in his mouth. Hearing Sophie identify herself as the Lord's daughter and it having no effect on the men. He stepped out and started killing the men.

"Who was first, and why?" Edward said, interrupting him.

Gerard stepped forward and pointed at the first dead man. "The biggest man, the biggest threat, also the one doing most of the talking. He was holding her by the ponytail and it pissed me off," Gerard said and earned the first small smile from Edward.

"Continue," he said.

"I shot him in the neck. I wanted lots of blood to scare the other men. Next I shot the man on her left side holding her arm. I shot him in the heart because I wanted to put him down fast. The third man charged; I gut shot him just to stop him. The fourth had stepped behind her and was using her as a shield with a knife on her neck. While he did that, I put a second arrow into the man who charged me to put him down for keeps. I closed distance on Sophie and the dead man holding her until I was thirty feet away. That is the distance we start every practice session at."

"The dead man?" Edward asked.

"He was already dead, I just hadn't put the arrow in him yet," Gerard said.

"Continue," Edward said.

"He was standing directly behind her, giving away nothing. He was right-handed and kept peeking out the right hand side. I drew and held on Sophie's right ear and waited. He was looking out every few seconds and then ducking back, but never showing me more than half an eye. I waited. Sophie was offering him money from her bags that I know she didn't have. He peeked out half an eye and paused to ask her something. I moved off Sophie's ear one quarter inch and took the shot. I took him in the cheek right below the eye, but I cut it too close. My arrow nicked her. I'm sorry sir, I would never do anything to hurt Sophie." Gerard took a moment to gather himself. "The man on the ground was still alive, but dead from the eyes down. I told Sophie to take a walk while I dispatched him but she refused. She said his life was hers to take. I tried to talk her out of it, told her how killing a person is harder like you said, but she was adamant. She asked me how to do it and I showed her, helped her. She stabbed him in the heart and that was that. I pulled the bodies off the trail, and decided we should head back. Sophie mentioned she was okay with pressing on and still hunting the rams today but I told her it was enough for one day, and you and Lady Joan would have my hide if I delayed your return," Gerard said.

Edward was quiet for a little bit of time. "Were you scared, boy?"

"No sir, not at all. I mean yes but. . ." Gerard stopped and arranged his thoughts. "I was not afraid for me sir, but I was terrified for Sophie. I have never been so scared in my whole life. Not even when that badger climbed the tree after me when I was five. I would do anything to keep her safe, and I would have gladly given my life to save hers today. It only took me a few seconds to realize the only way to save her was to kill them all and kill them quick. So I did."

Edward was looking at the men and the holes. He found the man with the hole in his cheek and the hole under his heart. He whistled once, sharp and loud. The guards up on the ridge snapped to attention and one of the soldiers inquired, "Yes, Lord Edward?"

"I want these men searched, turned inside out. Get me everything you can." He picked up the dead man's right hand and broke a finger sideways with a crack. "I want to know who they are, and where they came from." Another finger was broken. "If you have to cut off their heads and carry them around in a bag to show people, then do it." Another finger was broken. "Start with the nearest towns and work your way outwards." Another two fingers were broken loudy. "I want to know everything about them and your deadline was three days ago. Are we clear on this, Captain?"

"Sir! Yes Sir!" the man yelled. Lord Edward the Black dropped the right hand and picked up the left hand.

A short while later he led Gerard up the hill and back to the horses. He climbed aboard his horse and told Gerard to mount up and ride with him. The ride back was slow and quiet. Gerard was wondering how much anger the Lord held for him when Edward spoke. "I am not mad at you Gerard, so get that out of your head. You protected my Sophie, and for that I can never repay you. Thank you for doing what needed to be done."

"I am sorry I nicked her, sir," Gerard said.

"She is already showing it off like a war wound to the servants. She seems rather proud of it." Edward paused, his face grew stern. "I am angry because I am her Father. It is my job to protect her. I should have kept her from trouble, I should have prevented this somehow, I should have saved her."

"But you did protect her and save her," Gerard said.

"How do you figure that?" Edward asked.

"You entrusted her to me, and I would kill any man who tries to harm her."

8

Later at home Gerard's mother returned from the market and asked how the hunt went. He told her they didn't make it today and would try again another time. She didn't ask any further and he didn't volunteer anything just yet. He was afraid his parents would be mad at him and might not let him hunt for a while. His father was away for a few days so he didn't have to avoid him.

The next morning, he was having breakfast with his mother when he heard horses in front. They walked outside onto the porch as Lady Joan rode up with a group of four guards. One of the guards dismounted quickly and held her horse for her. She was helped down by another guard and walked deliberately towards the porch. She walked up and crushed Gerard in a hug and held him as she started to cry. She whispered thank you several times as her body shook, and eventually she stopped crying but still held him until she got herself back under control again. Gerard hugged her back but didn't know what to say. His mother was watching and looked terrified. When she was done she leaned back and kissed him once on the cheek before stepping back. Kathleen asked Joan if she would like to come in for tea and explain to her what exactly was going on. Joan looked at Gerard with a stern eye.

"And you didn't even tell your mother. You are in so much trouble." Joan winked at him. She walked towards Kathleen and looped her arm and directed them both inside the house.

"I would love some tea while we catch up," Joan said.

Gerard saw his chance and ran for the woods.

Later towards dusk he walked back towards home from the woods. He had several places where he liked to hide out and had spent the afternoon in one of them. There was a horseshoe bend in the river where it felt like the water whispered to you from all sides. He figured he wasn't in trouble, but some cooling off time for his mother was a good thing. At least the horses and guards were gone. He stopped on the porch and took off his boots, walking inside on soft feet. His mom was sitting in the rocker by the fireplace, reading a book. She closed the book when he came in and rose to meet him.

"Are you hungry?" She asked.

"No."

She held out her arms and he went to her and she hugged him tight.

"So proud of you, so proud," she said and rocked him back and forth.

The nightmares started not long after that. They varied in their structure but the common theme was always the same. Gerard was not fast enough and Sophie died. Gerard missed a shot and Sophie died. Gerard didn't see the fifth man hiding and Sophie died. Then there was the one that always woke him up with a scream nocked in his throat, Gerard's arrows caught the side of her face and he killed Sophie himself.

Sometimes the nightmares happened a few times a week; sometimes only a few times a month, but they never went away. He rarely got back to sleep after having one. Gerard found that shooting arrows in the dark helped calm his mind. After some nightmares he found he didn't need much light to hit the target. Some nights he didn't need any light at all. One night after a particularly bad nightmare he shot thirty arrows from thirty feet until he had a round where every one of them ended up in the center ring. Exhausted and satisfied he left the arrows where they were and staggered back inside wanting to lay down. He happened to wake up early the next day and found his mother outside crying looking at the arrows. After that, he made sure to collect his arrows and put the target away, no matter how tired he was.

9

Every time he saw Sophie after that day on the ridge, the first thing he did was reach up and tuck some hair behind her right ear. It allowed him to touch the light scar he had put there, and was a way for him to apologize without saying it aloud. She smiled every time he did it; it became their greeting. His relationship with Lord Edward the Black and Lady Joan also changed. He was ordered to call them Edward and Joan, and received glaring reprimands when he failed to do so. He received hugs instead of handshakes, and his birthday gifts bordered on outrageous. He got new handmade hunting clothes that repelled the rain. He got a musket with flint, powder and shot. He got a horse with a new saddle, so he could keep up with Sophie and her new horse and saddle. He was given books on sailing the oceans of the World.

As Gerard and Sophie grew older, they practiced and hunted together, but with less frequency. There was a time when they hunted a few times a week, and that tapered off to weekly hunts. By the time Gerard was fifteen and Sophie was thirteen they were down to one monthly hunt and archery practice on occasions.

Gerard led hunting trips a few times a week and was much in demand. He spent much of his free time tending to his family's house and their few farm animals. With any remaining free time he would go out into the forest on his own to search for new territory and explore parts of the forest he had not visited before. With rugged wilderness in every direction, there was always something new to see or explore.

He was miles from home when he heard the boar whining. It sounded like it was injured or being attacked so Gerard headed that way. His father was still the head gamekeeper of Dally Castle, but he was considered an apprentice gamekeeper as well. The animals in the forest were his responsibility. He heard voices before he got there and approached on soft feet to observe. At first it just looked like some of Edwards' soldiers had caught a boar to be killed and eaten. He was about to turn away when the boar started yelling again. The animal shouldn't be making that much noise, and it shouldn't be taking this long to put it down. Gerard crept closer to see what was going on. The boar was caught in a rope. Two of the men were holding it while a third was cutting and stabbing it. They weren't killing it; they were torturing it.

The three men laughed with the sounds the boar made as it cried out. Gerard moved fast and without thinking. He took off his bow, nocked an arrow and shot before advancing on the group. The man doing the stabbing had his free hand on the boar to hold it down. Gerard shot him in his hand. The shot went through his free hand and into the boar's chest, killing it and ending its misery. The man screamed and pulled his hand off the shaft and fletching sticking out of the boar.

"What the hell are you doing?" Gerard yelling is his fury walking towards the men. "That is Lord Edward's property! You should know that as you are his soldiers."

The man with the hole in his hand was wrapping it in some cloth torn from his shirt. "What bloody right do you have to spoil our fun, laddie?"

"I am one of Edward's gamekeepers. The animals of Kielder Forest are my charge. He will sack you and turn you out when I tell him about this," Gerard said.

The two other men moved fast and grabbed Gerard before he could get away. Gerard was not expecting an attack from his own soldiers so his guard was down. The men commenced with a beating that was brutal and thorough. He felt the rib break and had one eye swell up to the point of closing. The man he shot in the hand stomped Gerard's hand under his boot, breaking some fingers. He was starting to lose consciousness when one of the men said.

"Easy Glosston, ya dont want to kill em."

"Shut up Platt, you don't tell me what to do."

Gerard was left on the ground as the men tore apart his pack and broke his bow and then his arrows.

"We need to kill him or he'll rat us out for sure," one of the men said.

"I ain't killing no kid, that's a lot different than that pig you was stabbing for some fun," said the third man.

"I'll do it," the one named Glosston said, "you just need to help me hide the body somewhere."

Gerard had been weighing his options and realized he didn't have any. He would be dead in a few minutes if he did nothing, and might die in a few seconds if he tried what he was thinking. There was a dropoff thirty feet away that led down into a canyon. It was a long way down and there were several ledges along the way. The river was not wide or deep, and had rocks on both banks. Dead here or dead there.

Gerard already knew what his opponent's next move was going to be. It was checkmate. When you only have one move available to you, it makes the choice easier. He bit the inside of his cheek to stop his head from spinning and quickly pushed himself to his feet. He started staggering in the direction of the dropoff but only got a few feet before he heard the surprised yelling behind him. He heard the men crashing through the trees behind him and tried to speed up but didn't have the strength. With his last ounce of energy he dove forward towards the edge and curled himself into a ball to try and protect his ribs. He fell sideways on the edge and tipped over the side. It was a good twenty foot drop onto a steep slope with sand, gravel and rocks. His landing knocked the wind out of him and pain exploded in his ribs and chest. He rolled until he ended up laying on his back near the edge of the next dropoff looking up. He saw the three men above him looking over the edge down at him. Gerard tried to stay still and not move his eyes or his chest as he breathed.

"Is he dead?" one of the men said.

"We better be sure, I'll go down there and put my knife in him a few times," Glosston said. He started looking for a way down. Gerard turned his head to the side and saw the drop off for this ledge was only a foot away. He still only had one move available. Gerard closed his eyes and rolled over. As he went over the side into freefall he decided to keep his eyes closed and be surprised by the ending. He hit the water so hard it took him a moment to register he wasn't dead. The cold was also a surprise, much colder than he had anticipated. Gerard surfaced and moved sideways with the current and allowed it to take him around the next bend before trying to work his way to the bank on the far side of the river. He couldn't see or hear the men anymore and hoped they were lazy and not fully committed to making sure he was dead.

Reaching a gently curving bank Gerard crawled up on his hands and knees towards the treeline. He crawled under a low tree surrounded by downed leaves and branches. He pulled as much material on himself as he could before giving himself over to the pain and the cold.

When he woke, time had passed, the sun had shifted and was already behind some hills. He tried to move, but everything hurt. He was shivering uncontrollably and that didn't help. One of his legs was badly bruised. His ribs were hurting and he figured at least one was broken. One eye was swollen closed and his right hand throbbed. Crawling on his belly, he found some dry sticks and leaves. He made a small pile and used the flint from his belt pouch to get a fire started. Every strike of the knife on the flint hurt, but he knew he needed the fire if he was going to survive. Once the fire took he used what was left of his strength to gather more wood and sticks. He laid on his side, staring into the fire, trying to get warm. He faded in and out for a few hours waking up with the cold, and putting more fuel on the fire. He was hungry and thirsty, but did not have the energy to crawl back down to the river.

The night was half over when he woke up and felt all of his hairs standing on end. Across the fire were a pair of eyes. The wolf moved out of the darkness and around the side of the fire to get a better look at him. Gerard couldn't move his body much but his head and eyes tracked the animal. The wolf was beautiful, black with just a dusting of white on its chest and right foot. Its eyes were ice blue; it was like looking into a pure glacier. They stared at each other for a while.

"Hello, Midnight," Gerard said, and that earned him a snarl.

"I realize we just met, and you don't know me, but I would appreciate it if you didn't eat me tonight. I have so much to do. I don't have time to be dead right now."

The wolf watched him, and Gerard looked back.

"I'm going to take a little nap now, Midnight. I guess I'll see you later." Gerard closed his eyes and let the pain take him away. When his breathing evened out the wolf moved closer and sniffed a few times. The wolf watched him for ten minutes before slipping away into the darkness.

The next time Gerard woke up the dawn was turning the sky orange in the east. His fire had gone out. He thought about the wolf he met in his dreams. He had named the wolf Midnight and they had walked and hunted the forest together. They ran side by side, they caught a rabbit together, and they shared meat around a fire. It was a good dream. Gerard waited until sunrise before getting to his feet to start the long walk home. He stood up and had to lean over with the pain and effort. When he opened his eyes he saw the tracks. They were bigger than his fist.

"Oh," he said out loud.

After leaning against a tree for a bit to get his wind, he started walking home. His steps were slow, he made sure he didn't stumble or fall. He wasn't sure he could get back up if he did. The two hour walk out turned into a five hour walk home. He had to stop frequently to catch his breath; the pain in his side was nonstop. The shortest route took him past the castle. He hoped one of the guards he knew personally was working the gates. Maybe they could go get his parents to help him the rest of the way home.

Gerard came out onto the main road about fifty feet from the gates and the guards. He had trouble seeing but it looked like Davidson was on guard duty. That was good news because he was friends with Davidson. He raised his hand to wave and realized he should have used his left hand. When he raised his right hand the pain flared and his world went black.

10

Gerard woke up in a room he didn't recognize, and the bed was amazingly soft. Only one eye was working, but he thought he might be inside the castle. The window here let in so much light, and his house was very dark. He would have to see about getting his mother a window. He turned to the side and saw Sophie. She was crying. He tried to sit up but the pain stabbed him in the side. He tried to talk but his words sounded funny.

"Sophie, what's wrong?" Gerard asked.

"Are you ok?" Sophie asked.

"Yes I'm fine. Are you ok, what's wrong, why are you crying?"

"Well there is nothing wrong with his head, he's still as dense as ever," His mother said from the corner of the room. He moved his head now and saw his mom, Edward, and Joan standing together talking.

Edward came over and stood behind Sophie. "You look like you tried to steal a tooth from a bear while he was awake. What happened to you, son?" Lord Edward the Black said.

"Maybe just you alone sir, if you please?"

"It's back to 'sir', is it? Very well. Everyone out," Edward said with a tone that left no room for discussion. The three ladies walked out and Joan pulled the door shut behind them.

"Tell me everything, leave nothing out," Edward the Black said.

Gerard told him everything, holding back the two names for the very end. "When they were talking about killing me, two of the men called each other by names, so I know two of the three."

"Tell me," Edward said.

"They are your soldiers, sir. I don't want to come between you and your men. They have all taken an oath to you and . . ."

"Gerard," Edward interrupted gently, putting a hand on his shoulder. "You are my family; my family comes first. Now why don't you let your future king handle this and give me the names."

"Glosston and Platt," Gerard said.

The Lord nodded and patted him twice on the shoulder. "Rest up. You'll be on your feet in no time." Edward rose and headed for the door.

"Sir, What are you . . ." Gerard started.

"Edward, it's Edward. If I have to order you to call me that, I will. The answer to your question is, I will address the issue. The trick for a leader is to address an issue in a way so it never ever comes up again. Ever." Edward walked out of the room.

That night Lord Edward the Black ordered every soldier to report back for formation and announcements. Messengers were sent in all directions; nearly all of his men assembled. Over four hundred men stood on the warrior's belt two days later. The warrior's belt was a long thin strip of grass that ran along one side of the castle. They used it for training, summer festivals, and soldier formations. When told to get on the belt, everyone knew where to go. Today the belt was full of soldiers armed with swords, shields and armour. Edward rode onto the belt in his own armor with six house guards trailing, also on horseback.

He stopped in front of his men and waited for the horse's feet to quiet before speaking. His men were already silent. The six house guards dismounted and moved through the men like it was an inspection.

"Soldiers of Falstone, we have had a breakdown in leadership, and for that I must apologize. As a leader you must try and balance between being a kind leader and a firm one. I have tried to be both but I fear I have stepped too far towards kindness and allowed the honor and integrity of my soldiers to stray from the path I have set. That mistake will be corrected today."

"A member of my family was beaten and left for dead a few days ago." Startled gasps sounded from his soldiers. "He lives by mere providence and the mettle of his heart."

Near the back of the group, two men made a run for it, but were quickly captured by the house guards and stripped of their weapons. A third man was pulled out of formation and also stripped of his weapons.

"Gerard the gamekeeper is fifteen years old. He was beaten unconscious by three grown men. Soldiers! My soldiers! Soldiers who pledged to serve me, to represent me to the people of my kingdom. The reason for the beating? They were torturing an animal they had caught for sport. Gerard found them and stopped them. Gerard is my gamekeeper. He was doing what he gave his oath to do."

"This is the same Gerard who has promised to guard my daughter Sophie with his life. Two years ago he killed a group of men who threatened my daughter and saved her life. He is the reason my daughter is alive, the reason my heart still beats! My soldiers thought it was okay to beat him to death."

The entire assembly stood uncomfortably. Soldiers watched for what would come next.

Edward the Black had started out talking, but now he was yelling. His calm had unraveled; it was obvious he was losing what control he had left. He grew louder, angrier, and he visibly shook with rage. "Those of you with children, either sons or daughters, take one step forward now."

More than half of the soldiers took a step forward.

"I want Fury's Cage!" Edward the Black screamed.

The last time Edward had called for 'Fury's Cage' was after the assault on his daughter Sophie. His personal soldiers searched the surrounding area and located one father, one brother, and one uncle of the men who attacked his daughter. He asked them one by one what they had done to protect his daughter from their evil relative. None of the men had a good answer. After each one was questioned, they were put into the cage with a sword. The 'cage' was formed when his soldiers lined up to make a four sided box. The box had perfectly straight lines, with shields held to the inside to form a wall. Then Edward went into the cage with his sword. Fury was released in the cage. Fury and death. Only he didn't just kill them. He did . . . more. More than a few of his soldiers, veterans of wars and countless battles, threw up behind their shields.

All the soldiers with sons or daughters formed up the box and got the lines square and tight. It was large, maybe forty or fifty men across on each side. The first man was pushed into the box and a sword was thrown in after him. The lines reformed and everyone held their breath. Edward climbed off his horse and started walking, he dropped his gloves and started to jog, and pushed off his helmet and started running. He drew his sword and screamed as the near side of the box opened up and he charged inside. The box closed fast after his entry and every man watched. The condemned man inside the cage had not picked up the sword and just stood there with his hands out in surrender. Edward cut his left arm off near the shoulder on his first pass and was screaming at him.

"If you will only fight unarmed children then so be it, I don't want cowards in my ranks anyway." Edward moved in again and cut, and cut, and cut. The soldier was gone a long time before Edward stopped.

"Next man!" screamed Edward. A second man was pushed into the box and handed a sword quickly before the shield reformed. Edward charged him and ran him through where his neck met his chest. Edward the Black screamed, pulling his sword free as the man dropped to his knees. He swung in a wide arc and took the head off with his next swing. Then he went to work on the body. This lasted nearly a half minute. Edward the Black was mostly red and getting redder.

"Next man!" he screamed. The last man was pushed into the box and a sword thrown at his feet. He picked it up in his left hand because his right hand was still bandaged up. Edward screamed, charging the last man. This one was able to block the first swing, but not the next, or the next, or the next. He was cut down, and cut, and then nothing.

Edward was still on fire. He stabbed his sword into the red grass and started screaming at his men. "My soldiers do not beat children! My soldiers do not torture animals!" He picked up a head off the ground and threw it hard at the shield wall in front of him. It hit with a crunch sound and left a bloody circle on the shield. "My soldiers will do no evil until I order it!" It was dead silent in the meadow. Even the birds and the insects had gone quiet. Lord Edward the Black pushed the hair back out of his eyes and inadvertently smeared blood over half his face. He took a few deep breaths, then spoke in a reasonably calm voice.

"You men represent my honor, and my honor is important to me. The next time one of my soldiers tarnishes that honor, you will stand in my cage. But first it will be your father. And then it will be your mother. And then it will be your wife. And you shall be the last."

Lord Edward the Black walked towards his sword, picked it up, and resheathed it. "Starting today, my honor better be as important to you as it is to me." He started walking. The far side of the box opened so he could approach his horse. He mounted up and turned the horse to face the men.

"You are dismissed," he said softly. The horse turned and slowly walked away.

11

Gerard returned to his home after a week. His bandages came off his ribs and hand after two weeks. He was just getting his grip back in his hand when Lady Joan and Sophie stopped by to visit. Joan brought him a new bow and quiver. Sophie brought him a dozen new arrows. She made them herself; they were perfect. He tucked some hair behind her right ear and then hugged her, and also Joan. He told them both how much he appreciated the gifts. Sophie asked how the hand was doing. He said great, in fact he wanted to try out the new bow and arrows right away.

"Tomorrow," Sophie said. "I'll bring my bow and we can break them in together."

12

When Gerard turned seventeen, he started a campaign on his parents and Edward to be allowed to sail on a ship. For all his reading, he had never seen the ocean. He wanted to travel the world and have great adventures; he wanted more than his forest and the animals. His parents and Edward managed to put him off until shortly before his eighteenth birthday. Edward stopped by the house and invited Gerard to go for a walk on one of the trails near his house. Edward asked Gerard if he still dreamed of the sea.

Gerard told him yes, practically every night. He was set on going once he was old enough. Edward listened and nodded.

"I figured so. I have bought you a commission on a trade ship bound for Australia. The captain is a good friend, Captain Anthony de la Roche. His ship the St. George leaves port in two months. You can travel to Liverpool next month and spend some time meeting Captain Roche and learning the ship. You need to have a good knowledge base before you set sail, so you don't look so green in front of the crew."

Gerard had stopped walking, and now flug himself at Edward the Black and hugged the man tightly.

"Thank you so much, Edward! You don't know how much this means to me."

"I think I have an idea," Edward said. "I had hoped to keep you here forever, but the world is a big place. I know how powerful the call to adventure can be. Your family will miss you. All of your family." Edward said and put his arm on Gerard's shoulder.

"I will miss all of you too." Gerard looked down for a second. "I will miss her every day that I am gone."

"She said the same thing to me this morning when I told her. She is angry at me for letting you get away, but she understands this is your dream."

They walked in silence for a while and then Gerard asked something he had never thought to ask before.

"Have you ever been on a ship at sea?" Gerard asked.

"Yes, I have. It's better than your dreams," Edward said, and his eyes were blazing.

13

The journey south to Liverpool was a great adventure in itself. Gerard left with only one shoulder bag with the few things he thought he might need. Their buggy held four people but only three of them were on this trip. He shared the coach with two women who ignored him for the first two days, then spent the next five days telling him their life story. The trip was 175 miles and the horse team averaged twenty five miles per day. Gerard volunteered to help with the horses since he owned one, and he wanted to learn about the harnesses that connect them to the carriage. He tried to meet every person at every halfway house. He walked the towns they stopped in and explored all he could. By the end of the week the driver was letting him take the reins and drive the carriage while he slept or rested.

He was dirty, dusty and sweaty, and had never been happier. When the carriage reached the Liverpool station he learned it was on the wrong side of town from the docks. The coach driver offered to find him some free transportation to the docks but Gerard wanted to walk and see the city. He had never been in a city with more than a few hundred people; this city held thousands.

When he arrived at the docks he asked for the St. George and was directed to a tall ship halfway down the wharf. It was a beautiful ship, tall, new paint, clean canvas. He was stopped by a guard at the ramp where he asked for Captain Anthony de la Roche.

Captain Roche came out on deck and asked if he was Mr. Gerard?

"Just Gerard, please. It's nice to meet you sir."

"How is Edward these days?" Captain Roche said, shaking hands and then leading him up onto his ship.

"He is well, and he spoke highly of you."

"Welcome aboard the St. George, Mr. Gerard. Let me give you a tour and get you a bunk and trunk. We don't leave for a few weeks so you're in for some dry dock education. But worry you not, we will get you ship-shape before this ship sails."

The ship was being refitted and would not sail for another five weeks. Captain Roche took Gerard under his wing and began teaching him all things ships and sailing. He followed Captain Roche everywhere, asked questions, and listened as much as he could. Captain Roche made him do every job at least once. Roche explained what he was doing and why. He was a good man with a good heart. By the time the ship left port on June 29th, Gerard was already a knowledgeable deckhand.

14

The open sea was everything Gerard hoped it would be. He threw himself into the work and learned everything he could. He asked questions of other sailors and would offer to do their work if they would teach him while he did it. With the voyage came practice and experience. Captain Roche rotated Gerard through all stations on the ship and watched as his skill and confidence grew. The ship passed south of Cape Horn and turned right to battle the currents and the winds to push west towards Fiji and the South Pacific.

The storm following them was easy to see as it completely filled the horizon. Gerard had all day to watch it grow before it overtook them at dusk. The wind and the rain split the mainsail and the rest of the canvas was struck for safety. In the dark with the sails down the St. George was pushed steadily north, and further off course. The crew heard the waves crashing on the shoals long before they saw them, but by then it was already too late.

Just after dark the St. George ran aground on a shallow coral reef. The ship hung up and started to buckle. Captain Antony de la Roche ordered all men into the boats as the ship fouled and was lost. The ship was outfitted with two large boats called longboats and two smaller boats called jolly boats or jollys.

In the dark and confusion, Gerard ended up in a jolly boat with only three other men. Bothari was the master at arms. A hulking man crisscrossed with scars who didn't talk much, but always watched. Cuthbert was the younger of the two carpenters aboard the St. George. He was friendly enough and extremely clever. He was always making something or fixing something and was unhappy when he had nothing to do. Hudson was one of the many able-bodied-sailors. He always had a story to tell and boasted with the best of them. It sounded hollow to Gerard and he got the impression Hudson was nervous about his skill and knowledge despite being in his mid thirties.

The four men took to the oars and pulled hard south and west away from the wreckage and the reefs. They immediately lost sight and position of the other jolly boats, and the shouts and calls were swallowed by the wind. After rowing for an hour, they took a break to search the horizon for other boats. The dark, the rain, and the swells made it futile. The crew resumed what they thought was a westerly heading, but with no stars in view, it was anyone's guess.

Sunrise came and the brunt of the wind and rain started to peter out. Still nothing could be seen in any direction; no boats, no land, and no hope. Bothari had worn his sword while on deck and it was all he had brought into the lifeboat with him. Cuthbert had a shoulder satchel of tools he wore while on deck and had it with him still. It had some tools and string and leather and knives inside, but no food or water. Hudson had brought his boot knife and a sun hat for some reason. The hat didn't fit and kept blowing off in the wind. He was afraid of losing it so as of right now he was sitting on it.

Gerard wore a utility belt with necessities while on deck just as he had at home when he left on hunts. It held his small knife, a compass with a magnifying lens, and some flint. Gerard had also grabbed one water skin and one bag of hard tack when they first heard the waves crashing on the shoals. The water bag only had about six pounds of water in it, which was less than a gallon. Split four ways it was not going to last them very long. The hardtack could last them forever if they were desperate enough to eat it.

Gerard, Cuthbert and Hudson were discussing what direction to go, and each of them wanted a different direction. Bothari as usual just sat and watched and listened. Hudson was of a mind to go north.

"We need to go north. As the oldest one in the lifeboat that should put me in charge. North was the last direction the ship was headed and we need to keep moving that way," Hudson said.

"Yes, but I have more sailing experience than you do, so you should listen to me," Cuthbert said. "We should sail east and try to meet up with the other life boats and Captain Roche."

"I think we need to keep going west, towards Fiji and away from the shoals," Gerard suggested. "Our priority needs to be finding land and more water." He said nothing about being in charge since he was the youngest man in the boat. He figured going west was their best chance of survival.

The argument went around a few turns before Bothari grunted and got everyone's attention. He drew his sword and pointed it in Gerard's direction. He slowly pointed to the compass, the knife, the food, and the water, each movement punctuated with another grunt. Finally, he pointed the blade at Gerard's chest and nodded.

Nobody said anything for a moment before Cuthbert asked, "Are you sure about this Bothari? I know he's sharp, but he's still pretty green."

"He's not just sharp, he's lucky. Right now we need a handful of both." Bothari said. His seldom used voice was like gravel in the morning quiet.

Hudson looked like he wanted to keep arguing but then he looked at the water skin, licked his lips and remained silent.

"I guess that settles it then," Cuthbert said, turning from Bothari to Gerard. "What are your orders, Captain Sharp?"

Gerard looked at the three men now watching him. He considered all the things he had learned in Falstone from his parents and Edward. He thought about the crash course from Captain Roche. These men were putting their lives in his hands. They needed his leadership as much as anything. He handed the water skin and tack to Bothari. "Everyone eats something and then takes a small sip. We don't know how long we need to make that last so lets start small. Bothari, you're in charge of the rations."

He took out the compass and handed it to Cuthbert. "You have the most time at sea, I need you to keep us on a westerly heading."

Captain Gerard picked up a long scrap of wood laying in the bottom of the boat. "Hudson, we could use a spear in case we see any big fish near the boat. I need you to carve us one and attach some rope to it. Then you and I will take the first shift on the oars."

Gerard picked up some scraps of netting from the bottom of the boat and started cutting and retying the netting together. "What are you doing?" Hudson asked as he started work on his makeshift spear.

"I am going to make a fish trap that we can pull behind the boat as we row. I have some experience with trapping. If we're lucky, we can catch dinner while we row our way to Fiji."

Bothari gestured towards Captain Gerard again and grunted. "Sharp."

Captain Gerard had them row in shifts of one-hour on the oars, then a one hour break, then the next crew rowed. So, each man pulled a shift every four hours. They rowed from first light until past sundown as long as they could see the compass or stars. Cuthbert fashioned sun hats for everyone out of some leather from his pouch and canvas scraps in the lifeboat. Keeping them from burning was a priority they talked about the first day. Cuthbert also fashioned a drawstring for Hudson's hat to keep it from blowing away.

On the second day they found some rope and canvas adrift. Captain Gerard had them recover it and lay it out to dry. Nobody ate the hardtack. It dried you out rather than filled you up. The third morning on the boat brought heat and humidity, and the last of the water. The crew shared the last few sips until the bag was dry. Each man was alone with his thoughts as they stared out over the water. They rowed their shifts, talked little, and watched the horizon.

The fourth day they caught a medium sized bluefish in the trap that was quickly cut up and shared all around. The meat was good; the men cleaned it down to the bones. Captain Gerard took some of the inedible parts and tied the bait into the trap. Less than three hours later they had a five-foot black tip shark circling the boat, eying the bait. Bothari held the spear ready, waiting for a chance to use it, but the shark never got close enough for a good throw. The shark disappeared after a few minutes and did not return.

On day six Bothari woke early and checked the net trap. Sea grass had gotten tangled in the net overnight; it needed to be cleaned out. Just before he pulled the net into the boat, he saw movement under the water. A sea turtle was feeding on the greens. Bothari slowly grabbed the spear and pulled the net closer to the boat. When it was close enough, he used the spear and struck the turtle in the neck with a swift killing blow. The commotion woke the rest of the crew and they worked together to get the turtle and net inside the boat. The men were happier than they had been in days, but nobody was sure how to prepare or eat the turtle. Captain Gerard ordered Bothari to get the turtle out of the shell and start cutting the meat into strips. He asked Cuthbert to cut him some long thin sticks out of scrap wood. Hudson was told to cut up some wood chunks and make a pile of wood shavings. Gerard cleaned out the shell, placed it upside down on the bench and filled the bottom with wood shavings. He used his beveled glass and the sun to get a small fire going inside the shell. He put the meat onto sticks and then laid them across the shell over the fire.

As the meat started to cook and the smoke and smells filled the boat Hudson whispered in reverence, "Captain Sharp, I would follow you anywhere." Cuthbert nodded, and Bothari grunted in agreement, but he never took his eyes off the meat.

They ate most of the turtle that day, and cooked and dried everything they could use for later. For the first time in days they forgot about their thirst and relaxed with some degree of hope. Captain Gerard gave them the afternoon off from rowing. It was a selfish decision, because he was too full to row.

Two nights later, the rains came. One minute it was dry, the next minute they were getting soaked to the gills. Hudson started to wrap himself in the canvas when Captain Gerard ordered him to hand it over. At first it looked like Hudson was not going to give up his blanket but then he sighed and handed it over. Captain Gerard had the three men hold the canvas flat in the rain while he quickly ran his hands over the sides wiping it down. Once he was satisfied, he had them tip the canvas down at an angle and used the waterskin to catch the rainwater. In short order he had filled the water skin and quickly handed it to Hudson while tipping the edge of the canvas up to form a bowl. "Take a big drink, pass it on."

Hudson drank deep and passed the skin to Cuthbert. He also took a big draw and passed it to Bothari. Bothari tried to push the skin back to the Captain, but Gerard shook his head and pushed it back.

"Captain's orders, you drink first. I need my men in optimum shape."

Bothari smiled in the darkness, then drank most of the remaining skin. The skin was then brought back down to the canvas to be refilled again. When it was full again Gerard took his long drink and then sent the skin around for another smaller drink for everyone, and then back for refilling. They repeated this twice before the rain started to taper off and they used all the remaining storm to make sure the skin was topped off.

"Why did you have us hold up the canvas and wipe it down in the rain for so long?" Hudson asked and smiled. "Seems to me we wasted a lot of good rain water while you did your laundry."

Now it was Captain Sharp's turn to smile. It was fun when the prey just walked into the trap. He had the choice of embarrassing Hudson or teaching Hudson today and decided maybe a little of both would be in order.

"The canvas was in the ocean and therefore covered in dried salt. If we had just started drinking the water running off it, it would have been salt water and killed us within a day. I washed it just enough to get most of the salt off, so we were drinking freshwater instead. Although just in case I gave you the first drink, Hudson, since I decided you were the most expendable member of the crew."

The expression on Hudson's face was priceless. He went from confusion, to understanding, to horror, to anger, and finally to acceptance. When the corners of his mouth turned up Bothari couldn't hold it anymore and burst out laughing. They all joined in and even Hudson was laughing in the end.

Day 11 on the boat brought a morning fog with low visibility. The crew had just completed one rotation of lackluster rowing when the fog started to burn off and they saw the island right in front of them. They were less than two miles off shore and could just now hear the waves breaking on the shoals and beaches.

A cheer went up from three of them as Captain Gerard scanned the reef for an opening. The island was a coral atoll and appeared to be broken into sections. The perimeter was well guarded by jagged rocks, but they could see an opening further ahead. They pulled sideways hard for a few minutes and got past the reef and turned into a calm lagoon.

As they neared the beach a figure stepped out of the trees and walked towards the beach to meet them. Captain Gerard told Cuthbert to take over the oars for Bothari and told him to put on his sword and make ready for anything.

After nearly twelve days at sea the nose of the jolly boat bumped into the white sandy beach and came to rest. Captain Sharp climbed out first with Bothari right next to him. The sand was powder soft under their unsteady legs but they straightened up and stood tall to meet the island native. Under his breath he told Cuthbert and Hudson to stay in the boat and make ready for a quick exit if necessary.

The islander walking towards them was an intimidating specimen. Dark skin and muscles from a lifetime of hard work in the sun. Tribal tattoos covered most of his chest and arms. His long black hair was pulled into a braid that swung behind him as he strode towards the water. He wore what appeared to be a grass skirt held by a hemp belt with a good-sized knife on the side. He carried a single spear nearly six feet long with a blade that shone in the sunlight. Around his neck was a necklace made of some kind of teeth, and a single carved wooden figure made out of purple wood. He came to a stop about five feet in front of Captain Sharp and the two evaluated each other for a time.

Eventually the man's face broke into a wide grin. He stretched his arms wide as if to encompass the whole island and spoke to the newcomers in a loud booming voice. "Koo Koo Kushaw."

15

Koo koo meant 'welcome friend', and 'kushaw' meant everything I have is also yours. So the island greeting literally said 'welcome my friend, all I have is yours also.'

The language barrier was difficult at first but a few of the islanders already knew some English from previous visitors. With both sides eager to learn and communicate, they made quick progress.

The Sand Maru had lived on the island for at least five generations. They called the island Pukapuka, but knew that previous visitors called it Danger Island. Their island was part of the northern chain of the Cook Islands, and one of the most remote. They had not had any visitors to their island in over eight years. They were welcoming and happy to make new friends.

The village leader was named Mano, which meant Shark God. Mano looked to be in his 60's but was as fit and active as anyone. There were a total of 181 Sand Maru islanders living on Pukapuka, but six voyagers were gone on a trip to a neighboring island. The islanders had a long history of ocean voyaging in their double hulled canoe style boats. The boats were lashed together and featured two sails and two masts.

Captain Gerard explained their ship had broken up on the shoals at night and the crew became separated in the life boats. There had been 44 crewmembers on board the St. George when it left Liverpool, and they didn't know the fate of the rest of their shipmates. That evening Mano asked for two crews to sail east to look for other survivors. By the next morning two boats were rigged, stocked, and launched with some of the strongest rowers aboard. Leading the rescue team was Kai, one of their best sailors. The name Kai meant Sea, so he seemed well suited for the job.

The first night the crew slept in a large meeting hut that had a fire ring in the middle. The men were exhausted from the trip and the first good meal in days. Bothari asked Captain Gerard if he wanted to post a watch. The captain declined. If the Sand Maru intended any harm, they could have killed them already. Plus being outnumbered 181 to four, it seemed unreasonable to worry about something they had no control over.

Most of the village showed up the second day for a welcoming lunch and to start construction on the survivors' new huts. Everyone present wore one of the carved purple tiki's around their necks.

Captain Gerard had tried to protest the huts and explained to Mano that they probably would not be here very long. Mano did what turned out to be a common mannerism for him. He turned to the ocean, spread his hands and said, "Only the sea will see."

Four new huts were built over the next two days and when they were done another celebration was held. It seems the whole island had been busy making gifts for their new friends. Reed strung beds, bamboo chairs, wood tables, palm sandals, hand carved wooden bowls, and utensils. It was a heartwarming ceremony and each of the men were grateful for the gifts and the kind welcome. That night in his new hut, Captain Gerard slept better than he had since leaving home. He felt at peace, or as the Sand Maru called it, Malie.

The next morning after a shared breakfast with the villagers, Captain Gerard offered his men to help with the village tasks. At first Mano refused. Gerard explained that his crew wanted to repay the kindness that had been shown to them, and they were men of work and not happy when idle. Eventually Mano allowed it. Bothari had been working on a bamboo spear; he was eager to go with a group of fishermen to see if he could spear a big fish from the boat. Cuthbert went to the docks where repair work was being done on some boats and sails. He was jumping at the chance to learn about their boats, sails and rigging. Hudson volunteered to go with a group headed for the other side of the island for a beach sweep. Apparently, all sorts of things washed up on the beach and the islanders collected what they could use and repurpose.

Captain Gerard spent the day with Mano touring the island and meeting the villagers. Mano was also called Kupuna, or a village elder. Kupunas were easily identified as they were the only ones with tooth necklaces around their necks. Everyone who came to ask a question allowed Captain Gerard to practice his language skills. Like Captain Roche, Mano was a teacher at heart and wanted to share his knowledge with Gerard.

"Has anyone told you what your name means in Maru?" asked Mano as they walked. Gerard shook his head. Some names meant something, and others were just names.

"'Gerard' means 'luck' in Maru. You are known as Captain Gerard Sharp to your men, but you are known as Captain Luck to my people."

Early the next afternoon one of the island's rescue boats was sighted. Captain Gerard and Mano walked to the beach to meet them. The Sand Maru boat was towing a jolly boat behind it, which gave the captain a flicker of hope. The pair were on the beach of the lagoon when the crew paddled in and made landfall. Loto, the captain of the second rescue boat had a fast brief conversation with Mano, turned to Captain Gerard, bowed deeply, and went back to attending his boat.

Mano translated for him. "They found this boat drifting a day and a half ago. There were two men inside, both had already passed into the Lani, or sky. I am sorry for your friends."

The bodies had been purified in a traditional ritual called a Pi Kai, and then given to the sea. Gerard looked in the boat and saw a few knives, some garbage, but no water skins.

The following day Kai's boat returned, also towing a jolly boat. Again, Captain Gerard and Mano met them on the beach, only this time Kai took the time to practice his English and speak to the captain directly.

"We found a debris trail in the water and backtracked it until we found this boat. There was only one man on board, and he had passed into the Lani. I am sorry Captain Gerard."

Captain Gerard bowed his head and thanked Kai for trying to help his friends.

"There is more sadness. Come." Kai waved him over to the boat and for the first time he noticed that the other voyages had stayed far away.

The inside of the boat was covered with blood stains. There were broken supplies trampled at the bottom of the boat. He couldn't tell if it was one big fight, or several smaller fights.

"Here," Kai said, pointing to some garbage near the back of the boat. Bones, human bones, stripped of meat and left in a pile. He took a moment to imagine how bad the conditions had gotten on this boat in comparison to his boat. Which men were in this boat? Which men did this?

"This boat cannot be reused, and must be burnt. Too much kaumaha." (Sadness)

"I agree," said Captain Sharp. "Too much kaumaha."

The cursed boat was towed out to sea at sunset by the villagers with Captain Sharp and his crew following in their own jolly boat. The boat was to be lit with arrows and cleansed before allowing the sea to claim it. The fire lighting duty fell to the survivors of the St. George. When the boat had been towed out beyond the reefs, the islanders untied it and set it adrift. The islanders then paddled their boat back behind Captain Sharp and his crew's boat. The islanders stood silently giving them space. Along the beach, most of the villagers lined up and watched in silent reverence.

Cuthbert was the first to speak. "I thank the deep blue every day that I ended up in your boat, Captain Sharp. Where you go, I go."

Hudson cleared his throat. "I said it before in jest, but I say it now with my oath. I will follow you anywhere, Captain Sharp. When you sail off the edge of the world, I will stand beside you."

Bothari was looking down at his bow but grunted once to let everyone know he was thinking. After a pause he looked up and stared steadily into Gerard's eyes. "You saved me, I know this in my heart. As long as I draw air, I will owe you a life debt. Your path is now my path, and my sword is now your sword."

Captain Sharp nodded at his crew. "Thank you for your trust in me. I will find a way to get all of us home to England, I promise you." He lit the tip of his arrow and the others lit their arrows from his. "May peace be with our past, and may luck be with our future."

He fired his arrow into the boat; and his crew did the same.

That night after the pyre, the four men gathered in Captain Gerard's hut at his request. They sat on the grass mats around a small candle talking about the island until Captain Gerard was ready.

"We don't know how long we're going to be on this island. It could be weeks, months, or years. I see no reason to waste time worrying about something we have no control over. I came to the sea to learn things I didn't know. This may not be the education I was looking for, but I don't intend to waste my time here on this island. The Sand Maru have offered us a home, a family, and a place in the world. I vote that starting tomorrow; we embrace them and learn all we can. What say you?"

"Aye."

"Aye."

Grunt. "Aye."

16

Mano collected Gerard early in the morning and simply motioned for him to follow. They walked all the way through the village and into the jungle. The path was well traveled and weaved its way gracefully through the jungle and opened out onto the beach on the eastern side of the island. Mano turned south and started walking towards one of the other corners of the island that was overgrown and not inhabited. The cloudless sky lit up the white sandy beach; it was hard to see because it was so bright. The rumble of the ocean on the shoals was the only sound as they walked.

Pukapuka was shaped like a triangle with tropical jungles on its three corners. When they reached the southern corner, Mano stopped and stared at the tangled knot of trees and bushes in front of them. It was almost a solid wall of green against the white sand and blue sky. Gerard was also looking, thinking he was supposed to see something. Mano started walking towards the jungle and Gerard followed. The Kupuna found an opening between two trees that were both bowed out so it looked like they were climbing into a giant mouth. Gerard hadn't noticed this from the beach. Inside the treeline it was dark, cooler, and near silent. Mano moved forward slowly now on the skinny but well used trail of white sand. Gerard could feel the jungle pressing down on them as they made their way to its center. This part of the island looked untouched and unexplored, except for the well-maintained path they were on. Coming around a tangle of bushes, Mano motioned for Gerard to go first.

A circular clearing opened up in front of them perhaps thirty feet across. It was a ring of white powdery sand in the middle of a dense green jungle.

In the center of the clearing was a carved wooden idol nearly eight feet tall. The wood varied in color from violet, to plum to purple depending on the wood grain and weathering. It was the Purple Tiki.

"As you look at the Purple Tiki, the Purple Tiki looks back at you. You have questions about him, and he has questions about you." Mano stepped forward and knelt in the sand, motioning for Gerard to do likewise next to him. Gerard knelt down. Looking up at the tiki was even more intimidating from here. His wide eyes stared down at him, his teeth barred as if snarling. Was it a warning? A warrior's blessing?

"Close your eyes Gerard; and open your mind. The Purple Tiki only whispers to those who listen," Mano said.

Gerard didn't put much stock in a whispering totem pole, but closed his eyes and tried to clear his mind anyway. It was so very quiet in this clearing. "The Purple Tiki knows all because he sees all. He looks inside your heart, and sees the good inside you," Mano said.

Gerard wondered how the statue got here on Pukapuka. He wondered how long it had been here. Decades? Centuries? He wondered who carved it. What was it supposed to mean?

"The Purple Tiki never tells you everything he knows, but he tells you what you need to hear. When you are lost, the Purple Tiki will point the way," Mano said.

Gerard tried to listen and concentrate, but he was not getting anything at all. His mind wandered into one of his favorite daydreams: a beautiful ship sailing across the open sea. He could feel the wind in his hair and smell the spray of the sea. The white sails taut with wind against a blue sky. He felt the ship rock as it rolled over the waves. This daydream always came with a sense of calm and happiness.

"Captain Sharp," a deep voice said, and Gerard opened his eyes.

He was alone in the clearing.

Gerard jumped to his feet and looked around for the owner of the voice he had just heard. There was no one else here; Mano was gone. Gerard stopped spinning and looked at the Purple Tiki in front of him. They stared at each other for a very long time.

Gerard walked out of the clearing and back into the jungle. He followed the path and thought about the voice he heard. It was not one he had ever heard before. Strong, confident, maybe friendly? Of that he was not yet sure. He reached the beginning of the path and stepped out of the mouth of trees. Mano sat on the beach with his eyes closed. Gerard sat beside him and looked out over the sea.

Mano spoke without opening his eyes. "When I asked if you were ready to leave you did not respond. Did the Purple Tiki take you somewhere my young captain?"

"I don't know," Gerard said.

"Starting to believe what you don't believe is a good first step," Mano said. He opened his eyes and stood up, brushing the sand off himself. "Come back and visit anytime. The Purple Tiki enjoyed your company," Mano said, and began the walk towards their village.

The ceremony was held on the next full moon in a sandy clearing near the center of the island. Standing at the center were Mano and three other village Kupunas. Gerard and his three shipmates stood between the islanders assembled behind them and the kupunas standing in front of them. Mano prayed for wisdom and guidance for the newest members of the tribe, and that they would conduct themselves in a way that would make the Sand Maru proud. Each man held out his right hand, and each Kupuna cut a thin line on the palm. Then the elders cut a matching cut on their own palm and then embraced the men in a traditional handshake. Mano explained what was happening in his best English.

"The Maru word for blood is Koko. The Koko shared today binds us to each other for all days. We are connected by Koko, and Koko makes us family. Koko literally means family by blood. Welcome, Koko."

Four women of the village brought out purple tikis on trays held reverently high. The villagers bowed low as they passed. The tikis were carved out of the Purple Heart tree specifically for each man. The four men knelt in the sand at the feet of the elders as the strong leather cords were placed around their necks. Mano spoke with power as he addressed the village as a whole. "The Purple Tiki knows all. The Purple Tiki sees all. Let the Purple Tiki guide you, as he knows your heart and your mind. The Purple Tiki is wise, let his wisdom wash over you as well. Welcome my brothers to all that is mine. Koo Koo Kushaw."

17

Gerard was working in the growing field when the runner came for him. Several of the village Elders and craftsmen had joined Gerard on his newest project. For the last three weeks they had been building an Archimedes Screw to bring water up from a well into the crop fields. This would replace the current system of bringing up buckets of water one at a time from a nearby well. Some of the village's best woodworkers carved the blades of the screw to get it just right and fit tightly into the bamboo shaft. Gerard let Loto be the first to turn the shaft even though the honor was his if he wanted it. The first dozen turns produced nothing but you could hear water sloshing around inside. Fetu had just started to give Gerard some ribbing when water gushed out the top of the pipe. A cheer went up from the group; there was much hugging and back slapping. It seemed like everyone was lining up for a chance to turn the water screw. Naturally, the Kupuna pushed their way to the front. This was the culmination of months of planning and weeks of delicate work. It was good to celebrate.

The runner reported a sail had been spotted on the horizon and it was likely the boat was headed for the island. There was a large open lagoon on the lee side of the island and it would take the ship another hour or so to make landfall.

Mano the village elder had also been alerted by a runner and came walking through the trees into the crop field. They greeted each other warmly as Mano came over to inspect the new water screw. It had been over four years since Gerard and his crewmates stepped foot on the white sandy beaches of Pukapuka. In that time, they had not only become part of the village, but they had moved up in status. While too young to be considered an elder, Gerard was treated as such by most of the village. He had worked hard to learn not just the language but the traditions and old ways of the Sand Maru. Gerard had made it a goal to meet everyone on the island and learn their names and what they did. He also volunteered to do everyone's job for a day if they would stand next to him and teach him about it while he did it. Most of the village took him up on the offer. Others just found it annoying and wanted him out of the way.

Mano talked to him as an equal and even sought his counsel on certain matters. The water screw was just one more thing that Gerard had helped improve on the island. It was important to Gerard to introduce any new ideas slowly to persevere the traditions and essence of the Sand Maru and not upset the natural balance of things. Gerard had a quick word with one of the island boys named Kale. He asked Kale to deliver a message for him and the boy took off running back towards the village.

Gerard and Mano started for the lagoon in a slow easy gait. They had plenty of time to watch the ship approach and navigate the deadly shoals surrounding the island.

"Congratulations on the water project. It was a fine idea and will long serve our village and help us produce more food for everyone."

"I am happy to help as always, food for my family, food for my Koko."

"What are your thoughts on the ship that approaches, I would hear them," Mano asked.

"I am excited but cautious. I find I am protective of my sand and my Koko, but I would welcome new friends and a chance to return to my home, my other home."

"You will always have a home here. You know that," Mano replied.

"I do know that, and I thank you brother. These years have been good to me and my men, but we have another home, other families. My heart and my eyes would be glad to see them again. They have probably thought me dead for several years now."

"Gerard the Sharp killed in shipwreck? I think not. Not if they know you as I know you. They will know in their hearts that someday you will return."

They walked side by side in silence for a bit before Gerard spoke again. "I think being friendly and cautious is always a good stance, I think the Purple Tiki would like to hear their words and see into their hearts."

"Yes, that is what I was thinking also. I think this wise." They shared a smile and walked on. The Purple Tiki and the word wise were almost always used in the same sentence.

They stood hidden just inside the tree line and watched the ship as it approached. It was a good-sized ship with three tall masts and a second gundeck under the main. They could see men moving about on the deck as they worked to stow the sails and drift through the opening in the outer reef. Gerard could just start to make out the sounds of the captain yelling orders to the crew. It brought back fond memories of Captain Roche and his time aboard the St. George. He noticed the ship was not flying any flags. That was unusual. Normally the ship flew two flags: the flag of her country and the flag of her captain. Once the ship cleared the outer ring of shoals the captain's voice was easily heard. His threats and curses easily carried over the sound of the sea. His voice and tone caused a wrinkle on Gerard's forehead. Clearly this captain was not like his old friend.
Once the ship made the lagoon, they dropped the short anchor as the water was only thirty feet deep in the middle. One of the longboats was being hoisted over the side to be lowered into the water. Several men seemed to be arguing with the captain about who would be going with it. That was also unusual. Eventually five men climbed into the boat.

Gerard spoke to Mano in a low voice even though he knew they could not be heard. "I would like to try something with your permission. I would like to step out into the clearing alone and ask that you stay back in the tree line for now."

"Does Purple Tiki whisper in your ear Gerard the Sharp?" Mano asked with a grin.

"I believe he does."

"Very well then. Proceed,"

Gerard walked out of the trees and onto the beach where he could be seen from the ship. His dark tanned skin was in stark contrast to the white sandy beach. Years of working in the sun with the villagers had developed his body and made him look like one of them. Today he wore no shirt, and only had a small working knife on his belt. His leather shoes had been replaced years ago with rugged palm sandals favored by the villagers. Immediately shouts went up from the ship and the lowering of the boat stopped. He could feel the eyes on him and saw one man using a looking glass from the deck of the ship. Two more men armed themselves with swords and climbed into the boat for a total of seven.

"Interesting," said Gerard.

"Yes, very," whispered Mano behind him. "Many days have I taught you of my world and things known to me. I would follow your lead on this now as this is your world and things known to you."

"I am honored by your trust, my brother. Thank you," Gerard said under his breath. "Bothari?"

"Captain Sharp?" Bothari whispered from somewhere behind him. Obviously the runner had found him and sent him to the lagoon.

"I want four more Koa in the shadows right now with heavy steel. I want them on their toes with smiles on their faces. I also want Sefina with a sharking basket."

"Yes, Captain Sharp."

Gerard could hear just the runner's small footsteps going back into the jungle. Bothari would never leave his captain's side if there was any danger or a chance of a fight, for he loved both equally. Koa meant warrior, and the Koa of the Sand Maru were the warriors and protectors of Pukapuka. Koa was a title of respect and status among the islanders. Koa trained regularly with hands and weapons, it was an honor to keep your family safe.

"Mano, come join me on the beach and let us welcome our visitors and see if they would be our friends. Bothari, if the men stand before us as a group, stay where you are, but if they try to encircle us, you and the Koa may make your presence known."

Bothari grunted once in understanding; Gerard could tell he was smiling.

Mano stepped out of the trees onto the beach and caused more shouts from the ship to the longboat. They paused in the rowing to observe the newcomer and after a short discussion they resumed rowing for the beach. Gerard kept the smile on his face as he examined the crew rowing for the beach. Dirty hands and faces . . . mismatched clothing . . . most armed with blades of different origin. Their eyes were scanning the beach, the tree line, and the path back to the ship. Nervous.

Gerard the Sharp and Mano walked to the spot where the boat would make landfall. They stopped about thirty feet from the waterline to give the guests some room. As the longboat neared the shore the two men not rowing in front jumped out and pulled the bow of the ship up onto the sand. They stood back to let the others climb out, keeping their hands near their swords. The man Gerard had picked for the captain got off the boat last; he was marginally cleaner than the rest. He had a black eye that was going yellow and didn't wear a hat. Gerard had yet to meet a captain who didn't wear a big hat.

Gerard stepped forward and spread his arms wide and spoke the traditional island greeting with a smile. "Koo Koo Kushaw!"

The man with the blackeye walked forward a few steps, then stopped to check the distance between his men and himself. He faced Gerard and then yelled even though there was only twenty feet between the two groups.

"Do you speak the King's English?"

Gerard responded in the native tongue of the Sand Maru that he had learned well over the last four years. "Yes I do, I speak it very well."

One of the rowers spoke up next with his hand on his belt near the sword handle. "Aw shit, another dumb ass savage. Do you want me to kill him now or later Todd?"

The man with the blackeye turned and gave his man an angry look. "It's Captain Todd, you jackass. Let's see if they have anything worth stealing before we start killing anyone."

He faced the natives and began using hand gestures to mimic eating food and drinking out of a cup. Gerard let him go for nearly thirty seconds before he let out a "OOOOO" of understanding. He turned to Mano and continued to speak in the island language of Maru. "This man is either hungry or wants me to punch him in the mouth, I am not exactly sure which."

"It is wise to listen as the Purple Tiki does," said Mano. "Which path will you choose, my young elder?"

Gerard half-turned and whistled into the jungle behind him. "Have Sefina come forward, then have our Koa come forward when she reaches our group."

Some of the men from the longboat put hands on swords when Gerard yelled into the trees, but now they froze with rapt attention. Sefina stepped out of the jungle and slowly made her way down the beach with a basket of food. She was one of the most beautiful women Gerard had ever seen. The effect was not wasted on these men. Their mouths hung open as they watched her gracefully walk towards them. Sefina had long black hair that floated in the wind unbraided. She wore a short dress that started low on the chest and ended high on the thigh. Her smile dazzled as she had no fear, because Sefina had secrets. Secret number one was that her Koko were all around her. Secret number two was she was one of the most lethal warriors on the island.

"Blimey, would you look at that," one of the men whispered.

"We need to bring that treasure back on board for everyone to share," said another.

"We could sell her and make a fortune," said yet another.

"Shut up," ordered Blackeye Todd. "This one belongs to me."

Gerard shifted his eyes to Sefina and saw she heard and understood but her face never betrayed her. She spoke some English as her husband was the head Koa for the island, and had met travelers in the past. As a warrior she was great, as an actress she was better. She came to a stop before Mano and lifted the basket as she bowed her head. She raised her eyes and now looked directly at Gerard.

"May this food give you strength; and if you don't let me kill one of them, I will never forgive you." Her beautiful voice in Maru gave no hint to the lethality of her words.

"I think I will take this one back to the boat for myself," Blackeye Todd said and he started to walk forward towards Sefina.

One of Todd's men standing in the back let out a gasp and put his hand on the hilt of his blade, his eyes locked on the tree line behind them. Gerard didn't need to look back to know what was coming towards them. Four of the biggest bone crushers on the island. Bothari was a huge man covered with scars and now an assortment of tribal tattoos. He looked like violence waiting for a place to happen. The smile on his face looked forced and uncomfortable. Next to him was Pohaku, "The Mountain". Pohaku was huge by anyone's standards, just standing next to him made one feel like a child. It was well known in the village that Pohaku was one of the kindest souls and wouldn't hurt a fly. He didn't eat fish because he couldn't stand the thought of them suffering. The Mountain was covered in tattoos and his head was shaved. His smile was genuine, which made it just a little bit scary. The third warrior was Maleko, "The Quiet One". Maleko had the biggest arms of anyone in the village. He looked like he crushed rocks for a living, which was ridiculous, he only broke open coconuts. The fourth member of the group was Pale, of course. Pale meant protector. He was in charge of Koa on the island, and also Sefina's husband. He was tall and lean, and his speed was phenomenal. He carried a long spear he used as a walking stick that was nearly seven feet long. Pale was a smart man and a skilled fighter, but still had some scars put there by his beloved. He wore them with pride because Sefina pulled no punches when it came to training and the protection of the island.

Blackeye Todd stopped his approach when he saw the islanders and backed up into the middle of his group of men. Gerard watched from the corner of his eye and shared another smile with Mano. The Koa took up casual positions behind them; they looked casually deadly. The smiles pasted on the faces of the huge men did nothing to ease the tension of the visitors.

Pale spoke to the group in a quiet measured voice from the back. "I would ask my beloved that I be allowed to remove his eyes for the way he looks at you."

Sefina placed the basket at the feet of Mano, then did a low bow with her back to the visitors. This was not required and she was smiling as she did it. The men behind her gasped and seemed to lose all train of thought. She started to leave, but stopped directly in front of Pale. With a finger she beckoned his face down to her level like she was going to whisper a secret to him. Pale lowered his smiling face even though he knew what would happen next, this was all part of their courtship. She slapped the side of his face hard enough to make a cracking sound in the air. "No," she said softly.

With that she walked back towards the trees and the village. She seemed to be putting a little more swing into her hips than normal and it was appreciated by all the men on the beach.

"Jesus," one of the visitors said.

"What the hell was that?" said another.

"We can come back for her later, and any other pretties we find," Blackeye Todd said.

"Nobody said anything about kidnapping," said one of the dirty men in the back.

The rest of the group turned to look at him angrily. Blackeye Todd walked over to him and cuffed him on the cheek and whispered to the man low enough that nobody else could hear, but you could feel the threats in the words. By the time he was done talking the man hung his head and said no more. Gerard noticed he looked worse than the rest, fresh bruises, and a healing cut across his throat. He was the only visitor not carrying a sword and had marks on his wrists from either rope or shackles. Interesting.

Gerard sat down in the sand and invited the others to join him by hand gestures. Mano sat next to him and began unpacking the sharing basket. Blackeye Todd sat slowly and the other men followed suit sitting further behind him. The man in the back who Gerard now thought of as the prisoner remained standing and didn't join the group. Neither did the Koa.

Mano took items out of the basket and offered them to the visitors in a traditional manner. Each piece of food was lifted above them, broken in half, and then both pieces offered to the guests. Tradition called for the guests to take only one half, and leave the other half for the host, but the new guests took everything that was offered.

As they shared food, the visitors talked amongst themselves, feeling comfortably safe behind the language barrier. Much was said about the woman seen on the beach and the possibility of more women around. After one particularly explicit comment Mano asked Pale if he would be more comfortable going back to the village.

"No," replied Pale through gritted teeth. "I would not." His smile was that of an angry man rapidly losing his grip on his sanity. Gerard prayed for his strength, a change of subject, and a quick lunch.

The visitors openly discussed coming back after dark and to see if they could figure out where the village was and how many men were on the island. They also mentioned that they needed to replenish their fresh water supply. Drinking water was worth more than gold on the open sea. They discussed each man of the tribe in turn and boasted about how easy it would be to kill them when the time came. The Sand Maru just smiled and stayed on their toes.

As the lunch broke up, Mano thanked the guests for their company and warned them about the dangers of evil thoughts and deeds. This was accompanied by lots of arm waving and stomping on the sand. He told a nursery rhyme about a naughty child that got eaten by a monster and almost had the island men laughing and breaking character.

The visitors watched the display with some amusement before bowing and backing away towards the boats. The prisoner was loaded first and put on the oars, with Blackeye Todd and the rest of the men following. They pushed off and turned the longboat back towards the ship. The villagers on the beach smiled and waved until they were back at their ship. When Gerard and Mano turned and headed for the trees, the other men followed. Ten feet into the trees he found a dozen men with heavy bows and arrows.

"Just in case our guests wanted to take any souvenirs," Bothari said.

Some of the men laughed but Pale did not. Pale was the war chief of Pukapuka, and defining the island and its people was his responsibility. He made a hand motion and the men circled up in a huddle around him. Pale addressed some of the senior members of his Koa. "I want six eyes on the boat at all times with runners standing by. Bows and blades. I want Koa watching every beach they can access by boat. All villagers will sleep in groups of three tonight: two down, one up. Go."

The warriors melted into the trees in several directions.

"Is there anything you would add, Koko? I would hear your council," Pale asked in a humble voice.

"You are well prepared and well chosen," Mano said. "I trust you, Koko."

Gerard put his hand on the other man's shoulder. "You showed great strength on the beach. You honor not only yourself but your wife with your control. If it is within my power, I promise you his eyes when his time is at-end."

Pale looked Gerard in the eyes for a long time before letting out a breath and putting his hand on his shoulder. "Thank you, Koko," Pale said, then he too melted into the jungle.

Gerard and Mano started walking towards the village each thinking of the island's safety.

"I would hear your thoughts, Gerard the Sharp, for indeed the Purple Tiki was wise to open your ears and close your lips."

"We must be ready by sunset in case they come early. I saw only two longboats on the ship but we should probably plan for three or four. I counted fourteen men total but I do not think all of them are of the same mind. I believe the quiet one in back with the neck wound is a hostage or prisoner.

"Yes, I saw the rope marks as well. He was the only one to speak up for Sefina."

"True. I also don't think we should just wait around for our visitors to return; we should visit their ship ourselves, maybe pick a time when we think they might be otherwise occupied."

"Yes." Said Mano. "I think this wise."

18

Captain Sharp was in his hut getting ready when Roo walked in. She stopped just inside the doorway watching him put his sword belt on. Gerard offered her a smile but she did not give one in return.

"You are going to the ship then?" she asked softly, her face full of worry. News on the island spread as fast as always.

"Yes," he said.

"You are not Koa, I don't understand," she said with eyes ready to overflow.

"I asked to go," Gerard said.

The first tear rolled down her face and Gerard stopped what he was doing and opened his arms to her. Roo came forward and leaned her head against his shoulder. She didn't cry often and it tugged at his heart to see it now.

"It will be ok," Gerard said. "I will be ready for anything."

"I know Gerard, you see around corners," Roo said. She held him tightly for a minute and then relaxed some but didn't let go. Gerard dipped his head and nuzzled his face in her hair. "I was not ready to let you go," she said with a little hiccup.

"All will be well, Roo. I have five Koa going with me, including Fetu," he said.

"I mean from Pukapuka. In a week you will be gone and I will be alone again," she said.

Gerard opened his mouth to speak but then realized he didn't know what to say. He had been hoping for a ship for years now to be able to go back home, his first home. It was no secret he was going to leave, he just didn't know when it was going to happen.

"I'm sorry, Roo," he whispered, and he was.

His relationship with Roo started about six months after he was marooned on Pukapuka. As he learned the language and customs of the island, several of the eligible women had let him know his advances would be welcomed. Fetu was a great help with advice and information while he was adjusting to the cultural differences. Women outnumbered men on Pukapuka and so the women initiated most of the interaction.

Gerard deferred most of the offers in the beginning because he did not think he would be marooned on the island for very long. As the weeks stretched into months he found himself drawn to one woman in particular. Roo was 27 years old and hardly spared him a second glance at first. His strategy to win her over was slow and calculated. He made it a point to be where she was, he talked to her every chance he got. Today he had followed her to the gardens where she worked and offered to help her if she would help him practice the Maru language. She blushed red and told him perhaps he should ask Apona instead.

Apona was Gerard's age and had been throwing herself at him for weeks, stopping by his hut in the evening and asking if he wanted to talk, or go for a walk, or go inside and have sex. Apona was very pretty and very determined, but Gerard didn't have any feelings for her. His head and his heart were already full with thoughts of Roo. Gerard told her this and she just blushed and shook her head.

"How long are you prepared to pursue this quest Gerard?" Roo asked, looking at him in the eyes now.

"As long as it takes. I do not give my heart lightly as some do, so this offer is my whole heart for as long as you will have it," Gerard said.

Roo searched his eyes for a time before the corner of her mouth turned up with just the slighting hint of encouragement.

"What of my heart, Gerard? Do I give my heart to a sunset that is beautiful now but will be gone all too soon and leave me with only memories?" Roo asked.

"I can't promise you all of my tomorrows Roo, but I can promise you all of my tonights. It's all I have to give, but it is everything I have," Gerard said.

Roo reached out and took his hand and gave it a squeeze but didn't let go. The rest of the women working the gardens had given up pretending to work and were openly watching the couple now. Roo leaned forward and kissed him lightly on the cheek.

"Then I accept," was all she said, and then smiled. It was the first real smile she had given him and it was devastating. Gerard couldn't look at anything but her and his heart pounded in his chest. Roo turned and spoke to Kameo who was in charge of the gardens.

"I am taking this man to my hut Kameo, I won't be back today,"

Kameo looked at Gerard staring into Roo's face and gave a soft chuckle. Roo was a good friend and had been alone for a long time. It made the older woman's heart happy for her friend.

"You better stay home tomorrow too, that much youth and energy is going to take days to wear itself out," Kameo said.

The rest of the women in the fields either laughed or hooted for Roo as she led Gerard by the hand and towards her bed.

They didn't leave her hut for three days and only got out of bed for food and water. On the third morning there was a soft knock on the door frame that had Roo scrambling to put some clothes on and rush to answer it. She need not have worried, the person had knocked and ran away after leaving a tray behind full of fruit, bread, wine, and balm known for soothing sore muscles. Roo laughed until she cried from embarrassment but allowed herself to be pulled back into bed until late afternoon. Everything on the tray was used, including the balm.

Their relationship was comfortable and easy. They each spent a few days a week sleeping at the other's hut, but neither was willing to give up their own place or independence. They talked about everything and learned much from each other. Roo wanted to know about the outside world and cities and what women did and wore in other parts of the world. Gerard wanted to know about the island's history, and its culture. The only thing they didn't talk about was the future.

Captain Gerard the Sharp and his group of five other men pushed the longboat out on the far side of the island and pulled hard straight west into the sea. Joining Gerard on this quest were Bothari, Kai, Maleko, Fetu, and Tane. Gerard had hand selected his crew out of the many volunteers. Each man was picked for his individual skills, but the thing they all had in common was they were smart and fast on their feet.

They rowed until their island sat low on the horizon before turning the corner. They rowed in a wide circle, keeping the island on the port side at a distance of about ten miles. When they reached the opposite side of the island, they stopped to wait for full sunset. Each man ate and drank a little while they talked about their plan to attack the ship. They would split into two groups since most ships had at least two sets of stairs. Two Koa would move forward, one Koa would protect their backs. The first sweep would be fast, quiet and lethal. Then a second sweep would be slow and careful. Once they had control of the ship and the men were contained, they could start asking questions. Gerard was talking out loud trying to think of as many what if's as he could imagine. Eventually he felt comfortable that they had a plan for just about anything.

They held their boat at four miles off shore as they could still make out the outline of the ship's mast in the growing darkness. They wanted full darkness before approaching the ship from the ocean side. The longboat paused again at half a mile out as they watched the deck for activity and movement.

One hour after full dark they could just make out men lifting boats over the island side of the ship. It looked like two longboats and one small jolly boat, but it was hard to see in the darkness. The ship only had two lanterns on the deck, fore and aft, so it was near impossible to track the number of men or their movements. After the visitor's three boats moved off towards shore, Gerard waited another ten minutes before motioning his men forward.

The islanders brought the boat in silently, tying it off onto the anchor rope hanging off the sea side of the bow. This kept their boat mostly out of view from the deck and would keep it from bumping into the side of the ship. The men slid over the sides of the longboat and into the water without a sound. The lagoon was shallow here; there were no waves to make noise. They made the short swim to the starboard side and grabbed onto the rope netting hanging just above the waterline. Gerard motioned for himself and Bothari to go up the sides; the others would wait but be ready. The two men climbed slow and steady to keep the rope from creaking. As his head came level with the gunwale, he stopped to check the deck for movement while his eyes adjusted to the light. Nobody moved on the deck, the stairwell to his right was dark and empty. He hand-motioned for the others to follow and slipped over the side rail, stepping onto the deck as light as a feather. Next to him Bothari appeared and then melted into the shadows.

Gerard crept to the mouth of the staircase and stationed off to the side while his men swarmed over the rail, quick and quiet. He sent Kai, Maleko and Fetu towards the stairs at the stern, while Bothari and Tane waited by his side. When his men reached the far steps, they stopped and made eye contact. Gerard nodded once, and they crept down into the darkness.

Down one set of steps brought them to the cannon deck. No lanterns were lit but you could just make out the shadows of the cannons lined up along both walls. The next staircase down had some light coming from below, most likely crew quarters. Bothari tapped Captain Sharp on the shoulder and motioned for him to wait while he went first instead. Captain Sharp just smiled and shook his head. Bothari just shrugged his shoulders as if to say 'I had to try' and then motioned for him to go ahead. Still no sounds from the other end of the ship, just as he hoped. He drew steel and saw Bothari and Tane do the same. Gerard took off down the steps fast, keeping his head down and his feet light.

As he rounded the corner, he saw he was indeed in the crew barracks area. A quick glance showed six men in front of him and two more in the berth behind him. Coming off the bottom steps, the man closest to him sat up in his bunk and opened his mouth to say something. Gerard punched him as hard as he could with the handguard of his sword and felt the man's mouth give-way under the steel. Another man saw Gerard coming and yelled a warning as he rolled out of his bunk. Beside him, he heard a scream and knew that Bothari was going to work. Tane was guarding their backs, so Gerard didn't worry about the two men behind him.

A second man came out of a bunk with a blade in his hand, but he was slow and confused, while Gerard was fast and angry. He cut the man from collarbone to waist in a slash that pushed the dying body out of his way as he advanced down the row. Two men in front of him had time to arm themselves and square off in the narrow aisle. A scream sounded from behind them and both men took a quick look over their shoulder towards the forward bunks.

"Drop your swords or I will kill you where you stand," said Gerard in English. Another scream from behind them and the man on the left dropped his blade. The man on the right turned to look at his buddy and, in that heartbeat, Gerard stepped forward and took his neck with his sword. The man was bringing his hand up to check the wound when he fell face first onto the deck.

Gerard motioned for the smart man to kneel down on the floor and took a look behind him. Bothari had two men down and one at knifepoint on the ground. Further behind them Tane had dropped both his men and was standing with his back to Gerard, guarding the stairs to above and below.

Gerard turned back to the man on his knees and put his red blade against the man's throat. "How many men are on board?" he asked in English.

The man opened his mouth twice before he could find his voice. "I ain't that good at counting sir, but I think there is fourteen of us."

Fetu came around a partition in the middle of the ship and gave the all clear sign to Gerard. He spoke in Maru to Gerard over the man on his knees. "Four down, one prisoner."

"Five down, three prisoners," Gerard answered in Maru. His eyes went back to the man on the ground. "Where are the others?"

"I think we got old Hector guarding the prisoners below, I don't know where Mr. Price is."

Kai and Maleko lead their prisoner around the corner and they put the three of them on the ground next to the unconscious man with the ruined face.

Gerard still spoke in Maru. "Fetu and Maleko, at least two men still on board. They heard the screams so they'll know we're here. Slow and careful now." The two men nodded and started forward in a slow cautious crouch.

Now Captain Sharp switched to English for the benefit of his prisoners. "Tane and Kia, watch these men. If they move, kill them. If they say anything, kill them. If you count to 500 and I am not back yet, kill them."

One of the men looked like he was going to open his mouth and argue but then thought better of it.

A quick nod to Bothari and they stared down the steps into the hold. There was light near midship but at the bottom of the stairs it was dark. The smell was bad down here: shit, urine, and death. Gerard motioned for Bothari to look forward while he watched the stairs, midship and their backs. He smiled at the honor and crept into the darkness like an animal. He was back in two minutes and put his lips next to Gerard's ear to whisper. Storage area, some dry goods but mostly empty barrels. Gerard nodded and motioned for them to head towards midship and the light.

They came around a support wall and saw the brig crammed with men. Most were laying down not moving but a few were standing or leaning against the bars. A white-haired man sat on a box in front of the cell, with a flintlock musket pointed at some of the prisoners.

"Figured you'd be here soon enough. Now why don't you drop your weapons before I blow a few holes in your men." The white-haired man smirked as he watched Gerard and Bothari approach.

"Why don't you drop that musket and I will consider letting you live," Gerard replied in a flat tone.

"Now why would I give up my only advantage?" He laughed. "I will kill your friends and then where will you be?"

"Those are not my friends," Gerard said flatly, and tapped his belt knife. Next to him he saw Bothari slowly take out his throwing knife.

"Not your friends, aren't you here to rescue them?" He asked, confused.

"Nope. I have never seen them before in my life."

The man named Hector looked at one of the prisoners for clarification and the man just shook his head. "I don't know any savages Hector. Can't you see they're from that island?"

Hector looked back and forth between the prisoner and the islanders. "I don't see too good anymore, but I suppose this does change things."

"Let me clear things up for you then," Gerard said, pulling his own throwing knife. "I am going to kill you real fast if you don't drop that gun. Or I am going to kill you real slow if you shoot any of those prisoners. You have one second to decide."

"I just can't get a break," Hector said. He lowered the gun, gave a heavy sigh, and then dropped it onto the floor.

Gerard jerked the man off his box and sat him on the floor with his back against the bars of the cell. "Tie his hands behind his back."

One of the prisoners ripped a strip of cloth off Hector's shirt and went to work on the knots.

"Where are the keys?" Gerard asked as he patted down Hector.

"Todd has them," said a voice inside the cell.

Gerard looked into the cell and saw a young man sitting in the far corner against the bars. He was the one from the beach, with marks on his wrists and the cut across his neck.

"What is your name, sailor?"

"It's August sir. You seemed to have learned the King's English pretty quickly for a savage."

"I could speak it all along, I just decided not to."

"That is . . . funny actually," August said, smiling for the first time. He stood up with some effort. He had collected some new bumps and bruises since the beach. He walked forward gingerly stepping over men to get to Captain Gerard's side of the cell. When he was standing in front of Gerard his grin turned into a look of horror as he remembered something from earlier.

"Oh my God! You need to get back. Todd and his men are going to raid your village. That woman he saw earlier, your women . . ." he trailed off.

"Yes, we knew they were coming tonight. My family is waiting for him. All my family is waiting for them."

"Oh," August said, and the corners of his mouth turned up.

"What I could use right now is some information," Gerard said.

"What do they call you sir?" August asked, although he was probably about the same age as Gerard.

"I am Gerard the Sharp."

"Captain Gerard the Sharp," Bothari echoed from behind them.

"Well, Captain Gerard the Sharp, welcome to the Tawny Mane."

Gerard sent Bothari back to check on Tane and Kia and to help the others in the search. August told him that his ship had been captured by pirates about eight days ago. A good portion of the crew had been killed in the fight, including the first mate, Mr. Link. Captain Dominic was killed as soon as they took control of the ship. Most of what was left of the crew lay dying in this cell. His voice cracked at the end and he worked to clear his throat. Gerard spotted a water barrel half full nearby. He dragged it against the bars and handed the ladle to August.

"I am much obliged, Captain Sharp." He took a drink and then started giving sips to the other men in the cell. Some were wounded, some appeared to be unconscious, and some looked to be dead.

"I'll get you out of there as soon as I can, but right now you and your men need to just hold on."

Just then a crash and some yelling were heard from up above. The shouting continued, one voice Gerard had not heard before. He bolted for the stairs and ran towards the commotion. On the main deck he found Bothari squaring off with the missing pirate. He was holding a knife to Fetu's throat; Maleko was laying on the deck behind them either dead or unconscious.

Fetu was already bleeding from the top of the head and also from a shallow cut on his neck where the blade pressed home. Bothari circled to the right with his sword and the pirate was turning sideways to keep an eye on him. Captain Gerard pulled his throwing knife, took one step, and threw hard.

The knife gave a metallic ring when it buried itself into the side of the pirate's head. It entered just in front of the ear and sank to the handle. The momentum of the throw knocked the pirate off his feet and laid him out on the deck, leaving a dazed Fetu standing alone. Bothari stepped in quickly to grab him before he could fall to the deck; the man collapsed into Bothari's arms. Bothari lowered the injured Koko to the deck and started checking for injuries. Gerard walked over and retrieved his knife, using a foot on the dead man's head to pull it free. He cleaned the knife quickly as he had been taught, then cut off the dead man's shirt. This he cut and folded into two bandages, one for Fetu's head, and one for his neck. He returned his knife to his belt and knelt over Fetu to apply pressure to the wounds. Fetu was dazed but didn't appear to be seriously hurt.

"A good throw, Captain Gerard. I am pleased to see you have been paying attention to your instructor." Bothari gave a rare smile to his student for the last four years.

"Thank you my brother, your lessons saved a life today."

Bothari nodded once, then went over to check on Maleko. He was alive but unconscious, also bleeding from a wound on the head. Bothari followed Gerard's lead and cut more bandages from the dead man's clothing before going back to work on Maleko.

"What happened?" Gerard asked.

"I think he was hiding in the stays above. He dropped something on them and got a knife on Fetu before I could reach them. I would have thrown but he kept moving and it wasn't clear."

"It's okay. I think they are both going to live. That should be the last of them. Why don't you run down and double check our count with August. Ask him where we can find some food for his men and rope for the prisoners. Have Tane and Kia tie the men up next to Hector on the floor, and then have them report to me."

"Captain." Bothari tipped his head and was gone down the stairs.

Fetu's eyes opened and fixed on Gerard leaning over him. "Maleko my brother?"

"Alive but knocked out." A breath went out of Fetu as he relaxed some. "What do you remember?"

"The man dropped a wooden crate on us from above. He had a knife on me before I could clear my head, but I saw Maleko laying on the deck. Then Bothari was there and the two men were yelling back and forth. I saw movement out of the corner of my eye but before I could turn my head Purple Tiki whispered 'be still' and I was. Did the pahi (knife) fly true today?"

"The knife was true today; teacher is most pleased with himself," Gerard admitted.

Fetu sighed and relaxed his head back on the deck. "Yes, he will be bragging about this for many campfires to come." The men shared a laugh together.

"Thank you, my brother," Fetu said, "your best friend wishes he had not teased you so much about all the pahi practice you did."

"You were my first friend on this island, Fetu. You taught me the word pahi. It is an honor to help one's best friend," Gerard said.

"I will pay you back some day," Fetu said.

"You can pay me back by not turning this incident into a song and singing it to the whole island," Gerard said.

Fetu closed his eyes and rested his head on the deck. "You wound me Gerard, I would never embarrass you like that."

Gerard just waited because he knew his best friend too well. He watched Fetu's forehead scrunch up in concentration before he smiled and started to sing softly.

"Captain Sharp so bold and brave, and his best friend who he did save,"

"He sent that pirate to his grave, and with a knife his head did cave."

Fetu sang softly.
    "It needs work," Gerard said.
    "Don't disturb the master when he's creating," Fetu said.

Tane, Kia and Bothari came walking up the steps from below. Fetu asked for help standing up and after a few seconds of assistance, was able to stand on his own. The group circled up and Gerard listened to the updates from the men of his crew. Some food had been delivered to the men in the cell, and the prisoners were tied up along both sides of the brig. The men inside the cell were doing better, and were happy to help watch the new prisoners. They had to be persuaded to not kill them outright. These men had taken their ship and killed crewmates, including the captain. They respectfully asked the honor of killing them when the time came. Bothari had said it was up to Captain Sharp, but added it was a reasonable request. At this Captain Sharp just nodded, not deciding anything yet. They did not believe any other pirates were loose or hiding on the ship, as most of them had wanted to go ashore.
    "I don't know how much time we have before any of the boats return, if they return at all. If none have returned by sunrise, we will take a boat home and check with Pale. In the meantime, I want one man to watch the lagoon for returning boats. Take Maleko down to the barracks and put him in a clean bunk. One Koko stays with him at all times. We need to clear the deck of any opala (garbage) and secure any weapons on the ship. We need to be ready when the boats return, especially if we are outnumbered."
    Maleko was awake, and with help was able to walk down the steps mostly by himself. Fetu wanted to stay with him as he felt responsible for their injuries, and would stand the watch. Kia and Bothari dragged the body down to the cannon deck for now and hid it out of sight. Gerard and Tane went to check on the men locked up in the brig and ask about any additional weapons. August directed them to a small room at the back of the ship just left of the captains' quarters.

After persuading the door to open, they took inventory. Lots of swords here; the two men moved them to another room and hid them in some empty coffee barrels. There were also two flintlock pistols and four musket rifles with plenty of powder and shot. These were also moved to a different location and well hidden. Captain Sharp looked over the two pistols and saw that only one pistol was in working condition. He spent some time cleaning the gun, getting familiar with the action, before loading it and tucking it into his jacket pocket. It took three minutes to reload the flintlock pistol with another shot, and that was way too long. An interesting idea popped into his head and he spent some time seeing how fast he could move the gun from one pocket to another. He practiced until he felt he could do it fast and smoothly in a second or two.

Captain Sharp checked on Maleko and found him awake and nibbling on a snack on a bunk. Maleko wanted to come up on deck, but Gerard assured him there was nothing to do right now but wait. Fetu looked fully recovered except for the wet cut on his neck and the goose egg clearly visible on his forehead. Gerard assured the two men that they would not be left out if and when any more fighting occurred. He then walked back down into the hold for another talk with August. He had questions about Captain Todd and the men he had met on the beach. August answered what he could and gave more history of the ship and its crew.

The Tawny Mane sailed out of Plymouth, England several weeks ago, headed for New Zealand. Captain Reginald Dominic was a good captain but not overly friendly with anyone. He was stern, often remarking that he 'tolerated no folly'. About two weeks ago they came upon a 60-foot sloop that was taking on water. Todd and his men were aboard, but there didn't seem to be a captain. The men on the sloop explained vaguely that they'd hit something and were taking on water. They were unable to pump out the bilge fast enough and were running out of time. The 27 men were transferred over to the Mane. The ship went down head over boots eight hours later.

It was cramped with the extra men, but not letting the men aboard would have been a death sentence. Two nights later Todd and his men overpowered the sergeant at arms and the first mate and broke into the armory. Once armed, they had little difficulty taking the ship, since they outnumbered the crew. Todd captured Captain Dominic and ordered him to yield the ship. Dominic would give no ground. Todd didn't spare any time on parlay, ran him through and killed him. The master gunner spoke up about the killing and he too was put down by Todd and his men. Most of the remaining crew were put into the brig with a few kept out at a time to do the work and clean up after the pirates. Todd held both keys to the brig and kept them on a lanyard around his neck

Captain Gerard asked about the condition of the crew in the holding cell. There were 21 men in the brig, but two of them had already died from dehydration or injuries. Two more were still unconscious but being given water mixed with rations to keep them alive. The rest were doing better with the first food and water in days, but three men had serious injuries that needed to be attended to. The men included: a navigator named Cornelius, a master gunner named Smudge, one carpenter, and two coopers. A cooper's job was to make and maintain the barrels for food and water storage. There were also two cooks, musicians, and sail-men who worked up in the yards. August was one of the deck mates. He spent most of his time making sure ropes and pulleys were in working order.

Captain Gerard didn't hear Tane walk up behind him but was alerted when August's eyes shifted past him. "Small boat approaching, Captain Sharp."

Captain Sharp stood and turned to his Koko. "One small boat? Can you see how many men?"

"Too far away to see yet, two oars rowing."

"Ok, let's get into position. Maleko and Fetu?" Gerard asked.

"Already on deck sir." Tane turned to go.

"May luck be with you, Captain Sharp," August said, and this was echoed by several members of the Mane's crew.

Behind them in the dark Tane stopped walking and whispered loud enough for everyone to hear. "Captain Sharp doesn't need luck, he is the luck." He then disappeared into the dark.

19

On the deck they all watched the boat making slow progress towards the ship. They could see movement on the boat but still could not tell how many men on board. Captain Sharp and his men were hidden out of sight around the deck of the ship. They had discussed several scenarios depending on how many of the crew made it back to the ship. Waiting was hard.

They heard the boat bump the side of the ship and then the sounds of men climbing the rope ladders on the side of the ship. Finally, one man climbed over the boards, followed by a second. They were pulling something heavy with them and being assisted by the men below. They got two large bundles over the gunwale and dropped them on the deck, and then two more men climbed over the side. Four men, one wiggling bundle, one still bundle.

"I'm going to put my knife in the bitch that kicked me in the face," one of the newcomers said.

The four men started to untie the bundles as Gerard and Tane materialized out of the darkness. They got within about 15 feet before one of the men saw them and yelled a warning. Three of the men turned fast and pulled swords, a fourth was still struggling with the bundle.

Neither Gerard or Tane had pulled steel yet, but their hands were in the neighborhood. They couldn't see what the men had brought onboard until the last pirate stood up and turned to face them. It was blackeye Todd. He pushed the struggling form in front of him that had a canvas bag tied over its head as a hood. Todd pulled the bag off the head to reveal one of the females from the village. Her name was Pua (Flower); she was 12 years old. She had the beginnings of a bruise on her left cheek, and she had been crying.

Gerard took a slow calming breath and fought back the rage that threatened to overtake him. He thought about all his training, all the hunting, and all the traps he had ever sprung. This game was just bigger.

Tane had made a noise in his throat when he saw Pua, and had put his hand on his knife but not pulled it yet or charged. Gerard was going to have to commend him later for his control in the moment.

"Well well, if it isn't the village welcoming committee," Todd said and moved his knife to the neck of the small girl. "Drop those swords or I'll cut her right here."

"Todd the dead, I call your life forfeit. Release the girl," Captain Sharp said.

Todd's eyes went wide and so did three men with him, the same three who had been on the beach earlier today talking about the raid and the killing. "So you do speak English. Good, that will make things easier. Drop your swords. You're outnumbered, and we have hostages."

Gerard's voice had gone cold and flat as spoke to the men in front of him. "Actually, Todd the dead, you are outnumbered and your life is at-end. Drop. The. Sword."

Gerard didn't need to look around to know his Koko were coming out of the shadows with steel drawn. This had been discussed earlier and was part of the plan. They closed to a circle around the men and stopped when they were surrounded.

In a soft voice Gerard now spoke to Pua in Maru. "Fear not little Flower, Your Koko is here, and you are safe."

Pua looked at Gerard with the innocent face of a child. "I am not afraid Captain Gerard, for luck is with me today."

Gerard reached into his left coat pocket and drew the flintlock pistol, cocked it and took aim at Todd the dead.

Todd started talking as soon as he saw the gun. "Be careful now, you wouldn't want to risk hitting . . ."

Boom.

The shot put a hole in Todd's forehead two inches above his left eye. Todd the dead stumbled backwards in slow motion. The knife drew lightly across Pua's neck but not enough to cut. Todd's body hit the gunwale and pitched over the side of the ship. The splash meant that he hit the water and not the rowboat tied below.

Everyone had been following his death dance; Gerard the Sharp yelled to get everyone's attention back. "Next man!" He yelled, and all eyes turned to him. He made a show of putting the flintlock back into his left front pocket and then pointed at the second man with his finger. "Drop. Your. Sword."

The man hesitated for just a moment and Gerard said Bothari's name out loud. Before he could even finish the name a seven-foot-long spear shot out of the darkness and took the man through his chest and out the back by at least two feet. The man stumbled backwards two steps and tripped over the wrapped bundle. He went down awkwardly coughing blood with his dying breath. While everyone's eyes tracked the dying man's movements, Gerard quickly took the empty gun out of his left front pocket and transferred it to his right front pocket. When that was done he relaxed his hands at his sides and yelled. "Next man!" All eyes turned back to him.

Gerard reached into his right front pocket and withdrew the empty flintlock pistol. He cocked it and took aim at the third man. "Drop. Your. Sword."

The third man dropped his sword fast and then dropped to his knees with his head bowed in surrender.

"Next man!" Gerard yelled again, and took aim at the fourth man. "Drop . . ."

The fourth man threw his sword down early and dropped to his knees like his companion.

The islanders rushed forward to secure the two new prisoners as Pua ran and crashed into Gerard the Sharp with a full speed hug.

"I wasn't afraid," she said, crying into his shoulder. "I wasn't afraid."

"I know," Gerard said. "Your brothers all saw how brave you were, and Purple Tiki saw it too." He pushed her back a little because now he was in a hurry.

"Maleko was hurt earlier and could use your help. He is trying to be brave but I know he has some injuries. Will you help him for me?" Pua let him go and did a quick wipe of her eye.

"Of course I will," she said. She gave him a quick kiss on the cheek and moved past him.

Gerard quickly shed his outer layer of clothing and then bent to pick up the bag that had been used on Pua's head.

"Bothari, secure these prisoners tight and check who is in the second bundle. Clean the deck. You're in charge until I get back. If another boat returns, kill them all and kill them fast."

"Captain?" Bothari asked.

Gerard dove off the side of the ship and disappeared into the black water.

Inside the second wrapped bundle was a ten-year-old boy named Noah. Noah and Pua thought the idea of fighting pirates was high adventure and snuck out to one of the remote beaches to see if they could find some. This beach was not patrolled by the Sand Maru because it was guarded by reefs and not accessible by boat. In the dark Todd and his men didn't know this and ended up rolling over the reefs and nearly tearing the bottom off the boat. It's a miracle the trip in and trip out didn't kill them.

The pirates found the kids on the beach instead of the other way around, and had rolled them up like rugs. Pua explained that the men said they were dropping them off at the ship and then going back for more. On the return trip the men remarked how strange it was that they didn't see any other of their boats.

Noah came around shortly after being untied and was no worse for wear. He was however visibly upset at missing the shooting and stabbings. He felt his ten-year-old honor was forever damaged and sulked on a bunk.

Pua fussed over Maleko and his injuries. At first, he fought her until Tane whispered it was Captain Sharp's idea and probably a way to keep her busy so she did not dwell on the evening's terrors. After that Maleko found he did have some injuries. He even moaned a time or two as Pua cleaned the dressings.

The prisoners were tied up on the deck and told if they moved or made a sound they were dead. The deck was cleaned and the body was put down on the cannon deck next to the other one.

After about fifteen minutes Kia made a soft bird call that meant he had spotted Captain Gerard swimming back to the boat. He reached the side and climbed up the rope ladder. His men were gathered at the top by the time climbed over the railing.

"Prisoners secured tight with rope, Captain. Noah was in the second bundle. He is fine, pride might be a bit bruised. Pua is nursing Maleko back to health. He is enduring it as well as he can. No other boats seen yet."

Fetu was the one who asked the question on everyone's mind. "Where did you go, Captain Sharp?"

Captain Sharp reached into the hood he was holding and pulled out a leather cord with multiple keys on. "Keys for the brig. Let's get the crew out and help get the wounded into bunks. Once everyone is moved and stable, start putting the prisoners inside the cage one at a time. I want them sitting down inside along the walls, with hands tied behind their backs. Slow and cautious now. These are dead men with nothing to lose and they know it. I'll keep watch for boats while I catch my breath."

The other men walked away to their tasks except for Bothari who stayed and watched Captain Gerard with a critical eye. There was blood on his captain's shirt.

"What else is in the bag?" Bothari asked.

"A couple of souvenirs I promised to get for Pale."

Tane approached the jail cell holding the keys in his hand. One by one the crew of the Tawny Mane stood up in amazement and watched him unlock the door. As he swung the door open one of the senior men spoke.

"I never thought Todd would give up those keys to anyone. Thank you, sir. What do we call you?"

"I am Tane of the Sand Maru. The honor of the keys is not mine to accept. Captain Gerard killed Todd, threw him to the bottom of the sea, and then swam down after him to get the keys for you."

The men were quiet for a few seconds before another old codger spoke up from the group.

"That's a pretty tall tale Mr. Tane. Are you sure he didn't just take the keys off the dead body and then throw him into the ocean?"

Tane looked at the group hard for a few seconds. "I do not weave stories for Captain Gerard as it is not necessary. He simply does things others do not. Ask the prisoners on deck if you like, for they witnessed all."

With that he led the group of men up to the barracks, helping get the sick and wounded into bunks. He asked the able-bodied men to go get some food, some water, and blankets for the wounded. Tane sent runners about the ship to get medicine, bandages and supplies for the men too weak to move on their own. After most of the men returned to the barracks, Tane asked for a group of strong men to help transfer the prisoners into the newly vacated brig. He picked four men including August and led them up the stairs onto the top deck.

On the main deck Captain Gerard was talking to a group of his men from the island. The four men of the Tawny Mane followed Tane, but still approached the Captain's group slowly. They saw two of Todd's men on the far side of the ship kneeling down in front of guards holding them at sword point. Captain Gerard turned to face the group and gave a welcoming smile to the freed crew.

"It is good to see you free, August." The Captain stepped forward and grasped his forearm in a handshake that August was not familiar with. "Who have you brought to help us tonight?"

The men introduced themselves one at a time. Captain Gerard said each man's name out loud and then shook each forearm in a similar manner. "August, Stephan, Mr. Kim, and Jim-Jim, it's nice to meet you. I appreciate your help in this as we are stretched thin. We will be moving the prisoners down into the cell one at a time. Tane will get you a sword before we start. I don't need to tell you that all these men are dangerous. I have instructed my men to kill anyone who puts up a fight. Those instructions apply to you also. I don't want any of us getting hurt."

When he said the word 'us' most of the men jolted and looked up at Captain Gerard's face. "You are free men. Visitors who come to Pukapuka are friends first until proven otherwise. I would call you friends if you would have it?"

August croaked out a yes and wiped his eyes. The other three men said yes and were able to hold it together better. It had been an emotional day for everyone.

"Then get some steel in your hands and get this shit off my deck," Captain Gerard said, gesturing at the men on their knees.

"Yes, Captain Sharp!" The four men said as a group and moved off to follow Tane to the armory.

The two men from the deck went down first and were tied with no incident. The next man was also compliant and was tied securely. As soon as the fourth man was untied, he started fighting for his life. Maleko cut him deep on the shoulder and spun him around just in time for Mr. Kim. Mr. Kim stabbed him deep, and then slashed, and slashed and slashed. The Sand Maru men stepped back and let the fury of the Tawny Mane run its course. Mr. Kim came back to himself about 30 seconds later in the now red room. There was not much left of the man on the ground, and the floor was a mess. Mr. Kim was also covered in red. He started to apologize for his behavior until Fetu stepped up and put a hand on his shoulder ignoring the gore.

"Do not apologize for doing what needed to be done. If it would bring your friends back, we would join you in cutting these men to nothing."

Mr. Kim swallowed hard and got a hold of himself again

Fetu walked before the remaining men waiting to be moved into the cell. "That is what awaits you if you try and fight. Mr. Kim did a good job, but I can assure you that I will make a bigger mess out of the next one."

Nobody else resisted. Within fifteen minutes they had the remaining five members of Todd the Dead's crew tied up inside the cell. The unconscious man with the busted mouth had not regained consciousness yet, and was tied up on his side in the middle of the cell. The men made some noise about the smell and asked that the dead and diced body be removed.

Maleko just laughed and locked the cell door. "You can take that up with Captain Sharp the next time you see him."

Jim-Jim was crouched down next to one of the prisoners from the rowboat and asked him what happened up on deck. The men talked back and forth for several minutes with Jim-Jim asking several questions and poking him with the point of the sword. When the man on the ground finished talking Jim-Jim stood up and said he was ready to go.

The group of men left the brig and headed back up to the main deck. When Mr. Kim came into view several members of the crew stopped what they were doing and looked at him. Tane shook his head back and forth and everyone went back to what they were doing. Mr. Kim laid his sword and his shoes on the deck, climbed over the rail and jumped into the ocean for a bath. Captain Gerard met the group and waited for the update. Tane said all prisoners had been moved and secured. One fought back and was disposed of by Mr. Kim.

"Good work, crew. Everyone take a break, get some food or drink if you want. We are still going to wait until sunrise, then take a boat into the village. Until then rest up, get your strength back. That's an order," Captain Gerard said with a smile.

"Yes, Captain Sharp," the men said as a group, and then went down to the barracks. August tried to give his sword back to Tane who told him to keep it for now, just in case. August thanked him and followed his old crewmates down into the barracks. When he arrived, Stephen was already asking Jim-Jim questions and the rest of the crew had gathered around to listen.

"It was just like Mr. Tane told us. Todd had stolen a child from the village and was holding her like a shield with a knife to her neck. Captain Sharp was calm as pond water and shot him right between the eyes . . . with a handheld flintlock no less! It had to be at least twenty feet, at night, on the deck of a rocking ship. Todd fell over the side and into Davey's locker. Then Captain Sharp killed the next man in line and after that the last two men gave up right quick. Twas after that Captain Sharp shucked his boots, stood on the railing and then dove into the crushing blue by hisself. He chased Todd's body all the way to the gates of hell and took the keys away from him, he did."

Everyone was silent as they digested the story. One of the other men sitting on a bunk spoke softly to the group. "I was talking to that Kai fella earlier. He said Captain Sharp rode a shark once. Rode it around the lagoon like a kid rides a pony. I thought he was pulling my leg at the time but his face was serious as the tax man."

"Aw come on, that breaks it. Nobody rides a shark, that's just nonsense," one of the other men said. A few heads nodded with him but most of the sailors were still thinking about it.

The sailors started talking about what they were going to do. They had their ship back but didn't have a captain or a first mate. They had also lost the sergeant at arms, the master gunner and the doctor. They still had the navigator and could probably get back home, but they also lacked supplies like food and water for the return trip. The conversation continued into the night and one by one the men fell asleep on soft beds for the first time in a long time.

20

Bothari watched the sleeping crew of the Tawny Mane and had to smile. They were all sacked out on various bunks and hammocks, sleeping like kittens and snoring like alligators. The sun was just starting to come up and Captain Sharp wanted to talk with the crew from the ship. Bothari thumped his spear on the ground three times, producing a deep wooden thump. The sound woke the men without startling them out of a deep sleep. They have been through enough lately. When most of the men were sitting up and rubbing their eyes, Bothari addressed the men in bunks.

"The sun will be up soon and Captain Sharp will be wanting to go back to the island. He would like to talk to a few men up on deck. He asked for a group of trusted men who would speak for the rest of your crew. Take a few minutes to get yourselves sorted out and then meet us up top."

Before he could leave one of the crewmen yelled out what had been keeping some of them awake last night.

"Mr. Bothari sir?" said the weathered sailor. "Is it true that Captain Sharp rode a shark once?

"No," Bothari answered.

The men had just started to murmur among themselves when Bothari spoke again. "He's done it more than once. He says that sharks speak to him, but I've never heard them utter a peep." With that he turned and walked away. Several of the men had their mouths hanging open.

The four men who showed up on the deck were Jim-Jim, Cornelius, Hickory, and August. Jim-Jim was one of the oldest sailors on board with more sea time than anyone. He was known for spinning tall tales but was respected enough to be chosen as one of the representatives. Cornelius was the navigator and hardly ever talked, but was supposed to be incredibly book smart. Hickory was one of the coppers and well respected by the crew. He was the type to lend a hand wherever it was needed and the crew had taken notice. August had risen in status after his talks with Captain Gerard and was now considered the liaison between the Tawny Mane and the Sand Maru.

Captain Sharp, Bothari, Fetu, Tane, Kia, Maleko, were all waiting on the deck for the new arrivals. Maru handshakes were shared all around as the men were introduced to each other.

"We're returning to the island to check on our Koko, and to see what has become of the rest of Todd's men." Gerard said. "We would like to see if any crimes were committed by those in the brig before we deal with them. We would return later today if that is acceptable with you?"

The men all nodded.

"What of you and your crew? Do you have any plans for moving forward?"

The men all looked at each other a moment before Jim-Jim motioned for Hickory to speak for them.

"Well Sir, we spent half the night just kicking that thought around ourselves and we don't have a plan just yet. We lost some vital crew members, and have a few men on the doctor's watch. We are also short on supplies after being raided by Todd and his men." Hickory stopped talking and the rest of them remained silent. Three of the men dipped their heads as if they were embarrassed about their situation. August just stared at Captain Sharp with a look of hope.

"Hickory, Jim-Jim, August, and Cornelius. You have come to Pukapuka Island with empty hands and heavy hearts. The Sand Maru welcome you as friends. May our water replenish you; may our food strengthen you, and may our friendship mend your hearts. Stay as long as you like my friends. Koo Koo Kushaw."

"Koo Koo Kushaw," said the other Maru. And just like that, everyone was hugging.

Most of the crew of the Tawny Mane had come up onto the deck to say goodbye to their rescuers and new friends from the island. Captain Sharp had given one of the brig keys to Hickory for safekeeping. The six warriors climbed down into the longboat along with Pua and Noah. Once they got the weight distributed evenly, they moved the boat around to the island side of the ship. Kia let out a yell and the six men dug in with paddles and the boat moved forward. Pua and Noah were chanting a song and the rowers kept beat with the song.

Kia yelled "wikiwiki!" The singing sped up and the rowers kept time and the boat shot forward.

Another two verses brought another "wikiwiki" yelled by all the men this time. Now the boat was really moving and Noah's laughter carried back to the ship. The longboat flew towards home.

Halfway to the beach the Sand Maru started pouring out of the jungle. At first a few, then dozens, then it seemed like the whole village was coming out to meet them. Hoots and shouts went up from both the longboat and the beach. Noah was standing on the prow of the boat as it came tearing up to the beach.

Twenty feet from the beach Kia yelled "hoe!" and the rowers all lifted their paddles up above them with both hands. The keel of the longboat cut into the beach as the weight and momentum pushed the boat up onto the sand. Noah flew into the air and was caught by two parents who were both overjoyed and furious at the same time.

As the men got out of the boat Captain Sharp offered his hand to Pua to help her step out. She gracefully stepped out of the boat and then smashed into Gerard with another one of her full speed hugs. He hugged her back and got a kiss on the cheek again before she turned away. Her parents waited nearby and scooped her up as soon as she turned around.

Mano stepped forward and also crashed into Gerard in another Maru style hug. He stepped back and put his hand on Gerard's shoulder like a proud father. Those around him stopped to listen as the elder started talking. "I see that your visit to the ship was fruitful. Thank you for bringing our children home. If you had done nothing else, we would have been forever grateful. However, a whisper in my head says Captain Sharp has had good fortune on this night. What say you Gerard?"

All eyes went to him and everyone stopped to listen.

"I may have had a little luck," he said humbly. The villagers all cheered and then attacked him.

21

The village gathered in the largest clearing available to hear the reports from last night about the attack on the village and also the raid on the ship. The inner circle were all the village Kupunas, Pale and Sefina, and half of the Koa. The other half of the warriors were guarding what was left of the pirates. Gerard and his group of men were there, along with special guests Pua and Noah, who were allowed to listen but not talk. Roo sat next to Gerard holding his hand, she had not let go of it since his return. The villagers were 'hold your breath quiet' so everyone could hear all the way to the back.

Mano stood first and held the talking staff. He led them in a prayer thanking the Purple Tiki for watching over them and keeping the villagers safe. None of the Sand Maru were killed, and only a handful had injuries worth mentioning like Maleko and Fetu. He then thanked everyone who fought to defend the island, men, women and children. He handed the staff to Pale and took his seat.

Pale first thanked the village for their help in preparing for the attack and for following his recommendations for safety. Well, mostly following he repeated with a stern look at Pua and Noah. Then the whole story was told. About one hour after full dark the pirates came in three boats that spread out to different spots on the island. The smallest boat with only four men aboard came straight into the lagoon and beached where they had visited earlier in the day. The second longboat went further south and approached Akala (Pink) beach with six men on board. The third longboat went north around the point and came over the reef into a body of water called Haki (the break) with four men on board including the leader Todd. This beach was not watched because it was near suicide to go over the shoals in a boat.

The lagoon boat was pulled up onto the beach. The four men drew swords and crept towards the jungle. No torches were lit so the clumsy pirates had to feel their way to the dark tree line. A full dozen warriors hid nearby, watching them approach. When Pale moved on the first man, all the others moved as well. It had been pre-decided that the first wave of Koa would use clubs and knock them out with head shots. If any pirate still stood after the first hit, the second wave would move in and put that man down fast with steel. Pale had cautioned the men against swinging too lightly. A wounded man might kill a fellow warrior, but a dead kidnapper merely saved them from an execution the following day.

The four hits were on target and the men dropped like stones in the sand. Koa standing by with ropes quickly tied up the men, loaded them on shoulders, and carried them to the collection area set up ahead of time. This area was lit with torches and heavily guarded by more Sand Maru Koa. The four men were laid out in front of the guards. Two were dead, two were alive. The men back at the lagoon pulled the boat up into the jungle and hid it, covered the tracks in the sand, and collected any weapons dropped by the pirates. Pale finished telling his part of the tale and handed the talking staff to one of his senior Koa Pulima, (the fist). Pulima bowed to Pale who then sat down.

Pulima's voice was deep and carried easily to the farthest rows of listeners. He watched Akala beach when a runner reported that a boat was coming down the coast with an unknown number of men on board. Pulima and eight other men hid in the tree line; they watched the boat approach and then beach itself. The men started to walk directly into the trees, then changed direction and moved further south towards a clearing down the beach. Pulima and his men had to move quietly through the jungle as they paralleled the six men. At one point it looked like the men were going to turn south again away from the hidden warriors. Eventually, they turned back and moved slowly into the trees. Pulima and his men were not in perfect positions, but they moved fast on soft feet. Four men went down immediately and didn't utter a sound. A fifth man staggered around a few steps, until a Koa took him in the neck with his long blade. The sixth man ducked just enough to only get a glancing blow; he came up cussing and swinging. The warrior with the club stepped back as the Koa with steel stepped forward. It was over quickly and the dead pirate lay in the sand next to his crewmates. All six were tied, shouldered, and taken to the collection area. Four were dead, and two were still alive. The boat was moved and hidden, the area was swept clean, and weapons were collected. Pulima and one other man stayed on the beach to continue the watch.

Pulima reached down and helped another man to his feet, and handed him the talking staff. He bowed once and then sat back down. The new Koa was Honu (turtle) was younger, his voice less confident. He had been assigned the west side of the village with another Koa. He didn't expect any action because he was on the opposite side of the island from the ship. Half the night passed with nothing to report. Then a villager ran up behind him asking for help. Coral, the mother of Pua, reported that she was missing from the hut, and it was unknown if she had left on her own or had been taken. Honu sent Coral and the other Koa back to the village to wake one of the elders and start a search. A short time later they discovered that Noah was also missing. Since the two of them often hung out together, and the huts were not near each other, they determined that they had left together on their own. Parents paired up with Koa; they swept the area around the village working outwards. They searched for hours, finding no sign of the children. Pua and Noah had bowed their heads earlier; now were trying to disappear into the sand.

As dawn approached, the elders decided that two boats of Koa would be made ready for an attack on the pirate ship. They hoped to hear word from Gerard the Sharp before sending Koa into battle, but they also felt time was of the essence. Two teams of Koa had been picked out and armed when word reached them that a longboat was inbound from the ship. They all ran to the beach.

When Honu finished speaking, he handed the talking staff to Captain Sharp. He bowed once and went back to his seat. Gerard had been asked to give a full report since most of the islanders already knew what happened on the island that night. Word travels fast on small islands. However, nobody knew what happened on the ship; their ears were eager for every morsel of information. Gerard started by describing the row around the island and the approach in the dark from the ocean side. He talked them through boarding the ship and clearing the top two decks. He then spoke of the attack and how Bothari volunteered to go first, how Tane covered their backs. He talked about how Maleko, Kia and Fetu took their half of the ship with ease. He spoke of finding the brig at the bottom of the ship filled with the original crew of the Tawny Mane. He spoke of August, Jim-Jim, Mr.Kim, Stephan, Hickory and Cornelius. Good men in a bad spot. He explained how the cowardly attack on Maleko and Fetu caught them off guard and injured them, and how he and Bothari killed the man and together they secured the ship.

A boat was seen approaching the ship and the men hid for an attack. Todd and his men climbed aboard with Pua and Noah and were met by the Koko of the Sand Maru. Two of the men were killed including Todd, and the other two men surrendered. He took the keys from Todd's body and let the crew out of the brig; they moved the prisoners into bunks with food, water, and medical attention. He explained how the crew seemed lost with no captain and no leader, and running low on food and water. He spoke of how he offered friendship on behalf of the Sand Maru, and help with supplies. He told them he would return this afternoon and help them deal with the criminals.

Captain Gerard finished talking and went to return the talking staff to Mano when Bothari, Kia, Fetu, and Maleko all stood up at the same time. Everyone laughed and the four men came together and had a short discussion. Bothari, Kia and Maleko bowed and sat back down and Fetu held out his hand for the talking stick. Fetu was the better storyteller and Gerard feared the worst. He handed the talking staff over to Fetu, gave him a short bow, and then sat down. Roo kissed his cheek and then held his hand again.

"Thank you, Captain Sharp, for the very watered-down version of the events of last night. We honor you, we respect your leadership, but we feel it is a disservice to the Sand Maru that you do not speak of your deeds. Let me tell the Sand Maru what really happened last night, the whole story."

He could feel Roo looking at him but Gerard didn't look back at her. They had not been alone since his return and he didn't have time to tell her much except the bare bones of the story. He hung his head in resignation as Fetu launched into his tale of legend. The more Fetu talked the more he felt the weight of the village's eyes upon him. Fetu stayed mostly to the facts, and only bent the truth here and there, but it was bad enough. This was the first time Gerard heard that he swam all the way to the gates of hell and back, but by then Fetu was on a roll. Roo squeezed his hand a few times and Gerard squeezed hers back. She only gasped a few times. He wrapped up the story with Captain Gerard welcoming the crew as friends, and the crew members crying and hugging the warriors on the deck.

Fetu turned and walked over to Pua and held out the talking stick for her to take. She looked terrified to touch it and turned to look at Mano instead. He gave a go-ahead shooing motion and she allowed herself to be pulled to her feet. Fetu handed her the talking stick, bowed once, and then returned to his seat.

Pua took several deep breaths before she looked up and faced the villagers. Her voice was soft and cracking at first but she got stronger as she went. "I am sorry for making my village worry over me, I did not think about the consequences of my actions. I am sorry for putting our warriors in danger because I was foolish. I would never want anyone to be hurt because I did something stupid." Pua wiped her eyes and took another deep breath. "When the pirates jumped us on the beach and wrapped us up, I was never so scared in my whole life. All I could think about was protecting Noah. I fought the men but when I was hit in the face I fell down and couldn't think anymore. They covered my head and tied my hands and carried me away. I prayed for the Purple Tiki to help me but I knew that he would not. The Purple Tiki had warned me not to go out onto the beach, but I did not listen. I cried all the way back to the ship. I prayed to the Purple Tiki for a quick death, and that it would not hurt too much. I prayed that when my life was at-end, I would make the Sand Maru proud."

Tears were coming down her face now and some in the audience had tears as well. She turned to face Gerard now. "When the men got me onto the ship and pulled my hood off, the first thing I saw was Captain Sharp. He and Tane were standing right in front of us, facing down the four pirates. The moment I saw him the Purple Tiki whispered in my ear. The Purple Tiki said, 'fear not little flower,' and I was not afraid. I saw my Koko come out of the darkness and surround the pirates. Then Captain Sharp spoke to me softly in Maru. He was trying to reassure me that everything was going to be ok. He said 'fear not little flower.'"

Now she broke down and started bawling. Gerard rose and walked towards her, enveloping the young girl in a hug. She clung to him and cried a bit longer but fought to get herself back under control so she could finish her report. Nobody moved forward for the talking stick. When she was done,

Gerard pulled away to take his seat, but she would not let go of his hand and kept him standing next to her.

"I realized that the Purple Tiki had not abandoned me, and that Gerard the Sharp was there to rescue me. Luck was surely with me."

"When he raised the pistol and fired at the man hiding behind me I didn't even blink. I saw the shot pass over my head and saw the smoke trail it left behind. I felt the man's body jump as he died, and the knife pass across my neck as he stumbled and fell. I was not afraid then, I am not afraid now, and I will never be afraid again."

Pua let go of Captain Sharp's hand, then walked over to Mano and handed him the talking staff. Pua went back to her seat and Gerard sat back down next to Roo, and this time his hand sought out hers. Mano stood up and let a huge smile wash over his face.

"Gerard the Sharp, it would appear you need to learn more of our Maru language, for you left quite a bit out of your story."

Everyone laughed and a few around him clapped him on the shoulders.

"Let us speak of the criminals," Mano said, and the noise dropped to nothing. "Is there anyone caught in our nets who is not guilty of crimes against Pukapuka?"

Nobody moved or whispered.

"These criminals came to our island with blood on their hands and evil in their hearts. We heard the cruelty in their words yesterday; we saw their intentions last night. Many of them have already passed into the Lani, the rest will soon follow. Long has it been since the Sand Maru have had this burden. Long may it be before we see it again. I would hear your thoughts, Koko."

Pale stood up and Mano nodded to him to speak from where he was. "My Koa and I stand ready to serve the Sand Maru in all things. We would take these men and send them on their journey and let our island be troubled no more."

Most of the villagers nodded and Mano bowed to Pale who bowed back and then sat back down.

Gerard had been thinking of this problem all morning and working out the details. The pirates were already dead as far as the Sand Maru were concerned; that was a given. What Gerard wanted was a way to avoid the burden this would place on Pale and the other Koa. Any killing is hard, but the real problem was that it changed men in ways you could not always foresee. Gerard stood and Mano motioned him to speak when he was ready.

"My Koko, all these men have committed crimes against the island of Pukapuka. We stood together last night and protected our sands. Those who would do us harm have paid the price, and half of those dwell in Kehena (hell) today. I feel our honor is intact, and the debt to our people has been paid."

"Our new friends on the Tawny Mane have also had crimes committed against them. Their friends were killed, including the captain. They were beaten, imprisoned, and starved to death. Nobody has had to answer for those crimes as of yet. No opportunity for revenge has been available until now. Here a debt remains to be paid."

"If just one of our people had been killed by the pirates it would have been unspeakable," he said, making sure not to look at Pua. "If the killer had been caught by others, and they alone got to choose his punishment and carry out the sentence, our grief would have no end."

"The debt to be paid by these criminals is owed to the crew of the Tawny Mane. They have already asked for this honor. I would deliver these men to the crew, then assist them in any way they ask. The guilty will answer for their crimes. The crew will have their vengeance. And the debt owed will be paid."

Gerard bowed to Mano and sat back down. Most of the village was nodding, as was Mano.

"Anyone else wishing to speak?" Mano asked the villagers.

Pale stood again and Mano nodded for him to go ahead. He faced Gerard and spoke again.

"My brother speaks true as usual. The insult to us was mostly words and talk of evil deeds. The crime against the ship and her crew was murder and torture. The privilege of killing the criminals should be theirs."

Pale bowed to Gerard who stood and bowed back. Mano again asked if anyone else wanted to speak and nobody else stood. Mano motioned for the other Kupunas to stand and the men grouped in a circle to confer. In less than a minute the group broke up and Mano held his hands up for quiet although nobody was talking.

"The Sand Maru agree that the criminals belong to the crew of the Tawny Mane. We will offer them our assistance along with our friendship. This meeting has ended." He laid the talking stick down on the ground. "Malie my Koko."

The meeting broke up and most of the villagers started drifting away. Many of the islanders came to hug Gerard and offer him words of thanks. He accepted these with grace and kept saying that he could not have done anything without his Koko's help. Many others came close enough to lay a hand on his shoulder and thank the Purple Tiki for his guidance. Roo said she was going back to her hut but asked that Gerard stop by when he could. He kissed her warmly before letting her go. She held his eyes and whispered 'well done my captain' before letting him go. Mano had left earlier but told Gerard to stop by later on as they would make plans. Mano wanted to visit the ship and meet their new friends. Fetu came and embraced Gerard, joking that if he did not take proper credit next time, his tales would be exaggerated even worse and the old women of the village would start to burn candles at his door like the Akua. (Gods)

When Fetu left and Gerard was alone at last he set off towards the village for his last job of the long night. He was going to try and find a few hours of sleep before they went back out in the boats to the ship and to deal with the prisoners. It was another beautiful day on Pukapuka; everyone he passed had a smile and a kind word. He thought about his time here and how much he enjoyed his second family.

22

Gerard came to Pale's hut and did a traditional knock on the wooden doorway. Sefina came out and immediately hugged Gerard and started to ask about last night. He deflected a few questions as he always did and then asked if Pale was home.

"Ipo," (lover) she called into the hut.

Pale came out and seemed happy to see him. The men shook arms as always.

"I would speak to you privately if you have a few moments to spare," Gerard said and his eyes did a quick look at Sefina.

"Absolutely not," Sefina said.

"Sefina . . ." Pale started.

"I am your wife and I am your equal. I wanted to fight last night, but stayed in the village because you asked. When Pua was taken, I wanted to go after her in a boat, but I stayed because you asked. I am done being left behind. Either I am your wife and we share all things, or I am not, and we share nothing. Decide now, my husband." Sefina's cheeks were pink, her hands were on her hips. She planted a foot and glared at Pale. She was gorgeous on a normal day but with her anger up and the color in her face she was stunning.

Gerard had no idea how Pale handled a woman like this.

Pale rubbed his forehead; it looked like this was not the first time they'd had this argument. Pale looked at Gerard and shrugged leaving the decision up to him.

Gerard decided to forge on, but he was going to be evasive about it. "Thank you for your kind words in the clearing. I did not mean to keep any honor from you and the other Koa," Gerard said.

"Your arguments were valid and wise," Pale said and smiled.

"Speaking of honor," Gerard cleared his throat. "Do you remember the talk we had on the beach yesterday after the pirates went back to the ship?"

"I remember it well," Pale said. Sefina was looking back and forth between them trying to figure out what they were talking about.

Gerard reached into his pocket and pulled out a small canvas bag with a drawstring closure at the top. It was tied tight. He hefted it in his hand a few times before looking up at Pale. "I kept my promise."

"Indeed?" asked Pale with a look of wonder.

"Indeed." Gerard held the bag out for Pale, who took it softly and respectfully.

"What is in the bag?" Sefina asked.

"Souvenirs," both men said at the same time.

"May I see?"

"No," Both men said at the same time.

"Pale!" Sefina yelled.

Pale moved forward and embraced his brother.

"You honor me." Pale said when they parted.

"Pale, I want to see what's in the bag." Sefina said, getting angry now.

"And with that, I will leave you two alone," Gerard said, backing up.

"Coward," Pale whispered with a grin on his face.

"Guilty," Gerard whispered back.

"Pale, give me that bag right now!"

"Sefina, there are some things . . ."

"Pale Kalane Arturo, I am going to count to three. . ."

Gerard the Sharp, afraid of nothing, turned and ran for his life.

23

Gerard went to Roo's hut and managed a few hours of sleep before a runner woke him to meet down at the lagoon. Roo helped him get ready and prepared some food for him to eat along the way. Two longboats of men prepared to row out and meet the ship and their new friends. Several of the village Kupunas were going, along with two of the island doctors to see if they could help with the injured. Kai and Fetu were going back as was Bothari. They packed some food and wine with them, but they intended to invite most of the crew back to shore to share in the village's meal.

The boats pushed off and drifted out into the afternoon sun. Then rowers took over; the boats pulled steadily towards the ship at a much slower pace than the sprint home this morning. A shout went up from the boat and Gerard looked up to see several men on the deck waiving and hooting with joy.

The boats pulled along the lagoon side of the ship and this time they tied off to the rope ladders. Gerard climbed up the side first and was helped over by August and Hickory. The men remembered the handshakes and said they were happy to see him again. More Sand Maru came over the side; more crew emerged from below decks.

Eventually everyone had to move back to make room as the deck was filling up. Kia and Fetu moved through the crowd talking to friends they had made earlier. When the last villager was up from the boats, Captain Gerard waved over Mano and the other elders.

Gerard made introductions all around, including everyone he knew from the village. Hickory in turn introduced all the crewmembers on deck, including a few Gerard had seen but not met yet. It seemed that Hickory had been chosen as the temporary speaker for the crew, with Jim-Jim as his second for now. After the introductions, Mano formally greeted the guests and welcomed them to the island and village. He extended the invitation for meals on the beach, and told the crew they were welcome to travel back and forth between the ship and the village, whatever they were comfortable with.

Hickory thanked him for the kind welcome and offer of friendship. He said his men were doubly thankful, for both the rescue and the offer of aid and friendship. He then asked about the raid on the island and if everyone was okay. He specifically asked about the women and children, including Pua and Noah. Mano informed him that all was well and that the raid was 'unsuccessful.' At this many of the Koa laughed.

Mano promised him the full story later, but right now it was time to celebrate new friends. The islanders carrying food were led towards the galley by some crew where together they would start to prepare some meals. The island doctors checked on the crew members still confined to a bed. Bothari went down to check the brig.

Hickory gave the Kupunas a walking tour of the ship, pointing out interesting things and answering questions the men had. Gerard drifted to the back of the group to walk with August and see what was happening on the ship. August said the men had been cleaning the ship and putting things back in order. Stephan had begun an inventory of supplies to figure out what they had and what they needed. Hickory repaired the door to the armory and even made some improvements, August reported. They still had a few dead bodies to deal with and the mess in the hold, which nobody had cleaned up so far.

"There is one more thing, Captain Sharp. None of the men are willing to go into the captain's quarters. At first Hickory told everyone to stay out of there until we got things sorted out. When we started cleaning, some of the men didn't want to go in there out of respect for Captain Dominic. Others say it's bad luck to go into a dead captain's quarters. For now it's locked, but honestly nobody is trying to get inside. In fact, everyone is avoiding it if they can."

The tour had reached the crew barracks when word came that the galley was open and that dinner was being served. Mano joked with the wounded men stuck in bed. He told a story about getting gored in the butt by a wild boar when he was twelve. He'd spent the next two weeks sitting on aloe vera plants. Mano had all the wounded men laughing through their pain. One could see what made him a good leader; he was just so good with people.

Their group moved to the galley and joined the men already eating. Space was so limited that the party spilled out onto the upper deck and the barracks. Both groups seemed to be becoming quick friends; there was plenty of laughing on both sides.

After dinner Mano told Hickory they would like to talk about the prisoners and what happens next. He recommended that some other crew members participate in the conversation in order to cut down on rumors and help get information back out to the crew faster. The galley seemed large enough, so Hickory excused most of the men but held a handful back by name.

Hickory was joined by Stephan, Cornelius, Jim-Jim and August. Mano told them about the raid on the village last night and the defenses the Sand Maru had in place. The crew seemed pleased that it had gone so well for the islanders, and so poorly for the pirates. He finished the tale with the longboat returning this morning with the children and then nodded for Gerard to take over.

Gerard explained that they had killed half of the pirates and captured the rest. While they had no problem killing the rest of the men, the Sand Maru felt that the honor belonged to the crew of the Tawny Mane as they had also been wronged. The Sand Maru would help if asked, stand by if needed, or take care of the whole thing if that is what the crew wanted.

Hickory blew out some air and thanked the islanders. He took a moment to gather himself before he started talking again. "The crew has been talking about what to do with the men in the hold. We all agree that they need killing. We have not decided how to do it yet, but hanging and drowning are both on the list. We don't exactly have warriors on this ship, so your help is welcome. What do you think, Captain Gerard?

"I have been thinking about the problem all night and I think I have come up with a solution that everyone will approve of. I think we should sentence them to Piholo Mokupuni," Gerard suggested. The elders nodded and made affirmative sounds after he said this.

"What is that?" August asked.

"Piholo Mokupuni means the sinking island," Gerard said, "It's basically just a sandbar about forty miles east of Pukapuka. It's about eighty feet long and twenty feet wide with nothing growing on it. It lies in an area of exceptionally strong tidal currents. At low tide the highest point of the island is about six inches above sea level. At high tide, the island is about five feet under water. The island sinks twice each day."

"Ahhhh," said the crew of the ship.

Gerard asked the crew if the Tawny Mane could be made ready to sail by tomorrow morning. The men agreed it could be, but they were still short a few men needed for the sails and rigging. Gerard said the Sand Maru could help with that part. Cornelius left briefly, returning with charts and maps. He did some quick math and believed the trip would probably take five hours going out with the current pushing them, but less than four hours coming home with a fair wind in the sails. Gerard told the crew the plan he had for the prisoners, and then he told them what he planned on telling the prisoners. Everyone nodded in understanding when he finished.

"The villagers and I will return before first light tomorrow. To reach the tides we want we need to sail with the sunrise. We will bring the prisoners we have and their dead. We don't want these dead men buried on our island because they are evil. We don't want to put the bodies into the sea at our beach, because we don't want our sharks to associate our island with food. All will come with us, all will be left, and we will be done with them all."

Gerard, Mano, and Hickory entered the hold and relieved the guard sitting across the room from the prisoners. He did a head dip on his way out and headed for the stairs. The smell wasn't any better. The disaster made by Mr. Kim had been pushed off to the side but not cleaned up. The captured men began talking even before the guard was out of sight. With several of them talking at once it was difficult to understand but the gist of it was they were hungry, thirsty, had to go to the bathroom, and their arms were going numb.

When he was ready, Gerard held up his hand and made a motion for them to stop and be quiet. "We have talked with the crew members of the Tawny Mane and together we have decided your fate. These sailors are not warriors, as you knew when you took over the ship and killed some of them. They have no desire to line you up and chop your heads off one by one. We have decided to transport you to another island and drop you on the beach. There you can do whatever you want. Our only condition is that you never return to Pukapuka. You may live out the rest of your lives on that island in peace, or fighting amongst each other. We care not either way. We leave at first light."

Some of the men smiled during Gerard's speech, others were outright grinning by the end of it. They had escaped the blades of the island savages and would do or say anything to stay alive. Several started to ask questions at the same time, but Gerard held up his hand again for quiet.

"I will hear no questions from you. Tomorrow you will see your new home for the first time. I recommend you behave until then. It would be sad indeed if some of you were killed on the eve of your new dawn."

Gerard walked away, followed by Mano and Hickory.

On deck there was a flurry of activity as the men finally had a job to do and seemed grateful to be doing it. Maru and sailors worked side by side and talked back and forth like new friends do. Mano elbowed Gerard as they watched a team of men bring empty barrels out of the hold and up onto the deck. The sailors sang a work shanty and taught the words to the men from the island. When this one finished, the islanders started to sing one of their songs and the process was reversed. Another team loaded the barrels into one of the longboats to be taken to the Pukapuka and filled with drinking water.

On the poop deck Cornelius had the rest of the Kupunas in a group, explaining to them how the compass and sextant work. It looked like he was teaching two different men how to use two different things at the same time. He was going back and forth and talking a mile a minute but the Kupunas understood it all; these men were known for their brains as well as their leadership. Cornelius demonstrated how to use the sextant, pointing at the horizon and then the sky and back. He handed the device off to one of the men, showed him how to hold it, and what to look at. The rest of the men leaned in with wide eyes like kids around a new toy.

Gerard saw Kai working on a sail with another man and flagged him down. He pulled him aside and told him what was needed. Kai would check with Hickory and Cornelius to learn how many villagers they would need for the sail the next day. Kai would pick a group of men from his voyagers who were both good sailors and could help with securing and transporting the condemned. He would have these men back at the beach before sunrise, ready to go with swords.

Gerard and Mano went back to the island in one of the boats with only empty barrels, two sailors and two villagers. The rest of the villagers and Kupunas elected to stay on the ship for now as there would be many boats going back and forth this evening. Landing on the beach in the lagoon, the scene was similar to the one they just left. Crew from the Tawny Mane and villagers of the Sand Maru worked together lifting, loading, and laughing. Most of the sailors were familiar with the island handshake now and offered it every time they met a new person.

Many of the village women came to the beach to help with preparations and to meet the crew. Some of the men froze at the introductions but after some elbowing and shoulder punching by their new friends they got on with the work. Gerard found it interesting how many of the women volunteers fell into the category of 'unattached single women.'

Mano sent a runner to find Pale and ask him to meet them at the prisoner collection area. As they walked, Gerard looked for a way to bring up his concerns about the probable courtships between sailors and women of the island. Finally, he decided he needed to be blunt about it and dive in head first. "I do not know if it is my place, but I have some concerns about the women on the beach helping the sailors."

Mano stopped so fast that Gerard had to turn around to find him. Mano started to giggle, then laugh, and then started to completely lose it. He leaned forward with his hands on his knees, laughing with so much enthusiasm that eventually Gerard started to laugh with him. Mano had so much joy inside him it was contagious. When he wound down and wiped away a few tears he put a hand on his Koko's shoulder.

"Gerard the Sharp, there are many things on this island we do not know, but what happens when new men visit this island is something we figured out a long time ago. What do you think the women have been doing for the last two days? Olina, one of the elder female Kupunas, got most of the village women together yesterday and went over the rules of Kalepa (the trade). Our women have a list of rules that must be obeyed, just like the men do. If it will ease your mind young Gerard, know that the volunteers you see on the beach are just that, volunteers. They are of age, they are unattached, and they are looking to catch the eye of a lonely sailor."

It had been a long time since Gerard was embarrassed and felt his cheeks go pink. It was good to know he could still put his foot in his mouth if he set his mind to it.

"Your concern is appreciated Gerard, and I know you care for everyone on this island as they care for you. Olina mentioned to me in passing that I should talk to you about this, but I thought you already had too much on your mind." Mano started to giggle again.

Gerard put his hand on the shoulder of his mentor. "Thank you for reminding me that there is always something new to learn."

They started to walk again and Mano whispered under his breath. "When I tell Olina what you said, she is going to pee herself."

24

In the galley of the Tawny Mane nearly the entire crew had gathered for a meeting. Everyone was present except for the two men still on the doc's watch back in their bunks. Hickory told the crew about Gerard's plan to sail tomorrow morning and dispose of the pirates. Kai and several other voyagers of the Sand Maru would be returning in the morning to help them sail the ship. These men were all familiar with sailing boats between the neighboring islands. The islanders were also sending warriors to help deal with the prisoners and make sure they didn't cause any more problems.

"We have everything we need for tomorrow except a captain," Hickory said, looking at Jim-Jim.

"Don't look at me," Jim-Jim said waving his hands in front of himself, "That's a headache I want no part of. What about you Hickory? You could do it just fine."

A few of the crew murmured in agreement.

"I work with wooden barrels not wooden ships. Just the thought of it makes ma belly roll over," Hickory said. He turned and looked at the navigator.

"What about you Cornelius?" Hickory asked.

"No," was all the navigator said at first. "What about Captain Sharp? Seems to me he is not just qualified but battle tested."

"I think he would do a fine job but does he want the job?" Hickory said.

"He's from England and has been shipwrecked here for four years, he probably wants to sail back home," August said.

"He seems awfully young for a captain," Tanner added.

"Can we just ask him to be captain?" Edmund said.

"What if he says no?" Stephan asked.

"I reckon all we can do is offer him the job in the best way possible. How about when he arrives tomorrow morning we line up on the deck, salute, and nominate him as captain. He needs a ride home, we need a captain, seems like a fair-trade deal to me," Hickory said.

Most of the crew were nodding in agreement.

"Plus if we get lost, Gerard can ask a shark for directions," Jim-Jim said. He meant it as a joke but nobody laughed; some of the men just nodded like it was another argument in his favor.

Pale and Sefina waited for Gerard and Mano at the prisoner collection area near an old lava flow called Ahiani oi-oi (sharp glass). The lava flow split into two arms that formed a sharp jagged three-sided corral. The sides of the corral were fourteen feet high and made of jagged obsidian glass. This was one of the places where Sand Maru craftsmen came to make tips for their spears and arrows. Lots of torches had been lit and placed around the perimeter, and more than enough Koa watched the pirates.

Gerard and Mano stopped a distance away from the prisoners and waved Pale over to meet them. Pale started walking towards them and Sefina came with him. When they arrived, Pale looked serious but Sefina had a grin on her face. She came up to Gerard and gave him a hug that took him by surprise; he was expecting a punch. Gerard was very careful with his hands as he returned the hug and released it as soon as he thought it was acceptable. Sefina put her hand on his shoulder before stepping back.

"You honor my husband, and you honor me also." She leaned forward and kissed his cheek once. Gerard felt his face flush red for the second time in ten minutes. Sefina let go of his shoulder, made a small fist, and then clocked him not so lightly on the chin. "That is for not telling me what was in the bag before I put my hand inside." She didn't seem too angry. Still, his jaw was not working at one hundred percent. Sefina turned and beckoned her husband down to her level with a crook of a finger. Pale leaned down to her and she kissed his cheek also.

"I will wait for you at home, husband of mine." With that, she walked away.

When she was gone, Mano brought Pale up to date with what was happening on the boat while Gerard cleared his head. When he got to the part about the prisoners, Mano motioned for Gerard to take over. Gerard told him about the plan for the prisoners and the dead bodies. Pale was also happy with the arrangement. If the men could not be given a violent bloody death at his hands, then a slow, torturous death would be the next best thing. Gerard asked Pale to pass this onto his men, but to only tell the prisoners what they needed to hear for now. The dead bodies would be moved to the boats by guards during the night; the prisoners would be moved to other boats by armed guards before first light.

Gerard invited Pale to go with him in the morning on the Tawny Mane to help supervise the operation. Pale didn't even have to think about it.

"No thank you, my brother. It has been a long two days and I am going home to be with my wife and to get some much-needed sleep."

With a serious face Mano placed a hand on Pale's shoulder and said with all the fake concern he could muster. "I am afraid no sleep awaits you at home my brother."

The three friends cracked up laughing.

25

Gerard only got four hours of sleep before the nightmare woke him up. This time he had not brought enough arrows and Sophie was killed. His nightmares had become less frequent over the last few years on Pukapuka but he still had one every month or so. It had probably been three months since his last nightmare where his lack of practice led to a missed shot, and Sophie was killed. He knew it was coming though, the arrival of the ship had stirred up thoughts of home and his family.

"The nightmare?" Roo asked, lying next to him. Gerard nodded in the dark. They didn't need to specify as it was always the same. It had taken some time for Gerard to open up about it, but it woke them up often enough that eventually he had to. Roo was understanding and helpful, but talking about them didn't stop them from happening.

Done with sleeping for the night, he started thinking about everything that needed to be done today so he would be prepared. He looked forward to the opportunity to sail on a big ship again. He looked forward to being done with the problem of the prisoners and the dead men. 'After today,' he kept thinking. After today things change. He double checked the items he packed the night before in the canvas duty bag, kissed Roo goodbye, then headed for Kai's hut on the way to the lagoon.

He was just about to knock on the door when a woman ducked out and almost crashed into him. She pulled a cloak over her head and then took off in another direction. Gerard knocked twice on the door frame and Kai yelled 'komo' (enter) from inside. Gerard ducked in and found Kai putting the last of his clothing on. He looked sheepish; he knew Gerard had seen the woman just leaving. Kai was single and living the bachelor life.

"Friend of yours?" Gerard asked with a grin.

"Just wishing me luck on today's voyage," Kai said, tying his belt.

Gerard took in the messy bed and the condition of Kai's hair. "That must have been a hell of a sendoff," he said, grinning.

"You should talk, you keep Roo's neighbors awake half the night," Kai said with a smirk. Gerard's look of shock was genuine. Gerard knew she made a little noise, but surely they didn't . . .the neighbors couldn't . . . Kai started laughing out loud and slapped Gerard on the back.

"Take it as a compliment my brother," Kai said, "The hens whisper your name over tea and blush like coral."

"Aw shit," Gerard said.

"The legend of Gerard the Sharp!" Kai yelled and then laughed until he cried. Gerard hoped that Roo was blissfully unaware of all of this.

"Let's go," Gerard said "We don't want to be late."

At the lagoon there was a group of men taking care of last-minute details. Mano was there giving orders; Gerard wondered if he ever slept. The Koa had brought the last load of prisoners. Two boats full of them had already been transferred to the ship and secured. Pohaku the Mountain was in charge of this group; they appeared to be on their best behavior.

Kai's group had gone ahead and was already on the ship helping the crew with the canvas. Gerard got Pohaku alone and asked about the dead pirates. They had been loaded into one of the long boats; it was already tied to the back of the Tawny Mane. The crew on board had also loaded their dead pirates into the longboat and secured a canvas across the top. The dead crew of the Tawny Mane had been cleaned, wrapped in sheets, and stored on the cannon deck for a proper burial at sea.

Mano embraced Gerard before he left, wishing him success on his journey. He said the Purple Tiki would travel with them, guiding his heart and hands. Gerard turned to leave, but Mano would not let go of his arm. Gerard raised his eyes in question and Mano leaned in closer and lowered his voice.

"The men on that ship need a captain. They need a leader who is confident and fearless. They need somebody to lead them away from their darkness and into the light. You are that man, Captain Gerard Sharp. Your whole life has been practice for this moment. Go be that man!"

Gerard was rocked by the remarks from his mentor and friend. For the first time in a long time he was literally speechless. Mano handed over a large bag he was holding and embraced Gerard once more in a hug. Then he released him and pushed him towards the waiting boat. Gerard had considered asking to be the temporary captain for the journey today, but felt the position was above his reach. There were older men on the Mane. There were men with much more time at sea. There were men who knew more about sailing tall ships than he did. He thought about the options on the ship and thought about Mano's words. Nobody wanted it more than he did though. Nobody.

He was alone with his thoughts as his boat rowed out towards the waiting ship. The rest of the men were already aboard. This was the last boat with the last group of prisoners, Kia and himself. Gerard remembered the bag Mano had given him and opened it up. Inside was a black wool tricorn captain's hat. It was old, but well cared for. It had a gold pirate coin secured to one side of it. Gerard turned it around in his hands and thought about the next ten minutes of his life. All that practice for this moment. A flash of color caught his eye. Hand-painted on the inside of the brim near his right ear was a small Purple Tiki.

The longboat pulled up to the lagoon side of the ship; the prisoners were moved up one by one. The guards took no chances now. Each prisoner had two escorts. In a few short minutes, the last of the prisoners stepped over the rail and the rope ladder was clear. Gerard went to climb next when Kai asked if he could go first. When Gerard nodded, Kai grabbed Gerard's duty bag off his shoulder and went up the rope fast and over the gunwale in a flash. Gerard stepped off the longboat onto the ropes and then pushed the boat away from the ship with his foot. The two Sand Maru rowers gave a quick wave of thanks and then turned the boat and headed for home. Gerard climbed up the ladder, over the rail, and onto the deck.

The entire crew was on deck at attention. August blew the bosun's whistle for 'captain on deck'. The shrill sound cut through the morning air. When it was done, there was dead silence on the ship. Gerard looked over all the men on the deck. His men. Friends and family, new and old. He gave a silent oath to the Purple Tiki that he would not let them down.

"Thank you, crew. I promise you I will work hard to be a good captain. We will learn fast and we will learn together. By word and by deed I will put this crew and this ship first. Your trust in me is well placed and I will not forget this honor. We have a good beginning together with new friends and new opportunities." Gerard looked towards the horizon and saw the sun would be up soon. "The Tawny Mane has had some dark times. It's time to bring her back into the light."

Gerard reached into the bag and pulled out the captain's hat. He brushed some sand off the side and then got it settled on his head. It fit perfectly, of course. Captain Sharp took a deep breath and started yelling. "All hands-on deck! I want anchor up and canvas down! Cornelius, get on the wheel and get me out of this lagoon! Jim-Jim, run up the colors! Hickory, Bothari, status report now!"

Everyone started running.

Hickory reached him first. The ship had all the supplies it needed for two weeks if needed, but plenty for the one or two day run they planned. The one sail that had been torn more than a week ago had been repaired. They had a full complement of crew and everyone was ready to go.

"Thank you, Hickory. I know you are a cooper at heart, but I need a good quartermaster I can trust. Right now that's you. We will all be doing double duty for a while. The job is yours as long as you want it."

"Thank you, Captain Sharp, the crew and I are happy to have you onboard," Hickory said and moved off.

Bothari appeared in his place, clearly happy to be back on a ship. A cheer went up from the crew as they watched the flag hoisted up to the top of the main mast. The crew agreed on one flag for now: an English flag for their home port, as well as the home of their new captain.

"Bothari my brother, I have need of a First Mate and Sergeant at Arms. I can think of no other man I would want by my side more than you. Will you honor me with your service once more?"

Bothari bowed once, then moved in for a bone-crushing hug. Captain Sharp thought he heard a rib crack, but gave nothing away.

"Your path is my path, Captain. You honor me."

"You will probably be required to talk more, with me and the other crew members. Are you going to be able to handle that?" Gerard asked.

Bothari smiled and grunted once while shrugging his shoulders. It sounded like one of his yes grunts, so Gerard moved on.

"Very well then, give me a report on the prisoners."

"The men we captured on the Tawny Mane are still below, locked in the brig and tied to the bars. The men brought on board this morning from Pukapuka are on the gun deck tied to the cannons. I don't think either group is aware of the other group. All the dead pirate bodies are in the longboat being pulled behind the ship. We have armed Koa and sailors watching both groups. The crew worked most of the night getting the Mane in ship shape. They cleaned, made repairs, and restocked supplies from the island."

The boat moved slowly towards the mouth of the lagoon, consistently picking up speed. They reached the opening in the reef and the ship rolled over the first few breakers. The sun picked that moment to crest over the horizon and wash them in sunlight. Cheers went up from the crew, sailors and islanders alike. Captain Sharp walked back to the helm and checked with Cornelius. They were just cutting into the south equatorial current. Gerard could feel it pushing the boat along. Cornelius said they were running 2-3 knots. That should put them at Piholo Mokupuni in five hours, give or take. Captain Sharp thanked him and was about to leave when he stopped and addressed Cornelius.

"Cornelius, I am afraid I have taken your skills for granted. I never officially asked if you wanted to be my navigator." Cornelius started to say something but Captain Sharp put up a hand to stop him. "Cornelius, I need a man who I trust and who is qualified to navigate this boat. Right now, you are the only man on this boat who meets both those needs. I would be honored if you would agree to be my navigator."

Cornelius looked like he was ready to cry. "I have never been asked like that in my whole life. It would be an honor, sir. A real honor."

Captain Sharp grasped him in a traditional handshake and thanked him. He then made a tactful retreat as Cornelius got something in his eye that made them water profusely.

Captain Sharp walked the deck, taking note of the cleaning job the crew did and the newly repaired items. When he finished his sweep he went down to the gun deck finding Jim-Jim and three other crewmen watching the prisoners.

Jim-Jim gave him an update that all was well and the prisoners were well secured. "I almost forgot about these," Jim-Jim said, taking a lanyard off his neck. It was a leather cord with five keys on it. He handed them over to Captain Sharp and explained what each one was for. One key for the brig was given to him by Hickory last night. Two keys to the armory, with its new door and lock. Two keys to the captain's quarters. Captain Sharp put them around his neck next to the other brig key already hanging there and tucked them into his shirt.

"Jim-Jim, I need a second in command on this ship that I can trust, somebody the men respect and will listen to. I need somebody who will help me learn to be a good captain. I would be grateful if you would be my second mate."

Jim-Jim wrapped Captain Sharp in a hug and then followed it up with a Maru handshake. "You're already a good man, Captain Sharp, but with my help, you're gonna be great. I accept."

He thanked Jim-Jim and the other men guarding the prisoners and said he would check back with them later.

Gerard continued his tour of the gun deck and found the area neat as a pin, except for the pirates tied to the guns. Some of them tried to ask questions as he passed, but he didn't even look at them, much less talk to them. He finished touring the deck, noting the storage area had been cleaned and organized. At the bow were neatly stacked rope, pulleys, grease and ramrods. At the stern of the ship were powder barrels and cannonballs.

Captain Sharp went down to the barracks level and saw it too had been gone over: beds clean, personal items tucked away, blood washed off the floor. Only two men were still confined to beds; he stopped to talk with both of them. Foreword of the crew quarters was the galley, which had been scrubbed spotless. He stopped to talk to the men working there, thanking them for doing such a great job. The men were humble and could not believe the captain had thanked them personally. To the aft of the crew's quarters was more storage, food, water, spare sails and canvas. Everything was organized and secured.

Captain Sharp went down the last ladder into the hold. The horrible smell was gone. It smelled like plumeria flowers, which grew on the island in several places. He wondered if this was the work of Mano or Olina, and made a note to ask when they got home. He checked the front storage area first and found it as neat and clean as the rest. He walked aft, past the stairs towards midship and the brig. He could hear talking up ahead and stopped before coming around the corner.

"....day will come when we find you again mate, either on land or at sea. You could do yourself a favor now and loosen these ropes and I would spare you then, but if you don't, I promise you will die screaming," said one of the pirates.

"I'm not afraid of you, Earl. We got Captain Sharp looking out for us now," said the guard.

"Yes, but Captain Sharp won't always be around now will he?" said the one called Earl.

Captain Sharp went back to the steps and climbed up halfway on quiet feet and then stomped back down. He walked directly towards the brig and when he came around the partition everyone was quiet and looking at him.

Three sailors stood guard on this deck, all outside the brig. Two sat a ways off towards the bow stairs, one stood next to the bars of the cell. When Captain Sharp appeared, the other two guards walked back over to join him at the cell door.

"Any problems?" Captain Sharp asked as he took out the keys and unlocked the cell door.

"None at all," said one of the older guards. "Just a lot of talk and bitching."

Captain Sharp walked into the cell, looking around at the men. Some of them were sleeping, some of them were smiling, but none of them were afraid. "Which one of them is named Earl?" he asked, looking at the young guard.

The guard pointed at a man in the middle on the right side about the same time the man started talking.

"I'm Earl, why do you. . ."

Captain Sharp drew his sword and, in a flash, punched the man in the face with the metal handguard. Blood and teeth splashed on the man to his left and that man started to scream. Captain Sharp hit the guy on the left just to shut him up and ended up knocking him unconscious. He turned his attention back on Earl. He put the tip of his sword over Earl's heart and pushed it in until he was sure it had pierced skin. Earl's face was a bloody mess, his eyes wide and horrified. Better.

"I heard a rumor that Earl threatened one of my crew members. I am Captain of this ship. Nobody threatens my men! Nobody!" Captain Sharp yelled and pushed the knife another half inch. Earl made a low whine in his throat but didn't dare to move or breathe. After a few seconds, Captain Sharp stood and cleaned his knife off.

"The next man in this cell who smiles at me will have his head cut off and thrown over the side." Captain Sharp put his knife back on his belt. All the men in the cell now looked right terrified. That was progress. Gerard walked out of the cell and started to lock the door.

"Where did you hear that rumor, Captain Sharp?" One of his men asked.

Captain Sharp didn't want to admit he was eavesdropping, so he made up a completely unbelievable lie on the spot.

"I went for a swim and a shark told me."

Captain Sharp didn't see his crew members behind him exchange a look of absolute astonishment. He locked the cell door, checked it, and then turned to the guards.

"The next prisoner who talks, I want killed immediately. The next prisoner who talks after that I want killed immediately. Do you have any questions?"

The three guards all shook their heads. "No sir."

"Good. Carry on then."

Captain Sharp climbed back on deck and found everything had settled down into routine. The crew on deck were doing their jobs; the ones not needed had gone below. The ship moved along at a nice clip. The island was disappearing from view behind them. He found August coiling a rope line off a sail and went over to talk to him.

"A word with you, August."

He finished with the rope and turned to face the captain.

"That was a good bosun's whistle this morning. Was that one of your jobs for Captain Dominic?"

August blushed with the compliment. "No sir, that was my first time. Our bosun was killed by the pirates when they took the ship. When I heard we was taking the ship out today, I asked Hickory if I could try it. He gave me the whistle to practice and practice I did. Although, after a few minutes Hickory told me I had to go out in one of the jollys towards the ocean as I was killing the men's ears something awful. I'm glad I got it right Captain, I only learned a few of them so far."

Gerard smiled at his enthusiasm. "August, I know you were one of the deck mates before, but I have a new proposition for you. I need an assistant to help keep me and this ship running smoothly. Cabin Boy doesn't quite fit the job description. On the island we have runners who do all kinds of odd jobs to help, but none of them are assigned to any one man. I would ask that you be my runner and help me with whatever is needed. It's a new job and I would like to hire a man I can trust. I trust you, August. Will you accept the position?"

August was openly crying by the time he finished talking. "I would be honored sir, but I would be too afraid of making a mistake."

"August, I will let you in on a little secret, since I won't take no for an answer. I plan on making mistakes. Big ones. Huge, epic, disastrous public mistakes. Since we already know they are coming, how about you and I plan for them and just make the best of it."

"Alright then sir, where do we start?" August asked, getting himself together.

"Right now. New rule: no crying in front of the crew."

Captain Sharp gave August his first assignment and told him to report back in two hours. As he walked across the deck, he smiled at the crewmen working and nodded to Cornelius at the helm, who smiled and nodded back. Captain Sharp headed for the back of the ship and stopped in front of the captain's quarters. He pulled the keys from around his neck and unlocked the door. The door creaked as it opened; Sharp made a mental note to have Cuthbert fix that straight away. Captain Sharp walked in and shut the door behind him.

The room was a mess; it looked like the pirates had been using this area to eat, sleep and dump garbage. There was some broken furniture. All the drawers and cabinets had been emptied and dumped on the floor. The captain's desk and chair were unharmed, as was the larger maps table on the other side of the room. Five of the six chairs had survived and only one lay broken in the corner. The captain's bed lay in the back corner under the windows, opposite the desk. It looked comfortable enough, the posts going up six feet were very delicate and ornate. The top blanket was an ungodly mix of gold squares and lace fringes. The two sheets underneath were plain white linen; he decided he could keep those, after they had been washed. They stunk. Plenty of work to be done. Captain Sharp went to the back of the room, pulling back the curtains on all the windows for maximum light. He also opened the windows to let some fresh air into the stale room. There were two pegs on the wall just inside the door; there he hung his coat and hat. He took off his sword and belt and left them folded by the door. Then he rolled up his sleeves and got to work.

26

The two hours went by fast, but Gerard had made significant progress. He piled all the garbage up by the door. Papers, maps, and documents were stacked on the desk to be organized later. He fixed what he could on his own; what required Cuthbert's touch was set aside for him.

Captain Sharp spent some time going through the room and looking at all the drawers, cabinets and cubby holes. There was a great amount of space for storing papers, trinkets, and treasures. He found a small bag of assorted coins left behind by Todd and his men. He was looking at the bookcase thinking it was well made and sturdy. There was way too much storage space for his meager possessions but he thought he could put one of his warrior clubs on this long shelf in the middle. It was a bit too small as the sides had been built inward on both ends. He didn't see the reason for the additional woodwork other than decorative. He was running his hand over it when it shifted slightly. In less than a minute he had the secret panel opened and found the two large bags of gold coins inside. When he lifted one of the bags up there was a small piece of paper underneath it. Captain Sharp pulled it out and looked at the note with its elegant handwriting:

"Do not allow this money to fall into ATC hands."
-Reginald

The captain took a quick look inside the bags, saw the gold coins, and then re-tied the top. He put the bags back inside and closed the hidden door. He tried to open the other side of the bookcase in the same spot, but that side was solid wood and its only purpose was decorative. After this discovery Captain Sharp explored the room a second time much more carefully, looking for secret compartments. He found the captain's personal journal on this second sweep under a false bottom in the desk drawer. This he kept out and set aside to be read later, but dropped the small bag of coins inside to be found.

A knock at the door interrupted his cleaning. Gerard called out for the person to enter. The door opened; August stood in the doorway looking in. "Two hours sir, like you asked. I found the men you wanted and they are finished preparing. Hickory and Jim-Jim have a team standing by for the men. I think everyone is ready," August said and smiled.

"Excellent work August, thank you. Head out on the deck and pipe for everyone to come topside for the ceremony. I need just a minute to clean up and then I will join you."

August glowed with pride and then headed out to the deck.

Captain Sharp dusted himself off, then donned his hat, jacket and sword. Outside he heard the whistle for 'all hands' and heard men coming up the steps. When he was together, he opened the door and went back out onto the deck. Most of the men were already topside with a few stragglers still coming up. Captain Sharp walked over to the two men standing by the rail who had been found and recruited by August.

The deckhand Tanner was the drummer for the ceremony and he was dressed normally. Elyas had been recruited as the mortician and had found a black robe for the ceremony. He held a Bible in front of him with ribbons marking a few places. Captain Sharp had a few words with them, going over specifics. When he was done, they nodded and said they were ready. Captain Sharp nodded, and the drummer began playing a slow funeral march.

Captain Sharp removed his hat. Those on deck with hats followed suit. The crew was so still that you could hear the water lapping on the sides of the ship. Hickory and three others came up the stairs carrying the first deceased crew member on their shoulders. He was wrapped and sewn into white sailcloth. A second group led by Jim-Jim came up behind them holding the second crewmen above them. The two groups walked slowly and carefully towards the side rail where they lowered the men onto planks being held up with the edge laid over the railing.

The recruited deckhand and once actor did an excellent job as a makeshift priest. He was a performer and had no problem recreating a funeral. He said kind words about each man; he knew them personally and had sailed with both of them before. He read the appropriate Bible verses and had everyone bow and pray where they should. When he reached the last verse to read, he stopped and nodded for Captain Sharp to speak.

Captain Sharp spoke loud enough for everyone to hear.

"These men of the Tawny Mane were taken before their time. Some of those responsible have already paid for their crimes, others will soon pay. This does not however adequately compensate us for the loss of our crewmates. They died in defense of this ship and her crew. Their sacrifice will not be forgotten. Rest now crew, until we meet again. Malie, peace."

Captain Gerard nodded back to the priest, who nodded at Hickory and started reading.

"Unto Almighty God we commend the souls of our departed brothers, and we commit their bodies to the deep; in sure and certain hope of the resurrection unto eternal life."

The two groups of men holding the planks tipped them up as the priest started reading. The wrapped bodies of the men slid smoothly and quietly off the planks and down into the water with a splash.

Captain Sharp gave everyone a full minute of quiet before he stepped forward and put his hat back on, marking the end of the ceremony. "We have some hard business to handle later today. I want you to remember this moment when you do. The criminals we carry today are responsible for the deaths of your crewmates and former captain. They would kill you if they could. They deserve no mercy, so none will be shown to them. As of sunset today all debts will be paid, and the sea shall wash us clean. Crew dismissed."

As the men returned to their stations, Captain Sharp found Cuthbert and Bothari and held them back. He told August to find two deckmates and have them report to his quarters. Captain Sharp led Bothari and Cuthbert into his quarters. He pointed out to Cuthbert the items that needed replacing or repairing and set him to work. When the deckhands arrived, he had them remove the garbage and asked them to come back and help clean the floor. When they left, he asked August to close the door for a moment with their small group still inside.

"I have found two secret compartments hidden among the walls, drawers and bookshelves. I think more eyes and more hands would help me locate any others I may have missed. You are some of my most trusted men, so I am asking for your help and discretion. If you find anything, keep it to yourself until we are alone again. Okay, Let's get started."

When the deckhands returned to clean the floor, Captain Sharp got down on the floor and started helping. The crewmen were beside themselves with worry and kept telling Captain Sharp he was not supposed to help. He finally told them that he didn't plan on following any captain rules and they need to be flexible going forward. The three of them had the floor scrubbed and polished in no time while Bothari, Cuthbert and August continued to move around the room and knock on walls and test panels. When the deckhands were finished they took the buckets and rags and left but still looked worried like they had broken some laws.

Captain Sharp stood up and stretched out his back, and asked Bothari to close the door again. When that was done he asked them what they found.
    Bothari had found the false bottom drawer in the desk with the small bag of coins and a loose floorboard with nothing underneath it. August had found the fake panel on the bookcase and the false bottom desk drawer. Cuthbert had missed the desk and floorboard, but found a sliding wallboard under the coat pegs that contained a beautiful custom made sword. They pulled it out and examined it together. Clearly it was made by an artist with its matching scabbard and lots of filigree on the blade. The flat blade had no curve but was thinner than a traditional longsword. It looked like it was designed for speed. The handle and handguard were designed to be functional rather than ornate. An inscription on the handle read: "For Luck in Defense of the Ship." At the end of the blade it had a single word inscribed on the blade. Niho. (teeth)
    "This is not the sword Captain Dominic wore, the few times I saw him wearing one. He carried a rapier, but his hand was never near it. I got the impression that he was never trained to use it," said August.
    "A new sword for the new captain?" asked Cuthbert.
    "I don't know," said Captain Sharp.
    "Oh come on, Captain Sharp! That sword was meant for you, and you know it. Your name is on the handle, for Neptune's sake. What more of a sign do you need?" said Bothari.
    "What does he mean by that?" asked August.
    Gerard pulled the sword again and wrapped his hand around it, testing the weight and balance. It was beautifully made and felt good in his hands. He wanted it for sure, but did not know if he should have it. "In the Maru language, 'Gerard' means 'luck'. So one way of interpreting the inscription is 'For Gerard, in Defense of the Ship'."
    They were all quiet for a few seconds until August spoke again. "What does that little purple guy have to say about it?"

Captain Sharp returned the blade into the scabbard and started to attach the new sword to his belt. "New rule: it is called the Purple Tiki. The Purple Tiki says defend the ship with everything you have, including your teeth."

Two hours later, the island of Piholo Mokupuni lay just ahead and off the starboard side. The ship tacked sideways until they were one hundred feet from the island. Captain Sharp ordered the crew to drop anchor while the water was still deep enough. The island was nothing but a sandbar. At the moment the tide was low and the sea calm. Water gently lapped at the beach. It looked peaceful.

As soon as the ship was anchored, the crew put part one of the plan into motion. Four Koa of the Sand Maru climbed down into the boat they had been towing and paddled it to the beach. Once there they unloaded the dead pirates one by one, neatly stacked at the far end of the sand bar. Finished, the men rowed the boat back to the Tawny Mane and docked it on the farside of the boat at the bottom of the rope ladder.

Another armed crew began escorting the prisoners up from the gun deck and onto the far side of the boat. All the prisoners had their hands tied in front of them now, so they had to be helped down the ladder. Once the boat was full, two Koa rowed the boat while two other Koa guarded the prisoners. Bothari had asked to be in the transfer boat; his request was granted. As the longboat rounded the ship and their new home island came into view, some of the prisoners started to complain. Bothari hit one of the loud men on the head with a club. The crack was so loud it was doubtful the man would ever wake. The body slumped to the bottom of the longboat.

"The next one who speaks will have his head cut off and fed to the sharks."

This kept the conversation to a minimum for the rest of the trip. When they hit the beach, Bothari ordered the prisoners to get out and walk to the far side of the island. The men complied. Once they were out of range, the Koa tossed the man from the bottom of the boat onto the beach. Now empty, they rowed the boat back to pick up the next group of prisoners.

The second group were escorted on deck from the brig on the Tawny Mane. They loaded into the longboat and rowed around the end of the ship. When they saw the island and the prisoners already standing on it, and the pile of dead bodies, they started to yell. This time Bothari had to hit two men before everyone stopped talking.

"The next one who speaks will have his head cut off and fed to the sharks."

These prisoners were unloaded and ordered to walk towards the other side of the island. As they did, the first group yelled threats and insults back to the Koa in the longboat. They worked desperately to get their hands untied, but nobody had gotten free just yet. The bodies of the two complainers were tossed up onto the beach and the boat returned to the Tawny Mane.

The last group from the brig of the ship was brought up the steps and loaded down into the boat. Captain Sharp stepped down with Bothari and the men as the boat was loaded. They pushed off and went around the ship as before. When the island came into view it was surreal. A good size pile of dead bodies at one end, and a few dead at the other end, and a dozen men running around the middle screaming insults and curses. One of the prisoners in the boat started to say "What the hell..." when Bothari hit him on the head with his club and the man fell over like a stack of books.

"The next one who speaks will have his head cut off and fed to the sharks.

And why not? It had been working pretty well so far. As they approached the near end of the island most of the prisoners ran towards the far end, yelling over their shoulders. Two men stayed near the shore and had gotten their hands untied. As the boat hit the beach Captain Gerard and Bothari stepped off the boat. Now all the prisoners ran for the far side. The last batch of prisoners were unloaded and pushed towards the far side. The body of the last man to complain was tossed up onto the beach.

Two of the prisoners approached the longboat slowly; both men had their hands free. One of them was Earl from the brig. He appeared very unhappy with his face and his current situation. "What the hell is this?" said Earl through swollen lips and missing teeth.

"This is your new home. Welcome to Piholo Mokupuni," said Captain Sharp.

"This is bullshit! We never agreed to this. How are we supposed to survive here?"

"You are not supposed to survive here. You are supposed to die here. As for the agreement, we agreed to not chop off your heads and bring you here instead. However, if you are unhappy with the agreement I will gladly enforce the alternative." Captain Sharp put his hand on Niho; it was warm, it felt like it wanted to come out and play.

Earl thought about it for a moment but in the end decided to do nothing.

"Another time perhaps," Captain Sharp said.

Captain Sharp and Bothari walked back to the boat and climbed onboard. The Koa started to row them away and now all the men on the island started shouting threats and profanity towards the longboat and the ship. The men in the longboat said nothing; the men on the ship said nothing. The longboat reached the side of the ship and the crew tied it off securly. Nobody wanted to accidentally lose a lifeboat around here. They climbed up on the deck and walked to the railing overlooking the island. Most of the crew was on deck now.

Captain Sharp held up his hand for quiet and that only made the men on the island yell louder. He let them go for about half a minute and then started talking regardless of whether they could hear him or not. "Attention dead men, welcome to your last home: Piholo Mokupuni, the sinking island."

The prisoners on the beach went quiet and started listening.

"This island will be five feet under water at high tide. You will not survive the day, for you have committed crimes against the Tawny Mane. She now calls your lives forfeit."

Captain Sharp turned his back on the dead men and nodded to August who blew 'Attention' on the bosun's whistle. The rest of the crew turned from the rail and came to attention.

"Attention on deck! I want anchor up and canvas down! Cornelius, bring us around with the wind. Let's open her skirts and lengthen her stride. I want to see what this beautiful girl can do."

27

The crew unfurled just the topsail for the turn, then the forsail while coming out of the turn making the Mane lean over and push into the sea. When the men finally dropped the mainsail, that's when the fun really began. The Tawny Mane jumped and bucked like a colt while the crew tried to secure the sheet and clew lines below. It seemed like everyone on deck was yelling orders over the sound of the wind and the spray of the ocean. Captain Sharp went up to the helm and put a hand on the wheel next to Cornelius.

"Why don't you take a thirty-minute break and get something to eat, Cornelius?"

The old man smiled at Captain Sharp and elbowed him once in the side. "Running with the wind is always the best time to be at the wheel. Keep her as long as you want, Captain. She's your ship." With that he headed down the ladder and into the galley.

The view was magnificent, the wind was screaming, and the occasional spray from the bow cooled his skin. Flying, she was. Absolutely flying.

The ship moved along at a good clip, though the wind had dropped by a few knots. They were right on schedule and the ship was performing well. In the distance off the port side he could just make out 'The Wedge' coming into view. The wedge was an old lava cone that had its top sheared off long ago. It was eighty feet long and less than half of that wide. The high side of the wedge was more than forty feet above the water line, sloping down to the low end barely ten feet above the sea. The top and sides had been smoothed flat by eons of wind and water. The wedge was a well-known navigational landmark that all the island voyagers used.

Captain Sharp heard a whisper in his ear and yelled for Cornelius to come take the wheel. Cornelius came running up and took over the helm. Captain Sharp asked him if he could get within 200 feet of the rock formation and sail down the long side in one steady pass. Cornelius said of course he could, but looked confused by the request. Captain Sharp explained that he wanted to allow some hands-on training with the guns; they were going to pretend the wedge was an enemy ship. Cornelius' eyes got wide and he smiled.

"If this is practice Captain Sharp, then I would like to offer a suggestion if you don't mind?" Cornelius asked timidly.

"Please do, I would appreciate your suggestions and expertise on this."

Cornelius got excited and animated now, as he was talking he was using his hands to describe the angles and directions. "You don't want to just rake her down the side, that's for novices. Let's perform an axel twist maneuver. We come at the enemy like we are going to go side by side, but then when they are still up ahead of us we turn away slightly, putting our guns on her before her guns can see us. As we pass her, we turn parallel again, then as she goes past, we turn back towards her and keep our guns on her long after her gunners have lost sight of us.

Captain Sharp moved in fast and embraced the navigator in a hug and then released him. Cornelius was so surprised his mouth was hanging open.

"That is exactly the kind of expertise I was talking about. Thank you, Cornelius, you've made me a better captain and made the Tawny Mane that much more dangerous. If you have any more ideas like that, I want them shared with me immediately, you understand?"

"Aye-Aye Captain!" Cornelius said and saluted with a smile. He got back on the wheel and put his game face on.

There was a bell hanging on the mast next to them. Captain Sharp grabbed the rope pull and rang the bell hard and fast for five seconds. Then he took a breath and started yelling. "Enemy ship off the port bow! Gunners to your stations! Smudge! Get your ass up here!"

The crew on deck ran to the rail and started looking around. Smudge ran up the steps and headed straight for the port side bow.

Bothari appeared at his captain's side looking slightly confused. "Captain?"

"I think it's time for Pahi throwing practice, don't you?"

Bothari's face broke into a grin and he started laughing. "Yes Captain Sharp, practice time indeed." He watched as the group at the rail scanned the sea and found nothing.

Smudge turned around and shrugged with his arms and shoulders.

Bothari pointed at the rock wedge up ahead in full view. It was the only thing in full view. "There is your target, master gunner. It's a three masted Spanish Galleon with 60 guns on board, probably 42 pounders. We only get one pass so make it count!"

Smudge was not a slow man; he caught on immediately. If Bothari's face was happy, Smudge's face was ecstatic. He began yelling and herding his men down to the gun deck. "Move it, you lollygaggers! Get those port doors open and cannons drawn back! I need powder and pebbles at each station! We need more runners." He disappeared down the steps, yelling orders from below deck. Several men on deck turned to look at Captain Sharp and Bothari still up on the poop deck.

"Cornelius, do you need any help at the wheel as we pass that enemy ship?"

"I could use one man as a back-up Captain," he yelled, getting into the spirit of the moment.

Captain Sharp pointed at one of the men who he had seen helping Cornelius earlier today. "Marty, get up here, shut your mouth, and open your ears."

Marty ran for the stairs.

"The rest of you, get down on the cannon deck and help Smudge. Do not blow up my ship! Move!" The men ran for the stairs like excited kids. After the last man disappeared down the steps, Hickory's head popped up above the stairwell and yelled to Captain Sharp. "How many shots are we allowed, Captain Sharp?"

"How many cannon teams do you have down there?" Captain Sharp asked.

"We are setting up four teams manning four cannons sir."

"Eight shots then, two apeice."

"Aye Aye, Captain!" His head ducked out of sight.

August ran up on the deck from below looking flushed and excited.

"Orders, Captain?" he asked.

"Yes, get down on the gun deck and watch everything. I want a list of every mistake and recommendations for improvements when this exercise is over. I also want you keeping score. I want to know who hits and who misses. You are my eyes and ears down there, August. Don't miss a thing. Move!" August saluted and then ran back downstairs.

Captain Sharp and Bothari climbed down the steps and moved to the port rail. Crew members not involved with the gun deck came topside for a better view, as did most of the Sand Maru. Behind him he saw Cornelius put the young crewman on the wheel, talking him through every step. The Mane had been moving sideways to get within range. The wedge was coming up fast now. Gerard could hear a continuous monologue from Smudge below; what to do first, what to do next, what to do after that. The wedge lay a good three hundred feet ahead when the Tawny Mane turned starboard and brought her guns to bear.

The Tawny Mane was outfitted with twenty-four cannons: twelve on each side. The 32-pounder cannons were considered heavy caliber artillery as they fired a 32-pound shot. Each shot took eight pounds of powder wrapped in fabric. The 32 pounders had an extreme range of 2000 yards, but anything over 1000 yards was a lucky shot. Most ship-to-ship encounters happened with less than 50 yards between them. Just one 32-

pound shot could penetrate 36 inches of oak planks and send a shower of deadly splinters thirty yards in all directions.

The boom of the first shot caught everyone by surprise and lifted their feet a good inch off the deck. The Mane pitched back before rolling level again. The concussion was impressive as the gun fired was directly below them. The crew watched as the first shot arced over the sea and missed the wedge to the left by some thirty feet.

A chorus of "Aw!" came from the men on deck. Below on the gun deck they heard cannons rolling on wooden wheels as they were moved into position. They also heard Smudge barking orders to anyone who could still hear after that first blast.

The second shot came only a few seconds later; the crew could see it was true the moment it arced into view. The shot hit the wedge near dead center about three feet down from the top. The explosion of rock into the air was impressive as was the cheering and screaming on the deck around him. Men jumped up and down and shook their fists in the air, cheering their shipmates on. The third shot was also on target, hitting the wedge near the waterline, sending up a huge spray of water, rocks, and black obsidian. His crew cheered again and that's when the musicians joined in. Edmund played a fanfare on the horn celebrating the hit as the drummer pounded out a steady deep rhythmic beat. The two started to sing and a few of the men on board started to sing with them. It was not a song Captain Sharp had heard before.

"I went to school in cannon-dale. Where they teach you not to fail."

"They taught me how to shoot the mark. Lighting powder with a spark."

The Mane had been turning with the approach of the other ship and now the boats were broadside and parallel. The fourth shot came right as the boat evened out and it looked like it threw off the shot. The shot missed to the left, but by less than ten feet. The band kept playing, the men kept singing, everyone was stomping their feet. Smudge was either getting louder, or the men on the gundeck were having trouble hearing him.

"I shot my cannon day and night. Shooting till I got it right."

"And now I'm on the open sea. Shooting those who dare cross me."

Shooting out of a hot bore left a thicker smoke trail, making it easier to track the shot. Shot five came out hot and true. Nice and low with not much arc, it slammed into the back third of the wedge with a huge spray of black glass and rock. More cheering from the top deck and even some could be heard from the men below them.

"If we see the skull and bones. We shoot him down to Davy Jones."

"Protect my ship till I grow old. Retire with my chest of gold."

Shot six missed the wedge by being a little too high, and shot seven actually bounced off the water not twenty feet from the wedge and skipped up into it. It was a smaller crash of rocks and glass, but counted as a hit according to the crew on deck.

"When I'm done and shot me last, I'll marry me a bonnie lass."

"If I play me cards just right, I'll be shooting her at night."

The ship was just finishing its roll-around and turned to keep the guns on the enemy ship. Shot number eight hit the front of the wedge and notched a huge cut out in the front of the rock formation. This time it crumbled down into the ocean instead of exploding upwards. For this the crew let out the biggest cheer yet. The topside crew were still dancing on the deck when the gunners came up from below. Some were dirty, some were blackened, but all of them were smiling. The crowd on deck moved to greet them; there was much embracing and back slapping. Smudge moved through the crowd and stopped short of Captain Sharp to give him a smart salute. Captain Gerard saluted back and then crashed him in a hug.
    "Excellent shooting Smudge! You and your team did fantastic for your first training exercise."
    Smudge blushed red and literally said, "Aw shucks."
    "Great work everyone!" Captain Sharp yelled. "The Tawny Mane is indeed a fast and dangerous woman. You should all sleep better knowing we can outrun what we want to, and outgun what we need to."
    "Pukapuka is still about two hours away. I want this ship cleaned up and squared away before we arrive, but first we're going to crack open that cask of wine in the galley and celebrate our first victory together!"
    Everyone cheered. The band played. Some of them danced. Smudge was toasted by several members of the crew. Cannons were secured. Supplies were stored away. The Tawny Mane sailed towards the horizon.

28

Inside his quarters, Captain Sharp took inventory and made notes. Cuthbert had already repaired some of the items on his list. The rest would have to wait until they were back on Pukapuka, where Cuthbert had most of his personal supplies. The desk and the chair were in great shape and fit the room well. The meeting table and chairs were also sturdy and usable. There was an assortment of navigational aids that he was obviously keeping. There was a globe mounted on a swivel on the floor that looked up to date. There were a total of three sextants and four spotting scopes. The map collection had mostly been ignored by the pirates; the two maps he found on the floor earlier had been cleaned, rolled back up, and returned to the scroll racks. All the maps were well-made and would definitely come in handy in the future.

There were two trunks full of clothing that were going ashore and not coming back. Not only was the previous captain a different size, they had vastly different tastes in style. Out of all the clothing left behind Captain Sharp had only found a few things he decided to keep. One light jacket that was black with purple trim, and a heavy foul weather jacket in a deep blue. He did find two pairs of boots that fit, and kept all the socks that didn't have ruffles on the top.

The curtains were a thick red velvet and needed to go. He was sure he could trade them to one of the sewing women on the island for some white gauze curtains to let all the light in. He also had that obnoxious bed sheet that would probably be cut up and sewn into fifty dresses by the end of the month. There were three suitcases that were now empty, and he decided to only keep the one small one. The other two he was going to give away to the village. Other items he was going to donate to the village included two different sized end tables, a speaker's podium, a wooden coat rack, a padded foot-rest, and several books in both Spanish and French. There were also three hideous oil paintings that meant absolutely nothing to him.

The first painting was of a middle-aged woman with a stern face, possibly the old captain's wife but nobody knew because nobody had been inside his quarters to ask. If it was his wife, it explained why he chose to live a life on the sea. Although it could have been his mother, or grandmother, or great grandmother. The second painting was of a very old woman impeccably dressed, also frowning. The third portrait was of an old man, trying to look regal, but mostly looking frail.

Gerard piled everything going ashore near the door. The room was looking less like somebody else's. The secret panel near the door was now empty, as he chose to wear the teeth on his side instead of his old sword. The heavy bag of gold coins was left in its hiding spot for now. He figured it belonged to the Mane and might be used to buy her supplies down the road. The pile of paperwork and the captain's personal log were in his duty bag to go ashore. He was going to go over the paperwork back at home and see what he needed, organized what he could, and burn what needed burning.

Pukapuka came into view late in the afternoon but with plenty of sun still left in the sky. The wind pushed them straight into the lagoon past the reefs. As soon as they cleared the breakers, they dropped all the canvas except for the topsail. It was just enough to push them forward towards the beach. Captain Sharp chose to anchor the ship much closer to the beach than before. He dropped anchor in about twenty feet of water and only one hundred yards off shore. Supplying and maintenance would be easier if the ship was closer. Dozens of Maru turned up on the beach when they arrived, yelling and hooting to the men on deck. The crew of course yelled and hooted back. As they were securing the ship he saw a few men on the beach load into a boat and head their way. The last of the sails and ropes were secured as the boat arrived on the side. The islanders started to climb the ropes. Captain Gerard lined the crew up at attention and had August whistle a fanfare as the guests were helped over the rail. Mano, Pale, and Olina climbed up. Captain Sharp stepped forward and spread his arms wide as he welcomed the distinguished guests.

"Welcome my friends to the Tawny Mane. Koo Koo Kushaw". He then took off his hat and embraced his three old friends. Sharp dismissed the crew before they started talking about the events of the day and catching up.

"Before the men run off, I would like a word with them please," said Olina. "Perhaps in the galley? It's a little quieter and more intimate then the deck of the ship."

Captain Sharp nodded his assent.

In a surprisingly strong voice she yelled for all sailors from the Tawny Mane to assemble in the galley immediately. She then asked Bothari if he would do a quick sweep of the lower decks and make sure all the crew were in attendance. She marched off towards the stairs and Bothari left to check the decks below. Captain Sharp asked Mano what that was all about although he already had an idea.

"She is going to give the crew a short version of the Kalepa. Sharing a hut with Sand Maru women is a delicate dance. The men must be warned not to break any rules."

"I see," said Captain Sharp.

"You don't need to tell barracuda how to catch minnows," said Pale, "especially when the minnows are lining up to be caught."

"There is also a celebration tonight," added Mano. "We invite all the crew to come ashore tonight for a sharing fire. There will be food, drinks, music, and dancing. We will hear of your adventures today and tell stories of our own. Together we will drink until the island is crooked and we fall to the sand." He clapped Gerard on the shoulder and that was that.

Olinas' talk took less than five minutes. The men came back looking dazed but happy. They lowered boats over the side and prepared to go ashore. Captain Gerard put Bothari in charge and went ashore with Mano and Olina. Pale wanted to stay on the boat and have a look around as he had not been on the ship yet.

Mano asked about the trip; Gerard gave him the full report. He would have to repeat it later for the group but Mano wanted to know ahead of time if there were any problems. Gerard looked at the setting sun and calculated how many hours ago they had left the sinking island.

"Our problems are history."

The sharing fire was gigantic in both size and scale. With all the villagers and sailors it was well over two hundred people gathered. There were tables full of food and endless drinks to try. Some specialty desserts were made for the occasion along with a wild boar that had been put in the ground last night and baked all day. The drummers of the village beat out their songs and sang along. Tanner from the Tawny Mane had brought his drum from the ship and sat down with the group. He listened for a few seconds, started nodding his head with the beat, then joined in. Everyone cheered and danced. Pierre, one of the other musicians from the ship, had brought a violin and a mandolin. He played along with the group and also did some solo numbers, much to the delight of the crowd. The villagers had ever seen or heard a violin before.

The single women all wore colorful leis around their necks, woven earlier in the day. Sometimes after dancing with one of the sailors they would take the lei off and put it around the neck of a sailor and then kiss him on the cheek. It was not subtle; it wasn't supposed to be. Gerard danced with Roo and a few others when he was asked. The women of this island were truly beautiful. He didn't accept any leis though.

When everyone had eaten and the serious drinking started, they sat around the huge fire and told stories. Gerard told of the day's events on the ship. He told each story twice, once in Maru for his family, and then once in English for his crew. He gave a full account of dropping off the dead men, turning their backs, and sailing away. He talked about how great the Tawny Mane was on the sea, racing with her sails and leaping over the waves.

Then he broke into his story of the wedge. The encounter with the wedge was the most fantastic sea battle he had ever been part of. Here he grew animated and joked about how the wedge had snuck up on them and tried to broadside them. Only the courage of the crew and the cunning tactics of Cornelius and Smudge could save them. Cornelius sat near the fire and blushed pink at his name, but it also could have been the woman leaning against him twirling his hair on her finger. Smudge and his brave men attacked the wedge and peppered her with shots until she cried mercy and half of her fell into the sea. At this point all the men working the gunner's deck cheered and lifted drinks in the air. The wedge was left with a notch in its bow as a warning for others not to trifle with the Tawny Mane. There was much cheering after his story. Mano joked that his storytelling ability was improving rapidly.

Roo had had a long day and told Gerard she was going back to her hut. He asked if she wanted company and she kissed him and told him to stay. The celebration was for him and the crew and he needed to stay and tell stories. Roo said she would come find him in the morning, kissed him again and left.

Smudge gave his account from the gun deck complete with sound effects and him falling over every time a cannonball hit the wedge. There was much cheering after his story also.

Kai rose and told the story of the time when he and a group of others were rowing near a coral reef when a giant squid grabbed one of his rowers and plucked the man right out of the boat. Kai and his crew dove underwater with knives and cut their friend loose while fighting the other tentacles. It was an old story but a good one, followed by much cheering.

Getting into the spirit of it, Jim-Jim told the story of a whale he saw breach out of the water and land on a jolly boat, snapping it in half like a twig. Four men were killed, but the man at the bow of the boat was catapulted out of the jolly and up into the ship's rigging where he stuck like a bird in a net. Other sailors rushed up the ropes to get the poor lad before he woke up and accidentally fell to his death.

The stories went long into the night. Gerard noticed that every now and then a pair would slip away from the campfire and not come back. Eventually he looked to ask a question of one of the crew of the Tawny Mane only to find all of them gone. He drank with Mano, he drank with Fetu, and he drank with Pale and Safina. When the sky in the east started to get pink he staggered from the fire and headed to his hut. The island was crooked and several times he fell on the soft white sand.

29

Gerard woke up because his head felt like it was splitting in two. He was trying to figure out why, and then he remembered the sharing fire and the pele wine from last night. He went to rub his head and found he couldn't move his arm. Turning his head he saw an unfamiliar woman laying next to him still asleep. Well shit, that wasn't good. He couldn't remember anything after leaving the fire. He laid there for a moment and tried to clear his head. He had never been in this position before so he was not sure what the etiquette was. He did not know if he was supposed to wake her up and talk about it, or was he allowed to sneak out and deal with it later. He was wondering if he should have attended Olina's speech in the galley when an arm was thrown over his chest from the other side of him. He felt a body move against his back and did an internal groan. Shit, more than one of them. Now he was wondering if you had to make two separate apologies or could you just give one to both of them at the same time? Roo was going to kill him or worse.

The woman in front of him turned in her sleep, now facing him but he couldn't see who it was. Her long black hair covered her face, which didn't help since all the women on the island had long black hair. She put a hand on his chest just below the other arm and let out a soft sigh. Gerard was still trying to decide how to escape when the woman's hand started to move in slow circles. It felt nice but the problem was with each circle the hand was drifting lower and lower. Gerard wiggled around and was able to free one of his arms that he used to stop and capture the woman's hand before anything 'further' happened.

The woman giggled but didn't try to do anything else. The body behind him snuggled closer and the arm wrapped around his waist. That arm felt different and heavy so Gerard looked down to see what was going on. It was a man's arm.

"What the hell?" Gerard sat up quickly and pushed the man's arm off him, waking up both his bedmates. The woman pulled her hair away from her face and he recognized her, it was Coral, Pua's mother. She was naked and she was smiling like nothing was wrong. Gerard shifted around and looked behind him. It was Akoni, Pua's father. He was also naked and smiling like nothing was wrong. "What the hell?" Gerard said again and was trying to wiggle out of the bedroll they were in. When he realized he was also naked he stopped trying to get out of bed. Better to stay undercover naked than stand around in the morning light naked.

His head was thumping and he laid it back down and started rubbing his temples.

"You should have seen your face," Coral said, giggling.

"Will somebody tell me what's going on?" Gerard said, not opening his eyes.

"Let him down easy, Coral." Akoni said. He climbed out of bed and put some shorts on. He leaned over Gerard and kissed Coral. "I'll go warm up some firi-firi and coffee. You catch up loverboy on his busy night." They both started laughing as he walked out of the room. Firi-firi was like a donut twist. It was good on its own, but it was great when dipped in coffee. The thought of donuts and coffee helped improve his mood a little bit. He chanced to open one eye and Coral was smiling at him.

"Hello," he ventured.

"Good morning," she answered.

"Just exactly how did I end up in your bed?"

"It's a long story."

"I don't think I have any plans right now. I would love to hear the story."

"Are you sure you want to talk right now?" She put a hand on his chest and started to do the slow circles again. "We could relax for just a little while longer."

"Coral!" Akoni barked from the next room. "Stop torturing the poor kid."

"You're spoiling all my fun." She snapped back. Coral got out from the bed unconcerned with her nakedness and started sorting through clothing on the side of the bed. She looked great, even though she was probably around fifteen years older than Gerard. She talked while she dressed.

"Somebody got very drunk last night at the sharing fire and had problems finding their way home. First you went into Kalama and Puleeiite's hut, took off your sword, and climbed into bed with them. They were somewhat surprised but not exactly thrilled. They told you to leave and you did. You then went next door into Rangi and Enele's hut, took off all your clothing, and then got into bed with them. Rangi was not happy and dragged you out and pretty much threw you out the front door. You landed face down in the sand with your butt sticking up in the air naked. You were too drunk at this point to stand up so you decided to just stay there and go to sleep. Akoni and I were walking back from the fire when we found your naked butt sleeping just off the main path. Instead of letting the whole village have a look-see at you all night long, and possibly letting you wake up with a sunburnt ass, we dragged you to our hut since it was only a little way further. We put you to bed and that was that." Coral was combining her hair now, getting ready for the day.

"And nothing happened?" Gerard whispered.

"Well you did get a little handsy in the middle of the night," Akoni said from the next room and they both started laughing. Gerard covered his head with the sheet.

"Is it common for you to do things at night that you have no memory of the next day?" Coral asked.

"Nope, this would have been the first," Gerard said.

"Then I think your virtue is safe. Although I can't speak for the other couples you 'visited' last night."

Akoni lent him a pair of shorts to wear for the day, and his earlier panic eased off over breakfast. His head was almost normal again by the time he was ready to leave. He needed to go find Roo and explain what happened or at least what he thought happened before word got to her.

"We could never thank you enough for saving Pua from the evil men. We thought getting your naked butt off the main path would be a small token of our thanks, though," Coral said as they walked him out front. She hugged him and so did Akoni.

"Thank you, Gerard the Sharp," Akoni said. "We are forever in your debt."

"You are not in my debt. You are my family, Koko. Thank you for taking care of me when I could not," Gerard said. "Any chance we could keep this just between us?" he asked with hope.

"I'm afraid not," Coral said, smiling. There were four women walking down the path towards them including 'Ahoeitu the gossiper'. Coral threw her arms around Gerard and yelled with enthusiasm.

"Thank you Gerard the Sharp for the most amazing night of my life! We will never forget it!" she yelled.

Gerard's cheeks burned with embarrassment. Sometimes your family could be a real pain in the ass.

Gerard made the two required stops on his way home. He found Kalama at his hut and offered his sincere apologies. Kalama just laughed it off and said it happened to everyone once, but not to let it happen twice. Puleeiite was gone but he asked that his apologies be passed onto her also. The villager said he would as he handed Gerard back his sword. Kalama asked where it came from and Gerard told him the story and showed him the inscription and name on the blade. Kalama was impressed and they talked about knives and swords for a while.

Gerard's next stop was Rangi's hut where he and his wife were both sitting in front working on some reed projects. When Enele saw him she turned bright red and went back inside the hut Gerard went through his apology again noticing that he was being watched by a group of women sitting in the shade next door. Rangi was still a little angry but did admit that Gerard was so out of it he was barely able to stand or talk. He was upset that Gerard may have seen his lovely Enele naked and had to be assured that Gerard remembered nothing of the previous night. When the apology was finally accepted and the men shook hands Gerard asked if he could have his clothes back.

Rangi yelled for Enele and she came outside still pink. Rangi told her to go get his clothing and she ducked back inside. Moments later she returned holding his neatly folded clothing and walked it over to Gerard. Her blush had spread from her cheeks down to her chest and up to the tops of her ears. She handed Gerard the pile of clothing making sure she touched his hands way more than necessary. When Gerard got brave enough to make eye contact she batted her eyes at him before turning away and ducking back into the hut. Gerard fought to keep his own blush in check. He thanked Rangi for the clothing, and apologized again for the misunderstanding last night. With a final bow he turned and left and saw that the women next door were already in a huddle.

Gerard stopped by Roo's hut first and found it empty. He headed for his hut next hoping she was in his bed still sleeping. Gerad's hut and bed were also empty and he groaned with frustration. No matter where Roo was on the island, she was going to hear stories before Gerard found her.

He had several people he needed to find this morning and wanted to reach as many as he could. He went into the middle of the village and grabbed a few runners to help spread the word. After talking to the crew on the ship yesterday, they agreed to have a swap meet on the lagoon beach tomorrow. Most of the men had a few things to trade. This was something the village did a few times a year. The crew also had clothing and personal effects from the deceased crew members that nobody else wanted or needed. Pre-made clothing was always in high demand on an island where resources were limited.

Gerard made sure he found Natice and Sione who ran the seamstress group. He asked them about the possibility of trading the heavy red velvet curtains for some new light gauzy fabric curtains. They were very interested as this type of material was unavailable on the island. Then he mentioned the gold and lace bedspread and they were practically drooling. The two of the women asked if they could go out to his ship right now and see what needed to be done and take some measurements. Gerard told them they were welcome on the ship anytime and that he would row them out there personally if they wanted. They told him that wouldn't be necessary as crew and islanders were constantly going back and forth already. They would just hitch a ride with one of the boats. He asked if they had seen Roo and they both gave him a crooked smile but said no.

Gerard went looking for Cuthbert, only to learn he was already out on the ship working on some repairs. Gerard hoped he was doing the captain's repairs first, as the ship had a long list of things needing to be done.

Gerard decided to head to his hut and start to tackle that mound of papers found in the captain's quarters on the Tawny Mane. He knew Roo would eventually come find him either before or after she cooled off. Sitting at his desk, he started with the captain's personal journal since it was organized and undamaged. The chronological history would hopefully give him some clues about all the loose papers. The log book started with a previous voyage some 5 months before this most recent one. The Tawny Mane had left Portsmouth, England and traveled east through the Mediterranean Sea to the port of Alexandria, just outside Cairo, Egypt. The ship carried a half load of cut wood to exchange for a large quantity of fabrics, bags of dates, and barrels of spices. It listed the names of the local contacts and merchants. The log clearly spelled out the price of the goods, who the money was paid to and how it was paid. Captain Dominic made notes about his frustrations in dealing with his shipping company and employer. They expected him to bribe them to get the better shipping routes; bribe them to find his own cargo, and then come up with his own bribes on the back end. He was supposed to pay the harbormaster and cargo contact out of his own pocket.

On that trip the lumber was the bulk of the payment with a small bag of gold coins and a larger bag of silver coins added to balance the scales. Gerard didn't know if that was the true cost of the shipment or the coins were added to speed the transfer along. It was not uncommon for a bribe to be required in order for the harbormaster to find a berth or lost shipment. A handful of coins here and there was almost required in some places and was considered part of the cost of doing business.

The ship spent nearly three weeks in Alexandria. It was an uneventful sail back to England, but instead of returning to Portsmouth they docked at Southampton. Again the goods were unloaded and there was a 40 day break in the log book. It seemed likely that the captain and crew had left the ship and gone to travel or visit family.

The new entries in the logbook spelled out a trip to Wellington, New Zealand to pick up a shipment of sugar, rice, and tobacco. The bag of gold he had found earlier was to be used for the payment of materials since no goods were being brought down to trade. The Captain was supposed to make contact with the harbormaster Oliver Roe. Oliver would direct them to a warehouse run by a man named Benjamin Braxton. It had the expected dates of the trip and Gerard checked his calendar. As of today, the ship was only 5 days behind schedule. Interesting.

The log book documented the sail out of Southampton and running south and west across the Atlantic. They made the turn around Cape Horn without incident or bad weather. The ship sailed due west towards New Zealand when they came across the sinking ship and her men. There was a lengthy update around the events of the sinking ship. Captain Dominic expressed concerns about the lack of leadership of the men and the conflicting stories. He felt the men he had interviewed had been dishonest and asked his senior crew to be watchful. The next day he reported nothing unusual, but the extra men would be putting a strain on his water and rations until they reached Wellington. There were no further updates in the log. Gerard closed it and moved on.

Next he turned his attention to the papers. He tried to organize the documents into piles: general orders from owners and sponsors, purchase documents and receipts, private communications, and unimportant papers. Once he had everything in half a dozen piles, he organized them by date.

He was just finishing this task when there was a knock at the door. The sewers had returned from the ship, bringing the red curtains and gold bedspread with them. Two runner boys stood behind them loaded down with red velvet. The women deemed the material 'too valuable' to leave on the ship. This meant other clothing makers had heard about them and wanted them badly. They had taken the measurements for his new curtains and told him they would be ready in two days. The women would even take them out to the ship and install them themselves. Gerard began to think he had grossly underestimated the worth of the old red curtains. He thanked them and asked if they could help him with one more item. They seemed eager to make him happy so he took a chance.

He wanted a captain's jacket similar to the one Dominic had left behind, but one of his own to wear on the ship. He wanted black with purple trim, cuffs, pleats, gold buttons, the whole works. The women asked if they could cannibalize the coat left behind by the last captain and Gerard agreed; he would drop the coat off later. That was perfect, the sewers needed to take measurements before going forward. Gerard thought about his leverage and asked if the coat could be ready in three to four days? The woman gave him a stern look, but then looked back at their cache of red velvet. They told him four days, no less. They agreed and hands shook.

Gerard was still sitting at his desk when the next knock came. He went to the door to find a very angry looking Roo waiting outside for him. She never knocked, she always just walked right in. A small crowd was already gathered on the path near his hut, apparently they had followed Roo hoping for some entertainment.

"Am I not enough for you!" Roo yelled.

"Roo please," Gerard said looking at the crowd, "come inside and we can talk, it's not what you think."

"Inside your hut? How many women do you have inside your hut right now Gerard? Must I stand in line?" Roo yelled. She had a look on her face he could not decipher. He had seen her angry but this was different.

"Roo nothing happened, honestly," Gerard said softly.

"It sounds like nothing happened at least three times, and probably more. Exactly how much of this island do you plan on 'conquering' Gerard the Sharp!" Roo said loudly, waving her arms.

Gerard had no answer for her this time. He just stood there looking miserable and tried to think of what he could say to make it all go away. Roo marched up to him and pushed him inside the door and out of view of the crowd. She pushed him back towards the bed and then tackled him on it. She landed on top of him and he opened his mouth to start apologizing and explaining what happened. Roo put a finger on his lips and shushed him. Then she leaned down and tenderly kissed him on the lips. She moved her lips to his ear and whispered softly to him in the dark room.

"Coral came and found me first thing this morning and told me what happened. She knew the rumors would reach me soon enough and they started pouring in as soon as she left." Roo said with her crooked smile.

Gerard looked at her in confusion for a moment. "So you know nothing happened?" Gerard asked.

"Yes lover. Even after all the outrageous stories had reached me, I still would have talked to you before believing any of them to be true," Roo said and kissed him again.

"Thank you, but I don't understand why you were yelling at me on the porch in front of half the village," Gerard said.

"That was just a show for all the gossipers following me around all day," Roo said sweetly. "Now why don't you get me out of these clothes and really give them something to listen to. The legend of Gerard the Sharp continues to grow does it not?" Roo said and kissed him hard. Gerard growled at her and started to rip her clothes off as fast as possible.

"Yes Gerard!" she yelled way louder than necessary.

Later on after Roo left Cuthbert came by with the repaired chair for the captain's quarters. This would complete the set of six around the meeting and map table; the repair made was stronger than the original according to Cuthbert. He had finished the other improvements requested and even added a few of his own. Gerard thanked him and gave him a hug. Cuthbert then asked the questions that had been tickling the back of Gerard's brain for a few days now.

"So, when are we leaving?"

"I'm not sure yet," Gerard answered honestly.

"Ok, let me know. I'm ready." With that, Cuthbert walked away.

30

Gerard took his chair down to the beach and rowed out one of the small jollys left on shore. It took some work to climb up the rope ladder holding a chair but he managed. Some of the crew had made it back to the ship, but not many. Everyone appeared to be in a good mood; go figure. Captain Sharp carried his chair back to the captain's quarters and stopped at the door. Painted on the door in four-inch letters was his name: 'Captain Gerard Sharp'. It felt a little like being punched in the gut. He opened the door and went inside.

The change in the room was impressive. Gone were the heavy red drapes; the sunlight now steamed in the windows and lit up the room. The door didn't squeak anymore. Cuthbert had installed more hanging pegs on the wall near the door. Gerard hung his hat on the new hat peg above the coat hooks. He put the repaired chair next to the table and flopped down in it hard. It didn't creek or groan. He got up and pushed the chair under the table with the others.

The bed was much improved. Gone was the gaudy bedspread and the tall ornate bedposts. Cuthbert cut off the bedposts four inches above the bed frame, rounded them off, and then dyed them a similar color to match the rest of the bed. What was left was a common functional bed with short posts on the corners, just tall enough to hang a belt or sword off it. The down-filled mattress was exposed laying bare on the woven ropes that made up the bed frame. It looked to be relatively new and thick. Upon closer inspection it did not stink now that the sheets had been removed. He wondered where the sheets went. He hoped the sewing ladies had not taken those as well. He did need something to sleep on.

There was a wire loop sticking out of the wall near his desk with a scrap of paper on it that said 'pull me'. Gerard pulled on it and the wire ring came out about two inches. It felt like it was weighted down below but he didn't know what it did. He was going to have to ask Cuthbert about that. Not thirty seconds later a man from the galley knocked on his door.

"Yes?" Gerard asked.

"Did you need something Captain?" The cook asked.

"No," Gerard said. "Why are you asking?"

"The bell Mr. Cuthbert installed in the galley was ringing, we thought you needed something."

"I apologize, he didn't tell me what the device was for. I can assure you I won't be ringing that for anything."

"So we will be going back to the old system sir?" The cook looked worried.

"What was the old system?"

"Captain Dominic would stomp on the floor and yell 'Porter!' and one of us would run up here and ask what he wanted," the man said and frowned.

"What do you think of the new system and the bell?" Gerard asked.

The man's face lit up and he already had his answer. "It's ingenious sir, the stomping and screaming used to scare me half to death. I mentioned it to Mr. Cuthbert when he was having lunch in the galley. He asked me what I would prefer instead. Since your quarters are right above the galley, I suggested a bell on a string. He said 'wire would be better' and made the whole contraption in less than an hour. Mr. Cuthbert said I had a right fine brain in me noggin." The cook's smile was wide.

"I agree with Mr. Cuthbert, it is a grand idea. Let's keep the new system but I promise I won't use it very often, if at all," Gerard said.

The man looked like he might cry. "You don't like my bell idea sir?"

"No, I love the bell idea, I would just rather walk down to the galley and talk to you myself," Gerard said. This did nothing to cheer the man up and he continued to look unhappy. Gerard did a mental sigh and tried again. "How about we try the bell out for a short time, but you tell me if I am ringing it too much."

The cook's face lit up like sunshine. "That would be wonderful sir! Captain Dominic would yell for us at least a dozen times a day, but with that bell you could double that and we wouldn't even mind." The cook left happy, and Gerard made a mental note to use the bell at least once a day to keep his cook happy.

Rowing back to the beach, Gerard thought about his next move. His thoughts were all over the place; he felt like he was getting lost in his own head. He needed to talk to Mano, but maybe he should talk to Bothari first. That felt like a better plan; everyone knew Bothari was a good listener. Getting him to talk was the hard part. Pulling the boat up onto the beach, he headed off towards Bothari's hut.

Bothari's hut was set off to itself a short distance from the main group of huts. Most of the huts were grouped in neighborhoods made up of family or close friends. It was not unusual to change huts every now and then based on marriage, divorce, death, and really bad arguments. Bothari wasn't home, so Gerard sat on the porch and started whittling a stick he had been carrying. He was there about ten minutes when a Koa walking by saw Gerard and walked over to talk to him.

"Looking for Bothari?" he asked.

"Yes, do you know where he is?" Gerard asked.

"As a matter of fact I do. Saw him heading up to Pele's Porch about an hour ago."

"Thank you," Gerard said, standing up and brushing off his lap.

Pele's Porch was the highest point on the island. There was only one side of the volcano left standing and even that was only eighty feet tall. The path leading up to the top ledge was a short easy climb with lots of switchbacks. The view from the porch was incredible, looking out over the center of Pukapuka and the other two corners of the triangular shaped island. It was a place of quiet and contemplation. Nearly everyone in the village went up there from time to time to work out a difficult problem. Gerard had been here many times.

As he came to the top, he saw Bothari sitting near the edge with his eyes closed. Gerard sat down beside him. He arranged himself in a comfortable position, then closed his eyes and opened his mind. He had learned over the years that the Purple Tiki didn't always talk to you when you wanted him to, but he usually whispered something when you needed him to. Gerard tried to turn off his brain and slow his breathing. There was no sound up here but the light wind through the vegetation. Good air in: troubles out. He breathed.

After ten minutes Gerard was just starting to get deep-deep when Bothari asked him what was troubling him. He came back up slowly, keeping his eyes shut and his breathing slow and easy.

"I am not even sure what part troubles me yet. It feels like our course has already been set. We have been hoping for a ship for years and now we have one. We travel not as passengers but as owners. We have a loyal crew. We have family back home who we want to see again. There is no reason to not go except . . . saying goodbye to another family."

"Yes," Bothari said. "I have felt peace here like I have never known. Still, my eyes long to see the face of my sister and niece. I would see the streets of my home again. I have given much thought to spending my last days on this island with its soft sand and warm breeze. Yet the sea is not done with us. Captain Sharp has legends yet to be written."

Gerard opened one eye and looked at him sideways. He was grinning about what he said.

"Yes. The sea calls us again," Gerard said and stood up, brushing the sand off his pants.

"Tell me one thing," Bothari said with his eyes still closed in meditation.

"Anything," Gerard said.

"Did you really sleep with three couples in one night?"

At the bottom of Pele's Porch, he could still hear Bothari laughing. He headed for Mano's hut and was there in only a few minutes as it was close by. He knocked on the doorway and heard Mano yell 'komo' from inside. Gerard ducked under the doorway to find Mano sitting at the table with Mr. Kim. Mr. Kim stood up and thanked Mano for his time and the talk, then held out his hand for a shake. Mano bruised past it and embraced him in a hug. "Family," he said. "Koko." Mr. Kim left and Gerard sat in the vacated seat.

"I have been expecting you, Captain Gerard the Sharp. Your mind worries too much for one your age, but I knew it would eventually sort itself out.

"I am not sure I have everything sorted out yet, but talking to you always helps," Gerard said.

"You honor me," Mano said, dipping his head. "Would you talk or would you listen?"

"Definitely listen," Gerard said.

"You are leaving on the Tawny Mane as soon as she is supplied. Your loyal men go with you. Some of the Sand Maru may choose to go with you, to see the outside world. You will visit your home and see your family, but the sea now holds a piece of your heart. You are the youngest captain I have ever known; that is both an honor and a burden. Your life's adventures await you. So what part have you not figured out?"

Gerard had a lump in his throat. When you laid it out like that, it was pretty clear. It also cleared up what the issue was. He was going to miss his Sand Maru family.

"This family has been so good to me. I do not want to disappoint them by leaving," Gerard said.

Mano shook his head back and forth. "Gerard, from the beginning we understood we only had you for a short time. Your life lies out there. You will return to us; the Purple Tiki has told me this. You have been a good friend, and good family, that does not change just because you change huts."

31

The swap meet was a huge success. It seemed like the whole village had showed up and spread-out blankets with items for sale or trade. The crew of the Mane got rid of everything they brought; some even traded the shirt off their backs. They traded for other clothing, sandals, necklaces, knives and tattoos. There were two Kupunas working on new tattoos for two different crew members. The traditional process of island tattoos involved dipping a sharpened bone into ink and then tapping the needle into the skin one point at a time. The process was painful and slow but looked amazing and lasted a lifetime. The ship's men sipped pele wine to take the edge off.

Gerard gave Roo first pick on everything he had. She only wanted a few items and left after giving him a lingering kiss. Gerard traded away everything he could, and gave away the rest. The trunks went for a set of lanterns a voyager had acquired years ago. The old captain's clothing went for some new clothing for him, some already made, some promised to be made in the next few days. The lace socks he gave away to Enele and Puleeiite as a peace offering. The suitcases were traded to other voyagers to help transport goods back and forth between islands. In exchange he got a purple heart club with shark teeth set into the edge and a long spear with a nasty obsidian tip on it. There were nearly a dozen decorative throw pillows that he gave away to all his friends. Everyone wanted a throw pillow; it was the hot commodity of the day.

One of the Kupunas took the padded foot rest, and another known for his long stories took the speaker's podium. One of the tables he gave away to a newlywed couple, and another he gave away to Pale and Sefina. Mano took the coat rack and the books. He was talking about teaching himself French and Spanish so he could read them. Only one villager wanted one of the paintings, the other two were donated to the village as a whole. Maybe they could be hung in the meeting tent.

Gerard also brought everything from his hut that he was not taking with him. His hut itself and the big furniture pieces inside would be given to the next Maru coming of age and moving out or the next married couple, whichever came first.

Fetu walked through the crowds of people and embraced him warmly. He looked down to see everything Gerard owned laid out on the blanket for sale or trade. "So it is true then, you are leaving the island?" Fetu asked.

"Yes, the sea calls me again. I have a ship and the opportunity to see my first family again. I love my island, and my Koko; but my path lies out there."

Fetu nodded and was quiet for a period of time. He was looking down at the sand and trying to get his thoughts in order. "I also love my island and my Koko. I used to think I would spend my whole life on this island. Pick a wife, have a family, grow old and die. It all felt so simple and planned."

"Used to?" Gerard asked.

"The Purple Tiki sent me a dream last night. The most beautiful woman I have ever seen, only I have never seen her before. My Ipo (lover) I think. A woman not from this island. Skin as pale as our white sand, and hair as red as Pele's blood. She was wearing a green dress the likes I have never seen before. The wind was tossing her hair and the sun was lighting it up from behind her. Her eyes were the color of the sea. The sea! She was laughing at something she had just heard. Her laughter. . ." His voice broke and he stopped talking. "Her laughter. . ." He tried again but was unable to speak. He swallowed hard and took a deep breath and blew it out. "There is nothing I would not do to hear that laugh again," Fetu said quietly.

"It sounds like there is a beautiful future ahead of you, my brother." Gerard said.

"I hope so," Fetu said. "That is why I shall travel with you, my brother. You stood next to her in my dream. You were the one who made her laugh. It seems that your path is also the path to my future. From the moment my eyes opened this morning, nothing else mattered."

"Are you sure about this, Fetu? Sometimes a dream is just a dream. The Purple Tiki does not share everything he knows. There is always a chance that if you leave this island you will never return to your home."

Fetu smiled. "My home is no longer a place, it's a sound. I just haven't found it yet."

He embraced Gerard once and said he had much to do. He walked away with a determined step, about to give away everything he had ever owned.

Three more villagers came up to him during the event and asked if they could come with him on the Tawny Mane. The first man was Blaed, who was in his thirties and still single. Blaed had been accidentally cut across the face as a child and now had a long red scar from above one eye, down across his nose and past the corner of his mouth. He was a quiet one and did not appear to have much success with the village women.

The second one was Kolohe (trouble) and he was trouble. Gerard had said no immediately and didn't even think about it. The young boy then set out on a campaign to win him over. He talked about needing a change, a fresh start, and making a good name for himself. He needed to get away from the pressure of the village and the eyes of the Kupunas to be able to grow. He talked about how Gerard had been given the exact chance Kolohe was looking for, a fresh start in a new place where he would be judged on what he did today, not what he did yesterday. It was a good argument and in the end Gerard said he would consider it. He also told Kolohe he would have to talk to his parents before even considering it. Kolohe walked away looking hopeful and happier than Gerard had ever seen him.

The third one surprised him most of all. Vaheana (storm) was in her late twenties and one of the only female Koa on the island. She had been unattached as long as Gerard had known her and rarely spoke. She didn't smile, but did not appear depressed either. When she walked up and asked if she could have a talk, she didn't waste words.

"I wish to sail with you when you leave this island," she said.

Gerard waited for her to elaborate on her request, but that was all she had to say. "Are you asking to sail as a passenger to our next destination, or something else?" he asked.

"I wish to be part of your crew."

He was taken aback by the request, as it was very unusual. On most ships women were not allowed to be part of the crew because of tradition, superstition, and prejudice. He started to think of all the potential problems that could and would happen. The crew would undoubtedly argue against it.

He could think of no positives to her request and only negatives. He was leaning towards saying 'no' when a voice whispered in his right ear. 'Interesting.'

He realized he had been quiet for too long and she was waiting for an answer. He said the first thing that popped into his head. "Interesting. Why do you want to be part of my crew?"

"I want to see the world. I do not accept that there is only one life path for me on Pukapuka. The world is bigger and I want more than what is being offered to me here," she said.

"Is that all, I thought you were happy here?" Gerard asked.

"I am, or I was," she said, "I volunteered to guard one of the beaches the other night and was not selected. I have more experience than some of the Koa who were chosen. I am faster than some of the warriors who were picked. The opportunity to protect my Koko should have been mine. It was made clear to me that even though I am Koa in name, I am not seen as a warrior when it matters. There have been other incidents like this, but this was the most recent. I want to find a place where I matter."

"There are bound to be endless problems with your request. Let me ask you the two biggest ones that come to my mind. First, you will be the only woman on a ship full of men, are you sure you are ok with that? Second, you have to know that some of the crew would be against this and resent you for it."

"Yes I realize I will be alone on the ship. Feeling alone is something I have been familiar with for a long time now. As for the mindset of your crew, that is up to you Captain Sharp. You could tell them nothing, and have me win them over with my attitude and work ethic over the next few years, or you could ask them to give me a fair chance like any other member of the crew. Then it will only take me three months to win them over." At this she offered a hint of a smile.

"I will give your request proper consideration, Vaheana. What you ask for is uncommon but not impossible. However, my first duty is to my crew and my ship. If having you as part of the crew puts them in unnecessary danger, then my answer will be no. If I think this can be done with minimal disruptions, we will talk further. I will give you my decision by tomorrow morning."

"Thank you, Captain Sharp. I had hoped you would not dismiss my request out of hand. You already know my character; I would not be a liability on your ship." She grasped his arm in a traditional handshake. "I would be honored to be part of your crew. You put their safety and protection before all things. There is no other Captain I would choose to sail with."

Later on Hickory came by to see what Gerard had left on his blanket, having already traded everything he had brought. He also wanted to show off a new warrior club he had traded for. It was carved out of a length of wood with a round knot on the end. The shape and weight made it effective and lethal. It had decorative carvings on the side and a leather wrapped handle. He was talking of making a belt holster for it and carrying it instead of a sword. Gerard asked him what else needed to be done before she was ready to sail again.

"Nothing really, captain. We have been topping off supplies since we got back. We should be ready to sail as soon as your new curtains are ready." He had a smirk on his face when he said it.

"That sounds great. I didn't know everyone was aware of my new curtains."

"It's not just your stuff, Captain Sharp. Them sewing women walked around the ship and pointed out all the linens that needed to be replaced. Seems like half the crew ordered something: new sheets, pillows, curtains, hammocks. From what I hears, they have been sewing night and day to get it done in time."

"Interesting," Gerard said.

"Anyways, we can sail the day after tomorrow if you like. Problem is we don't know where to sail to. Unless you had an idea, sir."

"As a matter of fact I do. Let's have a meeting tonight on the Mane just after sunset. Make sure all the senior members of the crew are there. I'll fill you in on what I've learned. We have a destination and possibly a job waiting for us. I will tell the crew about it when we are together."

"Aye-Aye sir," Hickory said and started to leave but then thought of something else.

"Um Captain, there is something else I wanted to mention . . . but it's a delicate subject." He looked both ways before leaning in and lowering his voice. "Nobody has seen Cornelius since the big fire. Rumor has it that the woman who dragged him from the ceremony has him tied to the bed and won't let him leave. 'Course I never believe rumors meself."

Gerard tried to hide his smile. "Of course. I will track down Cornelius and let him know about the meeting. Thank you for letting me know."

Before finishing up at the swap meet that afternoon Gerard saw Olina and waved her over. He asked her if she would do a small favor for him and she agreed. When he leaned in and whispered the story to her, she laughed so hard he thought she was going to pee herself.

32

As the swap meet was wrapping up, Gerard made two trips back to his hut with things that weren't traded away. It wasn't much, but eventually somebody would want it. He had asked Mano to give away the rest of his

117

possessions if somebody wanted them, including his hut. Mano smiled and informed him that a certain young couple who had yet to announce their ho'ohiki (promise) to each other had been seen eyeing his hut. The knowledge that his hut would continue to be somebody else's home on the island made him feel better about leaving.

His hut was looking spartan, like it did when he first moved in years ago. Each time he went out to the Tawny Mane he carried more of the belongings he wanted to keep. He walked around, looking at the room and seeing the changes and improvements he made over the years. His hut was solid and well maintained; it would serve a new family for years to come. It had been a peaceful home full of good memories. He wanted to make sure he remembered the feel of it, because it was important to him. This is what home felt like. He would miss this home, these friends, and this island. He still needed to talk to Roo but he was putting that off for now. There was only a small pile left by the door now, along with the few items he traded for today. He put back on his hat and sword as he wanted to look official, and headed off towards trouble.

Havorn and Rauana had two children that some of the villagers referred to as light and dark. Tern was nineteen years old and of fair skin. She was nice to the point of being naive, and was much loved by the village. Kolohe was seventeen years old, dark skinned, and spent most of his youth getting into trouble. It wasn't like he set out to cause problems, but if something broke or something went missing, Kolohe was on the short list of suspects. He had shot up this past year and was at that stage where he was lean and clumsy.

Gerard stopped at the door and knocked twice. Rauana came outside and hugged him before welcoming him inside. Havorn was sitting at the table, but stood to shake arms with Gerard as he came in. Gerard took off his hat and set it on the table. The couple offered food and tea before anything else, as was tradition.

"Have you talked with Kolohe about our conversation today?" Gerard asked.

"We are sorry if he caused you any embarrassment. We told him it was a fool's errand and not to waste your time, but he would not be dissuaded," Rauana said.

"He speaks very highly of you Gerard, but we would not wish this burden on you," Havorn said. "He did not come home after the swap meet. We are hoping you let him down easy. He is a good kid but much growth is needed."

"I agree," said Gerard. "That is why I told him I would consider it."

The parents were more than surprised. Mom was the first to recover and speak.

"I don't understand, he is just a boy. He didn't choose to row at fifteen and is still half a year away from Winter's Day. Surely you don't have children on ships at sea?"

On Pukapuka there are two paths to adulthood. When you turn fifteen you have the option of rowing a canoe alone to the neighboring island of Suwarrow about 52 miles away. It takes about 2 days to get there and another 2 days home. Young rowers need a working knowledge of the stars since you row overnight. The elders of Suwarrow have a special shell that these voyagers bring back to Pukapuka as proof. The row is not easy and only a few try it, and not all of those are successful.

The second path to adulthood is the Winters Day celebration held on June 20th, the shortest day of the year. All the young adults turning 17 that year are welcomed into adulthood on that day. On Pukapuka this means three or four people per year.

"Actually, we do have children on ships but Kolohe is far from a child. He is on the verge of adulthood and looking for his way in the world," Gerard said.

Havorn shook his head. "It is bad enough he causes problems on the island, but he can't sink the island. I worry about the mess Kolohe would cause on your ship Gerard. It would break us to learn that men were hurt or worse because of his playing."

"I understand your concern but he will not be playing on my ship. He will be working with the other men and pulling his own weight. He will either learn to be responsible or I will throw him overboard myself." Gerard stared hard at the parents and did not smile.

Rauana touched the Purple Tiki around her neck and whispered 'Aue'. (oh dear).

"There are many dangers at sea and that is only one of them: storms, shipwrecks, pirates, sickness. There is a chance he will never come home. In a few months he will be old enough to be called a man. He will either do it here in the shadow of his past, or out at sea as a member of my crew. As long as he agrees to my conditions, and understands the consequences, I intend to offer him a position on the ship. I understand wanting a fresh start. You need to find him and talk about this. He needs to know this is not a game; this is the rest of his life."

"I understand, Captain Sharp," Kolohe piped up behind them in the doorway.

Both his parents stood up and rushed to hug him. He allowed it for a few moments and then walked over to where Gerard stood. He had a smirk on his face and he reached out for an arm-shake. Gerard moved fast putting a hand on his neck and pushing him back against a wall post. The house shook but held. The surprise on his face was genuine. The gasp from his parents was also real but they didn't move forward to interfere. Gerard held him tight enough to have him up on his toes, but not enough to cut off his air.

"The next time you eavesdrop on me, I knock teeth out of your head. Do we have an understanding?"

Kolohe looked afraid but he nodded.

"When I speak to my crew I expect to be answered. Do we have an understanding?"

"Yes sir," Kolohe said, and it sounded like he meant it.

"Ok, then." Gerard released him and stepped back. "We leave in two days. You're allowed one bag of personal effects and clothing. Get rid of everything else, including your attitude. If you disappoint me, the last thing you'll see is my ship sailing away from you."

Gerard put his hat back on and faced the parents, still frozen by the doorway. "It was nice talking with both of you. Thank you for the tea Rauana, it was excellent. Now if you'll excuse me, I have several other stops to make." With that he walked past them and out the door.

33

The sewing group was easy to find as it had grown into a group of fourteen women occupying two buildings in the common area. Natice was running around shouting orders like the leader of an army. Gerard asked for a word with her but still had to wait ten minutes until there was a lull in the action of the sewing frenzy. First he asked about his curtains and was assured they would be finished and hung tomorrow morning. Next he asked about his missing linen sheets off the bed. She said they had indeed been taken, washed, dried, and delivered back out to the ship earlier today. Apparently she felt guilty about the inequity of the bargain they had struck and threw in washing the sheets as a bonus.

Gerard told her they were leaving the day after tomorrow at sunrise. She needed to get everything else done by then or it would be left behind. She did some mental calculations and told Gerard not to worry, that it would all be done in time. Gerard thanked her, giving her a hug before moving off. She went right back to yelling orders and sending runners for additional support staff. It sounded like it was going to be a long night for the sewers.

Gerard headed out to the ship well before sunset with the last load of things from his hut. He also brought back the captain's log book and all the loose paperwork he had recovered. He put the log book back into the false bottom drawer where he found it. He organized the paperwork into different drawers and cubbies and labeled them with one of the fountain pens. He kept out a few documents he wanted to share with the crew and left those on his desk under a paperweight found in a drawer. The brass paperweight was a sand dollar: heavy and well-made. The bottom was rough, to keep the piece from slipping and sliding. The desk had also included a brass starfish.

The bed sheets had indeed been washed and returned. They even made up the bed for him. The linen looked brand new but more importantly smelled fresh and clean. He was tempted to lay down for a short nap and try them out, but decided to test the galley bell instead. He gently pulled the string two times. He didn't even make it back to his desk before Maurice rushed into the room and snapped to attention. Gerard had a quick talk with Maurice about what he wanted and was assured it would be no problem. Maurice left happier than Gerard had ever seen him.

Bothari arrived first and knocked on the doorway as he came in. Gerard had him sit at the maps table and they talked about the day. Hickory and August arrived about the same time and stopped and knocked in the doorway. Gerard called for them to come in and sit. Cornelius arrived soon after that, announced himself in the doorway, and was called to come in. His arrival was greeted with some good-natured ribbing and hooting. Jim-Jim arrived last and knocked on his way in, never breaking stride.

As the last man sat down, Gerard went behind his desk and lightly pulled the wire loop twice. Seconds later Maurice rushed in followed by Pierre. The cooks laid out trays of tea, mugs, snacks, cakes, and berries.

Gerard complimented Maurice on a fantastic job and he gushed at the compliment. The cook asked if there was anything else before leaving. Gerard asked him to close the door shut on the way out, which he did.

Captain Sharp began by explaining that on his island, talks and meetings always started with an offering of food or drinks like tea. It was a sign of friendship and a tradition he intended to continue while on the ship. Next he told them that in this room he wanted them to feel free to ask questions and to make suggestions. He didn't care about rank or age, what mattered was the sharing of ideas and knowledge. He knew he had much to learn about being captain, and asked his crew for help while he caught up. They all agreed to help speed up his education.

First he wanted to talk about spoken and unspoken rules. He told them he would prefer to be called Captain Sharp while on the ship, but was okay with being addressed as Gerard here in private, or when they were off the ship on land. He did not like the sound of Captain Gerard or Captain Gerard the Sharp. 'Too pompous,' he said and the men laughed.

The next item on his list was to let them know that if his door was open, they should just walk right in. He was already tired of the knocking. If the door was closed, then knock. The men all agreed this was reasonable. He wanted his quarters less formal than the previous captains' quarters.

Many of the crew had taken to coming to attention and saluting when they passed Captain Sharp on the deck and he asked for this to be discouraged. While he appreciated the sign of respect, he planned on walking the ship a lot and didn't want the men to stop what they were doing every time he passed by. This was especially true if he was preoccupied and pacing back and forth. The group started discussing this one with some arguments on both sides. In the end they agreed that coming to attention and saluting would only be used the first time the captain came aboard from land and the first time they saw the captain each morning. Captain Sharp agreed this was a reasonable compromise.

They covered a few more minor items before Captain Sharp asked if anyone had questions. Hickory asked when they were leaving and where they were going. The crew had been told they were sailing for New Zealand, but didn't know which port, or what cargo they were picking up, or from whom. It was a good segue; Captain Sharp went over to the desk and retrieved his stack of papers. He explained what he had found on the floor of the captain's cabin, and in the log book.

The Tawny Mane was headed for Wellington, New Zealand to pick up sugar and tobacco before a return trip to Portsmouth, England. If they left in two days, they would only be seven days behind schedule, a reasonable delay for a trip halfway around the world. Pukapuka was along the South Equatorial Current that would push them steadily west towards New Zealand anyway. A return trip to England required them to sail west to New Zealand, then south in the East Australian Current, and then back east along the Antarctic Circumpolar Current toward Cape Horn. As long as they were going that way anyway, they might as well pick up the cargo and get paid when they get back to England. The men all agreed this was a terrific idea. Jim-Jim asked how they were supposed to pay for the cargo in Wellington and all the men looked at Captain Sharp.

"Let me worry about that, I have a way of persuading people," the captain said. The men laughed and Bothari and August kept their secret.

There was one more item of business to cover before the meeting broke up. Captain Sharp had been thinking of how to handle it. His plan was to be evasive but honest, and catch the men with their own honor.

"There are four Sand Maru and two former shipmates of mine who want to join our crew. I told them I would talk to my crew first before giving them an answer. Do you men have any reservations about bringing new people aboard?" Captain Sharp asked.

"Not at all," Hickory said. "We are short a few crew members so we could use the help."

"On that point I agree with you," Captain Sharp said. "I do have concerns about the physical appearance of two of the people. I worry that their appearance will be held against them, and they won't be given a fair chance to prove their worth."

Hickory and Jim-Jim sat up straight, mouths open. Cornelius and August looked confused. Bothari sat with his face blank as usual.

"I don't think that's fair Captain Sharp," Hickory sounded insulted. "You haven't known us all that long, but surely you can see we are men of integrity. I don't care what a man looks like, as long as they can follow orders and do the job."

"What about you Jim-Jim?" The captain asked.

"I have seen some ugly mugs in my time, but that's never stopped a man from working hard. Do you know these people personally, Captain Sharp? Would you vouch for them?" Jim-Jim asked.

"Yes, I know both of these people personally, and vouch for them both. Strong, smart, hardworking, and good with weapons. I just want to be up front about my concerns before I gave my word and brought these people on board. You are my leaders on this ship; I expect you to set an example and keep others in line. I will not have my new people harassed about their looks. Are we clear on this?"

All the men around the table agreed.

"Alright, then. We leave at first light, the day after tomorrow. Tie up loose ends and get your affairs in order. Natice told me all orders will be done in time, so make sure you get your goods." Several of them smiled at this. "Say your goodbyes, for we sail with the tide."

As the group headed back for shore, Gerard, Bothari and August climbed into a jolly boat together. The other men had gone ahead and were out of earshot. "Are you going to tell me what that was about or is this going to be another Captain Sharp surprise?" Bothari asked as they rowed slowly towards the island.

"Vaheana asked to join the crew." Gerard said.

Bothari was quiet while he processed the information and then reviewed the conversations from earlier. He grunted to himself and then spoke his mind as usual. "You set your trap and caught every last one of them with their oath. This is going to be uncomfortable for a little while."

"Who is Vaheana?" August asked.

"A woman warrior, a Koa," Gerard said.

"Oh," August said. "I thought you were talking about somebody with a scar or birthmark."

"That was his plan," Bothari said. "Tricked and trapped them all right and good."

"It wasn't all a trick," Gerard said. "Blaed also asked to come. He has a long scar across his face. The important part is my crew has promised to overlook appearances, and judge the new crew on how hard they work."

"Wow, a woman on our ship," August said.

"Keep that information to yourself, August. You will hear many things in confidence that you need to keep to yourself, like the bag of gold coins. The less people who know about it, the better. The men will know about Vaheana soon enough."

"Is this one of those huge mistakes you were telling me about earlier?" August asked.

"Probably," Gerard said, but smiled.

34

The hut was set apart from the others much like Bothari's was. Gerard went to the door and knocked on the frame and then stepped back. Vaheana came out onto the porch with a lantern and searched his eyes for an answer. "If you are here to tell me no, you can do it here on the porch and get it over with, I have much work to do," she said.

Gerard stepped back up onto the porch and moved forward until he was inside her truth space. He dropped his volume a bit and spoke in a hard flat tone. "We have much to talk about before you board my ship tomorrow. One of those things is: can you follow orders and show respect like the rest of the crew? If you cannot, then our deal is done before it starts."

He watched her face as she realized her request had been granted. She was shocked. She had been so positive that he was going to say no, she hadn't even packed a thing. Relief washed over her as she realized she was really leaving. "Thank you, Captain Sharp. Would you like to come in and talk?"

Gerard smiled and backed up a step. "That would be nice Vaheana, thank you."

Inside they sat down at a small table with the lantern hanging nearby. "I am sorry I don't have any food to offer, but I could make some tea if you would like?" she said.

"It's nice of you to offer, but no thank you. Let's talk about the next two days of your life. If we both live through that, then we can have tea together."

"Okay."

"Let me tell you about my requirements, then we can see how well they fit with your expectations," Gerard said.

She made a go-ahead motion with her hands and sat back.

"I would like your transition into my crew to be as smooth and invisible as possible. I don't want you to stand out. I don't want the crew treating you differently. I don't want you to be the 'woman' or the exception on board. What I do want is for you to be a valuable member of the crew. I want you to find a job and excel at it. I want you to fit in, but not lose your identity in the process. You're smart and I want you to speak up when you have an idea. Part of your job is to make the Tawny Mane a better ship, and her captain a better leader." He finished. "What are you looking for on my ship, Vaheana?"

"I just want to get away from this place. I want a new start. I want to figure out who I am and not be told who I am. I don't want to be held back because of tradition or ignorance. The world is such a big place, I want to see more of it."

"I understand wanting to see the world, that is a dream we share," Gerard said and stopped for a moment. "Let's talk about the awkward stuff.

You will be bunking with the rest of the crew members. There is little or no privacy. There are no bedrooms on the ship except mine, and you're not sleeping there." He smiled. "Can you live with that?"

"If it means going with you, then yes, I can live with that," she said.

"For most other women I would be concerned about their safety, but I'm not worried about yours. Break a hand if you have to, but let me know if you have any problems. Everyone on my ship is under my protection. I will not tolerate any harassment," Captain Sharp said. "I have not told anyone about you yet except Bothari, and he keeps his own council. I want you to come out to the ship with me tomorrow morning. I will introduce you and the other recruits to the crew. Then we can get you a bunk, a foot locker, and a tour of the ship. We leave the day after tomorrow at dawn, so you don't have much time. You're allowed one bag for everything you want to bring. As for the rest, sell it, trade it, or give it away. Mano can help you if you ask."

"Thank you for this opportunity," she said, looking emotional for the first time.

"There is one more thing. I have laid the foundation for you to be judged on your work and not your appearance. There are going to be some awkward moments on my ship tomorrow. Personally I am looking forward to it. It is a good test for my crew. This will also be a test for you." Gerard stood up and Vaheana did also.

"Earlier today I threatened to kill a child in front of his parents if he disappointed me. I will now extend you the same courtesy. Do not let me down, Vaheana." He stepped forward and got into her truth space again. His eyes changed from friendly to feral. "If you become an issue on my ship, I will put you in the sea, and there you can be the shark's issue. Do you understand?" This was not the Gerard she had known for the last four years. This was the version she had heard about but never seen. This man was predatory, hard, and scary. She nodded and tried to step back but the table was blocking her path. Gerard closed the space between them again and she wondered if his eyes had actually changed color. "When I address my crew I expect to be answered. Do you understand me, Storm?"

She found her voice and much to her relief it was steady. "Yes Captain Sharp, I understand."

"Excellent." Gerard stepped back and his eyes went back to normal. It happened so fast she wondered if she imagined it. The smile was also back on his face.

"What you said earlier was true, you have much work to do. I will leave you to it. I will send a runner for you in the morning. Good night Vaheana."

"Good night, Captain Sharp," she said, and wiped the sweat from her brow.

Gerard had several more stops to make before going home for the night. The first two stops were at Blaed and Kolohe's huts. He found them and told them to be ready to go out to the ship tomorrow morning and meet the crew and be assigned bunks. Both meetings were friendly and without incident.

His next stops were Fetu, Cuthbert and Hudson. He told them they were leaving the day after tomorrow at first light. He encouraged them to come out to the ship with him tomorrow morning with the new recruits, but said they could report any time, just don't be late.

It was late when Gerard finally made it home to find a man sitting on his front porch. As he got close he could see it was Mr. Kim from the Mane. Gerard sat down next to Mr. Kim but didn't say anything. He gave him time to open up at his own speed. Gerard leaned back and looked up at the stars. They were so bright here on Pukapuka.

"I'm not going with you, Captain Sharp. I asked Mano if I could stay here and he said 'yes'. He asked me to teach him to speak French. I told him I would try, even though I am not a great teacher. I am done with the sea, and she is done with me." He hung his head.

Gerard reached over and put a hand on his shoulder. "I am happy for you my friend. My home is your home. The island is blessed to have you."

"You are not mad that I am leaving?" he asked, surprised.

"Not at all. Each man has a limit and only you know when you've reached it. I am happy you are putting down roots on my island Mr. Kim. When I return here, I will count you as one of my friends."

Gerard sat with Mr. Kim as he cried, and kept a hand on his shoulder.

35

When Mr. Kim left Gerard went inside to find Roo laying on his bed. She watched him in the dark as he took off his clothes and laid down beside her in the bare room.

"You're leaving me," she whispered in the dark. It was a statement, not a question.

"Yes. I'm sorry Roo. Everything is happening so fast now," he said.

"When?" she asked.

"Day after tomorrow. I am going out to the ship tomorrow morning to help get her ready. I will sleep on the ship tomorrow night and we leave first thing the next morning," Gerard said.

"Our last night then," she said softly. Gerard put his arms around her and pulled her into the nook of his shoulder so her head could rest on his chest.

"You could always decide to stay here," Roo said softly.

"You could always come with me," Gerard whispered back.

They held each other in the dark and listened to the quiet sounds of the island. Neither of them spoke, and neither of them slept for a long time.

The next morning Gerard woke up as Roo tried to slip out of bed without waking him. It was just getting light outside and he could see her collecting her things to go. He let her take two steps towards the door before he spoke her name.

"Roo."

She stopped and turned to him with tears already on her face. She dropped her head and let the curtain of hair cover her face.

"I did not want your last memory of me to be a crying mess," Roo said.

"I love every memory of you, even the messy ones," he said.

Gerard got out of bed and went over to where she was to hold her. She stood rock still for a few seconds before hugging him back tightly. They held on for a few minutes and swayed back and forth.

"Will I see you again Gerard?" Roo asked.

"Yes, I just don't know when," Gerard said honestly.

"Goodbye Gerard, until I see you again," Roo kissed him softly on the lips, then slipped out of his arms, out of his hut, and out of his life. It hurt a lot more than he thought it would.

Gerard cleaned his hut for the last time. He planned on sleeping on board the ship tonight so he was done with this hut and this home. It had been a good place for him; he wanted it to look great for the next owners.

The last of his belongings fit into his shoulder bag as he headed away from his home for the last four years. He stopped at the neighbors' huts to say goodbye and was surprised by the tears. This was going to take longer than he thought. He made his way towards the village center where he could find a group of runners. Many of the youth had taken over one medium sized meeting huts and turned it into their corral. Everyone knew if one needed runners, they headed for the corral. He found a large enough group for his needs and sent eight runners running. All of them were told to have their persons report back in one hour.

His next stop was the Elder's hut, where a few of the Kupunas held court every day. He stopped in and talked to the ones present, saying goodbyes and exchanging hugs. Mano had not made an appearance yet so he went looking for him. Mano was not at his house either. The neighbor didn't know where he went. Gerard figured he would have to come back later today and say goodbye to his mentor, it was not something he could leave without doing.

By the time Gerard got back to the clearing Bothari and Cuthbert were already there. The three men sat together at one of the long tables and talked. Gerard asked Bothari if he could oversee the bunk assignments process and make sure the new recruits were near him. Bothari grunted and nodded.

"How bad is it?" Bothari asked.

"I'm not worried about Blaed, he'll be fine. I want to keep an eye on Vaheana for the first few days just in case, but I don't expect any problems. I think after a week her being a woman will be a non-issue."

Cuthbert looked up. "Vaheana is coming?"

"Yes," Gerard said.

He smiled. "Outstanding, I like her."

"The third one could be trouble, since it's Kolohe."

"Aw shit," Both men said at the same time.

Gerard just smiled, since that was his initial reaction too. "We had a conversation yesterday where I choked him and threatened to kill him if he pissed me off, so I think he will be on his best behavior."

"I bet his mom would have freaked out if she saw that, her little darling." Cuthbert said.

Gerard nodded. "Yes Rauana was freaked out, but then so was Havorn."

Cuthbert continued to look at Gerard with a questioning look in his eyes.

"I was in their living room when I said I would kill him."

Cuthbert continued to stare at him. "Jesus."

Bothari smiled and grunted.

Fetu was next to arrive with a small bag, a spear, and some bamboo rods. He hugged Gerard and Bothari and sat down.

Blaed showed up next; Gerard got up and shook his arm. He nodded at each man already there, and then sat down without a word. Next to show up was Kolohe with his parents walking beside him. He stopped them a ways away from the group and did the final goodbye thing. His mother cried and his father looked worried, but Kolohe was determined. He took his bag from his father and walked over to join the group. Gerard stood and met him, shaking his arm. He welcomed him, ordering him to have a seat as they were waiting for a few more. Gerard waved to Havorn and Rauana but only Havorn waved back, and it was a half wave at best.

Cuthbert who watched the exchange whispered "Jesus" under his breath again. Fetu asked what was going on and so Cuthbert leaned over and started to whisper the story in his ear.

Vaheana showed up next with a large bag over her shoulder, a sword on her belt, and carrying a six-foot-long spear and a bundle of bamboo shafts. Nobody paid attention to her until Gerard stood up and welcomed her with an arm shake. He invited her to have a seat as they were waiting on a few others.

She dropped her bag and the bamboo, stuck the spear in the ground, and sat down at the table.

"What is she doing here?" Kolohe asked with the attitude that only a sixteen-year-old could manufacture.

"She is a member of my crew. Is that going to be a problem for you, Kolohe? If it is, you are welcome to go back home to mommy and daddy," Gerard said in his flat voice.

Kolohe didn't say anything but his neck and ears went red. Bothari chuckled. Vaheana stared straight ahead at nothing. Gerard put his game face on and stood up, then started to move towards Kolohe slowly while keeping his eyes locked on him. "I asked you a question, crewman Kolohe."

Cuthbert, who had known Gerard as long as anyone, played his part perfectly. He scrambled away from his seat next to Kolohe like death was about to happen in a large messy way. On the other side of Kolohe, Blaed also got up and also moved away. Kolohe suddenly realized his life was in danger and started yelling with his hands up in front of him.

"It's not a problem! It's not a problem! I just asked a simple question!"

Gerard advanced until he was right next to Kolohe and leaned down to speak softly. Vaheana was watching now with wide eyes. She was fairly certain he was about to execute the boy to make an example. "I was going to grant you one mistake before I killed you, and you just used it up. If you open your mouth again, you won't live to see my ship."

Hudson picked that moment to walk up and say hello. When nobody moved or answered him he looked disappointed. "What did I miss?"

Gerard moved towards him, welcoming him with a smile and an arm shake. "It's good to see you, Hudson." Behind him everyone started to breathe again.

Hudson looked over the group and then looked back at Gerard. "Vaheana and Kolohe coming with us?" he asked.

"Yes," Gerard said, waiting.

With a straight face he asked, "Do we have to take Kolohe?" Behind him everyone laughed. Well, almost everyone.

Sione came walking up just after that holding a wrapped bundle of several orders. Natice was too busy to leave so she sent her second in command to give Gerard the update. They were on schedule and should have everything delivered by the evening. He thanked her for the report and reminded her that they were leaving the next morning, with or without any unfinished orders. She smiled and said that every moment he kept her here, was time she could be using at the sewing hut. She handed Gerard the bundle that had several name tags on it. Gerard bowed low and then stepped forward and grabbed the old woman in a hug.

"You have been a good friend Sione, I will miss you."

She immediately started crying and had to pull out a handkerchief to dab her eyes. "I always knew this island was too small to hold you. Malie Koko." And she hugged him again before hustling off.

"Ok crew, let's go." Gerard grabbed his bag and headed for the lagoon, not looking back. They would either follow him or not.

It took two boats to get everyone and their gear out to the ship. Gerard helped toss up bags and bamboo from the boat before climbing up the ladder. When he vaulted over the rail his entire crew was standing on deck at attention.

August piped for Captain on board; the whistle was sharp and clear.

In the quiet that followed, Captain Sharp thanked August, put on his hat, and then faced the crew.

"Good morning crew, and at ease. Thank you for the welcome as always. I have a few announcements, then we can all get back to work. First of all, Mr. Kim has decided to retire and stay on the island of Pukapuka. He wanted me to pass on his thanks for your friendship while he sailed. Pukapuka will embrace him and welcome him like family. That is an option to all of you when your traveling days have ended. The Sand Maru always have room for new friends and family."

"We have six new crew members joining our ship today. I want you to make them feel welcome. Some of them you may have met, some may be new to you, but all of them are known to me." He turned to face the new crew members. "Welcome to the Tawny Mane. Koo Koo Kushaw."

Gerard started down the line of people calling out their name, shaking their arms, and giving some details about each. "This is Cuthbert the carpenter. I have sailed with him before. His skills will be much appreciated on this ship. Welcome."

"This is Fetu, a warrior. I have sailed with him and have fought by his side. His skills will be welcomed on this ship. Welcome, brother."

"This is Hudson, a seasoned sailor. His experience will help our ship. I have also sailed with him before. Welcome aboard."

"This is Vaheana, a warrior and a voyager. Her skills and knowledge will be much valued on this ship. Welcome." Gerard heard some whispering but didn't pause a moment.

"This is Blaed, a warrior and a hard worker. Welcome to the Tawny Mane."

"This is Kolohe, eager to listen and learn to be a good sailor. Welcome."

"Hickory, Jim-Jim, Bothari, August, front and center."

The four men came forward and stood before the new crew.

Captain Sharp introduced each one of them and indicated they should shake arms with the new crew members.

"This is Bothari, my first mate and sergeant at arms, any problems with the crew go through him."

"This is Hickory, my quartermaster, anything you need, you go through him."

"This is Jim-Jim, my second mate. If you can't find me, talk to Jim-Jim."

"This is August, my runner. He keeps me on time so I can keep the Mane on time. If you need to get word to me about anything, talk to August."

After the last set of handshakes were completed, Gerard addressed the crew as a whole again. "We sail first thing tomorrow morning, get my ship in ship-shape. Dismissed!"

"Hickory, Bothari, will you take the new crew below, get them bunks and trunks, and then give them a tour?"

"Yes sir," both men said, and led the group off.

"Jim-Jim, August, status report."

Jim-Jim and August walked up and stopped before the captain. Captain Sharp indicated that Jim-Jim could go first.

Jim-Jim considered what he was going to say, then looked around the deck. "A word with you in private Captain Sharp, perhaps in your quarters?"

"Of course." Gerard picked up his bag from the deck and led the way. Once inside his quarters he hung up his hat and bag on the pegs, and then leaned against the desk. Jim-Jim chose his words carefully; August had the good sense to shut the door.

"A woman on a ship is supposed to be bad luck, Captain," was his opening salvo.

"So I have heard, but my name means luck, so I think we balance out," Gerard said.

"I don't know if all the crew will be happy with this arrangement. It's a bit . . . unusual," Jim-Jim tried next.

"I know it's unusual, but I am not concerned with doing things the way other captains have done them. As for the crew being happy, that is up to them."

"Some of the crew might refuse to work with her," Jim-Jim said.

At this Captain Sharp stood up straight and looked hard at his second mate. "Do you mean to tell me that because of her physical appearance, some of my crew might not give her a fair chance?"

Jim-Jim went to answer and stopped when the words hit home. He spent some time wandering around in his own head, then smiled when he spoke.

"That was a right fine trick you played on us sir, and we took the bait like hungry guppies we did." He was not angry; he sounded impressed.

"Yes, you did. All I'm asking is you give her a chance, like any other newbie. I'm also asking that you lead by example."

"Aye-aye captain," Jim-Jim said. "It's just the damnedest thing though."

"I agree it is. I am also trying to imagine what she is going through. Having the courage to ask me to join the crew, to leave everything she has ever known to work on this ship, to be alone on a ship full of men. Have you ever met a braver woman, Jim-Jim?"

Jim-Jim looked like his brain had just exploded inside his head. He spent a good thirty seconds thinking about the captain's question. "No sir, I have not."

"Excellent. Why don't you take over the tour for Hickory and have him report to my quarters . . . and Jim-Jim, don't spoil the surprise for my other guppy."

Jim-Jim laughed all the way out the door.

When Hickory came in and August shut the door Captain Sharp asked how things were going. Hickory explained that Bothari wanted the newbies near him in case beatings were needed. He put Kolohe in the bunk above him and Vaheana in the bunk next to him. Blaed was in the next bunk over towards his feet. Hudson, Cuthbert, and Fetu were allowed to pick any bunk they wanted. When he finished the update, Captain Sharp just waited.

"When I saw that man Blaed come over the rail with the scar on his face I wondered why you made such a big deal over it. As far as scars go it's almost nothing. I got a bigger scar on my leg from a fork. Then Vaheana came over the rail and I immediately thought to myself 'she has no business being on this ship.' I was thinking of how to talk to you about it when the puzzle pieces fell into place. You never said men yesterday, you kept saying 'people'. That stuck in my head as weird. So after I ranted and raved about how fair and honest I am, I can't really say anything about her now."

"Give her a chance, Hickory. She is a good person, a good sailor, and a hell of a Koa," Captain Sharp said.

"I plan to Captain Sharp, but probably not for the reasons you're thinking. When you said you knew them personally and would vouch for them, that was all I needed. I trust your judgement sir." Hickory smiled.

"Thank you, Hickory. For the record, I only vouched for Blaed and Vaheana, Kolohe is on his own. I already threatened to kill him once today."

As Hickory was leaving, Captain Sharp told him to leave the door open. He took his bag off the peg and started to put the last of his stuff away. He told August to talk while he worked. August reported that the ship was ready to go. They had plenty of food and water. In fact several times a day the villagers were coming out with more 'offerings' of food for the trip. The crew were back on board except for three sailors at last count. Those three had 'lady friends' on the island and would be back at the last possible minute.

Captain Sharp asked about the temperature of the crew and had to explain what that was to August. He wanted to know what they were saying, what they were talking about, what was on their minds.

Once August understood, he told the Captain what he was hearing. The men were excited to leave and get back to sailing. They had heard that there was cargo to be picked up and they might even get paid despite the pirate attack. Most of the crew thought Captain Sharp was an upgrade over their last captain, though he lacked the experience.

A knock at the door interrupted them; Captain Sharp called for the person to enter. One of the crew named Tanner came in and asked to speak with Captain Sharp privately. "August is my assistant and helps me take notes. You'll need to say your peace in front of him." Tanner decided pretty quickly and started talking.

"You have to get that woman off this ship," he said, rolling his hat around with his hands.

"Why?" Captain Sharp said.

"Because she's a woman!" Tanner replied nervously.

"Yes, I know she's a woman. Why do I have to get her off the ship?"

"Because . . . because I am married, sir!" Tanner said exasperated.

Captain Sharp waited but Tanner didn't say anything else.

"Perhaps you could elaborate a little more?"

"I can't have this woman sleeping with me when I am a married man and my wife is at home, sir!" he said in a rush.

"Oh okay, I think I understand. Vaheana has asked to share a bed with you?"

"Certainly not. I have not even talked to the woman," Tanner replied.

"So you're not sharing a bed; you're just sleeping on the same ship."

"Exactly!" Said Tanner.

"What exactly are you afraid of, Tanner? I still don't think I understand the problem."

"Well it's at night sir, anything could happen. Anything!" Tanner practically yelled.

"Are you afraid Vaheana will attack you during the night?" Gerard asked with a reasonably straight face.

"Well that is just one thing sir. What about the men, all the other men?" Tanner said.

"You're worried one of the men might attack her?" Gerard asked.

"Of course!" Tanner said confidently now.

"You're worried that one of my sailors is going to attack a Koa, a trained weapons expert, at night, in a room full of her friends and crew mates?"

"Um . . ." Tanner was less sure of himself now.

"How about I talk with Vaheana personally. I will have her swear an oath to not attack you at night. Will that do, Tanner?"

"But the other men," he said softly.

"Let me tell you a bedtime story about Vaheana that might ease your fears. Years ago, Vaheana was friends with a younger woman in our village. This young woman was smitten with an older man who was known for his temper. He liked to drink and he liked to brawl. Vaheana tried to warn her friend about the temper but the girl was in love, and could only see what she wanted to see. One day Vaheana went to visit her friend who was said to be sick and had not left her hut for days. The friend talked through the doorway and told Vaheana to go away, she was not allowed to see anyone, but Vaheana is a good friend and went inside anyway. The young girl had a black eye and a split lip."

"Vaheana left and went in search of the man who had harmed her friend. When she found him drinking with a group of other men, she knocked him off his chair and warned him. If he laid a finger on her friend again, she would kill him. This was his only warning. Days passed and then weeks passed with nothing until one day the young girl didn't come to visit. When Vaheana went to check on her friend, she found her resting, with bruises on her neck from the man's fingers. Vaheana went after the man and caught him alone. Legend says that she tortured the man for hours. They say she cut off all his fingers with a knife and made the man swallow them one by one. When all ten fingers had been eaten, she stabbed him in the stomach and cut it open and pulled the fingers out again. Then she made the man eat them again, over, and over, and over, until he died."

"I am not worried about Vaheana's safety. If somebody were to make her angry, she might kill a lot of crewmembers in a fit of rage. I should probably talk with her about that."

Captain Sharp pretended to be deep in thought. "Tanner, thank you for bringing this to my attention and voicing your concerns. I will look into this matter. You are excused."

Tanner got up and swayed on his feet. He looked ill. He walked out the door looking like he was going to throw up.

August looked a little shocked himself. He got up and shut the door after Tanner left. "Did Vaheana get in trouble for killing that man, Captain Sharp?" he asked.

"Most bedtime stories are made up, August. You make them up in your head and just tell them." Captain Sharp smiled. "When I made up that story, she didn't get in trouble."

36

Captain Sharp sent August for Cornelius. While he was gone Bothari stopped by to give an update.

"The new crew is settled in: they have bunks and trunks, they got a full tour of the ship, and now they are having a sit down with Jim-Jim in the galley. They are talking about what skills they have and what kind of jobs they can do on the ship."

"Any issues?" Captain Sharp asked.

Bothari knew what the captain was asking. "No. Some of the men have been speechless when they meet her, but she is pretending not to notice. Nobody has said anything negative to her, and so far she is all business. I may have to kill Kolohe later today, it's still up in the air."

"Whatever you think is best," Captain Sharp said.

Bothari nodded and left, leaving the captain's door open.

Cornelius knocked at the door and walked in hesitantly. Captain Sharp got up to greet him and directed to the maps table where they could both sit down.

"You asked to see me sir?" Cornelius asked, sounding nervous.

"Yes I did, and thank you for coming. I want to be the best captain I can be and for that I need your help. On my last ship I did just about every job and got a well-rounded education, but I didn't get much time to learn to chart, and navigate. I would be grateful if you would teach me."

Cornelius seemed overwhelmed by the request. He started to get worked up and Captain Sharp had to put a hand on his shoulder. "Cornelius, I don't know what kind of relationship you had with the last captain, but I am guessing it wasn't very close. I'm your new Captain, and you're my new navigator. We have different jobs on the ship, but I would also like us to be friends. We are going to spend a lot of time working together, so I need you to get past this and get comfortable with me." He patted him on the shoulder while he got it together.

"Now, when we are in this room talking as friends, you can call me Gerard."

"I don't know if I could do that, Captain Sharp," Cornelius said with a small smile.

"It's up to you, but that's the kind of thing friends do," Captain Sharp said. "Now let's talk about navigating."

A knock at the door had them both looking up, it was Vaheana standing in the doorway.

37

Earlier Jim-Jim had a meeting in the galley with the newest members of the crew. He wanted to know what job they were looking for on the Tawny Mane. He wanted to know what jobs they had done in the past, and what sort of jobs they were good at. When it was Vaheana's turn, she said she enjoyed being a Koa, but was also skilled at navigating boats. Jim-Jim asked if she used a compass or sextant in the past. She explained that she navigated by the sun, moon and the stars. When they traveled at night and the clouds blocked the sky, she relied on her knowledge of known currents and the wind. Jim-Jim told her he was going to pair her up with Cornelius and expand her navigational expertise. He sent her topside to find Cornelius who was usually at the helm, even while they were parked in the lagoon.

Walking up on the main deck she saw the poop deck was vacant and nobody was at the helm. August was walking by and she flagged him down.

"Do you know where I can find Cornelius?" she asked.

"Sure do, he is in the captain's quarters with Captain Sharp," August said with a smile. "If the door is open, go right in."

"Thank you," Vaheana said.

"I agree with Captain Sharp," August said, stopping her before she walked away. "I think you are the bravest woman I have ever met, and I'm happy to have you on our ship."

"Captain Sharp said that?" she asked, somewhat bewildered.

"Sure did, he said it to another crewmember, I was standing right there," August said.

"Thank you, August. I'm happy to be here too."

Vaheana walked towards the captain's quarters, slightly dazed. She had never really stopped to think what Captain Sharp thought of her. She assumed the captain thought of her as a burden, and had stuck his neck out just bringing her on this ship. This information was curious.

Arriving at the door, she saw Captain Sharp sitting with another man who she figured was Cornelius. The man was openly crying; she wondered what the captain had done or said to him. She remembered the captain standing nose to nose with her, threatening to kill her if she became an issue. It made her wonder what Cornelius had done. She knocked on the doorframe and got their attention.

"Yes?" Captain Sharp said.

"I told Jim-Jim that I was a lead navigator on several voyages to neighboring islands. All my training is with stars, currents and wind. He thought it would be a good fit if I worked with Cornelius and learned some of your people's navigational techniques."

Captain Sharp stood up and welcomed her into the room. "Excellent timing, Vaheana. Cornelius was just about to teach me about charts and navigation. Please have a seat." He pulled out a chair for her and she sat down next to Cornelius. "Two students instead of one, what do you say, teacher?"

Cornelius composed himself, taking a deep breath. "Let's get to work, we have a lot of ground to cover."

Two hours into it they had just covered the basics. Captain Sharp's head felt full but Vaheana was soaking it up. He got up from the table and went behind his desk to the wire loop. He pulled it twice softly then went back and sat down. Vaheana was wondering what he did when the cook rushed into the room with a tray loaded full of a teapot, cups, biscuits, cookies, and sweet bread. The man was so happy his cheeks were bursting pink and he was talking a mile a minute.

"I knew the three of you were in here working and I didn't know what you wanted so I made an assortment of choice foods. Captain Sharp, I talked with Mano and he told me about your favorite tea so we got a supply from the island. If you want something heavier I can bring up dinner or have something brought in from the island?" He finished all this in one breath.

Captain Sharp got up from the table and helped the cook with the tray. He grabbed the man's arm just to hold him still for a moment and to thank him. "Thank you Maurice, this is wonderful. You have outdone yourself; your captain could not be happier." Maurice blushed to the tops of his ears and thanked him. Then he turned to Vaheana and Cornelius.

"Did he tell you about my bell? I was the first to think of it and then Mr. Cuthbert. . . " and proceeded to tell them the whole story, twice. He even coaxed Vaheana to come over and pull the lever.

Once Maurice was properly complimented and ushered out the door they had something to eat and got back to work. They had been at it for less than an hour before August walked into the room and cleared his throat.

"Boat approaching sir, looks like Mano and some of the elders, maybe all of the elders." August smiled.

"Thank you, August. Get everyone on deck and ready for visiting dignitaries." Gerard stood up, grabbing his sword and hat.

August nodded and headed out. Cornelius and Vaheana stood up and Cornelius asked what they wanted.

"No idea, but we are going to find out shortly. Let's go." He ushered them out of the room.

38

The crew was on deck when the boats docked on the side and the Kupunas climbed up the side. Most of them were present, including Olina and Mano. Also joined the group were Natice and Sione, along with four men carrying mountains of fabric. As the last of them were helped over the rail, August blew a welcome fanfare.

"Welcome, my family and friends. You honor me with your visit," Captain Sharp said smiling. Mano walked forward and went right for the bone crushing hug. Captain Sharp let out an oof and everyone laughed.

"I am sorry I missed you earlier Koko, but with so many children somebody is always crying," Mano said. It was an old joke of his that everyone on the island younger than him was a child, and they all cried for attention.

"I was going to come find you later tonight. I would not leave without saying goodbye," Captain Sharp said.

"Of course, but you need not, for we are here." Mano turned and addressed the crew on the deck. "Let us start with the sewing that has consumed our wives and women for many days and nights now." He waved the sewing women forward and the porters followed them. Natice came forward and hugged Captain Sharp while Sione called out names of the crew, who rushed forward to receive their orders. It was like Christmas on the main deck. It was shocking how many packages had been finished and were being handed out. When nearly all of them had been handed out and the men were oohing and aahing over their new stuff, Natice addressed the crew.

"Thank you for your patience everyone, these gifts were well-made with love from the women of this island. We hope this material will serve you well, last a lifetime, and remind you of our home." The men clapped and cheered and Natice and Sione both bowed deeply.

"I had one last order to complete and it has been finished as promised. It is my wish that this gift not only inspires you on the Tawny Mane, but protects you and keeps you safe. Captain Sharp, if you please."

She indicated he should step in front of her and he did while facing her. She smiled, then roughly turned him around to face the crew instead. The crew smiled and laughed. Gerard was looking forward towards his crew when their eyes went big and they all said, "Ooh!"

Behind him Natice had shaken out the new captain's jacket of black velvet with purple trim on the cuffs and collar. The gold buttons on the front were a sharp contrast to the field of black; the jacket had large pleats on the bottom of the same purple fabric that caught the light when it moved. Natice put the jacket on Captain Sharp, checking the fit; of course it was perfect as it had been measured for him. Captain Sharp looked down at his jacket with wonder. It was everything he hoped it would be. He stepped forward and did a half twirl and the jacket flew out behind him in waves of black and purple. The men cheered as Captain Sharp scooped up Natice again and spun her around a few times.

"You honor me," he whispered in her ear, setting her down.

"Just as you have honored us for many years," she said back. She reached up and lifted the edge of the purple collar on his right-hand side. On the underside of the flap hidden from view she had painted a small Purple Tiki. She smoothed the collar back out and kissed him on the cheek before stepping away. Sione came over and gave him another hug.

"Thank you, it's perfect," Captain Sharp said.

"No matter how far you travel, this part of your home island travels with you," she replied, releasing him. The old woman was tearing up again.

Natice stepped forward now with one last small bundle and raised her voice. "One last gift to the crew of the Tawny Mane from the island of Pukapuka. The women of the Sand Maru have made you a flag. It is the flag of our home, and now the flag of your home. It was created from our hearts, so wherever you go, our heart goes with you." This she presented to Hickory who took it reverently and then leaned down to hug her.

Mano stepped forward again and raised his hands for attention and everyone got quiet. He motioned for the other Kupunas to come forward with him and they did. Olina was holding a flat wooden box with a tooth on it in front of her that Gerard had only seen once before, and now his mouth got suddenly dry.

"On Pukapuka only the oldest and wisest are chosen as Kupunas. It has been our custom for many generations that the Kupunas lead our people, show wisdom in all things, and teach others what they have learned. It has been many years since the last Kupuna was chosen."

Olina stepped forward now. "Kupunas are not just leaders, but are ambassadors of Pukapuka to other islands. They are authorized to make treaties, to buy and sell goods, and their word is law."

Anuk'ia stepped forward now. He was the oldest Kupuna on the island somewhere north of ninety. He moved slowly but his mind was still sharp. "Heavy is the burden of wisdom teeth. One must know when to lie through your teeth, and when to grit your teeth. One must know when to sink your teeth in, but not bite off more than you can chew. One should always be armed to the teeth, and defend our home with tooth and nail."

Hiapo stepped forward with a barrel and turned it upside down and poured out sand onto the deck of the ship in a round circle.

Mano stepped forward again. "Gerard, come forward and kneel on the sand of Pukapuka island."

Captain Sharp removed his hat and knelt in the soft sand of his island. Olina opened the box exposing the new necklace of teeth. Anuk'ai took the necklace and placed it over Gerard's head while Mano spoke from beside him.

"May the wisdom inside you lead us, may the light inside you guide us, and may the teeth inside you protect us. Arise Gerard, Kupuna of Pukapuka."

As Gerard stood the Sand Maru started yelling and the crew joined in. There was much cheering, hugging and back slapping. The teeth indeed felt heavy. The islanders were lining up to hug him and wish him well before heading back for the boats. Mano hung around to the end of the line.

"I don't understand, why do this now when I am leaving for who knows how long?" Captain Gerard asked.

"Do you think you will stop serving Pukapuka just because you voyage far away from us?" Mano asked with a smile.

"No . . ."

"We do not think so either." Mano crushed him in another hug and stepped back. "I will miss your council while you are gone but I look forward to the stories you bring when you return. The legend of Gerard the Sharp will continue to grow." Mano said. "The Purple Tiki has told me this."

"Then I shall make you proud, Koko. Thank you for everything, there are not enough words."

Mano headed for the ladder and climbed down into the boat. Everyone got situated and they turned the boat around. Olina was already sitting in the boat looking up at the side of the ship and the crew looking down at her from the rail. She yelled out, "What does the cannon sound like when it fires? I have always wondered."

Gerard smiled down at her and yelled back. "If you are on the beach at sunrise, you'll find out." At this his crew cheered and the islanders on the boat cheered back.

The captain's bed was so comfortable it was going to take some getting used to. It was also too warm with the down feather mattress bag. Roo would have loved this, he thought. He tried to think of a way he could have handled the situation better or differently. Gerard was half in love with her, of that he was sure. It was the other half that had him sleeping on the ship tonight. He loved the sea and he loved sailing. He was eager to be sailing again, and a chance to visit home.

He kicked one sheet off right away, and kicked the second sheet off not long after. He might need to string a hammock above the bed until the ship got into some cooler weather. Gerard thought about how nice it would have been to have the down mattress back home in Falstone when it snowed.

Home. He hadn't thought about home in a long time. He wasn't there yet, but returning was at least a possibility now. He was looking forward to being on the open sea again, excited about this new game he was going to play. It was important for him to win at the game of being a ship's captain. It felt like the most important game he had ever played.

39

Sounds of soft movement on the ship woke him up. It was still dark outside, but the sky in the east was just starting to soften into pink. He could hear the crew moving around, waking up, and going up and down the stairs. Moving day. Gerard got up and made his bed as had been his habit on the island. He folded up one of the sheets and stored it in a drawer. He dressed quickly, making sure he looked sharp and neat. He put on his belt and sword, his new captain's jacket, and finally his hat. He opened the door and August fell inside. He had been sleeping sitting down with his back against the door and they surprised each other.

August scrambled to his feet and came to attention. Captain Sharp was trying to suppress a grin when he asked what he was doing.

"I didn't want to be late for our first day, sir. I was so excited that I couldn't sleep. I thought maybe I would sit right here so I didn't miss anything," August admitted.

"Good thinking," Captain Sharp said. "Of course, next time you could just ask the person on late watch to wake you at first light."

"I'll remember that for next time, sir," August said. His hair was flat on one side. He looked like he had been sleeping against a door all night.

"Why don't you run down to the galley and get us some tea and a small breakfast? I won't do anything important until you get back."

August snapped a salute and took off. Captain Sharp walked out onto the deck and dealt with the rush of salutes and men snapping to attention. Cornelius was just walking up the stairs with Vaheana, already talking with his hands, teaching her on the go. She nodded along with him and fired back questions as fast as he was answering them.

"Good morning!" Captain Sharp called, waving them over. "How are we looking today?"

"Good morning, Captain," they both responded, and then Cornelius continued on: "Everything looks good; we are ready to set sail. We will be sailing out of the bay, cutting into the current and running with it. It should push us along at 4-5 knots. If we can find some wind out there and catch it in the canvas, we could do better. I think eighteen days is still our target but we could be two days either way, depending on wind and weather."

"That sounds great," Captain Sharp said. "I wouldn't mind making up a few days if we can, but only the sea will see."

Vaheana's face showed surprise as she recognized the familiar saying from Mano. "Using the Kupuna cliches already, Captain Sharp?" she said.

"Yes," Captain Sharp said. "I think this wise."

It was the first time Captain Sharp had ever heard Vaheana laugh, and she laughed like a donkey. It was so hilarious and infectious that he laughed along with her. Cornelius just watched. August ran up with two mugs of tea and some pastries. Captain Sharp told his navigators he wanted to pull anchor and start moving out of the lagoon about ten minutes before sunrise. They nodded and headed off to the helm.

Jim-Jim and Fetu spoke with a group getting ready to head up the ratlines. They had everything they needed and were just waiting for the word. Captain Sharp explained what he wanted and they all nodded. He told them to carry on and walked away. He sent August for Smudge as he went to the rail to look back at the island. Villagers were already gathered on the beach of the lagoon.

Smudge appeared and the captain asked him if a sendoff cannon shot was ready for the beach viewers. Smudge smiled and said he had something a little special planned, it would be ready when the captain gave word. He looked so excited that Captain Sharp had to clarify.

"You're not going to blow up my ship are you?" he asked.

"Probably not, captain, but I would feel much more comfortable shooting over water than over parts of the island. I don't want to catch the island of Pukapuka on fire as we are leaving," Smudge replied. He didn't seem worried, more like this was an afterthought.

"I agree. How about once we are moving towards the mouth of the lagoon, take your shot off the starboard side? That side is all rocks and ocean with no vegetation."

"Excellent, Captain Sharp. I will wait for your word," Smudge said, and headed below.

Captain Sharp checked the horizon to the east and saw it was orange, going yellow. Not long now. He looked at the beach now full of Sand Maru. He closed his eyes and listened to the sound of the waves and the wind. He took a deep breath of island air to hold it in and remember it. He could smell the flowers, the sand, the smell of his home. Captain Sharp took one more deep breath, turned from the rail and started yelling.

"All hands-on deck! I want anchor up and sails down! Cornelius, Vaheana, get me out of this lagoon! Jim-Jim, hoist our flag! Smudge, stand by on the cannon. There is a berth in Wellington with our name on it, let's get to it!"

Six men got on the capstan and the anchor was drawn up in short order. The crew in the stays got the flying jib out and the wind started to push them around. When they came out of the turn, they also dropped the forestay sail. That pulled the ship towards the opening in the reef.

Jim-Jim ran up the colors of their new flag. It had three horizontal stripes, red, white, and red. In the middle was a circle with a palm tree on a white sandy beach: the flag of Pukapuka. The crew cheered as the flag was hoisted. Captain Sharp could hear an echoing cheer from the beach. He checked his starboard side and saw they were in the clear of anything that could catch on fire.

"Smudge! Whenever you're ready!" Captain yelled. Captain Sharp waited about ten seconds and was about to repeat the order when the cannon roared. It sounded like a double powder shot because his ears were ringing from his spot on deck. He felt the ship pitch left before rolling back level. The object was shot impossibly high, probably 60 degrees or more, and arced up over the rocky shoals and out over the sea. It looked like a burning cannonball dripping red and silver sparks as it flew. It was one of the most beautiful things he had ever seen. He took a quick look around; every member of the crew was frozen with their mouth hanging open, watching it fly. The flight lasted nearly nine seconds before it exploded with a boom. Sparks rained out like a blooming flower in the sky. There was about three seconds of calm before everyone on the ship went nuts: cheering, jumping up and down, hugging. Smudge ran up on the deck and was mobbed by the crew. Captain Sharp looked back at the beach and they were also going crazy. He cheered along with his crew.

Not five minutes later the sun burst over the horizon and lit up the ship and waves. Captain Sharp realized the timing was perfect; if they had been a few minutes later, some of the fire and sparks would have been lost in the light. He wondered if Smudge knew that, or they just got lucky. In the end it didn't matter; the shot had been perfect. It was another few minutes before a modest and ruffled-up Smudge made his way over to where the captain was standing. He was embarrassed by the reaction, but proud at the same time. Captain Sharp pulled him into another hug and thanked him for the display.

"Thank you Smudge, you do us honor, and you honor the Sand Maru."

Smudge looked back at the beach where he could just make out the villagers still jumping in the air and dancing. "Yeah," he said. "I figured they would like that."

"What exactly was that?" Captain Sharp asked.

Smudge was overjoyed at being able to brag about his work. "I got that from a Chinese fella I met a while back. He was the gunner on a junk ship and needed to trade for some flint. He gave me four of those pretty cannonballs as a trade. That was only the second one I ever shot. The first one didn't work out so well, because I didn't arc it high enough. This one was better."

Captain Sharp put his hand on Smudge's shoulder. "That one was perfect. Thank you. Do you have any other little surprises you think your captain should know about?"

Smudge blushed again and thought about his response. "How about this: if I have something I think will help us out of a tight spot, I'll let you know."

"I can live with that," Captain Sharp said.

40

Captain Gerard walked the deck of his ship, talked to his crew, and watched the waves roll past. In less than two hours Pukapuka was out of sight and the ship was moving smoothly. Vaheana was at the helm, with Cornelius beside her talking back and forth. She had color on her cheeks and seemed to be loving what she was doing. Hickory and Jim-Jim both said all was well and had nothing to report. Captain Sharp asked Hickory for an updated inventory list of supplies on board. Hickory said he would get on it right away. The captain told him there was no rush, but he wanted it accurate. Bothari sat at his bunk, teaching Kolohe how to sharpen a knife.

Captain Sharp returned to his quarters and hung up his hat, jacket and sword. He sat at his desk and looked at the wooden box with the tooth on it. He opened the lid again, looking at the wisdom teeth inside. Twenty sperm whale teeth slivers had been cut, polished and strung onto a cord of braided coconut fiber. He ran his fingers along the teeth and the braid; it was woven tight and would last a lifetime. He closed the lid and put the necklace in one of his empty drawers. It was indeed an honor, but not something he was going to wear every day. Not while on his ship anyway.

He pulled the captain's personal log out of the drawer and turned to the last entry. He re-read it one more time. He turned to the next blank page and started writing. He gave an account of the taking of the Tawny Mane as August had described it. He listed the names of the crewmen killed, provided by Hickory. He described how the pirates locked the crew on the bridge and then ransacked the ship. He wrote about the ship finding Pukapuka island and the first meeting on the beach. He gave a one-sided version of the boat raid and the attempted raid on the island. He described how the crew and the islanders agreed on the punishment, and how that was carried out.

Next he recounted assuming command of Tawny Mane. He told of the honor and responsibility of the position, and his commitment to the protection of the crew. He wrote a brief autobiography, and noted that all future journal entries would be made by him.

Lastly, he described finding the captain's personal log book, the shipping documents with names, dates and locations. He thought about mentioning the hidden money, but something told him to keep that to himself for the moment. The ship had a job to complete; they were still on schedule. They had the means to purchase the supplies waiting for him, and he needed a ride back to Europe. Their course was set and they sailed forward.

He closed the book and placed it back in its hidden drawer. He stood and stretched and noticed how much the sun had moved. He grabbed his jacket and hat and went out on deck. There were only two men on deck, one laying down watching the sails, and one sitting down watching the sea. He looked up and saw Vaheana alone at the helm and climbed up to the poop deck. He did a slow 360 and scanned the ocean in every direction. Nothing to see but the deep blue sea.

"Where is Cornelius?" He asked.

"I don't need Cornelius watching over me every moment. I can handle going straight on my own," she snapped.

Her tone was unexpected; he wondered what happened while he was in his cabin. It seemed awfully early for her to use up her free chance but he was not going to let this slide. It would set a bad precedent. Captain Sharp stepped forward and put his hand on the wheel.

"Vaheana you are relieved of duty, get off my deck."

She looked at him and realized she had made a mistake. She opened her mouth to start talking but Captain Sharp was quicker.

"I was making friendly conversation with a member of my crew. I was going to offer to take the helm while you got something to eat or drink. Steering this boat is a privilege and one you just lost. You are excused." Captain Sharp stared straight ahead.

"Captain Sharp I am sorry, I thought . . ."

"Vaheana, don't make me throw you overboard on the very first day. Go." The last word had some edge to it. She climbed down the steps and walked for the stairs. She kept her spine straight until she got below and then hunched over with disappointment. She had really messed up. She headed for the galley to get some tea to warm up her hands. 'Idiot!' she thought. She was pissed off at Giles, not Gerard.

So far this had been the perfect transition for her. She was treated as an equal and given a bunk with the rest of the men. She made sure she kept everything low-key and didn't speak out. Most of the men were cordial or ignored her, which was fine either way. She was careful at bedtime to not take off too many layers and keep everything covered. She was offered a position which thrilled her and gave her some status among the crew. All was going well.

Cornelius told her he was going below to get a few hours of downtime, and would come up and relieve her later on. She readily agreed and set him on his way. She loved being at the helm, especially by herself. The wind in her face, her hands on the wheel, it was exhilarating. Using the training she had with the stars and sky, and now incorporating some of Cornelius's tools from the ship, she didn't believe they could get lost if they tried. She was having the time of her life until Giles climbed up the stairs.

"Hello," she said, not having met this sailor yet.

"Hello. Getting along, okay?" he asked.

"Yes, thank you. I am Vaheana," she said, offering her hand.

"Giles," he said back and shook her hand, but did not release it. "Now that we have that out of the way, how about a look at that chest of yours dearie?" he said. He pulled her towards him; she had to let go of the wheel to keep from falling over.

She put both hands against his chest to keep from falling into him. Giles used that moment to pinch her butt rather sharply with his free hand. Beside her the wheel started to turn on its own as the ship was pushed to port. His assault had been so unexpected it had taken a few seconds for her to catch up, but she was caught up fast. She made a fist and brought it straight up and caught Giles under the chin hard enough to make his teeth snap together. He released her and stepped back, bringing his hand to his mouth. There was blood on his lip; he had bitten his tongue.

"Now why did you have to go and do that?" Giles mumbled, angry now.

"You have no right to touch me, nor to speak to me that way," she said, backing away and putting a hand on the wheel. She turned it back towards where they were supposed to be and kept an eye on Giles.

"We are all alone on the deck, nobody topside but you and me." Giles said. "A woman asking to be on a ship full of men surely wants to be handled. If it's a matter of money, I have some. Were you a professional before?" He reached for her again. This time, without taking her hands off the wheel, Vaheana kicked him right in the groin. Giles went down in a heap and curled up to protect his injuries.

"Get away from me before I cut you. If you come near me again, I'll gut you like a fish," she said, getting full angry now.

"You're going to pay for that," Giles said, climbing to his feet. He backed away from her and went down the ladder gingerly. He walked to the stairs and disappeared below. She felt a small shiver go down her spine now that he was gone and rubbed her sore butt. The incident didn't scare her, but it made her angry. She had been having such a great time. Everything had been perfect. Damn Giles! Now she would have to be more careful of her surroundings. Ships were like jungles: they had lots of dark hiding spaces.

Not even thirty minutes later, Captain Sharp had climbed up to the poop deck and stood next to her. Her temper got the best of her and she snapped before she caught herself. Vaheana sat by herself at a table in the galley and put her head down in her arms. She had messed it up already.

She decided to ask the Purple Tiki for help and closed her eyes and tried to empty her mind. She was breathing nice and even when a hand on her shoulder made her jump. She looked up to see one of the cooks standing next to her. She didn't know his name yet but he had a serving tray full of tea and biscuits. The smile on his face was genuine. Maurice set the serving tray down and poured each of them a cup of warm tea. Then he sat down at the table across from her and pushed the biscuits between them. Vaheana wrapped her hands around the warm mug and took a sip; it was tea from her island and it was delicious.

"My name is Maurice; I am the head chef on the Tawny Mane." He extended his hand.

"Vaheana," she said, shaking his hand and trying not to think of Giles earlier.

"It's nice to meet you."

"Rough first day?" Maurice asked.

"I just pissed off Captain Sharp on my very first day. He relieved me of duty," she said.

"Oh merde!" Maurice said. "This calls for something more than biscuits." He reached into his apron pocket and started fishing around. He pulled out a small wax paper tube and untwisted one of the ends. Very carefully he shook out a few sugar plums. She had never seen them before so she asked him what they were.

"O sweetie, you need to eat one right now. A sugar plum is candy that has layers of sugar built up over a nut or a seed. These are almonds with six layers of sugar coating and dyed yellow at the end. I just love yellow. It's my favorite color." Maurice pushed one forward to her; she picked it up and examined it before putting it in her mouth. She knew what sugar was but had never had anything like this before. She closed her eyes and made a yummy sound and Maurice patted her hand.

"That's why I hide them. They would be gone in a minute if the crew knew." He looked around suspiciously.

Vaheana finished her first sugar plum and eyed the remaining three on the table. Maurice pushed two of them towards her and kept one in front of himself and started talking. "Well, he didn't throw you over the railing so that's a good thing," Maurice said, looking for the positive.

"He did mention doing it though," Vaheana revealed.

"Oh, dear," Maurice said, and pushed the last sugar plum over to her side of the table. "He is a great man, but there is definitely some darkness in there. I think if you give him some time to cool off, you should be able to talk to him about it."

"It's all my fault. I was mad at . . . someone else and Captain Sharp was the first person I saw after that and I snapped at him."

"Is somebody giving you a hard time Vaheana ?" Maurice asked, getting his hackles up.

"Nothing I can't handle," she said and patted his hand this time. "I appreciate the sentiment though."

"Well, you let me know if you need any help. I could be just as mean as Captain Sharp if I had a mind to." He stood up and twisted the ends of his stash of candy and tucked it back into his apron while looking around for spies. "You stop by any time, Vaheana. My door is always open." He took the tray but left her the tea and the biscuits and headed back into the kitchen.

41

Captain Sharp had been on the wheel for three hours and was loving it. The ship was running great and the sea was calm. There was a light wind pushing them from the back, but not enough to fill a sail. He spent some time thinking about the Vaheana problem, but didn't get anywhere. She had some personal things she needed to clean up. She needed to keep her temper to be able to communicate with her captain. She also needed to either handle her problems or ask for some help. More communication. Captain Sharp worried he may have made communication more difficult with the death threats, but surely everyone knew he was just kidding, right?

Cornelius and Stephen walked on deck together for the afternoon watch. The men parted at the rat lines with Stephen going up the rope and Cornelius coming up the steps to the helm. Cornelius asked if there were any problems. Captain Sharp shook his head. He turned over the wheel to Cornelius and asked if he and Vaheana had any problems earlier.

"None at all; she is quick as a whip. I think she does just as good off the sun as I do off the compass."

"No arguments or disagreements then?" the captain asked.

"No, nothing. Why?" Cornelius asked, looking worried.

"I'm not sure. She snapped at me earlier, so I relieved her and sent her below. I don't want her at the wheel until she figures it out and fixes it. You can have Marty help you rotate in and out until that happens. It shouldn't take long, it looks like she loves it up here."

"Yes sir, I would agree," Cornelius said.

Gerard climbed down the stairs onto the main deck and headed for his quarters.

"Just a moment, Captain!" Gerard heard from behind him. He stopped.

Edmund was climbing down from the crow's nest where he just finished his shift on watch. When he got to the deck, he jumped the last few feet and walked over to where the captain stood.

"I was wondering if I could talk to you in private, Captain Sharp," Edmund asked.

"Do you want to get something to eat first?" he asked.

"It can wait, sir," Edmund said.

"Very well, let's go to my quarters," Captain Sharp said and led the way.

After Edmund left, Captain Sharp stood up and walked to the rear windows of his quarters. He pushed aside the blinds and opened one of the windows to let the air in. He stared at the receding sea as his ship sailed on. He was angry; angry he had to deal with this issue so soon, and angry Vaheana didn't trust him enough to tell him. She probably wanted to deal with it on her own, he mused. He could understand that, but on his ship, everyone was provided his protection. . . until they weren't.

Gerard considered how to handle it. Neat or messy? He wanted to make an impression on the rest of the crew: a lasting impression. One of the lessons he had learned growing up was that if you beat an opponent badly enough, sometimes they never wanted to play with you again. This was one of those games. He wanted this to be the last time he played it.

He first went looking for August. When he couldn't find him, he went looking for Bothari himself. Gerard found him sitting on the floor next to his bunk stretching and exercising. Captain Sharp gave a head tilt. Bothari understood immediately, and followed him the captain forward into one of the storage areas. Captain Sharp looked around to make sure nobody else was in the dark storage area. When he was sure they were alone, he led Bothari into the back corner and whispered to him what he needed. It was time to have another practice drill.

On the way back to his cabin, he thought of another idea for Cuthbert. He hoped that August would like it as much as Maurice did.

42

Captain Sharp had a restless sleep, but the bed did feel better than the first night. One sheet was plenty; he didn't overheat as badly as he did last night. He was up with the sun and got himself dressed and ready for the day. He opened the door slowly, but August wasn't sleeping against it. Gerard considered this progress. He left the door open and he finished straightening up his room and made the bed. That done he walked behind his desk and gave the ring two soft pulls. He guessed it would take twenty seconds and it took fourteen. Maurice breezed into the room with warm tea and some kind of pastry.

"Good morning Captain Sharp, another lovely day at sea," he said, putting the tray down on the map's table and pouring the captain a mug of tea. "I was thinking that if you tell me what you like for breakfast, or give me a few options, I could tailor your meals and bring you exactly what in the morning without any delay on my part or waste on your part." He handed the captain a mug of tea and folded his hands in front of him expectantly. Captain Sharp took the mug of tea and sipped it: perfect, warm, glorious.

"Thank you Maurice, I don't eat much in the morning. For breakfast, I would prefer just one small biscuit, or a piece of fruit and tea. Always tea. Lunch is my biggest meal. I like to have meat when it's available. Meat, bread, half a potato would be perfect. Dinner can be a smaller affair, like soup or cooked vegetables. Coming onto this ship, I expected dinner to consist of whatever you had leftover in the kitchen from that day. I am not a picky eater, and will probably eat whatever you put in front of me. Ideally, I would like to eat the same food you are serving the crew, so I do not appear above their status. I realize this is all an adjustment for you and I don't want to be too much trouble."

"Trouble? Are you mad? Dominic had me cooking four custom meals a day for him, plus desserts! Captain Sharp, I simply cannot bore you to the level you are requesting. You are going to have to make allowances for better meals, or my talents will atrophy and I will slip into the vapors of boredom. However, I think there is some common ground. We can try and meet somewhere in the middle. Now, let's talk about the Vaheana problem."

Captains Sharp's head snapped up from his tea. "The Vaheana problem? How do you know about that?"

Maurice poured himself a mug of tea and sipped it gently. "I know everything that happens on this ship. Half the crew come into the galley to talk about rumors with me; the other half come into the galley and talk about rumors in front of me. Either way, I hear it all. Vaheana feels terrible about snapping at you, but it wasn't her fault. The other crew member just made her so angry."

Captain Sharp looked at Maurice with a new and critical eye. This was an untapped resource of information he had not counted on. "Do you know who this other crew member is?" he asked.

"Right now I don't, but if I don't have the answer by lunch, then you can dip me in saltwater and call me hardtack," Maurice said.

"I know who it is," said the captain with a smile, calmly sipping his tea.

"Ooh, do tell!" Maurice moved over and got shoulder-to-shoulder with the captain. "I would love to take a wooden spoon to that scoundrel myself if I had the time to spare."

"I can't tell you who it was, but . . ." Captain Sharp paused.

Maurice's eyes were so big, and he was leaning in so far their heads were nearly touching. "Yes?" he said breathlessly.

"I was going to deal with it today during morning announcements. I know that normally you stay below in the galley and work on breakfast, but perhaps today you should be up on deck with the rest of the crew. I wouldn't want you to miss the show."

Maurice clapped his hands together, he was so excited. "Captain Sharp, you are the bee's knees! I wouldn't miss this for anything." He picked up the empty tray and headed for the door.

"Maurice," The captain said. "Not a word to anyone. We don't want to spoil the surprise."

Maurice motioned, closing his lips, locking them, and throwing the key over his shoulder. With that he danced out the door.

When August came in, Captain Sharp told him they were going to have some announcements on the main deck and that attendance was mandatory. He told August to blow for all hands and do a sweep below to make sure everyone was there. August went outside and the bosun's whistle sounded. Captain Sharp put on his sword and his hat. It was showtime.

Five minutes later the crew was on deck. The captain walked towards the forecastle deck at the front of the ship so all eyes would follow him. He stopped at the base of the stairs and turned to address the crew. Most were awake, some were half awake, some were sipping coffee to stay awake.

"Good morning, crew. We are off to a good start and a bad start at the same time. The Tawny Mane is sailing well, making good time, and performing without incident." He paused here. "My crew, on the other hand, is struggling to follow the rules and keep their honor and integrity intact. I must say this has made me a bit angry." He let his voice go flat as he said this and let the anger come forward. Everyone was awake now. Everyone paid attention now. At the back of the ship Bothari climbed the ladder to the poop deck holding a cork float bag.

"Last night I learned that one of my crew members was assaulted by another crew member." A few gasps emanated from the crew. Captain Sharp started to walk down the line of sailors as he talked. "The victim did not come forward to report this. It was reported by a witness watching from the crow's nest. I hope that each and every one of you knows you are under my personal protection. This is not an obligation that I take lightly. You should feel free to come to me if you are being harassed or threatened. Nobody, I mean NOBODY!" He screamed, "Fucks with my crew!"

Captain Sharp stopped in front of Giles. Giles was pale and already shaking. He put his hands out in front of him in surrender and started to talk.

"Captain Sharp, I didn't think. . . "

Captain Sharp grabbed him by the collar and his belt, pressed him into the air, and threw him overboard.

There was a short scream, cut off by a splash, then nothing. Captain Sharp turned back towards the crew and adjusted his hat that had been knocked askew in the moment. There were alot of wide eyes and open mouths now. He saw Bothari casually throw the cork float off the back of the ship in the direction of the departed passenger. Captain Sharp let the smile come back to his face and felt his eyes return to normal.

"Does anyone have any questions?" Captain Sharp asked. He looked for Vaheana and saw she was as pale as the rest of them. He counted to thirty in his head, giving everyone time to think. "Assault on one of my crew members will not be tolerated. This will be my only warning on the subject."

"Now that we have that out of the way, we have an opportunity for a drill this morning. Jim-Jim, you're in charge. Man overboard. If he's not found in five minutes he's not found, you understand me?" Captain Sharp asked and Jim-Jim nodded vigorously.

"Very well then, carry on. I'll be in my quarters." Captain Sharp walked past the frozen crew towards his door. It took at least ten seconds before Jim-Jim started yelling. "Move it people, get one of the jollies over the side. Cornelius, bring us around, can anybody see him?"

Bothari was waiting at the door and the two men went in together. Captain Sharp pulled the door shut behind him only to have Maurice come bursting in moments later. He embraced the captain in a hug and then kissed him once on each cheek. "Sacree Merde! The stories would not have done it justice. Thank you, captain. Can I bring you anything?"

"No thank you, Maurice," the captain replied.

The cook started to leave and then paused at the doorway. "Do you know if Giles knows how to swim?" Maurice asked.

"I have no idea." Captain Sharp said, and let the wolf smile out.

"Mon Dieu!" the cook said, and closed the door.

"When it comes time to throw Kolohe overboard, I want to be the one to do it," Bothari said.

Captain Sharp thought about it for a moment and then nodded his head. "You got it. Why don't you pull up two chairs before the next visitor shows up. Shouldn't be long now." Bothari pulled two chairs over from the maps table to the captain's desk and sat back in one and relaxed.

"That should take care of any discipline problems around here for a while. Was it as fun as it looked?" Bothari asked.

"Oh hell, yes. With me being angry, I didn't even feel his weight. I probably could have thrown him farther if I wanted." Captain Sharp smiled. "You should have seen the crew's faces when I turned back around."

"I saw plenty of them in the back, eyes nearly popping right out of the sockets," Bothari said.

There was a knock at the door and Captain Sharp yelled 'enter'. August poked his head in and pulled the door shut behind him. As he walked over to the desk Captain Sharp whispered to Bothari, "maybe one more chair." Bothari nodded and dragged over one more chair.

Captain Sharp indicated August should take the new chair brought over on the right and leave the chair in the middle vacant. August sat down and looked at both of them.

"Wow, that was something. Did you know you were going to do that before the assembly this morning?" August asked.

Captain Sharp just nodded.

"Oh, wow. Did you know you were going to do that last night when you heard about it?"

Captain Sharp nodded again.

"Oh, wow. I don't know how you go from calm to furious in the blink of an eye, but it sure is something to see." August glanced at the empty chair. "Are we expecting somebody?"

"Yes, I think Vaheana will be stopping by for a short conversation."

"Do you want me to leave?" August asked.

"No, I think it will be educational for everyone involved." Captain Sharp said.

"Had anyone spotted Giles before you came in?"

August perked up. "Yea, he was spotted a ways back bobbing in the ocean holding a cork float bag like a dying man. He looked right scared he did."

"Good," Captain Sharp said. "That reminds me, I had an idea last night I wanted to ask you about. What do you think of the bell that Maurice and Cuthbert came up with in the galley?"

"I think it's a grand idea," August said. "Everyone used to hate the way Dominic would go off. If you were sleeping and he started up it would scare the bejeezus out of you."

A knock at the door interrupted them; the captain yelled for them to enter.

Vaheana walked in and closed the door before turning around and seeing Bothari and August already seated. "I was hoping I could have a word with you in private, Captain Sharp."

"Bothari is the First Mate, and Sergeant at Arms. I think this concerns him also. August is my assistant. He sits in on most of my meetings. You are going to have to get used to that. Why don't you have a seat." Captain Sharp stood up and indicated the empty chair in front of him.

She noticed the vacant seat for the first time and did some fast thinking. "Who were you expecting?" Vaheana asked.

"I was expecting you to stop by and want to talk," Captain Sharp said, motioning to the empty chair again.

Vaheana tilted her head back in exasperation and groaned loudly, then walked over and flopped in the chair. "Do you already have my apology worked out too?" she said with a little bit of tone.

"Easy, Vaheana. You get a little latitude this morning, but not that much," Captain Gerard warned.

"I didn't come to you because I wanted to handle it on my own. I didn't want to be the person on your ship for only one day already asking for help. Plus I'm a Koa, he didn't scare me, he just surprised me. When he limped away, I felt we had an understanding."

Captain Sharp nodded but didn't speak, waiting.

"I'm sorry I snapped at you. Giles had just left. I was still angry that he got the best of me for a moment. You came up and the first thing you did was ask where the real navigator was, and my temper got out before I could stop it," Vaheana explained.

"Do not put words in my mouth, Vaheana. I simply asked where Cornelius was. You need to stop looking for the hidden meaning in my words, for there is none. If I am unhappy with you, you will know it immediately," Captain Sharp said.

"Yes. That lesson has been demonstrated," she said, grinning. "I would like to resume my training as navigator. I realize it's a privilege and one I will take better care of. I am sorry I snapped at you, you have been nothing but fair to me. I will work on my temper."

Captain Sharp looked at her for a moment, then asked Bothari what he thought.

"I think the issue has been dealt with, and I think she knows she is out of chances," Bothari said and looked at her. "You need to work hard on that temper. Lashing out at the captain undermines his authority, and hurts the ship."

Vaheana nodded.

Captain Sharp turned to August. "What do you think?"

"I want you to make her navigator again," August replied with a grin.

"Thank you, August," Vaheana said.

"When Captain Sharp throws you off the poop deck, it will make an even bigger splash," August said nonchalantly.

"WHAT?" yelled Vaheana.

Captain Sharp and Bothari absolutely lost it.

43

Giles was fished out of the ocean and brought back on deck. The crew took him below to dry off and warm up. Just about the time he was feeling normal again Bothari showed up and came up to speak with him nose-to-nose.

"Are we going to have any more issues, Giles?" he asked.

"No, sir," Giles said.

"I would avoid Captain Sharp for a few days if I were you. He is still pretty angry over this incident."

"It won't happen again sir. I plan on avoiding Vaheana," Giles said.

"I meant you being able to swim and being rescued, that incident," Bothari said and walked away.

After Vaheana and Bothari had both left; only August remained in the captain's quarters. Captain Sharp went back to talking about his idea from earlier.

"I went looking for you last night and couldn't find you," Captain Sharp said.

"Sorry sir, I was helping Hickory with some inventory last night, I will try to. . ."

Captain Sharp waved him off. "It's okay August, I don't expect you to be available for me every minute of the day. You have friends, you have free time, and you have other duties on the ship. What I was thinking was a way for me to call for you without yelling and stopping my foot on the deck. What would you think of me having Cuthbert set up something similar for you?"

"Another bell sir?" August asked, looking happy. "I think that's a great idea, sir."

"Maybe not a bell, but something similar. I don't want you to feel like I am calling you with a servant's bell, but if we could find a way to let you know when I wake up, when I need your help, it would help both of us."

"Would you like me to talk to Cuthbert about it sir?" August asked, looking excited with the project.

"Yes I would August, thank you. Let me know what the two of you come up with."

44

The next morning Captain Sharp was still in bed when there was a soft knock on the door. He took a look at the sky and saw it wasn't full dark anymore, but sunrise was still a ways off.

"Yes?" He called.

"Ohe hana," (bamboo work) a voice called out.

"Five minutes," He called back. Soft footsteps walked away. He got out of bed and put on some light clothing designed for movement and exercise. He washed his face and headed onto the deck.

Sitting on the deck, already stretching out were Fetu and Vaheana. He sat down next to them and started working on his arms and shoulders. Bothari came up the stairs, pushing a very grumpy looking Kolohe in front of him. They joined the group. Bothari led Kolohe through a series of warm ups.

When he was ready, Captain Sharp went over to the pile of Bamboo sticks and picked out some of the three-foot-long ones. He spun these in his hands and swung them across his body. After a few minutes Fetu came over to stand next to him, holding one of the shorter sticks in his hands. Captain Sharp put the extra stick back in the pile turned to square off with Fetu. The two of them started a series of swings and blocks with the practice bamboo swords. The rhythmic clacking of the bamboo stick was soon joined by another pair as Bothari and Vaheana went through their drills. Kolohe was off to the side trying to mirror the movements as the odd man out.

A few minutes into the drills, some of the crew came on deck to investigate the noise. They watched for a time before drifting back down below. One of the watchers was August. He stuck around. After a break in the routine, Captain Sharp paired off with Vaheana before the next round of drills. He caught Bothari's eyes and nodded toward August watching off to the side. Fetu went to work with Kolohe, while Bothari walked over to August.

Five minutes later, August had a bamboo stick in his hands and was learning the basic patterns. They rotated twice more before everyone put the bamboo sticks in a pile. Each of them picked up one of the bamboo staffs: six feet long and solid. They started drills again, incorporating August into the group. The basic movements were done slowly at first, then with increasing speed and force. Soon the deck was full of the deep thrums of bamboo-on-bamboo hits. They changed partners twice more for the staff drills before calling a stop. A few more of the crew had drifted up to watch and had stayed until the end. Bothari went over to talk to them and to gauge interest for next time. They had 'ohe hana' or bamboo work every three days, and it was always early in the morning.

The only injury the first day was August's left hand, squashed once and bloodied by Kolohe. One of the elements of the drill is control. It was a mark against your honor to injure somebody else. August said it was no big deal and shook it off, but Bothari made a note of it in his tally book. A second injury to August by Kolohe would require a 'hookaa' (payment). This meant Bothari would squash Kolohe's hand in a similar, but likely harder manner. One didn't want to be in the tally book, and one definitely didn't want Bothari to call him out for a payment.

Later that morning, Cuthbert and August came by to brainstorm about the communication system he wanted. Captain Sharp explained that he wanted a system where he could alert August with three or four different requests: to let him know when he was awake and open for business as Captain of the Ship; when he needed him in the capacity as a runner or personal assistant. He also thought it would be beneficial to have a status report option, where August would know it was time to walk the ship, check with the senior crew, and then report back to the captain. The three went back and forth for a time before the junior men left to continue the discussion in the galley with the help of Maurice.

The Tawny Mane pushed steadily west, aided by the South Equatorial Current. The 'SEC' flows due west and well north of New Zealand Island. Ships would routinely miss the islands unless they caught enough canvas to push them far enough south. With good wind and sails you can catch the west side of New Zealand before being pushed past it. If the wind was not in a ship's favor, they'd float west to Australia before the current turned south and then east again. This route brought you back out to the west side of New Zealand, but at a delay of anywhere from two weeks to a month.

The Mane had three masts along with her lateen sail in the front. The lateen was a triangular sail off the foremast and strung out onto the lead boom. This allowed the ship to tack against the wind when necessary. In all the Mane had 11,000 square feet of canvas when she dropped all her skirts and they caught every gust of wind they could find.

Jim-Jim ran the crew on the deck: that now included Fetu, Blaed and Kolohe. They were learning the ropes, rigging and canvas. Jim-Jim had been at sea for over fourteen years. He had a good feel for the ship and the sea. He touched base frequently with Cornelius. Captain Sharp listened and learned all he could.

Stephan ran the night crew, commanding the deck from sundown to sunup. He was much quieter than Jim-Jim and did not yell when communicating. If he needed to send instructions aloft, he would just climb up and tell the crewman what needed to be changed. Captain Sharp made it a point to ask Stephan questions and get him talking when he could. He was talking to Stephan just after dark when Cuthbert found him and said he had a communication system figured out in his head.

Captain Sharp asked what he decided on. Cuthbert replied that he would rather install it first and just show it to him after the fact. Captain Sharp agreed and told him to move ahead, and that he would make his quarters available tomorrow morning if Cuthbert needed it. Cuthbert said that would be fine, and started to leave.

"One more thing, Cuthbert." Captain Sharp removed one of the keychains from around his neck and handed it to Cuthbert. "I want you to keep hold of the backup set of keys. I would give them to Bothari, but he and I are together much of the time. If I go ashore, I want a trusted man on the ship with keys to the armory. I trust you Cuthbert, and I know you will keep them safe."

Cuthbert put the leather cord around his neck and tucked the keys into his shirt. "Thank you, Captain Sharp. It's an honor. I will keep the Tawny Mane safe in your absence." The men shook arms and Cuthbert moved off to go below.

Stephan watched the exchange and asked Captain Sharp about it. "I notice you give your crew more latitude than most other captains, but you don't seem threatened by it. It doesn't bother you to have smart men thinking for themselves working for you?"

"Absolutely not. I want to be surrounded by intelligent crewmen. It's the best way to ensure this ship is successful. In the process all of us are going to be cross-trained and get smarter. I don't have time to be an expert on navigation, sails, and cannons, or anything else. I expect my crew to be experts at their jobs, and I will rely on them when I need to. For example, I know how to steer the ship, but that does not compare to Cornelius's years of experience and all the secrets and tricks he has picked up. The same goes for you, Jim-Jim, Smudge, or even Maurice. I need all of you to be great at what you do. When you all perform well, our ship performs well and we get to New Zealand on time and without incident. I learn more every day, but unfortunately it takes years of different experiences to make a great captain. All I can do right now is learn everything I can on board and rely on my past job skills and experiences to keep us safe."

Stephan thought about this and seemed satisfied. "What job did you have before you became Captain Sharp?"

"I killed for a living," Captain Sharp said, and the wolf smiled.

45

The next morning the captain was up, dressed and ready to go when August showed up. He sent his runner back down to set up a meeting in the galley with his senior crew, Smudge, and the rest of the cannon firing team. Just before he left, Cuthbert showed up with a bag full of stuff over his shoulder. He had a big smile on his face. Captain Sharp knew he was going to like whatever Cuthbert came up with. The men said their good mornings and the captain left him to his work.

Captain Sharp entered the galley and found a dozen men already assembled. Maurice and Pierre were laying out coffee and breakfast while Smudge and Hickory stood talking near the door. Before Gerard could reach them, Maurice walked by and put a mug of tea and a small biscuit in his hand and never broke stride. "Expert," he said under his breath.

Captain Sharp told everyone to sit, and asked that Smudge and Hickory sit at his table near the front of the room. After everyone got settled and quieted down he started on his agenda.

"Thank you Maurice and Pierre for catering our impromptu meeting this morning. The crew and I appreciate your efforts and your work." He raised his mug up in a toast; all the men present did the same with a small cheer. Maurice blushed scarlet and Pierre fled for the kitchen.

"I want to talk about the shooting exercise we had the other day on 'The Wedge'. I want to cover what we did right, what we did wrong, and what we can do better next time. I am not that concerned with mistakes at this point, so nobody needs to feel threatened. It was our first exercise with a mixed crew, so mistakes should be expected. What I want, and what you should also want, is for us to be ready when it really matters. Smudge, give me your summary. Then we will hear from August. After that I'll open it up for questions and general discussion."

He sat down with a paper and quill and motioned for Smudge to stand up and give his report of the events. As he started to talk, August leaned over to speak softly to Captain Sharp.

"I'm not very good at speaking before a group, sir. Perhaps I could talk to you later in your quarters?" August whispered nervously.

Captain Sharp leaned closer to August and whispered back, "You're going to give your report next and you are going to do just fine. Look at me, and talk to me. Pretend it's just you and me in my cabin. Talk loud enough for everyone to hear. If you mess up, I throw you overboard." He gave a normal smile when he said it, so hopefully August knew he was kidding.

"For our first time out of the barrel I think we did pretty good, always room for improvement. I think once we fired the third cannon, the crew knew what to expect and what to do next, so we got into a rhythm. I think five hits out of eight shots was damn fine for a training run," Smudge said.

"Five out of eight? Are we counting the skip shot then?" Captain Sharp asked with a grin.

"Of course! Shots near the water line are considerably more damaging, and it did hit the target. . . eventually," Smudge justified.

"Okay then, five out of eight. What do we need to do to make it eight for eight next time? Tell me what we need to do differently," Captain Sharp asked.

"Well, I could always use more men. . ."

"Smudge," Captain Sharp started slowly, "of course we are going to train more men. We need to utilize all of the cannons if we are attacked. That's a given. I want to know what we need to do differently to be more accurate with every shot we take. I have said before that the protection of this ship and its crew is my top priority. Five out of eight is pretty good, but it's not good enough for me. I want eight out of eight. When we are fighting for our lives, and taking fire from another ship and my crew are dying, I want eight out of eight. If we are pretty good, maybe only half the crew dies. That is just not acceptable. Now let's start over. I want us to be the best. I want other ships to know our name. I want pirate ships to cower in fear. When I tell you to shoot the mast off another ship, I want to see that twig floating ten seconds later. So Smudge, what do we need to change to be the best?"

"I'm not exactly sure, Captain Sharp. I haven't been in an actual canon battle just yet, so far it's all been practice and pretend, and not much of that," Smudge admitted.

"That's a good beginning, Smudge, thank you. More practice and more drills. I'll be asking everyone for ideas later, so you can all start thinking of things that will help. I don't think that one man should have all the answers. A good idea is a good idea, no matter who it comes from. Remember: we are not here to place blame or point fingers; we are getting better and saving lives down the road."

The crew nodded, following along.

"August, I'd like to hear your report," Captain Sharp said.

August stood and looked at the men seated behind him. Captain Sharp cleared his throat. When August looked back at him, he repeated himself.

"I want to hear your report, talk to me."

August turned to face Captain Sharp directly and took a deep breath and began talking. "It was dark down there sir. I think having more shutters open would help the men to see."

"That's good, what else?" Captain Sharp made some notes for himself and motioned for August to keep going.

"Mr. Smudge was the only one who knew what was going on. Everyone else was just standing around waiting for him to give orders.

Captain Sharp made more notes and motioned for him to keep going.

August looked a bit more relaxed. "We have twelve guns on each side. We need to find a way to be able to use all of them quickly if needed." He paused and looked at Smudge now. "I used to work in a factory. They had teams of workers going from station to station to make things faster. I think if we did the same kind of thing here, we could be more efficient."

"Outstanding, August! This is exactly the stuff I am looking for," yelled Captain Sharp.

August smiled, growing more confident. He mentioned that if the navigator could give warning when the ship was going into and coming out of turns, the gunners below could be better prepared and shoot more accurately. He thought that four teams of gunners, with at least two men trained to aim and fire them would be most effective. It was his next suggestion that excited Captain Sharp the most.

"Since we need to train at least three other master gunners, I would like to volunteer for one of those positions," August said, as he sat down.

Captain Sharp waited a few seconds for anyone to argue, but nobody did. August had risen in status among his peers even if he didn't realize it. He was a respected member of the crew. They took what he said at face value. Captain Sharp stood and looked at the men sitting around the galley. They looked to him for leadership, but he thought it might be time he spread that around some. He took a chance and asked August why he wanted to be a master gunner.

August stood up and took a moment to get his thoughts in order. He looked at the captain with some real steel in his eye for the very first time.

"This ship is full of brave people who I look up to everyday. Someday I want to be thought of that way too. I asked one of the people I admire how to do brave things when you're so afraid all the time. She told me three things: volunteer for something that scares you, bust your ass to be the best at it, and don't let anyone or anything get in your way. I've decided I want to protect my ship and my crew, and nothing is going to get in my way."

The cheer from the men was so loud that it caught August off guard. Captain Sharp introduced August to the Sand Maru smash hug. The others came over to pat his shoulder or ruffle his hair. It was a great moment; Captain Sharp had a lump in his throat. He wanted greatness for all of his crew. This was a good beginning. When everyone was back in their seats, he let August go and had him sit. Captain Sharp stood in front of the men. He had one more item to cover before they moved on.

"August," he said, getting the room's attention, "that someday you talked about, it started today."

Captain Sharp opened up the questions to the group and got several more good ideas. One of the men used to hunt wondered aloud why the cannons did not have an aiming system on the top like some of the newer muskets. The group talked about making and attaching some kind of sight pins front and back, which could help improve accuracy. Presently the gun was aimed by the cannon master from behind, looking across its top. Another man had worked in a foundry where it was too loud to talk to each other, so the workers used hand signals. He thought it could be useful below since after the first shot nobody could hear.

The group decided that they wanted four teams loading and positioning the cannons, and three or four cannon masters to do the final adjustment and firing. Two more men volunteered quickly after August's earlier example. When they had most of the details worked out, Captain Sharp left Smudge in charge. He told them the priority was to spend some time working on the most efficient station rotation and hand signals. Once they had a good handle on that, he wanted some non-firing training time every day for the next few days. They would meet again in three days to talk about the progress, and see if more changes needed to be made. They would also look for opportunities for live fire exercises if targets presented themselves. This left all the men smiling and ended the meeting on a happy note.

Back in his quarters, he found Cuthbert sleeping in his comfortable captain's chair. He thought about tipping it over, but decided Cuthbert had probably been doing jobs all over the ship at all hours and he could afford to cut him some slack. He brought another chair over from the maps table and sat in front of his own desk. He needed to write down some notes from the cannon meeting before they slipped his mind. He was just about finished when he saw Cuthbert's body jerk awake out of his peripheral vision. Cuthbert stood and stretched before moving around from behind the desk.

"Begging your pardon Captain Sharp, I only sat down for a minute," Cuthbert said.

"It's not a crime to sit in my chair, Cuthbert. Don't worry about it. Now if I caught you napping in my bed, I would have tossed you overboard without a thought," Captain Sharp said and smiled. He closed his notebook and put the quill down. "Now why don't you show me what you and August came up with?"

Cuthbet led him behind the desk and off to the side near a blank spot on the wall. He had drilled a small hole in the wall. Coming out of the hole was a sturdy, braided rope with a brass ring tied on the end. Above the hole in a vertical line were six wood pegs for the ring to hang on. Five of the six pegs had been labeled in Cuthbert's neat handwriting. The bottom peg said 'awake'. The next peg up said 'open'. The next peg up said 'runner'. The next peg up said 'status'. The fifth peg was blank for now, and the top peg said 'emergency'.

Cuthbert explained that when the captain woke up in the morning he should move the ring to the awake peg. Down below on the wall next to August's bunk, a similar ring moved up the wall and centered on the word awake. As the peg was moved up or down, the brass ring circled the request in the captain's quarters as well as August's bunk. Open for open, runner for runner, and status for a status check. He left one blank for future use without having to redo the whole system.

The emergency hook was special because when the rope was pulled all the way up to the top ring, it pulled a bell off its resting spot below making it ring. When Captain Sharp had an emergency, the bell would ring next to August's bunk, waking him up or getting his immediate attention.

Captain Sharp asked to see the other end of the system, and they moved the ring to the 'runner' peg before leaving. They walked to the crew quarters where three people were already gathered around the new invention. The ring was strung between two beams and couldn't move side to side all that much. The brass ring was indeed centered on 'runner'. Cuthbert pulled the rope up from the top, exposing the bell hanging below and making it ring. He also showed the captain the weights tied at the bottom of the rope to keep it tight and from slacking. Gerard followed the path of the rope up the wall and turned through a well-sanded hole in a beam. It ran along the ceiling, into the galley, disappearing into the wall that ran up behind his desk in his quarters. He thanked Cuthbert for another fantastic job and asked what his next project was. Cuthbert said he was caught up and was looking for something to do, that's why he was so excited to get to work on the signaling system. It was the only interesting job he had to keep him busy. Captain Sharp mentioned that he might want to go up to the gun deck and talk to Smudge about a sighting system for the cannons. Cuthbert's eyebrows went up, and then he was gone.

That afternoon he met with Hickory and received an updated list of the ship's stores, supplies and rations. After topping off in Pukapuka they were supplied for a long journey if needed, but had more than enough to get them to New Zealand. They were overstocked on a few items, which they agreed they might be able to trade while in New Zealand. Gerard had asked Hickory to make a second copy of the inventory so he could include it in the ship's log.

Next, the two of them spent some time figuring out what additional supplies would be needed before starting the long trip back to England. They brought in Cornelius and had him map out a rough estimate for the trip home. They had 26 crewmen on board. The return trip would take between 80 and 110 days, with a target date of 92 days. It all depended on the doldrums.

The doldrums is the area at the equator where the wind doesn't blow, as the northern and southern trade winds meet and cancel each other out. The band extends as far as five degrees north and south of the equator. For sailing ships, the doldrums could be a nightmare. An unlucky ship might get stuck for weeks without a whisper of a breeze. The doldrums cost you time, water, and sanity.

Captain Sharp asked Cornelius and Vaheana how the southern push was going. Both of them agreed the southerly wind was pushing good so far, perhaps even ahead of schedule. Cornelus said they were building up some current credit and that they might need it for later. Vaheana asked what that meant and he explained it to both of them.

The Southern Equatorial Current pushed the Tawny Mane at a steady rate on a steady course. The wind was the biggest variable in the equation. With no wind at all, they would drift west and miss New Zealand on the first pass. They needed to catch the wind to push them south while the current pushed them west. If they caught enough wind the first twelve days, and then the wind died, they might still catch the northern tip of New Zealand since they had built up enough south credit for the current to push them into the island. If they didn't build up enough south credit and the wind died, they would drift right past New Zealand with no way to make landfall. Some ships had gotten close enough to see the island, only to be swept past on the SEC. Cornelius wanted to build up as much credit as he could; since you could count on the wind to be unpredictable.

46

The next day about midmorning the man on watch sighted land and called out below. Captain Sharp came out with his eyeglass and spent some time looking for himself. The island looked small from here, probably too small to support any people. What it did support was coco palms. The island was so dense with coco palms that you couldn't see more than five feet into it. The beach appeared to be full of coconuts: some laying in the sand, some tumbling in the surf.

Captain Sharp yelled for Hickory and Jim-Jim and they had a short conversation. The captain wanted to know about the trade-resale value of coconuts in New Zealand. Jim-Jim sent for another sailor named Hans Michael, who had been to New Zealand before. When he arrived, the four of them talked about the opportunity. Hans Michael told them coconuts didn't grow in New Zealand and therefore the value was high. They had to be imported. Since the current pushed towards them, it was difficult and costly for a ship to get them.

Coconuts were valuable because they had so many uses and could be resold several times throughout their processing life span. Everyone knew about the high calorie food aspect, but they were also a high calorie potable drinking water source. The husk fiber could be removed and spun into ropes and heavy-duty braided cord. The thinner fibers were used in jewelry applications, like bracelets and necklaces as they were strong and unlikely to break with everyday use. The hard shell of coconuts could be turned into coal and burned as fuel. Depending on the buyers in New Zealand, this single product could be resold several times after the initial sale, making the initial investment substantially higher than most other imported foods.

They decided to stop at the island and gather what they could, to be sold when they made port later on. Captain Sharp climbed up to the helm and talked to Vaheana, who was on the wheel. He wanted her to come around on the back side of the island and stop in the eddy of the current. He told her to try and get close but not to beach his ship. She gave him her annoyed look but didn't say anything this time. He had August pipe for all hands and got the crew on deck.

"Crew, we have a unique opportunity at the island up ahead. The trees, sand, and beaches look to be full of coconuts. Hans Michael says they have significant trade value at our next stop in New Zealand. We currently have no cargo and plenty of room to store what we find. Once we are anchored on the lee side of the island, I want crews in boats going to the island to pick up all we can. I want this delay to be no more than half a day. Once we get to New Zealand and the cargo is sold or traded, that money will be divided among the crew of the Tawny Mane. That should give all of you some walk around money while we are there."

A cheer went up from all the men on deck; they quickly went to work un-securing the boats tied on the deck. Jim-Jim was put in charge of the shore detail and would be going out with the first boat. Hickory said he would check in with his other copper to start figuring out the storage below.

The meeting broke up and Captain Sharp climbed up onto the poop deck to watch Vaheana work. She posted two leadmen on either side of the ship towards the bow. The leadman's job was to drop a length of rope into the water called a 'sounding line' and read off the depth. The rope had a lead plummet on the bottom and different color ribbons tied off every three fathoms to mark the depth.

The ship eased past the island on the port side, then swung around to come up behind it. The leadmen were alternately calling out twenty plus fathoms in a steady calm rhythm, then the starboard side yelled fifteen fathoms on the mark. Port side confirmed fifteen fathoms and the crew in the stays started dropping canvas es fast. The depth dropped to twelve fathoms and was matched on the opposite side. Vaheana yelled for the anchor to be unlashed from the side of the ship and allowed to hang free. They were still some distance away from the island. Captain Sharp wanted to be much closer. The port leadmen called out nine fathoms, but the starboard side was holding at twelve. Both leadmen called out six fathoms at the same time. Vaheana turned to look at Captain Sharp. Her eyebrows were up in a question. He told her to drop and hold at three fathoms. He walked away and climbed down the ladder. Vaheana yelled to stand by on the anchor and secure all sails.

As soon as the first leadmen called out three fathoms she yelled drop anchor and the crew up front released the chain. The anchor caught fast in the sand and the ship stopped and did a half turn while she settled.

Jim-Jim and his crew were already going over the starboard side with the two longboats. Others put the two smaller jollys over the port side. Most of the crew was on the deck to either help get the boats over or to stand by to receive the cargo. Everyone else watched and waited. The first boat pushed out and headed for the island beach, less than two hundred feet away. They were already pushing through coconuts floating in the calm water on the backside of the island.

Vaheana climbed down from the poop deck and came over to where Captain Sharp and Bothari were supervising.

"Can I go to shore on one of the jollys sir?" she asked.

"Homesick?" Captain asked with a smile.

"I just want to look around, get some sand between my toes."

"You're one of the crew, Vaheana. You don't need my permission."

She smiled and ran towards the side of the ship where the boats had already been lowered and vanished over the rail.

"A good bit of luck to fill our holds just before making port," Bothari said, putting a hand on Captain Sharp's shoulder.

"Yes, the Purple Tiki has guided us with a fortunate hand," Captain Sharp agreed.

One of the longboats came back first, bursting to the rails with coconuts. The crew set up a relay system for throwing them up onto the deck and then tossing them man-to-man down the stairs and into the holds. Soon both sides of the ship were unloading coconuts as fast as they could and they were being tossed down both flights of steps in ones and then two's.

Vaheana was on the beach picking up coconuts with the rest of the men when she found one of the biggest conch shells she had ever seen. She set it aside to take back with her later and went back to work. A few minutes later she found another one, and then another one. She yelled for Jim-Jim and they had a short conversation, before he referred her to Hans Michael. She found him on the beach loading boats and asked him to come over and take a look. She showed him what she had found and after some discussion they started wrapping the conch shells in palm leaves and stacking them up on the beach. The two of them started spreading the word and soon there were several rows of the bright pink and orange conch shells wrapped up in palm leaves on the beach.

When the last few boats were heading back, Vaheana and Hans Michael carefully hand loaded the conch shells in the boat and rowed back out to the Tawny Mane. Once tied to the side, Vaheana climbed up with one of the shells and flagged down Captain Sharp. She showed him the shell and said they needed to store them in the drawers and cubbies in the captain's quarters so they would not be damaged or broken. He started to ask why when Hans Michael joined them looking excited and talking fast. He said it was an incredible find. The shells were rare and extremely valuable as collector's items. The size and coloring of these shells were some of the best he had ever seen. Vaheana said she had traded for shells like this on other islands in the past. They headed off towards his quarters with a line of people behind them carrying more wrapped shells. Captain Sharp followed them to make sure none were stored in his bed. The crew had found a total of 46 fully intact conch shells to bring on board. His room was going to stink to high heaven.

The coconut loading took five hours to complete and stuffed the ship to the gills. The crew was tired but happy, and everyone was covered with sand. There were lots of cuts on hands from the coconuts but no other injuries to report. News of the conch shell find went through the crew rapidly and after the fifth person came to his quarters to look at them, Captain Sharp unwrapped one and sent it off with the crewmen to show everyone on the ship.

Cornelius was at the helm when they pulled anchor and turned out of the eddy and back into the current. The wind was less than it had been earlier but still enough to keep them moving south by southwest. Cornelius kept tracking numbers and taking readings and said there was nothing to worry about for now. That night for dinner some of the dishes included baked coconut, toasted coconut, and coconut milk. Captain Sharp figured they had a few days before the men would be so tired of coconuts, they would start throwing them overboard.

47

It was dark when the knock came. "Ohe Hana." This time Bothari didn't wait for an answer before walking away. Captain Sharp got up, dressed and headed out onto the deck.

Bothari, Vaheana, Fetu, August and Stephan were on the deck getting loose. Kolohe came up the stairs begrudgingly and joined them a few minutes later. After warming up, they paired off and began with the short sword work while Bothari went through the basics with August and Stephan. On the third rotation, Captain Sharp was paired up with Fetu. They ran through the drills quickly. Fetu asked if he wanted to go 'weliweli' (dangerous) and gave his best smile. Captain Sharp smiled back and said he would enjoy that. Captain Sharp called over to Bothari, who was working with Kolohe again. When the teacher looked up, Captain Sharp asked 'weliweli?' Bothari nodded, then instructed the rest of the group to stop and kneel off to the side of the two men. He stood between the two and looked at each of them. "Control," he said once. Both men nodded.

Bothari clapped twice, and Fetu and the captain began circling each other. They both swung some test swings that were blocked with loud deep thuds. Fetu tried two straight jabs that were blocked, followed by a side swing that hit Captain Sharp hard just below his ribs. His ribs were unprotected because he was swinging a down strike that caught Fetu on the right shoulder. The two came together with a series of swings and blocks. The loud booms reverberated in the morning air. Fetu went for a leg sweep; Captain Sharp absorbed the hit in order to connect with another one of his own that caught Fetu on the ribs. The next time they came together, Captain Sharp was swinging and Fetu's block caught the captain on the hand, smashing it good. Captain Sharp let go of the staff with that hand and immediately Bothari clapped once. Both men stopped and relaxed. Bothari stepped in and looked at the injured hand. Captain Sharp was bleeding from three fingers, one of them from above and below the fingernail. "A good swing and block, no fault." Bothari said.

Fetu looked at the smashed fingers. "Sorry about that, Captain Sharp. If it helps, my shoulder feels like ground meat." He was smiling when he said it.

Captain Sharp gave Fetu a half hug, keeping the blood off of him. "A good round indeed, it's been awhile. Thank you, my brother." As they separated he could hear several voices talking and turned to look. The top of the stairs was crowded with spectators. The loud sparring had woken most of the crew and they all came up to watch. Great. He turned around to use the other stairs only to find that one full of crew members also. On the bright side, the doc's apprentice was one of the spectators in this direction.

Later on in his quarters Gerard tried to ignore his left hand, but it thumped in time with his heart. His ribs ached in places, but it was the hand that annoyed him. It had been awhile since he had gone weliweli, but it had been worth it. He had seen Fetu limping earlier. That improved his spirits greatly.

Captain Sharp looked over his notes from the meeting with the cannon crew. It sparked something he had thought of the other day. He got up and walked outside his cabin to the armory door next to it. He unlocked it and went inside. It was a very small room or a very large closet, depending on how one looked at it. On the floor against the wall were two barrels full of swords. It looked like enough for the whole crew, but he counted them to be sure: thirty one in total. Next to these lined up along the wall were four flintlock rifles. On a side shelf were the two flintlock pistols right where he'd left them. On the upper shelves were extra flints, a liquid shot mold, extra wadding and three small barrels of powder. More than enough for this trip and some practice thrown in.

He was about to lock up the door when he noticed a sliding door brace being held up by a wire hanging down from the ceiling. It looked like the wire went up and then turned towards his quarters. He locked up the armory door and went back into his quarters and started looking for where the wire went. It was easy to find since he knew what to look for and was getting to know Cuthbert better. Inside one of the bookcases there was thin wire that ran down the back corner of the cabinet. Tied at the bottom of the wire was figure eight loop and that was hooked on an old nail that came out of the wall sideways near the bottom. It looked like leftover construction material or just garbage at first glance.

Captain Sharp unhooked the wire and let the weighted door stop pulling it higher until it reached the top and the cabinet and the oversized knot prevented it from going any further. Captain Sharp then went back and tried to open the armory door. It would unlock, but it would not open. The doorstop inside was wedged between the door and some exposed ship ribs and probably would take a battering ram to break it down. He locked the armory door and went back into his quarters. He pulled the wire back down and resecured it on the nail at the bottom, lifting the door stop in the armory next door.

Captain Sharp went back to his desk and looked at his notes again, then he turned to look at the brass ring that was hanging on the 'open' peg and had been since he had returned from seeing the doc. He leaned over and moved August's brass ring to runner and sat back. Less than two minutes later August walked in and asked how his hand was.

"It hurts. Let's move on. What was the name of the man from the cannon team who said he used to hunt as a child?"

"That would be Ambrose, sir," August said, happy to know the answer.

"Ambrose, of course. Do you know any other men who used to hunt or know how to fire flintlock rifles?" Captain Sharp asked.

"No, but I could ask around and find out."

"Make the rounds and talk to every person on this ship. I want everyone with long gun experience here in my quarters in one hour."

"Yes, sir," August said and headed out.

An hour later August returned with six other men, including Ambrose and Giles. Captain Sharp had them all sit around the maps table and asked each man about his shooting experience: the type of gun used, and how long it had been since they shot.

Ambrose was in his late twenties and grew up hunting on his parents property in Kelso, south of Edinburgh. He hunted meat to feed himself and his family. He was familiar with muskets and flintlock rifles but had not shot either in at least five years.

Perkins was in his early thirties and had some shooting experience from nearly ten years ago. He spent a summer in the country outside of Bristol and learned to hunt birds. He admitted he had only shot maybe twenty or thirty times, but had managed to knock down birds once out of every three tries.

Gideon was in his late twenties and was from Watford, north of London. He served two years in Her Majesty's Guard. They did proficiency shooting twice per year. During his service he was involved in one combat engagement that lasted for six days. He used a flintlock rifle exclusively.

Elyas was thirty three, from Coventry, outside of Birmingham. His parents belonged to a hunting club. He accompanied them on several hunts for both birds and wild boars. He last shot about fifteen years ago and even then only a handful of times. He was only familiar with a musket.

Giles was twenty six and from Brey, Ireland. He had shot occasionally when he was back home but nothing in the last three years. He was familiar with both musket and flintlock rifles. He didn't meet Captain Sharp's eyes when he talked and didn't add anything further to his short report.

Pascoe was twenty six and originally from Calais, Belgium, but had relocated to Plymouth with his family about ten years ago. He hunted when he was younger and was even hired by other families in his small village to hunt for food. He admitted he probably wasn't very good anymore since it had been a dozen years since he had shot. He was only familiar with flintlocks.

Captain Sharp explained to the group why they were here and what he was looking for. They had four good flintlock rifles on this ship. They were just one more tool they could use to defend the ship if necessary. He wanted a team of shooters available in the event of an emergency. The shooters would be trained and used in a variety of ways. They would be used to hunt meat for the crew while on land. They might be asked to bring down geese or other birds flying over the ship. They would definitely be used to repel other ships threatening the Tawny Mane. This included shooting other men from ship to ship. He wanted to make sure they understood that this was a necessary component of the job, and could ultimately save lives on the Mane. He asked if anyone wanted to opt out of the group at this point.

Nobody did.

Captain Sharp explained that his team of shooters were expected to have cool heads, follow instructions, and above all be good shots. The team would be trained with the guns available on the Tawny Mane and would receive ongoing training. When nobody had any questions he led the group out onto the deck.

At the back of the ship on the poop deck Bothari stood next to a small table he had set up with two flintlock rifles and shooting supplies. Cornelius roped off the wheel in a fixed heading and climbed down to the main deck to watch the show. Captain Sharp sent Ambrose and Giles up to the poop deck while himself and August walked towards the bow. A sheet had been hung sideways at the front of the ship with two targets painted on it. The distance from the poop deck to the target sheet was one hundred feet. Captain Sharp had walked it off himself. Hastily painted on the sheet were two targets. The first was a rectangle about two feet wide and three feet long, roughly the shape of a man's torso. The second target was a circle twelve inches across. It represented a goose, a barrel of powder, or a man's head.

On the poop deck Bothari told the men they would get four shots apiece: two at each target. After each shot, Captain Sharp and August would measure the shot and record the results. He mentioned they need to be careful to not shoot the ship, or Captain Sharp since he would be standing not too far away from the target. He smiled at Giles when he said this.

Bothari told the men to load up and watched them handle the flintlocks. Ambrose spent some time looking over the gun and checking the flint and frizzen before loading up. Giles just started loading his gun and was thus ready first. Bothari lifted a red flag over his head and told him to go ahead and take his shot.

At the far end, Captain Sharp and August made sure they were as far away from the target as they could get. Giles took his shot. The crack was loud in the quiet air. After the shot Captain Sharp and August measured the shot with a string, marked in inches and recorded the results: eight inches outside the box, low and to the left. Captain Sharp had August circle the hole and mark it 'Gil 1'. This way they would not confuse this shot with new holes. They stepped away and Captain Sharp raised his hand for the next shooter. Bothari told Ambrose to shoot while Giles reloaded and they changed positions. Bothari raised the red flag while Ambrose took aim, let out a slow breath and fired. The shot was just inside the box and level with the centerline. They recorded the distance from the dead center and moved back out of the way.

This was repeated for the large target and then for the two shots on the smaller target. Bothari thought Giles was thinking about his last shot too long and took a step closer to him. Giles heard it and that seemed to help him make his decision and he fired shortly thereafter, missing wide right and low of the circle. After Ambrose took his last shot, he sent the men down and yelled for Perkins and Pascoe to come up and have their turn. Elyas and Gideon shot in the last group.

After the last shots were taken, and Elyas and Gideon had climbed down onto the deck, Captain Sharp invited the group to come up and look at the target sheet. The men came up to take a look and see how they fared against each other. There was some good-natured ribbing as they compared shots and some debate about which shots were closest to center. He gave them a few minutes to look at the target and then took the sheet down and folded it under his arm. He was going to take this back to his quarters for closer inspection. Captain Sharp told the shooters he would get back to them in a few days and excused them. The group left still arguing about if it was better to shoot a torso high and right in the heart area, or low and center for a gut shot.

Bothari took the flintlocks back into the captain's quarters to be cleaned before being returned to the armory. The rest of the supplies had already been put away back on the shelves. Cornelius was eager to get back on the wheel and make sure they had not deviated from their course.

Captain Sharp, Bothari, and August spread the sheet out on the maps table, looking over the shots and the scores. Captain Sharp asked Bothari about his observations and anything he noticed. Bothari reported that Elyas didn't know how to load the gun and had to be helped. He thought that Gideon rushed his shots and probably could shoot better than he did if he had taken his time. He also mentioned that Giles took a long time with his last shot, and his sights may have been drifting around the deck some.

Captain Sharp smiled at this. "Yes, I thought I felt my hair stand up before his last shot. Interesting."

"You mean he was going to shoot you, sir?" August asked, somewhat surprised.

"Aiming at me and shooting me are two completely different things August, but it is something I will keep in mind."

Pascoe had the best scores, with Ambrose close behind. Both men were good shots and hit the targets four out of four times. Pascoe was just a bit closer to center with his group of shots. After that Giles and Gideon were just about even for accuracy marks, with Perkins ranking below them. Elyas ranked last and only hit the rectangle once, and missed the circle both times. He didn't miss by much, but it was still the worst of the group.

48

When the Tawny Mane woke up the next day, the wind had disappeared: gone without a trace. The canvas hung limp off the yards and the sea was flat as a skillet. Heat and humidity both rose with the sun; everything felt hot and sticky by mid-morning. Not a whisper of breeze could be found nor felt. Cornelius said it happened from time to time and wasn't worried just yet. They still had time and credit on their side. They searched all day for ripples on the water that could lead them towards a breath of wind, but found nothing.

The next day was just as bad: no wind, no southern push, and no escape from the heat. Captain Sharp climbed up into the crows' nest himself to have a look around for signs of wind. Nothing but a flat ocean as far as the eye could see, and from up here he could see a good long way. They sweated and waited together. It was a long day. Nobody lingered long on the top deck.

Captain Sharp was on the deck early the next morning, doing some bamboo work with August. His hand still hurt but at least he could grip the swords and staff. It was still dark; the sun was well below the horizon in the east. The western sky was still cloaked in darkness. They were half way through the workout when the watchman called down to Stephan who was on the wheel at the end of the night watch. He asked Stephan to come aloft and he was up the ratlines in a matter of moments. He was back down in a few short minutes and came straight over to Captain Sharp.

"Storm coming up behind us, sir, and it's a big one. Clouds blocking out the horizon top to bottom and side to side," Stephan said.

Captain Sharp turned to look at the horizon but it was still dark and unreadable. He thought he could just make out the clouds in the sky, but it was impossible to tell just yet. He walked over to Bothari and told him they were done for the day and to wrap it up. He told August to pipe for all hands. August said he had left his whistle at his bunk along with the rest of his day's clothing.

"Even better," the captain said. He told August to go down to the barracks and pipe away. "Tell the crew a storm is coming up behind us. Have everyone get dressed, get a fast breakfast, and then start securing the ship for heavy winds and waves. Get Cornelius and Vaheana up here too. We've got a few hours, but I want to be as ready as we can be when this hits."

August bolted for the crew quarters below.

Gerard relayed the news and instructions to the men on deck and sent them off on their way. He heard the bosun's whistle below and the ship came to life. Captain Sharp headed back to his quarters to prepare for the day.

When Captain Sharp came out onto the deck shortly thereafter, the sun was nearly up in the east. The sky was clear and bright. The western sky was a horror show. A white haze on the waterline blocked out the horizon and two anvil shaped thunderheads rose up out of the clouds like monsters from the deep: a white squall.

White squalls brought strong winds, hail, rain, thunder and lighting, and steep choppy waves. It was still dead calm on the deck of the ship but that wouldn't last much longer. Captain Sharp headed to the poop deck to talk with Cornelius and Vaheana.

Cornelius had been through a number of these and said it was dangerous, but not overly worrisome. The safest way for the ship to navigate in the storm was at a forty-five-degree angle; that worked perfectly for them. If the storm was pushing west to east, they would sail south-by-southeast across it and let the storm pass above and below them. They might even make up the push south they had lost over the last few days. He seemed excited about the prospect of this. Cornelius recommended they only drop canvas on the main mast and the lateen for right now, as they didn't want to outrun the seas and have waves coming over the stern. Captain Sharp told him he would find Jim-Jim and send him up for instructions.

Captain Sharp climbed down the stairs and looked to the west. It appeared that the squall was noticeably closer in just the last few minutes. He found August and told him he wanted a man with a life ring positioned near the captain's quarters. The man needed to be ready to throw either side at a moment's notice. He grabbed another crewman walking by and told him to find Jim-Jim right now and have him report to the helm double quick. He also wanted Hudson found and sent his way immediately. The man snapped a 'yes, sir' and headed below. The first gasp of wind in days blew across the ship, then died and the air went back to the dead calm they had been stuck in for days.

Within the hour an easy breeze started up from the west and the seas below them started to move and roll. The wind was intermittent at first but became steady within a few minutes. The wind picked up from three knots, to six knots, to nine knots over in the span of ten minutes. The sea built into waves. White caps could be seen between them and the storm. Everyone on deck felt the temperature drop by ten degrees as the leading edge of the storm pushed into them. The cool was a nice break from the humidity of the last few days, but they all knew they'd be soaked to the bones before this was over.

Hudson found Captain Sharp on the deck and was given his instructions: find a few good men and head below to the bilge pumps at the bottom of the ship. Sharp wanted to make sure it was pumped dry before the storm hit and to make sure Hudson and some crew were standing by in case they started taking on water. Hudson said he was 'on it' and headed below.

Captain Sharp needed to yell to be heard over the wind now. He called for all non-essential personnel to head below and to clear the main deck. The wind was up to fifteen knots, the ship had started to lean over with the tack that Cornelius was making across the waves. A gust of wind came up from the back and Captain Sharp felt the boat fishtail as it was pushed over by the wind. He looked up at the helm. Cornelius was on the wheel fighting it but didn't look concerned. He was talking to Vaheana next to him, still teaching from the looks of it.

The ocean roiled now, the waves taller and closer together. The Tawny Mane tipped and pitched over the crests as she rode sideways across the storm as it grew nearer. The leading edge of the squall closed on them now. Captain Sharp could see the wall of water moving towards them as it fell from the sky. The wind had to be thirty knots, and what little canvas they had out snapped and cracked in the wind.

Captain Sharp yelled one last warning that they were out of time and for everyone on deck to hold on. He followed his own advice and gripped the ladder rung at the base of the poop deck. The wall of hail hit them like a slap in the face and tipped the Tawny Mane up on her nose. The mast groaned as it bowed under the stress before righting itself. That first blast of wind had to be fifty knots as it pushed the ship over. Captain Sharp looked over the starboard side and was looking down into the churning sea. Looking over the port rail showed nothing but clouds and hail.

He yelled for Cornelius to ease up on the tack to reduce the strain on the ship, but the wind and waves carried off the sound. The navigators never looked towards him. He saw Vaheana help brace the wheel and try to hold them on their heading. He took a look behind him in the doorway of the armory and saw August holding a cork float and watching the deck. Next to him, Bothari held another cork float bag with a rope tied around it. He had a hundred feet of rope coiled over his shoulder; the end of the rope was tied around his waist. The hail was the size of marbles. The exposed crew on the deck were taking a beating.

The wind shrieked as it tore through the yards and rigging. Lightning lit up the clouds and the thunder crashed down on them immediately. It sounded like the two anvils had been smashed together. The flash and the crash happened simultaneously as the storm was right above them. A thirty foot wave hit the port side of the ship. The top five feet of the wave broke on the deck and washed the deck to starboard. Captain Sharp watched water pour down into the stairwells and hoped that Hudson was pumping his ass off down below. There were just two crewmen on the main deck and they were holding tight to the ratlines. There were two additional men up on the forecastle deck who were getting plenty of spray but escaped the wash over.

Captain Sharp turned and screamed to the men behind him. "Watch the two men on the main deck on the ratlines! They are the most exposed."

Both men nodded so he thought they heard or at least understood him.

Another wave broke on the side of the ship. The spray blasted into the air and pushed her over at the same time. Captain Sharp looked up at the three sheets of canvas they had left out; they were bowed and taunt. He chanced another look over the side and saw they were tearing sideways across the water. The sea was a cauldron of white froth and the Tawny Mane screamed across the top of it. The ship felt like a rock skipping over water after a very hard throw. The boat had pitched over thirty degrees by now, and they were in danger of broaching. Broaching occurs when a ship is running with the waves and is pushed so far over that the rudder or keel loses its grip on the ocean. The boat will heel over to the side and come to a sudden catastrophic stop. There is a good chance the mast will snap off, sails will be lost, and crewmen will be thrown into the sea.

Captain Sharp fought the wind and hail, making his way up to the poop deck to Cornelius. The navigator was going back and forth between the wheel and one of his gauges attached to the mizzenmast behind the wheel. He noticed Captain Sharp and broke into a wide smile.

"We are building up some credit now, Captain Sharp!" he yelled, and he had never looked happier.

"We are too far over, she's going to broach!" Captain Sharp yelled. "Straighten out the tack and run with the wind."

"No she's not, Captain!" Cornelius yelled back and waved him over to the angle gauge. "She is only tipping between thirty-two and thirty-six degrees, but she can take forty-one in a pinch!"

"Have you had her this far over before?" Captain Sharp yelled.

"A time or two," he replied, but did not sound as confident as Captain Sharp would have liked.

Captain Sharp looked at his navigator and then back at the angle gauge on the mast. He leaned over to yell into Cornelius's ear one more time. "Thirty-eight degrees: that is my limit, so that makes it your limit too. Thirty-eight, no more! Straighten her out if you have to!"

Cornelius nodded and went back to the wheel to help Vaheana. She fought the wheel with everything she had and was loving every second of it. She laughed at the rain and yelled every time a wave slammed into the side of the ship. Her hair was plastered to her face and her smile was radiant. She laughed to herself as the weather chewed them up. Every time thunder crashed or a wave hit the ship she yelled in Maru. "I am Vaheana! I am the storm!"

Captain Sharp shook his head and went back down the ladder, trying not to fall into the boiling sea. His feet had just hit the deck when another wave broke over the rail and slammed his legs out from under him. He held tight to the ladder but scrambled to get his footing again. He quickly looked for the two sailors on the side ratlines and was relieved to see they were both still there. Soaked, but hanging on. The hail turned to rain and the wind continued to push them across the waves like a skipping rock. The Tawny Mane was beaten and soaked over the next hour and a few gusts pushed her over near tipping. He was pretty sure his navigator was exceeding the limits he had set, but Captain Sharp had intentionally set them low knowing that he might. Gerard had to trust his navigator and his experience, and he did. Mostly.

Ninety minutes into the squall, the wind throttled back some and the rain lightened up. He sent August below to have a quick word with Hudson and went to stand next to Bothari.

"Coming out the other side I think," Bothari said.

"Agreed. Although I wouldn't mind if the wind hung around a bit longer," Captain Sharp said.

Another half an hour saw the rain taper off as the anvils moved past them and continued to sweep west. Behind them to the west the sky was blue with scattered clouds and a clear horizon. The wind dropped down to fifteen knots but continued for another three hours before dropping under ten knots again. The white foam from earlier burned off in the afternoon sun and four hours later there was no evidence of the storm that had passed.

There was no damage done to the ship. One of the fishing nets used to hold the coconuts in one area broke free and a few thousand coconuts scattered themselves around the hold of the ship. This was cleaned up in short order and the rest of the crew went around the ship checking everything from sails and yards to ropes, pulleys, railing, and deck boards.

Two of the conch shells didn't survive the storm and were set to be tossed overboard. Fetu saw this and rescued them just in time. He wanted to use them to make jewelry, like his mother did when he was younger.

Just before watch change, Captain Sharp went to find Cornelius and ask how much distance they had made up. Vaheana was at the wheel and didn't know the answer, but said Cornelius had gone below over an hour ago. Captain Sharp found him asleep in his bunk, snoring soundly. The captain let him sleep. He had earned his money today.

49

Days passed and the Tawny Mane made time. They had a few days of light winds and variable winds, but nothing of the hot sticky stillness they had experienced for three days before the squall. The ship tacked south towards New Zealand and the SEC pushed them west towards Australia.

Pascoe, Ambrose, Gideon and Perkins had been called into the captain's quarters for the meeting. He had them sit at the maps table that had already been supplied with tea and sweet bread. August sat at the Captain's Desk making notes, while Captain Sharp joined the group at the large table. He welcomed them and announced they had been selected as his shooting team. He asked each man individually if he understood the duties of the job and still wanted to be part of the team. All four men agreed. He then asked Ambrose if he would be willing to serve as the team's leader. That role might change or rotate down the road, but for now he would be in charge. Ambrose agreed, but asked Captain Sharp why he wasn't on the team himself. Word among the crew was that the captain was a dead eye shot. They had all heard the story about him shooting Todd in the head.

Captain Sharp explained to them that if and when the shooting team was needed, he would probably be busy doing a dozen other things. He did say he wanted to practice with the shooting team when they did drills, to keep up his own skills. He reminded them that he wanted cool heads until it was time to start shooting, but once the shooting started, every shot needed to be spot on. They talked about training and decided to shoot once per week as long as they had the supplies. At this point, they had more than enough.

Captain Sharp was at his desk doing paperwork. He had just finished updating the captain's log, and was making notes about his recent inventory. Several days before he gave Hickory the impossible task of counting all the coconuts on board the Tawny Mane. Hickory had groaned and collapsed into a chair but after a brief discussion he understood it needed to be done. When they reached port they would need to know exactly how many they had for sale. Unfortunately nobody had thought to count them as they were being loaded on the ship. Captain Sharp told Hickory to recruit as many men as he needed, but that it needed to get done in the next few days.

Captain Sharp had a sit down talk with Hickory, Jim-Jim, and Hans Michael about selling the coconuts in New Zealand. They were undecided if they were going to sell the whole lot to a single vendor, or split the cargo up among several merchants. Inevitably it would come down to the price they were offered or what kind of trade deal could be worked out. He asked Jim-Jim, Hans Michael, and Vaheana to oversee the sale and trade of the coconuts and conch shells when they reached port. Both men had some previous experience with this and said they would be happy to do it. Jim-Jim was fast on his feet and Captain Sharp knew he would be a fierce negotiator. Hans Michael knew some local merchants from previous visits and that would help to open doors for the team. Vaheana had traded on other islands and the conch shells were her idea, so he would let her run with it. Captain Sharp and Hickory would be in charge of finding their contacts at the harbor and supervising the buying, delivery, and loading of goods for the return trip to England.

Hickory had come into his quarters this morning and gave him the numbers he was waiting for. The round number was they had fifteen thousand coconuts on board. The exact number was 15,287. Hickory admitted that the number might decrease by a few every day as Maurice was picking out a few each day to incorporate into meals for the crew.

"Holy shit, that's a lot of coconuts," Captain Sharp said.

"We filled all seven storage areas and used nets and canvas to hold all the buggers in place. We even filled the brig up to the ceiling with coconuts, so I hope you don't need to lock up anyone between here and New Zealand. The crew and I figured if anyone got into that much trouble, you'd just throw 'em overboard anyway," Hickory said with a smile.

"You throw one guy overboard and suddenly you have a reputation." Captain Sharp mumbled. Hickory laughed on his way out.

Seventeen days out of Pukapuka, they sighted land not two hours after sunrise. Cornelius checked his charts and calculations twice before announcing to Captain Sharp they had arrived at their destination.

50

New Zealand is actually two separate islands broken in half by a strait of water fourteen miles wide. The northern half of the island had the large port cities of Auckland, Tauranga, and Wellington. The southern island had the growing cities Otago and Dunedin. Wellington was nestled in the straight between the two islands, so it was accessible by north and south.

They had caught enough sail that the island was well ahead on the starboard side and they were able to sail south down its eastern side. They passed the eastern most point of the island marked with the East Cape Lighthouse and hugged the island as it bent towards the middle and their destination. The Tawny Mane reached the middle and turned into the strat between the two islands. Just after Palliser Bay the port of Wellington came into view.

The port of Wellington was one of the busiest in New Zealand due to its access from both sides of the long thin island and its proximity to the southern island for the distribution of goods and passengers. Access to Wellington Bay was a channel nearly a mile wide and considered very forgiving for cargo ships. The bay itself was four miles across and the perimeter was lined with cargo docks, slips of all sizes, and shipyards in the process of building and repairing other ships.

They drifted into the middle of the bay and struck all canvas effectively coming to a full stop. Captain Sharp ordered Jim-Jim to take a longboat into the harbor and found out which berth was supposed to be theirs. As Jim-Jim and the rowers were getting into the boat, he told them to keep any other information to themselves for the time being. They would deal with all questions and answers in good time. Jim-Jim said he understood, and got the group of men headed for the largest dock and hopefully the harbormaster.

Captain Sharp went into his quarters and opened the secret panel on his bookcase. He removed the two heavy bags of gold coins and held it for a moment. Something told him it wasn't safe in its current location and he was trying to figure out what to do with it. After a few seconds of looking around he walked out of his quarters with the bag and down into the galley. He handed the bags full of gold coins to Maurice and told him to hide them well.

"Mon Dieu! I could buy a whole restaurant with this and retire to the French Riviera!" his cook said.

Captain Sharp nodded. "You could if the money was yours, but it belongs to the ship and crew. Stash it somewhere safe and tell no one. I have a feeling that somebody may come looking for this."

"Oui Oui, this much gold is not soon forgotten," Maurice said and took the bag and headed into the kitchen.

Captain Sharp found Hans Michael on the rail and asked him to tell him everything he knew or remembered about New Zealand. He was still talking ten minutes later when Jim-Jim and the longboat came back and pulled up to the side. The men climbed back aboard and started pulling the longboat back up the side to be re-secured. Jim-Jim came over to Captain Sharp and passed on the instructions.

Their berth was just left of the main docks and next to the slip used for the daily ferry from the north island to the south. The harbormaster didn't ask about the delay and they didn't volunteer anything either. He welcomed them to New Zealand and said he would have flaggers at the berth right quick. Sure enough as they looked across the bay they could see two men waving red flags on each side of the berth. Captain Sharp yelled up to Cornelius and Vaheana to get their attention. When they looked at him, he pointed across the bay to the flag wavers. They saw it and nodded in understanding.

"Nice and slow!" Captain Sharp yelled just in case.

Vaheana waved him off and Cornelius never even looked his way. They yelled for one topsail and one jib and the sail crew got to work. After screaming across the top of the white caps during the squall, this trip across the bay seemed to take forever. They moved slowly and cautious and came into the forty-foot-wide berth right up the center. Once the nose of the Tawny Mane was inside the mouth of the slip, the dock workers yelled for lines and ropes were tossed from bow and stern. The rope at the stern was quickly tied off around one of the huge mushroom shaped bollards on the dock. As the rope went taunt and the ship stopped, the bow line was secured and the ship was essentially caught. Hand woven rope bumpers were secured between the ship and the dock and the Tawny Mane settled against the side of her new home. Two additional lines were secured off the opposite side of the ship to the far side of the berth to keep the boat from crushing the bumpers and to maintain a set distance for the gangways to be placed. Once that was done, the dock men started to roll the wide gangway ramp towards the side of the ship. The crew onboard the ship took out a section of railing large enough to accommodate the gangway and it was moved into position. Ropes were secured on each corner of the gangway to keep it from moving or tipping.

While they were waiting in the middle of the bay, Captain Sharp sent August to find Fetu and Blaed. When both of them were present on the deck Captain Sharp told them they would be in charge of ship security while in port. He wanted an armed Koa posted on the ship side of the gangway. Nobody was allowed on board unless cleared first by himself, Hickory, or Jim-Jim. They nodded in understanding and went below to get some steel on. He would need to come up with more guards and a rotation so he didn't wear out the few Koa he had.

Captain Sharp went into his quarters and put on his sword, hat, and captain's jacket. He picked up the stack of documents he had laid out earlier in the day and secured them in an inside pocket. He had the purchase agreement that had been filled out before the Tawny Mane sailed. He had the names of both the harbormaster and his contact at the local warehouse for the materials to be purchased. He had a list of the supplies the ship needed before heading back to England. He also had a list of the surplus items the ship was willing to trade, including the coconuts and conch shells. He brought the small bag of coins left behind by Todd and his men, but left all the gold on the ship and hidden for now. As he walked out of his quarters, August and Bothari were waiting for him. August looked nervous but excited and was holding a new note pad and quill that Captain Sharp had given him earlier. Bothari was strapped with steel and looking ready to brawl. He reminded Bothari this was a friendly stop and most likely they wouldn't be allowed to kill anyone. This did nothing to improve Bothari's mood. They stopped and had a quick chat with Jim-Jim about where to find the harbormaster's office and then headed for the gangway. Fetu was sitting on a barrel at the top of the ramp sharpening his sword with a pumice rock. He nodded to the three as they walked past and asked Captain Sharp to keep his eyes out for any red-haired beauties. The three men walked off the Tawny Mane and into the city of Wellington, New Zealand.

51

Oliver Roe the harbormaster sat in a small shack where the dock met the edge of town. The room was barely eight feet by eight feet and was dominated by his desk and chair. Behind him, the entire wall was shelving and cubbies from floor to ceiling. Each shelf and nook was stuffed to overflowing with papers, documents, maps and scrolls. If he had a system of organization, Captain Sharp had no idea what it was.

Oliver welcomed them to New Zealand and asked how the trip fared. Captain Sharp said it was mostly routine, but reported they were nearly tipped by a squall not two weeks ago. Oliver launched into a story about a typhoon that hit them three years ago that nearly laid down every tree and building on the island. He said they had ships washed up three hundred feet into town that had to be dragged back into the bay on rollers. After his story, he stopped and took a good look at Captain Sharp for the first time. He remarked that he looked awfully young to be a ship's captain. Captain Sharp just brushed it off and said he had adequate leadership experience. He also said this wasn't even the first ship he had been made captain of. This made Bothari make a noise somewhere between a grunt and a laugh, but he didn't add anything.

Captain Sharp asked Roe about the tobacco warehouse they were looking for and where they could find Benjamin Braxton. Oliver gave them directions and said if he wasn't at the warehouse, he was probably at the Whistling Sisters Tavern on the corner of Grey and Featherston streets. Captain Sharp asked a few more questions about the goods he was looking to trade and also who might be interested in some conch shells and coconuts. Mr Roe said he was trying to think of a name or two but it just wouldn't come to him. As he leaned back in his chair and pretended to think, he pushed a jar forward towards Captain Sharp's side of the desk. On the side of the jar was written 'coins for orphans'. Captain Sharp reached into his pocket and pulled out his bag of coins. He selected a few, saw Oliver watching him, and selected a few more. He dropped them into the jar with a loud rattle. As it turned out Oliver remembered two traders who might be interested in the shells, and two other distributors who would definitely be interested in the coconuts. Oliver also mentioned that Captain Sharp would need to be ready to bribe the employees of the ATC or they would forget his appointments, lose his paperwork, and misplace his cargo. Nobody enjoyed working with the ATC, but they were a fixture in the shipping business and something most people chose to work around rather than with. Captain Sharp thanked him for his time and his candor, and they shook hands to leave.

The walk to the warehouse took less than ten minutes as it was only a few blocks west off the pier. There was no name on the building, but Oliver had told them to look for the red doors with a white 'X' painted across them. This building had two huge doors with rollers on the bottom. One of the doors had been rolled sideways leaving half the entryway open for large carts and wagons. There was a large white 'X' painted on each of the doors. The three men walked just inside the door and stopped to let their eyes adjust to the dark interior. The huge warehouse was divided into several sections. On the food side of the building Captain Sharp could see tea, sugar, flour, rice, salt, and coffee. Crates and barrels were well organized and marked. On the other half of the warehouse he could see stacks of canvas and linen, brightly colored silks, lumbered wood, metal tools, nails and wagon parts. It looked like a small part of the warehouse was dedicated to assembling wagons from the surrounding piles of deck beds, wheels and axles.

There were three men assembling a wagon in the corner. Captain Sharp waited until they were at a stopping point before whistling. The three looked up and one of them started walking their way. He was brushing the sawdust off him as he walked and was reasonably clean by the time he arrived.

"What ken I do for ya?" he asked.

"I'm looking for Benjamin Braxton," Captain Sharp said.

"Found him ya did, call me Benji," he said.

"It's good to meet you Benji, I'm Captain Sharp of the Tawny Mane, we just docked this afternoon." Captain Sharp moved forward to shake hands and introduced his crew. "This is my first mate Bothari, and my assistant August." Hands were shaken all around.

"Kia ora," Mr. Braxton said and smiled. "It means be well on my island."

"Then I should probably add 'Koo Koo,' that is a welcome from my home island," Captain Sharp replied.

"Did ya say the Tawny Mane? I thought Captain Dominic was bringin' her in?" Mr. Braxton asked.

"It's a long story," Captain Sharp said. "Do you have someplace where we can sit and talk privately?"

"Sure do, follah me." He led them towards a three-sided office on the other side of the double doors.

The Captain, August, and Braxton sat while Bothari stood and hovered near the open side of the office to discourage any listeners from coming too close. Captain Sharp filled Braxton in on the events of the last two months on the Tawny Mane. He explained about the pirates and the killing of the captain and some crew. August helped with first-hand accounts and details here and there. They talked about the boat landing on Pukapuka and then the attempted raid on his village. Captain Sharp was vague but said all pirates were killed.

After this he went backwards and explained that himself, Bothari and others had been marooned on Pukapuka for nearly five years. He talked about finding the paperwork that laid out their route, destination, and contacts in New Zealand. The crew needed a captain and based on his previous Captain's experience; he was the default choice. The ship left Pukapuka and Captain Sharp, his marooned shipmates, and several of the Sand Maru joined him as part of the new crew of the Tawny Mane.

Benjamin Braxton listened quietly to the story and sat back when Captain Sharp stopped talking. He looked at the men sitting in front of him and then at Bothari standing off to the side. "Ya look too young to be captain of tha ship." Braxton said.

"I have adequate leadership experience," Captain Sharp said flatly.

"How many pirates did ya kill?" Braxton asked.

"Twenty-seven," August said before Captain Sharp could stop him.

"All of them," Captain Sharp said flatly.

"Bloody hell," Braxton said.

They sat there looking at each other while Mr. Braxton digested the story. In the end he did what any good business man would have done in the same situation. "Do ya have any money?" he asked.

Benji said he was willing to honor the original agreement but Captain Sharp would need to get authorization from the Atherton Trading Company. The Tawny Mane was not technically owned by the Atherton Trading Company, but it did fall under its umbrella of proprietary property. Mr. Braxton was in a partnership with them and could not risk the alienation of their good graces. He said if they signed off on the deal, they could move forward. Benji warned that Captain Sharp should expect to pay a bribe as the ATC was crooked as a dog's hind leg. Captain Sharp got directions to the office of the Atherton Trading Company and the name of the person they should talk to.

"Now," Captain Sharp said, "let's talk about the coconuts."

"Coconuts?" Braxton asked and his eyes were wide.

52

The men from the Tawny Mane found the offices of the Atherton Trading Company with little difficulty. The building was huge and the letters "ATC" were painted on the front at least ten feet high. They were asked to wait outside while the front watchman went inside to check and see if their contact Caleb Mason was available. The crew waited nearly twenty minutes before the doorman came back and said Mr. Mason had left for the day and they should try again tomorrow. Captain Sharp was able to keep his anger in check, but just barely. August, who was not as experienced, asked why they were made to wait so long before being told he had already left. The doorman gave a big smile and said, "that information is company business, it's none of your concern."

Captain Gerard talked loud and clear for the doorman to hear. "I'm afraid it won't be possible to come back tomorrow for we will sail with the morning tide. I guess I will hold onto the money for Mr. Mason until the next time the Tawny Mane stops in New Zealand. Let's go, men." He grabbed August's arm and hustled him away from the building.

"Wait," the doorman yelled. "Wait!" The doorman had opened the door and was yelling inside, "Mr. Mason!"

Captain Sharp, August, and Bothari walked away fast and made a few quick turns. They stopped behind a building next door and heard running footsteps go by. Captain Sharp led them back out onto the street and they started walking in the opposite direction.

"Let's find someplace to get a drink and a good meal. We all need to swear that nobody tells Maurice, agreed?" Captain Sharp asked.

"Agreed," both men said.

"Excellent. I have the feeling Mr. Mason will be waiting at the Tawny Mane no matter how late we are," Captain Sharp said. "I plan to keep him waiting longer than twenty minutes."

They walked back towards the dock in a roundabout way, exploring the city of Wellington. They passed an open-air trade market that reminded Captain Sharp of the farmers markets back home. You could buy just about anything if you knew who to talk to. Back in Falstone the farmers market was run by an old woman who knew everyone and everything. She assigned the spots vendors could set up. Everyone treated her like royalty. His mother had once commented that she had her hand in every pie; it was years later before Gerard understood that meant she controlled everything.

The cities or ports could change, but there was always somebody in charge who ran the show. This sparked an idea in Gerard's head. He started looking around at the different vendors and booths for the person who might be in charge. Every group had to have one; it was all a matter of finding them. He found the old woman in a prime spot near the middle of the market. There was only one good tree in the area. Her booth and her chair were in the shade from that tree. He watched her while he shopped at other booths and saw more than one local approach her to ask a question before moving on.

Gerard approached her table and examined the handmade jewelry on display. It was good work, but nothing exceptional. He picked up a few pieces and studied them. The thin fibers of some local plant were woven into a braid. Strong . . . but not coconut strong.

"Kin I hep ya find somethin, lil lamb?" Her accent was strong.

"The jewelry is beautiful! Did you make this yourself?" Captain Sharp asked, giving her one of his better smiles.

"Me and ma family," She said sweetly.

"It's good work, I wish the braid was coconut fiber to make it stronger." Captain Sharp said.

"Ah lil lamb, dar ain't no coir on dis island," she said, shaking her head.

"Coir?" He asked.

"Braided coconut fibers. Coir," she confirmed.

"What if I told you I had a boat full of coconuts right there in the harbor, and I was looking to trade them?" Captain Sharp asked.

"What ya lookin to trade for?" She said, looking very interested now.

"Information," Captain Sharp said.

"Jarom!" she yelled out. A boy about eight years old came running up out of nowhere. "Git my lamb a chair, an bring us somthin cool." The boy took off running and the old woman held out a cool hand to shake.

"I'm Mama Ruby," She said as they shook. "Les do som biznez."

The restaurant was excellent, as he knew it would be after Mama Ruby's recommendation. They had fresh kiwi meat pies that were bubbling hot and drizzled with a chocolate sauce. They also had a dessert called Pavlova which was a toasted flaky pastry with a marshmallow center, covered with a meringue layer topped with fresh chopped fruit. When Captain Sharp had tried to pay Omar the owner, he waved him off and said Mama Ruby had taken care of it. Captain Sharp tried one more time to pay and the man looked slightly afraid.

"Mama Ruby said no-take money," Omar said and waved his hands in a defensive manner.

"Fine, but if you wont take money, could I interest you in some coconuts?"

"Coconuts?" Omar said, and his eyes got big.

When they were still two blocks away from the dock they could already hear the yelling and quickened their pace. To call it a riot would be an overstatement but it did have some of the same qualities. The two groups were squared off with shouting going back and forth. On the Tawny Mane it looked like the whole crew was armed and on deck. Near the rail were Fetu, Blaed, Kolohe, Vaheana, and Stehpan armed with spears and bamboo staff. Blaed had some blood on his nose and lip and looked like he had been at the front of the disturbance at one point. Behind them were Hickory, Cornelius, Cuthbert, Hudson, and a dozen other men armed with swords. Up on the poop deck were Pasco and Ambrose with flintlock rifles casually laid across their arms, and back on the forecastle deck were Gideon and Perkins with flintlocks.

The Gangway had been cut from the Mane side and pushed off the ship and now hung down from the dock wall towards the water. Standing on the dock were no less than twenty men yelling threats and insults to his crew. The group on the dock consisted of Oliver Roe the harbormaster and six men in fine waistcoats with a ruffled kerchief around their necks. There was a good-sized group of dockworkers, and four constables with billy clubs already in hand.

One of the men with the ruffled kerchiefs had a bloody nose he held a cloth to, and one of the dock workers had a knot on the side of his head consistent with a bamboo staff. Captain Sharp knew this from personal experience.

Captain Sharp walked with purpose into the middle of the group on the dock. His crew on the ship relaxed to a degree when they saw him, but nobody on the dock side had noticed him yet. He waited until he was right next to Oliver before he started yelling.

"What the hell are you men doing with my ship?" Captain Sharp yelled. His crew had gone quiet with his approach and now everyone on the dock shut up and looked at him. Oliver looked both embarrassed and exasperated at the same time. Several men behind him started to talk at the same time but he was only looking at the harbormaster.

"Shut up!" Captain Sharp yelled. Surprisingly, everyone behind him did.

"Why is one of my men bleeding?" He growled at Oliver Roe and stepped forward into his truth space.

Oliver couldn't find the words, but pointed at one of the ruffled collars standing next to them. Captain Sharp moved fast and really leaned into the punch. He hit the surprised man in the jaw as he was opening his mouth to speak and laid him out on the deck like a wet bag of fish.

"Nobody touches my crew!" he yelled in the quiet that followed.

One of the constables stepped forward and put a handheld flintlock pistol against his chest and told him he was under arrest for assault.

Captain Sharp ignored the man and yelled to his ship.

"Shooters make ready! Target only the men in ruffled neckerchiefs."

On the deck his four shooters took aim at the well-dressed men on the dock, who started screaming and tried to hide behind the constables. Captain Sharp looked at the constable in front of him and noted that he was confused and scared, definitely not the one in charge.

"Take aim!" Captain Sharp yelled. Now everyone on the dock started screaming while some of the well-dressed men laid down on the ground and tried to curl themselves into the smallest shape possible. Captain Sharp was wondering how far this bluff was going to go when one of the older ruffled neckerchiefs came forward and pushed away the gun the constable was holding on him.

The man pushed his way in front of Captain Gerard and spoke fast and loud. "For hell's sake Captain, we just want to talk." He looked sideways at the constable like he wanted confirmation, and the constable nodded back at both of them. "Can't you have a civilized conversation before you resort to violence?" The old ruffled kerchief asked.

"Fetu?" Captain Sharp asked in a normal voice.

"Yes, Captain Sharp?" Fetu answered from the Tawny Mane.

"Who resorted to violence first?" Captain Sharp asked in the now dead quiet evening.

"The man you laid out on the deck. He punched Blaed in the face when he wasn't allowed on the ship."

"Is that your idea of civilized conversation?" Captain Sharp asked the man in front of him.

"Percival acted impulsively and without authority. He will be dealt with when he wakes up. Would you please have your men lower their guns so we can talk like civilized men?"

Captain Sharp raised his eyebrows at this and held the old man's stare.

"Civilized men who don't punch each other is what I meant," the old man said.

"Shooters stand down!" Captain Sharp said. On the ship, his men relaxed and lowered their guns.

"I am Captain Gerard Sharp of the Tawny Mane." he said, extending his hand to shake.

"I am Samual Astor of the Atherton Trading Company. We own the Tawny Mane and everything on board." he said.

"On that point, Mr. Astor, we can agree to disagree, but we don't need to argue out here on the dock. Would you and a few of your men care to join me in my quarters for some tea?" Captain Sharp asked.

Samual Astor seemed surprised at the sudden change in direction but he was a businessman and recovered quickly. "That would be lovely, thank you."

Captain Sharp turned towards the dock workers standing off to the side.

"If you men would be so kind as to pull up the gangway and put it back where it belongs," Captain Sharp said to them and then turned away before they could argue.

He then addressed his crew. "Crew of the Tawny Mane: thank you for your defense of our ship today, you do yourselves credit. Ambrose, Cuthbert: will you see that the weapons are returned to the armory? Blaed: tend to your injuries. Kolohe: You have security detail on the gangway. Bothari, August, Vaheana, Jim-Jim and Hickory: please join me in my quarters. Crew dismissed."

The crew immediately broke up and started moving away from the rail and below deck.

Counting Mr. Astor, there were five men from the Atherton Trading Company. One was currently sleeping on the deck, and another man was tending to him.

As soon as the gangway was laid back in place Captain Sharp indicated that Mr. Astor and his three men were welcome to come aboard the Tawny Mane. Several of the dock workers and constables came forward, only to be stopped by Captain Sharp.

"Only these men, the rest of you are dismissed," Captain Sharp said flatly.

One of the constables argued, saying they were worried about the safety of the men boarding the ship.

Captain Sharp gave him a flat stare. "Only one side has initiated violence this evening, and it was not me and mine."

The men all hesitated, looking to Mr. Astor for guidance. He waved them off and they walked away slowly and reluctantly. As Bothari joined him going over the gangway, he told Bothari to stand in front of the hidden cabinet when they got to his quarters. The group moved across the deck and Vaheana opened the captain's door and led them inside.

It wasn't crowded, but it certainly felt less roomy than it had been in the past. Mr. Astor and his three associates were invited to sit at the maps table while Bothari and his crew stood off to the side. He ordered August to sit at his desk and take notes. Captain Sharp walked behind his desk and pulled the ring twice, aware the four visitors were watching his every move. He walked back to the table and sat with his guests. Mr Astor opened his mouth to speak, but Captain Sharp held up a hand for him to wait a moment. No sooner had he done that then Maurice and Pierre bustled into the room loaded down with trays. For once Maurice was not talking a mile a minute. The captain made a note to thank him for his restraint. In short order, each of them had tea poured in front of them, and two platters were on the table with biscuits, sweet bread, coconut cookies, and toasted coconut slices. Maurice hustled Pierre out the door, then asked Captain Sharp if he needed anything else before leaving.

"No thank you Maurice. Your treats continue to amaze me. Thank you for showing our guest the best side of the Tawny Mane."

Maurice blushed a deep red, bowed, and then backed out the door. Once the door was shut, Captain Sharp helped himself to one of the biscuits in front of him.

"Please help yourself gentleman, my chef is quite extraordinary," Captain Sharp said.

Mr. Astor and one other man picked out a treat. The other two men sat ramrod straight.

"I don't know if you had time to meet everyone while you were on the deck, but let me introduce you to my crew members. This is Bothari, my first mate. We have sailed together many times. Next to him is Jim-Jim, my second mate. That is Hickory, my quartermaster. This is Vaheana, from my island of Pukapuka. She is a warrior and also the navigator of this ship. This is August, my personal assistant and one of our cannon gunners."

Each of the crew members nodded at the introduction. They were trying for an expression between friendly and bored but it wasn't working out too well. Bothari looked upset that he missed a chance to fight. Captain Sharp was thinking they needed to have drills on smiling practice.

The other ruffled collar who had picked out a treat took a bite and made a moaning noise before he could help it. The other two men looked at Mr. Astor and then reached for the trays themselves.

"I caught your name Mr. Astor, but who else have we here?" Captain Sharp asked.

"I am terribly sorry, Captain Sharp. I seem to have forgotten my manners today. Yes, I am Samual Astor, head of the south seas division of the Atherton Trading Company. You may call me Astor. This is Caleb Mason of our English branch, I believe he just missed your visit earlier today."

Caleb nodded and had the good graces to blush at the obvious lie.

"This is Tobin Wayne, our barrister on the island, and Harvey Lockland, our banking representative."

"It's nice to meet you. What do I owe the pleasure of this visit?" Captain Sharp asked.

"We have a number of questions for your Captain Sharp, but first and foremost: where is Captain Reginald Dominic?" Astor asked.

Captain Sharp directed August to answer the first part of that question. August stood up and gave the same recount of the story they told earlier in the day: pirates, murder, starvation, and Pukapuka. Jim-Jim and Hickory helped fill in parts of the story also. When he finished his part, August nodded to Captain Sharp who took over. Captain Sharp gave them a rundown of his side of the story: marooned, pirate raid, execution, voyage documents, captain, New Zealand. The story was getting cleaner and more precise even in the condensed version. When he finished, he asked Mr. Astor if he would like to see the captain's personal log book.

Astor looked surprised at the offering, but quickly nodded. Captain Sharp went to the desk and pulled it out of the hidden drawer. He placed the book in front of Astor and opened it to the day Captain Dominic found the other ship. Astor immediately started to page through it and read it.

The men were quiet for a few minutes until Harvey leaned over and whispered to Astor.

"Yes Yes, I was getting to that," he said, clearly upset by the interruption. Captain Sharp, it appears that some of your story is corroborated by the crew and the log book, but there are other sensitive items we need to discuss. Perhaps in private." Astor looked at the crew standing behind Captain Sharp with some disdain.

"I trust my crew with my life. Whatever it is you have to say, you can say it in front of them," Captain Sharp said, not budging.

"Very well then. What about the money?" Astor asked.

"What money?" Captain Sharp said. He enjoyed a good game of poker.

"The money hidden on this ship to buy the supplies," Astor said.

"I am unaware of this pile of money you speak of," Captain Sharp replied.

Harvey cleared his throat and looked at Astor for permission. Astor waved him on and he spoke out loud for the first time.

"It is standard practice to have a hiding spot in the captain's quarters for this money. Would you mind if I had a look?" Harvey asked.

"Be my guest," Captain Sharp said. "Just be careful of the conch shells. We have them stored in my quarters until we can find a buyer for them. If you break any, you've bought them, and I haven't set a price yet."

Harvey got up and went right to the bookcase. Captain Sharp motioned for his crew to move out of the way and over by his bed. It took Harvey less than ten seconds to find the hidden panel and open it: empty. He then started looking at floorboards and in less than two minutes, had found the loose board and pulled it up: also empty. He cursed under his breath, replacing the floorboard and returning to his seat. It would seem that hiding places were standard on ships and their locations known to the bankers at each end of the voyage. . . though they didn't know about the sword panel near the door.

Captain Sharp rose and went over to the bookcase panel, opening and closing it a few times. "Interesting," he said. "How much money are we talking about?"

"Ten thousand guineas!" Harvey let slip before Astor elbowed him.

Captain Sharp did some quick math in his head. "At 21 shillings per guinea, that's two hundred ten thousand shillings. That is a lot of money."

"The exchange rate is actually 22 shillings per guinea now." Harvey said and got elbowed again.

"Those pirates had the run of the ship for over a week, Captain. I guess we should have searched the bodies before we dumped them in the deep," August said with a straight face.

"You didn't search the pirates, then?" Harvey asked, already knowing the answer.

"I do not make a habit of turning out dead men's pockets," Captain Sharp said.

"Exactly how many pirates did you dispose of, Captain Sharp?" Astor asked.

This time August didn't say anything.

"All of them," Captain Sharp said flatly.

After a few moments of silence, Mr. Mason said, "at our offices you mentioned having money to give to me. To what were you referring?"

Captain Sharp reached into his pocket, pulled out a handful of coins and dumped them on the desk. "I have been in Wellington for less than half a day, but have already been told by several sources that bribing employees of the ATC is not just commonplace, it is expected. It is apparently the only way you can be seen, heard, or have your cargo located."

Mr. Mason had turned red, sitting back, looking embarrassed and angry at the same time. Astor looked upset, he may have not been aware of the depth and breadth of the problem with his employees. The two other men looked like they wanted to disappear into the floorboards.

"So if I understand it correctly, the only reason you came by my ship tonight was to collect the first round of bribe money from your employees?" Captain Sharp asked.

"Certainly not! I think you have misunderstood local rumors and complaints of our competitors," Astor said.

"It just seemed like too much of a coincidence that we were told Mr. Mason had left for the day, but when I mentioned I had his bribe money, he came running out from the back with his hand out," Captain Sharp said looking honestly confused.

"This is an internal issue and company business. I can assure you it will be dealt with and is none of your concern," Astor said.

Tobin spoke up for the first time. "You look too young to be a ship's Captain."

"I have adequate leadership experience," Captain Sharp said flatly.

"In any case it would appear you have wasted a trip though, Captain Sharp, for you have no means to buy the goods for your return trip to England," Astor said.

"I never said I was without means. I plan to stock this ship as full as possible before we sail for England," Captain Sharp said.

"You have your own money then?" Harvey asked, and they all watched him closely.

"I have means," Captain Sharp said.

"I'm afraid that will be impossible. The Atherton Trading Company will most likely replace you with another captain before the Tawny Mane sails for England," Astor said.

"And crew," Vaheana said.

"Excuse me?" Astor asked.

"You will need to find a new crew also. New navigator, sailors, sail-men, cooks, carpenters, quartermaster, and cannon gunners to fight off the pirates hunting for you. Where Captain Sharp goes, the entire crew will follow," Vaheana said.

"You speak for the whole crew, do you?" Caleb asked with a sneer.

"She does," Jim-Jim and Hickory said at the same time.

"Down to the last man I reckon," August added.

"If you would rather send an empty ship home to England with a replacement crew that may or may not make it, that's your business," Captain Sharp said. "I was going to supply the ship myself, take it back to England myself, and let the actual owners decide if they wanted to keep me or not. But if you speak for them and are willing to cover their losses, so be it. I can have my cargo and crew off the ship in a week at most."

"Cargo?" Astor and Harvey said at the same time.

"This ship was empty leaving England, what could you have possibly found in the middle of the ocean?" Astor asked.

"Good luck," Bothari said.

Vaheana laughed like a donkey.

The visitors asked a few more times about the cargo and Captain Sharp deflected their questions. Sharp told them it was ship's business and none of their concern. His crew would handle the sale, unloadiing, and delivery of the cargo. He said it might even be possible for them to buy another ship and sail back to England on their own. That way they would not have to split the profits with anyone, the captain mused out loud.

Captain Sharp stood up and signaled the end of the meeting. "Thank you gentlemen for coming aboard and spelling out some options for us, I appreciate your time."

Astor stood and asked if he could borrow the captain's log book to share with some of his partners at the trading company. Captain Sharp handed it to him.

"As a token of friendship and goodwill, of course I will loan you the log book from the Tawny Mane. I would like it returned, however. I will need it when I return to England and give my report to Lord Edward the Black." Captain Sharp said.

Caleb Mason was walking towards the door, but stopped dead in his tracks. He turned to look at the captain with a different expression on his face. "You know Lord Edward the Black?"

"Of course I know him. I have worked for him nearly all my life. I consider him a good friend. He was the one who commissioned my first trip to the South Pacific."

Captain Sharp ushered them out of his quarters and onto the deck. He steered them towards the gangway and was not surprised to see some dockworkers and constables hanging out on the docks not too far away. The unconscious man identified as Percivall was long gone. The suits from the trading company headed down the ramp and back to the relative safety of the docks.

Astor paused at the top of the gangway. "You have given us much to think about Captain Sharp. I will be in touch." He turned to leave but was stopped by Kolohe, laying his spear across the gangway.

"You forgot to say 'thank you'," he said.

"What?" Astor said.

"You forgot to say 'thank you'," Kolohe repeated, looking seriously pissed off.

Captain Sharp was about to say something when a voice in his ear whispered 'wait'.

Kolohe explained: "Thank you for bringing your expensive ship back. Thank you for doing the honorable thing. He could have gone anywhere you know. He could have kept the ship for himself. He could have turned pirate and robbed your other trade ships with the Tawny Mane. He could have sailed back to England and told you to 'get stuffed' in the process. Instead, he brought your ship back to you, and you forgot to say thank you. You are not civilized as you claim to be, Samual. You have no honor. Get off my ship." Kolohe moved his spear out of the way and turned his back on Astor. It was dead quiet on the docks; everyone had heard. Astor walked down the gangway and stopped at the bottom. He turned to face Captain Sharp and the crew of the Tawny Mane.

"I must apologize again, Captain Sharp. This has been a most confounding day. Usually I am the one pointing out how uncivilized other people are. It is not often that I am shown to be a doongi (dumbass). Thank you Captain Sharp for returning our ship to us, and getting her crew here safely. Your actions are unprecedented. That can be my only excuse for my lack of manners. Good evening." He bowed once and walked off.

Nobody said a word while Astor and his men left the dock area.

Bothari had come up next to Captain Sharp during Kolohe's speech. Now he spoke softly. "Where the hell did that come from?"

"No idea, but we can't throw him overboard now," Captain Sharp said.

"Dammit, and I was going to throw him so far." Bothari shook his head as he walked away.

Captain Sharp called a meeting of all senior crew to be held in the galley in five minutes. He sent August below to spread the word and start pushing people towards the galley. He walked over to where Kolohe was standing and got into his truth space.

"You don't speak for me, and you don't speak for this ship. You need to be careful with your words, they hold weight and power. What has been said can not be unheard."

"Yes, sir," Kolohe said.

Captain Sharp slowly put his hand on Kolohe's shoulder. "That was well said my brother, thank you. The man inside you awakens. I would call him friend if you would have it," Kolohe's eyes got shiny and he nodded. "Yes sir."

"Guard the ship, and keep your mouth shut. It would be a shame to throw you overboard when you're finally moving the right direction."

In the galley, Captain Sharp asked for a report from Jim-Jim, Hans Michael and Vaheana about what they found in town. Hans Michael found two of his old contacts and put out feelers about the coconuts and the conch shells. They were supposed to come by the ship tomorrow morning and talk numbers. They stopped by a seafood processing plant and talked to the foreman about his interest in the coconuts. He wanted to get in touch with an investor friend of his and asked the crew to stop back by tomorrow. They had stopped by one jewelry store. The man said he might be interested in the coconut fibers and a few shells, but in limited quantities only.

Captain Sharp and August shared information about their meeting with Oliver Roe, and how he would honor the contract if the Atherton Trading Company gave their consent.

Vaheana asked if the company might really take the ship away from him and replace him as captain. This caused an uproar, as most of the crew present were not present for the earlier meeting.

Captain Sharp had to jump forward and fill everyone in on the meeting with Astor and his men. The story was covered quickly. He told the crew not to worry, and that he was not even worried at this point. The game had just begun. He had several tricks to play and traps to lay.

They got back on the subject of their earlier walkaround. August gave Jim-Jim the list of dealers that Oliver gave them after his 'memory improved.' Next, Captain Sharp talked of his meeting with Mama Ruby. He explained to the crew that at first glance Mama Ruby ran a small jewelry table at the open-air market, but it was more than likely that Mama Ruby ran the entire black market in New Zealand. She had asked him not to sell any coconuts until tomorrow so that she might ask around and see if she could come up with some investors.

Sharp wanted all the sellers to keep checking back in with the ship for prices, information, and quantities. He guessed that once the town started buying the coconuts, they would all go in a rush.

Lastly, the captain wanted to discuss shore liberty. All crewmembers were allowed shore leave, but no more than half the ship could be gone at any one time. This evening's festivities were a good enough reason why. Stephan was put in charge of creating and maintaining a leave schedule. The roster would show who was on leave, and who was in line to go next. All crew members were to report to Stephan when coming and going. Captain Sharp also recommended that everyone going ashore traveled in groups of two or more. He had not seen evidence of thieves and muggers, but every port town had them.

He asked Blaed to come up with a duty roster for ship security among the willing and able-bodied men aboard. He wanted at least eight people on the rotation, with six-hour shifts. That way no person would have to work more than one shift every other day. A few more questions were tossed around and then the meeting broke up.

Captain Sharp thought about his first day in New Zealand. So far only one riot and one gun pointed at him. It felt like things were getting off to a slow start.

53

Kolohe lay awake in his bunk, just before sunup. He had quickly grown accustomed to the movement of the ship. It felt different being tied up in the berth. He worked security last night and had the day for himself. Stephan had told him he could go ashore this morning, so he was eager to get out and explore the city. He had spent his whole life on Pukapuka and had been amazed when they pulled into port. Such buildings! Some of them were two stories tall. He saw men riding horses, carts being pulled on wheels, and women dressed in billowing outfits of vibrant colors. Everywhere he looked there was something new to see. He wondered how much longer he would have to wait in his bunk when he saw movement in one of the bunks further down.

It looked like Giles was getting dressed in the near dark and trying to be quiet about it. He carried his shoes in his hands and tip-toed up the steps at the far end of the room. Kolohe vaulted out of his bunk and quickly put on a few layers of clothing. He took a coin bag out of his locker and put it around his neck. He grabbed his own shoes and headed for the stairs at the opposite end of the bunkroom. Peeking up on deck he saw Giles have a few short words with Gideon guarding the gangway before heading down the ramp and across the docks towards town. Kolohe pulled on his own shoes and headed across the deck.

Gideon saw him coming and said, "You're supposed to be paired up with somebody."

"Where is Giles going?" Kolohe asked.

"He said he had an early appointment with a prospective buyer," Gideon answered.

"Will you tell Stephan I headed out early to have a look around?" Kolohe said over his shoulder as he hurried down the ramp and turned towards.

There were only a few people moving about this time of day. He saw Giles walking up ahead and hung back in the shadows. He grew up in the jungle and had never been in a city before, but following people and staying out of sight, that was a transferable skill he already had. Kolohe tailed Giles for several streets before he turned a corner and realized Giles had disappeared. There were several doors on this street. He didn't know which one Giles had gone into. Something about this didn't feel right and he thought the Purple Tiki might be guiding him. He looked for a place to wait and watch, but the street was mostly clear. There was a drunk across the street curled up under an awning of a store. Kolohe crossed the street and moved into the awning next to him. He sat where he could see the street and borrowed the sleeping man's reed hat that had been laid aside. The hat was tipped low to hide his face. He settled down to watch and wait.

A few doors opened as people came and went, but it was nearly 45 minutes until a door opened and Giles walked out. In the doorway, he shook hands with a dark man mostly hidden in shadows who then gave Giles a folded yellow piece of paper. Giles walked away and the dark man looked around and then went back inside.

Kolohe gave Giles a half minute head start and then sprang up and followed him. He was easy enough to find as he headed straight back towards the ship. Giles stopped at the edge of the dock and talked to one of the younger street kids fishing off the pier. He showed the kid the yellow note and then held up a coin for him to see. He pointed to the Tawny Mane and the kid nodded at the instructions. He handed over the note and the coin and the kid ran off towards the Tawny Mane. Giles walked away quickly.

Kolohe was torn between what he should do. He decided to let Giles go and see what happened at the ship. The kid ran down the docks and turned up the ramp to his ship. Gideon stopped him at the ramp and they had a short conversation. The kid handed over the yellow paper and then ran back the way he had come. Gideon opened the note, gave it a quick read, and then tucked it into his pocket. He didn't yell or sound any alarm. He sat down and did nothing.

The idea of hiring one of the local kids was a good idea. Kolohe decided to use it himself. He tried to find the same kid Giles had used, but he had disappeared to spend his new money. He found another boy not much younger than himself, fishing on the bank. Kolohe walked towards him and started talking about fishing. After a few minutes the boy mentioned that if he didn't catch anything, he wouldn't eat today. Kolohe definitely heard a whisper in his ear that time. It was a great idea. He made a deal with the boy that, if he could help Kolohe with some information, Kolohe would pay him back with breakfast on his ship. The boy clearly thought he was being fooled but after some back and forth he agreed that he didn't have much to lose, and possibly a breakfast to gain.

"I'm Kolohe from the Tawny Mane," he said, shaking arms with his new friend.

"I'm Dart," The boy said. "What's first?"

"A friend of mine went into a building in town, I was wondering if you could tell me who lives there," Kolohe said.

The two walked through town comparing stories of trouble and mischief. It sounded like they had followed similar paths in life. Dart's dad was a drunk and a hitter, so Dart spent as much time away from home as he could. Dart's mom defended her husband at every opportunity, but tried to sneak Dart some food when he would come around.

Kolohe was unsure about the street he was looking for, but they found it after only one wrong turn. From the far side of the street Kolohe pointed out the door to Dart who immediately grabbed his arm and started walking them back the way they came.

"That friend of yours is into some bad business," Dart said. "That's the smugglers guild: thieves, kidnappers and murderers. It's not safe to look at the door and it's very unhealthy to point towards the door." Dart steered them back to the main street and back towards the dock. They talked back and forth on the way to the ship with Dart asking lots of questions about life on the ship.

"Do you miss your home and your family?" Dart asked.

"I thought I would, but to be honest I have been so busy learning things that I haven't had time to miss them. At home, I always seemed to be getting in the way. My sister was perfect, pretty and helpful, she could do no wrong. Everything I touched broke or turned to shit. The Tawny Mane has given me a fresh start. Here I am not Kolohe the troublemaker, I am just Kolohe."

They walked out onto the dock and up the ramp. Gideon was still on duty and stopped the two young men at the top. "Sorry Kolohe, no visitors are allowed on the ship unless cleared by Captain Sharp," Gideon said.

"Could you call Captain Sharp out here? I'm sure he will approve this."

"No can do, he left the ship about a half an hour ago," Gideon said.

"How about Jim-Jim?" Kolohe asked.

"Him and Hans Michael left about ten minutes ago," Gideon said.

Kolohe grew frustrated; he had given his word to his new friend. Dart watched the exchange patiently; he had not given up hope on free food just yet. Just then Fetu walked up onto the deck. Kolohe told Dart to wait here and he would be right back. He walked over to Fetu and asked if he could talk to him for a moment, it was important.

Fetu stopped and said "sure, go ahead."

Trying to decide what to tell and what to leave out was hard, in the end he took a short cut and hoped his new reputation outweighed his old reputation. "I am working on something important, Dart has been helping me and in exchange, I promised him breakfast on the ship. Can you help me keep my word?"

"Important to you, or important to the Mane?" Fetu asked.

"The Mane and her crew, sir," Kolohe said.

Fetu held his stare for a moment, then nodded.

"Let him pass Gideon, I'll keep an eye on him, on my honor."

"You got it," Gideon said. "Welcome aboard, young man. Koo Koo Kushaw."

Kolohe guided his friend towards the galley, but still had a moment to speak to Fetu who was following them. "Thank you, my brother, you honor me."

Fetu didn't know what to make of the change in Kolohe, but it was an impressive turnabout from the kid he knew on the island.

The group sat next to Stephan in the galley and waited for Maurice to make an appearance. He came out two minutes later to meet the new guest and talk about the morning menu. Dart just nodded at everything he rattled off. In the end Maurice said he would bring out a selection of food for the young men to sample. While they waited for the food, Fetu asked Stephan what was happening so far this morning.

"One of Mama Ruby's runners came for Captain Sharp and Bothari. They went off to meet with her thirty minutes ago." Stephan said. "Jim-Jim and Hans Michael went to meet a different potential coconut buyer not fifteen minutes ago. Vaheana got a note from somebody who wanted to meet up and buy all the conch shells. She left about five minutes ago to go meet them in town."

Panic hit Kolohe in the gut as pieces fell into place in his head. He stood up so quick he knocked the bench over behind him. "Vaheana's in trouble, we need to go right now!" he yelled.

Fetu was on his feet and asked how bad.

"Bad. I'll tell you on the way. We don't have time for the armory, let's grab some bamboo and run."

Kolohe turned and spoke to Dart. "You can wait here if you want, but there's going to be trouble."

Dart stood up and smiled. "Trouble's my middle name."

Maurice walked out of the kitchen one minute later to find an empty galley. "Well, merde."

Blaed and Elyas were laying on their bunks when the group ran in and started grabbing the bamboo, yelling Vaheana was in trouble. Less than fifteen seconds later they were armed with sticks and staffs and running topside. Elyas and Dart each had one of the three-foot-long bamboo sticks. Blaed and Fetu each carried one of the long bamboo staffs. Kolohe carried two. The five of them ran through town towards the Smuggler's Guild.

They rounded the last corner. There was a large man standing outside the door facing the street. His arms were folded across his chest and his body language made it clear he was guarding the door. "That means they are doing business inside," Dart yelled as they ran towards the door. Blaed was in the lead and the first person to reach the door. The man guarding the door pulled a knife when he saw the group coming and stood his ground. Blaed never slowed and jousted the man down with the butt end of his staff to the face. The man went down hard and did not get up.

Blaed tried the door and found it locked. He backed up three steps just in time for Fetu and Kolohe to join him. The three men lowered their shoulders and hit the door together in a rush. The wood snapped, the hinges groaned, and the frame gave up its grip in the doorway. The door and frame flew into the room and clattered to the ground loudly in a cloud of dust and dirt. Blade, Fetu and Kolohe stumbled into the doorway with their momentum behind the wreckage, but were able to keep themselves from falling to the ground.

Everyone in the room stopped what they were doing and looked at the newcomers. One man lay on the ground unconscious next to a broken wooden chair. Four other men had Vaheana backed into a corner. She was holding them at bay with another chair. She was bleeding from the nose and had a goose egg forming on her forehead. One man in a white suit stood off to the side, giving orders.

As Elyas and Dart came in the open doorway, the four henchmen moved away from Vaheana and closer to the white suit as if to protect him. Two of the men pulled knives out of their coats, one man already had a billy club out. They stood facing off with Blaed, Fetu, Kolohe, and Elyas. Kolohe tossed a bamboo staff at Vaheana who dropped the chair and caught it out of the air.

The guy in the white suit was furious. "What gives you the right to come into my . . . "

They never saw her coming.

Vaheana took a full swing while she moved towards the group and connected with the head of the man holding the billy club. The bamboo made a deep crunchy sound when it hit. Everyone who heard the sound knew that man would rise no more. She was already reversing the staff for another swing before the group realized the real danger was behind them and not before them.

Fetu told Elyas to watch the door, then charged into the fray. The man closest to him was holding a knife out in front of him ready to stab as soon as Fetu was in range. Unfortunately for him, Fetu had a seven-foot-long bamboo staff that he butted into the man's face and put a three inch hole where his nose used to be. That man fell in a shower of red as his face gushed with blood and bone.

Kolohe ran forward to the henchmen directly in front of him and performed the first move Bothari had taught him, the same move he had practiced over and over, even long after Kolohe said he had it down. Holding the staff sideways he charged and then pivoted the staff to swing up between the man's legs. The moment the bamboo connected between the legs, he reversed his swing and brought the top of the staff forward now striking the man in the head as he doubled over from the first hit. In practice, it felt slow and clumsy, but today his staff was fast and the hits sounded loud and deep with a rapid-fire boom-boom sound. He could tell the moment he hit the man on the head he was unconscious as his eyes lost focus and he teetered slowly to the side. While his body was deciding which way to fall Vaheana, took a two-handed swing from the side and tried to knock the head off the body. Kolohe was sprayed with a pink mist as the man was lifted out of one shoe and tumbled out of their way.

Elyas ran outside and grabbed the body of the guard and dragged him inside the room. Dart picked up the door and tried to lean it against the opening to muffle the sound of the fighting inside. He thought it was interesting that the men from the smugglers guild were yelling, screaming, and cursing; but the Sand Maru were quiet, not making a sound as they swung and fought. The only constant in the room was a symphony of bamboo hits. Boom boom boom boom.

Blaed stepped towards one of the men holding a knife and hit him with a side sweep, breaking his hand and sending the knife skittering across the room. Blaed took a look behind the man, then got the hell out of the way. Vaheana was coming for him. The smuggler sensed her approach and wheeled to face her. Vaheana had gone past the place where anger holds you in a fist and squeezes the emotions out of you. Vaheana had become a storm of calm death. The man raised his hands to defend himself until he saw her eyes. They were empty, and he knew he was already dead. He closed his own eyes, the warrior moved, and darkness took him.

The fight didn't last half a minute. In a fight between six-inch knives and six foot staffs, reach always wins. The doorman and the four enforcers were laid out on the floor either unconscious or much worse. The white suit was conscious but bloody. His right arm appeared to be broken, and he was making wheezing sounds when he tried to breath.

Dart came over and identified the man in the white suite. "That's Simon, one of the three leaders of the smugglers guild. There may be another man above him but nobody knows him, he keeps out of sight."

"Are you going to kill me, because I cannot let this unprovoked attack go unpunished," Simon said.

"Unprovoked?" Vaheana asked coolly.

Now that he had a chance, Kolohe told his group the whole story starting with waking up and following Giles off the ship. When he got to the part where Stephan said Vaheana had gotten a note from Giles to go meet a buyer, Fetu nodded along. He finished with the race through town and the taking of the doorman for Vaheana's benefit.

"So Giles and his money are the cause of this misunderstanding?" Simon asked.

"Misunderstanding!" Vaheana yelled.

Fetu put a hand on her arm and hoped she could hold it together. "Yes it would appear that Giles has brought this trouble to your door."

"Then my issue is with Giles and not you," Simon said.

"What of your men? I fear some of them went down too hard to ever come back up," Fetu said.

"The cost of doing business, for which Giles prepaid," Simon said with a casual wave of his left hand. "None are family, and not my smartest guards either."

Fetu turned to Dart standing nearby. "Is Simon a man of his word? Does he have honor? Or does he lie every time his mouth opens?"

Simon tried to glare at Dart, but the boy was only looking at Fetu. "Simon is a man of his word. His handshake is a contract."

Fetu held out his left hand in order to shake Simon's left hand. "So we will let this misunderstanding pass between us and steer clear of each other in the future?"

"My word," Simon said, and shook.

"Then we shall leave you and not trouble you again," Fetu said. Vaheana glared at him but he ignored it. "You will take care of the Giles problem for us?"

"That will be my next order of business," Simon replied. "It has just become my number one priority." He smiled.

"Would you like me to stop by the surgeon's house, ask him to come check on you?" Dart asked.

"That would be very kind of you Dart, thank you," Simon said, wincing with a deep breath.

The group moved through the door frame, and Fetu moved the broken door back into place. He told Kolohe to escort Dart to the surgeon's house, and then report back to the ship immediately, both of them. He sent Blaed with them to make sure the boys didn't get lost. He asked Elyas to fast walk back to the ship and let Stephan know everyone was all right and they were on their way back. Elyas headed off, and Fetu was left alone with Vaheana. They started walking back to the ship slowly with their bamboo staff laid over their shoulders.

"It's a small town," Fetu began. "A lot of people saw us running through town. I'm sure some people even saw us go inside the guild. If we kill everyone inside, eventually somebody is going to come looking for us. Constables, upset family, other members of the guild. This was our best option for getting away from the incident clean."

"I know," Vaheana said. "I know it was the right choice, but that doesn't mean I can turn off the anger. They said things to me before you got there: bad things, trying to scare me."

"And you killed them for it," Fetu said. "Two for sure that I saw. I was wondering why they got special attention."

"I'm also mad at Kolohe."

Fetu just waited.

"He saved me," she said. "It's like being saved by a baby turtle. It's just so embarrassing."

54

Jarom showed up just after sunrise to collect the captain for an early morning meeting with Mama Ruby. Captain Sharp and Bothari followed Jarom though the town as it was waking up. They passed through the narrow streets and started up a dirt road on the far side. The small farmhouse was neatly kept and surrounded by sugar cane fields. The one story house was painted with a whitewash finish, but the door was bright blue. Three steps led up to a front porch complete with a rocking chair and sewing basket. Jarom went up the steps and opened the door without knocking and ushered the men inside.

The main room held a large table and there were already five men sitting around it. One of them was Omar from the restaurant last night. Captain Sharp went to Mama Ruby first and bid her good morning, then made it a point to shake Omar's hand and thank him by name for the wonderful meal last night. Jarom dragged a long bench in from another room; Captain Sharp helped him move it to the long side of the table. The men scooted their chairs out of the way and made room for it.

Once Captain Sharp and Bothari sat, Mama Ruby introduced the others at the table. Omar and another man were both restaurant owners who wanted to buy coconuts for the food and milk alone. Two of the other men worked for local banks and were interested in the investment opportunity. The last man was a private investor looking for something to spend his money on. After the introductions, Mama Ruby asked Captain Sharp to recount their conversation from yesterday in the market concerning the coconuts.

Captain Sharp told the group his ship was full of coconuts: over fifteen thousand of them in all. All of them were in good shape and hand collected not two weeks ago. He discussed the fibers of the exterior being used for rope, braided cords, and fine jewelry chains. He described the meat and milk inside as delicious and filling. The milk also had medicinal applications. Coconuts were self-storing. They could be stacked for months and possibly years before being used. Finally, the used husks could be burned as fuel. A single coconut could be sold three or four times while its different layers were used up.

When he finished, Mama Ruby asked Captain Sharp and Bothari if they could wait outside for a few minutes while the group talked. They thanked the men for their time, and went out front. A second chair had been pulled up next to the rocking chair. Captain Sharp took it, leaving Bothari the rocking chair.

Ten minutes later, the front door opened and the men walked out, each stopping to shake hands with Captain Sharp and Bothari. The last man out was Usain, the private investor. He lingered with Mama Ruby while the other men walked off towards town. Once they were out of earshot, Mama Ruby caught the crew up.

"Dey will decide today if dey buy, an how much, but dey wanted to hear da sales pitch. Astor an his spies were askin bout you last nite, an he knows bout da coconuts. He ken offer you mor money den me an ma group. He likes to hold all de strings. Likes to be 'n control 'e does. He will come by yer ship t'day 'n make his offer," she said.

"It's too bad for him that my entire stock has already been spoken for by Mama Ruby and associates. His loss really," Captain Sharp replied.

Mama Ruby met his eyes with a hard look of her own. "You givin up a lot of coin just to piss dat man off lil lamb. Ya sure ya want to do dat?" she asked, giving him a way out.

"I'm sure," Captain Sharp said. "They put hands on my crew. That is unacceptable."

"I'll make ya a fair deal lil lamb, but yer pockets won't be saggin like dey wood be from Astor's coins."

"Let me worry about my pockets, Mama Ruby. Honestly my concern is remaining captain of the ship, and being allowed to sail back to England with my crew. I don't care about money right now, it's not important."

"Money not important?" Mama Ruby laughed. "Ya sur don tink like a ship's captin, but i'll treat ya fair neway."

"I am waiting for word from Astor on whether I can remain captain or not. If the Atherton group allows me to stay on as captain, then you wont need to give me any coins at all. The money I was going to turn around and give right back to you, if you could help me fill the ship with our supplies of sugar, rice and tobacco. If we can exchange supplies for supplies and keep the money out of it for now, I think we will both do better in the long run," Captain Sharp said. "If Astor wants his empty ship, then I will need the money and not the supplies."

"Now ya talkin like a capin."

"Speaking of money . . ." Captain Sharp said, reaching into his pocket. He withdrew five gold guinea coins. "Can you help me break these down into pennies and shillings? I want to give my crew some pocket money to visit you and the other ladies in the marketplace."

Mama Ruby looked at the gold coins and cackled with laughter. "O corse new money aint importen to a captain wid pockets full o money already." She softly took the coins out of Captains Sharp's hand and looked them over carefully. Usain leaned over her shoulder to have a looksie too. She slid the coins into her front apron pocket and looped her arm in Captain Sharp's arm and turned him back towards the front door of the house.

"Yer lucky, I jus happen to hav sum coins stashed in ma kichen," she said and led the way back inside.

Usain followed them both back inside. "You wouldn't happen to have any more of those gold guineas that need to be broken down do you? As it happens, I also keep lots of coins stashed in my kitchen."

When Captain Sharp and Bothari arrived back at the Tawny Mane, several people were waiting. Omar the restaurant owner stood at the top of the ramp talking to Maurice and Blaed, who was on watch. Caleb, Tobin, and Harvey of the Atherton Trading Company stood on the docks well away from the ship and crew. The ruffled kerchiefs saw Captain Sharp approaching and moved to intercept him before he even reached the ship. Caleb had a big phoney smile plastered on his face and held out his hand to shake with the captain.

"Captain Sharp, so good to see you again," Caleb said, completely ignoring Bothari. "I am happy to inform you that Astor and the Atherton Trading Company can give you top dollar for your cargo of coconuts. I have brought along Tobin to help us with the contracts and Harvey to authorize the transfer of funds to your account."

Up on the ship Blaed whistled to get the captain's attention. He made the hand signals for the words 'talk' and 'important,' then went back to his conversation with Maurice and Omar. Caleb kept talking, so Captain Sharp held up a hand to stop him.

"That was very thoughtful of you Caleb. Bothari and I have been walking for a long time. I would like to sit down and take a rest. Let's discuss this further aboard my ship." He led them down the dock and up the gangway ramp, nodding to Blaed at the top. He asked Bothari to escort the men down to the galley, noting that he would be along in a few minutes. He needed to have a few words with his crew first. Bothari led the men towards the stairs towards the galley. When they were out of sight, he faced Blaed and said, "talk."

"Kolohe, Fetu, Vaheana and Dart are waiting for you in your quarters, sir," Blaed reported.

It was the first time Sharp had ever heard anyone put Kolohe's name in front of another; it was always said last. That could be good, or it could be bad. He had no idea who Dart was.

Blaed's face was giving nothing away, so Captain Sharp just nodded and headed for his quarters. He went across the deck quickly as he didn't want to keep the delegates below waiting long. Bothari was not a great conversationalist on a good day. His door was open. Sharp found four people sitting at the map table having tea.

The one named Dart turned out to be just a waif of a boy no older than fifteen. He was thin from hunger and his clothes were old and torn, but his eyes were wide awake and alive. He looked nervous, but not scared.

Kolohe had some blood on the side of his face, but he didn't appear to be injured.

The rest of his crew were smiling, but Vaheana had blood on her shirt and her lip was swollen. She also had a raised bump on her forehead, but otherwise looked okay.

Captain Sharp pushed the anger down and tried to be as calm as possible. If Vaheana had been attacked, he would have to kill people. That would complicate their stay in New Zealand. He pulled out an empty chair and sat as Fetu poured him a cup of tea. He thanked Fetu as he gripped the mug and took a sip, trying to stay calm. Putting the drink down in front of him, he leaned back in the chair and looked at the group. "Tell me everything, leave nothing out."

Fetu and Vaheana both looked at Kolohe, who didn't look like he wanted to talk either. Fetu made a go-ahead motion and the young crewman spoke.

Kolohe covered his story from waking up and following Giles, to being in the galley and hearing that Vaheana got a note. He motioned for Vaheana to pick it up there and she recounted the note being delivered to the ship for her. The note was from an anonymous woman who wanted to meet Vaheana privately and buy all her conch shells. So Vaheana went by herself to meet the other woman. When she knocked on the door and was let inside the door was quickly closed behind her and several men were waiting inside the room for her. She broke a chair over the head of the man closest to her and grabbed another one to hold them off. She backed into a corner so they could not get behind her, but the men rushed her as a group. She got hit on the head by a club and punched in the face but would not go down or let go of the chair. She still had a knife on her belt but was saving that as her last resort when it got down to hand to hand.

She nodded for Kolohe to continue, so he picked up from there. Kolohe and Fetu grabbed some bamboo and picked up Blaed and Elyas on the way and ran through town towards the smugglers guild. They knocked out the guard outside, broke down the door, and ran inside.

Vaheana broke in here and picked up the story. When her Koko broke down the door, the first thing Kolohe did was toss her an extra staff. The smugglers turned their backs to her; that's when she started killing them. Fetu and Blaed helped with the clean-up and they were left with one bleeding and broken crime boss. They had a short discussion with the man who was very unhappy with Giles buying this trouble. He held no grudge for the crew of the Tawny Mane, and said he would take care of the Giles problem personally.

When they got back to the ship Vaheana had her injuries looked at, and then they all ate breakfast in the galley. They had just come to the captain's quarters to talk about career opportunities with Dart when the captain returned.

Captain Sharp relaxed some and sipped his tea, thinking about his response. It sounded like the incident had already been handled and handled well. He remembered a saying often heard from Edward the Black: 'the reward for a job well done is another job.' Sharp needed to get back down to the galley, but thought he might reward Kolohe with another job.

"That is all well and good, but are you sure about this Dart person? We don't know him, and none of us know his history. Who will vouch for his character?" Captain Sharp asked the group.

Fetu had already opened his mouth, but Captain Sharp made a stop gesture on the side of the table where only he and Vaheana could see it. He didn't have to wait long.

"I will vouch for his character, sir," Kolohe said.

"You? Are you sure you are willing to be responsible for him, teach him about the ship, find him a job and help him learn his way?" Captain Sharp asked.

"Yes, sir," Kolohe said with conviction.

Vaheana had to hold up a napkin to her face to hide her smile, and Fetu was obviously biting his lip.

Captain Sharp stood and walked around to Dart who also stood up.

"In that case, welcome to the Tawny Mane Dart. Koo Koo Kushaw." Captain Sharp showed him how they shake arms. "I hope you can follow the rules, Dart. It would be a shame if I had to kill you, and then kill Kolohe because he vouched for you." Captain Sharp turned and headed for the door. Before he was out of earshot, he heard Kolohe speaking to his new charge.

"Don't worry about it, he threatens to kill everyone at first."

55

Captain Sharp stopped on deck to have a quick word with Blaed who was still working ship security. "Giles is no longer a member of my crew, and no longer allowed on my ship. If he attempts to get on board, he is to be knocked unconscious or killed. I don't care which. Make sure the other members of the security team are aware of the update," Captain Sharp said.

"Yes sir. I have been keeping an eye out for him. I was kinda hoping he would try and come back during my shift," Blaed said, and smiled.

"Carry on." The captain headed below.

Down in the galley, Bothari, Caleb, Tobin, and Harvey sat silently at a table. It looked uncomfortable; they had probably been like this for a while. Captain Sharp walked over and sat with the men. "I apologize for keeping you waiting, that was not my intent. We had an emergency that needed to be dealt with. Caleb, you said you had an offer for me?"

"Certainly Captain. The Atherton Trading Company is authorized to pay you top dollar for your cargo of coconuts. According to our trading records and the latest information from England, coconuts are being traded at 4½ pennies per head. Mr. Astor has authorized us to pay you 4¾ pennies per head for your entire supply," Caleb said. "We can begin offloading tomorrow morning. Mr. Lockland can have your funds available at his bank by the end of the day tomorrow." Tobin pulled contracts out of his satchel and laid them out on the table.

"Four and a half per head, I wasn't expecting that," Captain Sharp said. Caleb smiled.

"I was expecting a much higher offer."

The smile disappeared.

"I received a better offer already. I'm going to go with that one. I am sorry to waste your time gentleman," Captain Sharp said, standing up.

"Wait, wait, wait! That was actually our 'opening' offer," Caleb said, looking nervous. "I am authorized to go up to 5 pennies per head for your cargo. That is well above any price you could find on this island, sir."

Captain Sharp was still standing. "Only 5 pennies per head? I am sorry Mr. Mason, that's still not a better offer. I must decline."

"5¼!" yelled Caleb.

Captain Sharp shook his head. "The other offer is still better."

"5½ pennies per head! Nobody can touch that price, not on this island. Five and half pennies and we can sign the deal right now." Caleb Mason said, looking exhausted from the exchange. He was sweating at the temples and seemed to be out of breath although he was sitting down.

"That is still not a better offer. Please pass along to Astor that I appreciate the offer, it was very generous." Captain Sharp started to walk away.

"Mr. Sharp," Harvey Lockland said. "Nobody on this island can possibly afford to pay more for your cargo than Atherton. How much more money do you need to agree to this contract?"

"It's not about the money; it never has been. In fact, the deal I accepted pays less than your original offer. The other party offered kindness and friendship. Neither of those things were offered by you or the Atherton Trading Company. That is what made the other deal better. Good day, gentleman. Bothari will show you out." Captain Sharp spun and walked away, their mouths still open. Taking less money was something they could not understand.

Captain Sharp went up to the main deck and was relieved to see the restaurant owner still talking to his ship's cook. He walked over to them and apologized to Omar for the delay. "I know your time is important Omar, but I had a few things I needed to take care of first. Would you like to come down to the galley and have some tea?"

"Perhaps another time. I should be getting back to my restaurant. I would like to take you up on your offer to purchase some coconuts. I have talked to Mama Ruby. She agreed to let me buy some of the stock before she takes the rest. She informed me and the other investors that the set price for your coconuts is 4 pennies per head, and nothing lower will be allowed. I spent some time talking with my staff about what we think we can use in the next four months and have come up with a number. The coconuts are 4 pennies per head, or 3 heads for a shilling. I would like to purchase 180 coconuts for 60 shillings." Omar looked pleased with his careful math.

About this time, Bothari escorted Caleb, Tobin, and Harvey past them and off the ship.

They watched Captain Sharp reach out and shake hands with the restaurant man. "Omar, you got yourself a deal."

They were still looking over their shoulders as they went down the ramp and across the docks. Omar pulled a bag of coins out of his inside shirt pocket and handed them to Captain Sharp who immediately tucked the bag into his own shirt.

"You are not going to count the money?" Omar asked.

"No. You are an honorable man and a friend to the crew of the Tawny Mane. When do you want the coconuts? Would you like us to deliver them to your restaurant?"

"I will come back later today with some men and a cart. They owe me a favor and have volunteered to do this errand for me. I am still working with my team on how to prepare and serve the coconut meat, but Maurice has been very helpful with advice," Omar said.

Maurice blushed again and said he was happy to help another man who loved to cook.

Captain Sharp had an inspiration. "Maurice, why don't you take the afternoon off and go with Omar back to his restaurant? I'm sure it would be easier for you to show his staff some of your coconut creations than to describe how to make them second hand."

Maurice's face lit up. Captain Sharp knew he had made the right call. "Oh Captain Sharp, that would be wonderful! Thank you so much. I will go tell Pierre he is on his own for a while."

"Omar, why don't you go to the galley with Maurice? He can give you a quick tour of the galley before you head back. Plus, you can help him carry some coconuts back for the preparation demonstrations. Take four coconuts back with you, no charge," Captain Sharp said.

Omar was all smiles. "I would love to see the ship's kitchen-galley, thank you Captain Sharp. I do not think I can accept your gift of the four coconuts for free, Mama Ruby is very strict."

"It's not a gift Omar; it's a trade. In exchange for the four coconuts, you will teach Maurice how to make that amazing Pavlova dessert. I liked it so much, I want to be able to share it with my crew."

Captain Sharp went into his quarters and sat at his desk. He took out the bag of coins from Omar and dumped them out on his desk for counting. He knew it would be exactly sixty shillings, and it was. Next he got out some paper to work some calculations on.

When Captain Sharp first went through the log books and ships documents he had come across the breakdown of shares on the Tawny Mane. The log book listed the profit shares as follows.

Ship's Captain	6 shares.
First Mate	2 shares.
Second Mate	2 shares.
Quartermaster	2 shares.

Navigator   2 shares.
All others   1 share.

    Captain Sharp had already decided to lower his allotted shares from six down to three. This put more money in his crew's pockets, and did not make him feel so far removed from the men. Now he just needed to figure out the distribution of the money from the sale of the coconuts today.

    The Tawny Mane had 21 survivors after the pirate attack. Captain Sharp and seven others from Pukapuka joined the crew afterwards, for a total of 29 crew members currently on the ship. He wrote down 29 and then stopped. He thought of Giles, scratched that out, and wrote 28 instead. He was about to move on, but thought of Dart. He scratched out 28 and put 29 down again.

    So 29 people on the ship had at least one share for a base total of 29 shares. Then two extra shares for the captain, one extra share for Bothari, Jim-Jim, Hickory, Cornelius and Vaheana for their senior positions on the ship. This made a total of 36 shares on the ship.

    There are twelve pennies per shilling. Omar had just paid the Tawny Mane 60 shillings, or 720 pennies. 720 pennies divided by 36 shares was an even 20 pennies per crewman. Every crew member of the Tawny Mane had just earned at least 20 pennies. The five members of the senior staff earned 40 pennies, and Captain Sharp earned 60 pennies. Now all he needed was a banker. He leaned over and moved August's rope peg up to the runner position and waited.

    When August came in, the captain asked if he knew anyone on board with banking or accounting experience. August said he did not, but would ask around. Captain Sharp told him to ask everyone on the ship, and make a list of the persons off the ship on shore leave. August said he would get right on it and ducked back out.

    August was back in about twenty minutes and reported that he had checked with fifteen people currently on board. He found two men with accounting experience. Tanner was one of the sailors, who worked aloft in the sails and rigging. Arlo was a crewman who worked the deck, tossed sounding lines, and had volunteered to be on the cannon team. Captain Sharp had met both men, but had not gotten to know either one well. He asked August his opinion of both men, and if the crew had formed any opinions about them. August sat down and thought about what he was going to say before talking.

    "Tanner is a good man and a hard worker. I have had no issues with him and I haven't heard any bad things about him other than he comes off across as stuffy," August said. "Arlo is also a good sailor and will help out without being asked. He is quiet and doesn't talk much, but is respected by the other crew members. I haven't heard anything bad about him either."

"I need to appoint somebody as a banker for the crew and their money. This person needs to keep accurate accounts, hand out money to the crew, and be trustworthy," Captain Sharp said. "Which one would you pick and why?"

"I would pick Arlo, but it's not for a very good reason. The only thing I have against either man is that Tanner wanted Vaheana off the ship without giving her a chance. It's not much, but I think that makes him less fair in my own head," August said.

"That was well thought out August, thank you," Captain Sharp said. "I didn't have any feelings one way or another, but that is as good of a reason as any. Why don't you find Arlo and bring him back to my quarters?"

When August and Arlo came back, Captain Sharp welcomed them in and had August close the door behind them. Captain Sharp sat at his desk, with two chairs set up in front. He had a blank piece of paper on his desk and a quill pen and ink.

"Thank you for coming in Arlo. I was having problems with some calculations and was wondering if you could help me out," said Captain Sharp.

"Of course captain, what can I do?" Arlo asked.

"We just got paid for a sale of coconuts and I don't know how to figure out what each man gets. I don't understand the shares and how to break down the money into smaller amounts. I am not good with numbers and can just barely read and write. Can you help me figure this out?" Captain Sharp asked.

"Sure. Why don't you tell me what information you have," Arlo said.

Captain Sharp went into a story about selling some of the coconuts. He said they were paid 4 pennies per coconut, and sold 180 of them. Arlo picked up the quill and started writing things down. There were a total of 29 crew members on the Tawny Mane who earned at least one share. Five members of the senior crew earned two shares, and the captain earned three shares. How much money did they each make?

Arlo did some quick math and replied that each crewman earned 20 pennies, with the senior crew earning 40 pennies, and Captain Sharp earning 60 pennies. Captain Sharp pretended to not understand and asked Arlo to explain how he arrived at that number. Arlo took the time to explain it again to the captain, genuinely patient about it. When he was done, Captain Sharp pulled his piece of paper out of his desk drawer and laid it next to Arlo's paper.

"Yea, those are the numbers I got too," the captain said. "Arlo, I need an accountant and a banker on this ship to handle the crew's accounts and to hand out money when they need it. Are you interested in the job?"

Arlo looked at the captain's notes and then back up at the captain. "So you're actually very good with numbers and can read and write just fine?"

"Yes and yes," Captain Sharp said. "I already knew I could trust you, but I wanted to make sure you were good with numbers and could explain it to a crew member if they did not understand. This is not a job I want. Besides, I am away from the ship fairly often while we are in port. I want the crew to have access to their money when they go ashore."

"Okay," Arlo said.

"Just okay?" Captain Sharp asked. "Do you have any questions?"

"No, this is all straight forward stuff. I enjoy working with numbers, so I appreciate you choosing me for the job. Do you have a ledger where I can keep the crew's accounts by name?" Arlo asked.

Captain Sharp opened the top left-hand drawer and pulled out a ledger book. It was older and used, but since the first dozen pages had been ripped out and were missing, it was now blank and unused.

"Quills are here in my top center drawer. You may use my desk or the maps table when you are updating accounts. You can update accounts with others in the room, but I am requesting that when you need to access the money, you make the crew member wait outside. I think the fewer people who know where the money is hidden, the better. Don't you agree?" Captain Sharp asked.

"I agree," Arlo said.

Captain Sharp got up and went over to the secret panel by the door where his sword had once been hidden. He slid the moving part of the wall aside and exposed the hidden compartment behind it. There were already two bags of coins inside, labeled 's' for shillings and 'd' for pennies.

"Now that is just brilliant," Arlo said and smiled.

"Right now we have forty shillings in the bag marked 's.' I had the other twenty shillings broken down into 240 pennies inside the 'd' bag. The crew can withdraw any or all of their money whenever they want. If somebody is out of money and needs a loan, come talk to me first. I am willing to help out the crew if it's a reasonable request," Captain Sharp said.

"Ok, I will get started on this right now," Arlo said, pulling the ledger in front of him.

"A few things you need to know: first, Giles is no longer a member of this ship. Second, we have a new crew member named Dart. Once you have the ledger set up, take some paper from the middle drawer and write an announcement for the crew to be posted in the galley. Let them know we have been paid from our first sale of coconuts. Everyone's accounts have at least 20 pennies in them. They can request the money from you before going ashore. I expect those accounts to grow many times over the next few days."

"I think you should let the crew know you dropped your shares from six to three. They will all be excited to hear that," Arlo said.

"Do whatever you think is best, Arlo. You are now the official bank and accountant of the Tawny Mane. I will be relying on your wisdom and expertise in these areas to make things run smoothly," Captain Sharp said.

When Captain Sharp walked back out onto the deck, he saw Mama Ruby making her way down the dock towards the ship. She moved slowly, but with purpose. Her young assistant Jarom helped her on one side, while a large man held her arm on the other. Captain Sharp waited for her at the top of the ramp.

"Good afternoon," Captain Sharp said. "Welcome to the Tawny Mane. Koo Koo Kushaw. That is a traditional greeting on my island of Pukapuka. It roughly translates to 'welcome to my home, you are family.' "

"Tank ye lil lamb. Need to talk to ya bout dis mornin miss-unduhstandin wid da criminals. Is yer crew memba alrite?"

"Yes, everyone is fine. Why don't you come into my quarters and sit down and have some tea?" Captain Sharp suggested.

"Dat wood be lovely. Lead on," she motioned.

Captain Sharp asked August to find Vaheana and have her report to his quarters. Once inside, he helped Mama Ruby settle into a chair and invited her escorts to sit as well. The other male with her today was Tawhiri, one of her nephews who was also her personal security. The captain went behind his desk, pulled the bell twice, then joined her at the table.

In less than a minute, Pierre appeared and the captain requested tea and snacks for six. Pierre nodded and hurried off; he was definitely less talkative than Maurice. Mama Ruby asked about his sudden appearance. Captain Sharp explained the bell and how the galley is directly below his quarters. She was impressed with the set up and the way Cuthbert had turned an idea into a tangible thing.

When Vaheana arrived, Captain Sharp invited her to sit and join them for tea. He made the introductions to everyone in the room as Mama Ruby examined her fat lip and bruised forehead.

Mama Ruby clucked her tongue. "O child, ya gonna get sum good color up 'n dere. Ya alrite deer?"

Vaheana glanced at Captain Sharp, who nodded and told her to go ahead and give a short version of her side of the events. So Vaheana told her story again. Captain Sharp made it a point to watch Mama Ruby's face when Vaheana started killing the smugglers. The old woman's eyes got wide and she reached out and took ahold of Vaheana's hand. When Vaheana finished, Mama Ruby looked at her with less sympathy and much more respect.

"Aint dat sumdin, deh was thinkin ya was the lamb, when all along ya was de lion. I'm happy for ya child. I heard a woman was teken from de ship an I fear'd da worst."

"Vaheana was one of the trained warriors on Pukapuka. I am lucky to have her on my ship," Captain Sharp said. "She is also one of our lead navigators who steers the ship and plots our course. I know she can take care of herself, but six versus one was too much for anyone to handle, man or woman. She kept her wits about her and hung on until my crew could get there and help out."

"Lawd now I dun herd it all. Now child, tell meh about des conch shells," Mama Ruby, said getting back to business.

Vaheana pulled one of the conch shells off the shelf and unwrapped it for Mama Ruby. The old woman ooo'd and ah'd over it while turning it over in her hands. Vaheana told her about voyaging to other islands in the past and having shells like this traded back and forth. Shells like this were very uncommon on Pukapuka, but they found a few washed up on the beaches over the years. Mama Ruby agreed that they were remarkable and the colors were like a sunset on fire. She mentioned that this would make some beautiful jewelry.

That jogged something in the captain's mind. Captain Sharp asked August to go find Fetu to ask if he had completed any of his handmade jewelry pieces. If so, would he be willing to show them to Mama Ruby?

August left just as Mama Ruby told Vaheana that broken shells might be worth just as much as the full shells to the right artisan. Mama Ruby asked if she could take one of the conch shells when she left today to show it to some of her contacts in town. Vaheana quickly agreed, saying she would appreciate any help in the selling of the shells.

August came back a few minutes later with Fetu and introductions were made again, including Jarom and Tawhiri. Captain Sharp explained that years ago, Fetu's mother created handmade jewelry and taught Fetu to do it as a child. Mama Ruby asked what kinds of jewelry they made.

Fetu described the different things he and his mother made: necklaces, bracelets, pendants, rings, earrings, hair combs, hair pins, and more. Fetu brought a rolled-up black felt cloth that he now laid on the table in front of them. He unrolled the cloth. Everyone in the room made an "Ooooo" sound, even the menfolk. Fetu had completed four bracelets and two necklaces; they were amazing. The broken pieces of conch shell had been cut into similar sizes of long, thin strips of brightly colored shells. These were rounded and smoothed until they looked uniform in size and shape. Small holes were drilled into each end of the shell strips, then strung together on a thin, delicate braid. The braid was made of coconut husk fibers, of course. What made these amazing were the colors of the conch shell. Fetu had arranged the shell strips so that the pieces in the middle of the necklace were the darkest of the red and orange. The colors got lighter as they moved away from the center in a soft rainbow of fuchsia, orange, coral, salmon, pink and yellow. The effect of the jewelry laid out on the black felt background was stark and brilliant.

Mama Ruby said as much. Fetu nodded, explaining that it was intentional. His mother learned over the years that colors stood out best against a black background, so she always carried a black felt cloth with her when she sold or displayed her handiwork. It was a technique Fetu still used.

"Mey I?" Mama Ruby asked before touching the pieces.

Fetu nodded.

Mama Ruby carefully picked up the necklace, running her fingers over the edges. She brought the necklace up to her eyes, examining each link individually. "Ow much wud ye charge fo des one?" Mama Ruby asked.

"That one I can't sell because I made it for my wife," Fetu said. "The others are all for sale. I made them with the intention of selling or trading them. As for how much money to charge, I have no idea. I am still learning about money. I know what they are worth to me, but I don't know what they would be worth to someone else."

"Your wife?" Vaheana asked.

"A story for another time," Captain Sharp said.

"I can tell you dis Mr. Fetu, som frens of mine wud giv haf a year's pay for a neklis lik dis, and dey be som rich frens," Mama Ruby said. "Wud ya like me ta help ya sell yer works of art?"

"You honor me, Mama Ruby," Fetu said and bowed. "I would appreciate your help, thank you."

"Dis ship of lambs needs ma help mor den I thot. I don't want nobody takin advantage of ma flock." Mama Ruby asked Fetu if she could take one of the bracelets with her to show off to some friends of hers who collected jewelry and pretty things. Fetu agreed, and revealed he had a few more unfinished pieces in the works.

When they were done talking shells and jewelry Fetu and Vaheana left so the captain could wrap up his business with Mama Ruby. She explained that the investors came to an agreement on the price of coconut; they set the bottom line at four pennies per head. She allowed two other local restaurants to buy some stock today and tomorrow before her group took the lot and moved them off the ship. In two days' time, a group of workers would be at the dock at sunrise with carts and wagons. They should be able to unload the ship in half a day, if the crew of the Tawny Mane were willing to help. Captain Sharp assured her that they would. Mama Ruby had secured storage space in a nearby building with a clean, cool sub-basement, perfect for the long-term storage of a boat load of coconuts.

"Ave ya heard bak from de ATC yet?" Mama Ruby asked. "Do ya know if dey will let ya stay on as captin?"

"No word yet. I should have an answer in the next few days. It would be nice if they let me know before we offloaded the coconuts. I would rather trade cargo for cargo instead of money, but they may take that option away from me. If that's the case, I may be in the market for a ship. You don't happen to know anyone with a ship for sale do you?"

"Les just say I kno enuf people dat everybody got somtin fer sale. I will bring ya money for de coconuts in two deys time unless I hear from ya," Mama Ruby said.

"Thank you," Captain Sharp said.

"You jez bedda watch yaself wid the ATC. Evrabody knows dey steal a baby's milk if dey cud get a penny for it," she said shaking her head. "Now dat biznez is dun, how 'bout ya give meh a tour of dis lovely ship of yaws."

"It would be my pleasure," Captain Sharp said.

56

Caleb was sent to fetch Captain Sharp later that same day. He was stopped at the ramp by the Koa, and another crewman notified the captain of his presence. Captain Sharp grabbed his personal effects, including his sword and hat, and headed out onto the deck. Somehow Bothari had also been notified and stood near the ramp, ready to go. He was outfitted to be a casual guard who might just have to start a war on a moment's notice. There was a lot of metal hanging from his body.

Caleb would only say that Astor wanted to speak to him, but would not say what it was about. He also refused to say if it was good news or bad news. Captain Sharp told him to 'lead the way,' then he and Bothari followed Caleb back towards the Atherton Trading Company.

Upon arrival, they were escorted into a meeting room with a large table. Astor was already sitting, and stood when they entered. He welcomed Captain Sharp and his 'man' and thanked them for coming. He offered them a glass of ice water, which they both accepted. Captain Sharp had not seen ice in nearly five years.

"Captain Sharp, I am happy to announce the Atherton Trading Company has agreed to keep you on as captain for now . . . provided certain conditions can be met. You will, of course, be required to sign a temporary contract of employment. You also need to sign a binding agreement that you are financially responsible for the ship and its safe return to Plymouth, England. You mentioned previously that you planned to supply the ship yourself. We have written that into the contract. Finally, there is a contract that entitles you to a portion of the proceeds upon your return to England."

"Do you have these contracts for me to look at?" Captain Sharp asked.

"Of course," said Astor. He slid a handful of papers over to Captain Sharp, who flipped through them quickly. When he came to the document he was looking for, he stopped to read it carefully.

Astor pushed a quill and inkwell across the table towards Captain Sharp. "I need your signature on the bottom of each sheet. The contract of employment has two copies: one for us, and one for you to carry back to England with you."

Captain Sharp held up a hand, indicating that he needed more time to read the document. He came to the part he was looking for and slowed down, trying to hide the anger. The Atherton Trading Company would allow him to purchase the cargo with his own money. They would allow him to sail the ship back to England. After all that, they were generous enough to give him fifteen percent of the profits for all his troubles. He read it twice to make sure he understood it correctly.

"Mr. Astor, your offer has been declined. You can explain to the shipowners how you fired their captain and crew and denied them any chance at recouping any losses or profit. Good day, sir."

Captain Sharp stood up fast, tucked the contract into his jacket, and walked from the room, with Bothari close behind. Mr. Astor tried to call him back twice, but Sharp was pissed enough to keep walking. He had already been thinking about his alternative plan. Now he was going to have to move forward with it.

He would take the money for his cargo and begin looking for a ship to rent or buy to get himself and his crew back to England. While he appreciated the crew's willingness to jump ship with him, he would not hold them to that pledge. They had lives and families to get back to; he didn't want twenty-six people stranded because of his temper tantrum. He was also giving serious thought to torching the ship and letting it burn right where it sat in the harbor. Unfortunately, he had fallen in love with the Tawny Mane. She was a beautiful ship, and she was, at least for a little while, his.

After the meeting with the investors the other day, Usain had pointed out his house from Mama Ruby's front yard. The house was not far off and also up on the hillside above the harbor. It was distinctive by its orange terracotta roof. Captain Sharp saw the house as they walked away from the trading company office and he now detoured towards it. Bothari didn't say anything as usual and just kept up. The walk was not far, but allowed Captain Sharp to rein in his temper while he walked. A fifteen-shilling return on his one-hundred-shilling investment? The captain walked to the front door, knocked loudly, and waited. A small woman opened the door and asked if they had business with Usain.

"Yes, I do," Captain Sharp said, and was ushered inside. Bothari and Captain Sharp were shown into a library and told Usain would be along in a few minutes. She asked if they wanted anything to drink. Both men declined. She walked away on soft feet, the same way she had come. The library was impressive: lots of books and maps. He was looking at a map detailing the 'Estrecho de Todos los Santos' when their host came in.

"Captain Sharp, Bothari! What an unexpected surprise. What do I owe this pleasure?" Usain said as he came into the room and shook hands with each man.

"I was wondering if you had a ship for sale? It looks like I will not be the Captain of the Tawny Mane any longer. I would like to get my crew, myself and our cargo back to England," Captain Sharp said.

"Are you quite sure about that, Captain Sharp? I had a reliable source tell me not long ago that you were indeed going to be the captain of the Tawny Mane and would be returning to England at her helm," Usain said, looking surprised.

"Astor just made me an offer to remain captain, but I turned him down," Captain Sharp said.

"Can I ask why?" Usain said.

Captain Sharp described the meeting they had just left. The employment contract and the agreement to get the ship back to England were standard and he was fine with those. The Atherton Trading Company expected him to fully stock the ship with supplies bought with his own money, and upon delivery in England, he would be entitled to fifteen percent of the profits.

"What?" Usain said. "You must have misread that."

"I read it twice to be sure, and then brought it with me as proof." He pulled the document out of his jacket and passed it over to Usain. "They will just have to hire a new captain and crew, buy their own supplies, and then get it around the horn and back to England safely," Captain Sharp said.

Usain was reading the contract and said out loud, "This is absurd!" and continued reading.

"Amelia?" Usain called out. The woman who opened the door for them earlier appeared at the library entrance. She must have been standing nearby. "Please send for Joshua and Marcus at once. Tell them it's a coffee emergency." Amelia nodded and walked away.

"Would you be willing to stay and have something cool to drink, Captain Sharp? I think I can help you with your problem. I just need some time for some friends of mine to arrive," Usain said.

"If you could help with our problem, I would be grateful. Since I am no longer captain, please call me Gerard."

"Let's not give up on Captain Sharp just yet, but I will call you Gerard, my friend," Usain said.

"What is a coffee emergency?" Captain Sharp asked.

"It's an old joke between friends. Joshua is a friend who was poor all his life, and then suddenly became very rich. His education took longer to catch up to him. He used to say he needed to fill his coffees instead of the word 'coffers.' Marcus and I let it go on for years before somebody else corrected him, and he called us out. Now when we say it's a coffee emergency, they know it's about money, or in this case, serious money," Usain said.

"Marcus is probably the richest man on the north island. He owns a good portion of the Atherton Trading Company. He is essentially one of Astor's bosses. I have it on good authority that he was supposed to officially hire you as Captain, and to see if we could get any more cargo space on your ship before it returns to England," Usain said.

"While we wait, what can you tell me about the 'Estrecho de Todos los Santos'?" Captain Sharp asked.

"Ah yes, you mean the 'Straight of All Saints'. I would tell you I highly recommend it for safe passage."

Joshua and Marcus showed up in twenty minutes and found the men gathered around the map in the library. Once introductions were done, Usain asked Captain Sharp to repeat the events of his earlier meeting at the Atherton Trading Company. Captain Sharp repeated his story from earlier. Marcus's ears turned red. When Usain handed him the contract to look over he went from red to purple.

Marcus mumbled 'tuhinga' (asshole) under his breath.

"Thank you for the information Usain, I will remedy this straight away. Perhaps Captain Sharp would be interested in Joshua's services for this afternoon. I will see you tomorrow morning for Chinese dominoes." Marcus shook hands and headed off.

Usain told the group. "A group of us have a standing game of bone tiles every Sunday right after church. We like to start off the new week by getting those first few sins out of the way. So we get together and we drink, we cuss, and we gamble. The pastor prays for us, but he won't call us out on it because we fill his coffees."

"Asshole," Joshua said, but both men were smiling.

"So Joshua, what do you do?" Captain Sharp asked.

"I am a solicitor for the courts. I give advice, draft documents, conduct negotiations and prepare cases for trial. The barristers do all the flashy work inside the courtroom. My work is boring. I'm usually hunched over a desk working by candlelight," Joshua said.

"What would you charge for some advice and possibly some help drawing up a contract for a ship's captain?" Captain Sharp asked.

"That depends," Joshua replied with a smile. "Is there room on your ship for more cargo?"

A few hours later, Captain Sharp and Bothari walked back to the Mane in a much better mood. They made new friends, had a fantastic dinner, and heard good news, all in a few short hours. Imagine their surprise when they found employees from the Atherton Trading waiting for them on the docks near the ship. Samual Astor, Caleb Mason, Tobin Wayne, and Harvey Lockland all looked like their asses had been half chewed off. They sat on a board that had been laid across some buckets. They had been waiting a good long while.

The group jumped up when they saw Captain Sharp coming. The men lined up behind Mr. Astor like ducks in the water. The ruffled kerchiefs watched the sailors' approach with some apprehension.

"Good evening, Captain Sharp, might I have a word with you?" Astor asked.

"I turned down your offer, Mr. Astor. I don't think we have anything further to discuss," Captain Sharp said.

"That was technically our opening offer. You see we really do want you to remain captain of the Tawny Mane," Astor replied.

"Your last contract would indicate otherwise. In fact, it was downright insulting."

"That was a misunderstanding on my part. I wrote down the wrong number and I apologize. I think our new offer will be much more to your liking."

"I don't think I am interested in working for you, Astor," Captain Sharp said. "Find another captain and crew."

"I'm afraid we don't have another captain or crew available sir. I realize we got off on the wrong foot and I apologize for that. My only concern is helping you and your crew return to England to be with your families," Astor said.

Captain Sharp pretended to think about this unexpected turn of events. "Well, that is very kind of you. Why don't you come aboard? We can look over the paperwork and sign the contracts."

"That won't be necessary," Astor said, pulling out a single piece of paper. "I only need you to sign this notice of employment and you can stay captain and be on your way. We don't need any other contracts."

"I didn't mean yours; I meant mine. I have retained the services of Joshua Stevedore, Solicitor of the court. He helped me draw up a contract that is much more to my liking."

According to his new friend Joshua, the contract was simple and straightforward, but the wording and language was complex. The Atherton Trading Company agreed to officially hire Captain Gerard Sharp and name him captain of the Tawny Mane. Since he assumed command during the first leg of the voyage, he is to be paid at the rate of 75% the median salary of a ship's captain upon their return to England. Upon the ship's arrival in England, the owners can choose to extend his contract for another voyage, or buy out his contract and release him from duties. If the owners chose to buy out his contract, they will be required to pay him 50% of the established captain's salary, or provide him with transportation back to his home island of Pukapuka.

Any and all goods transported back to England that have been paid for by the Atherton Trading Company shall be the property of the Atherton Trading Company, and they shall receive 100% of the profits of those sales.

Any and all goods transported back to England that have been paid for by Captain Sharp shall be the property of Captain Sharp. He shall receive 95% of the profits of those sales. 5% of those profits shall be paid to the Atherton Trading Company, its investors, and the ship owners.

Astor was obviously unhappy with the contract and asked for some additional concessions, to which Captain Sharp refused. Tobin, the lawyer for the firm, said it was a grotesque contract and advised Astor not to sign it. He whined that they were giving away money, but Astor had his orders, and he signed the contracts soon enough. Captain Sharp only had time to get one copy of each document done before returning to the ship. He explained if Astor and his men wanted to stay onboard and write copies of the contracts, he would allow it and sign them for the trading companies records. Astor said that would not be necessary, they didn't want a copy of these.

"I believe we have concluded business for the evening and I will now take my leave," Astor said as he stood up.

Captain Sharp remained seated and asked, "are you sure we are not forgetting anything?"

"I can't think of a thing," Astor said.

"What about the wax seal mark placed on all signed documents of the Atherton Trading Company? The mark that makes the documents official and binding. The wax seal you wear around your neck at all times." Joshua had told Captain Sharp about this and reminded him to make sure it was stamped. It was a common tactic used by the ATC where they forgot to put the seal on new contracts or lopsided contacts not in their favor, and then try to wiggle out of them later. It was common enough in the trade business that people talked about getting 'waxed' by the ATC.

"O yes, that. It must have slipped my mind," Astor said, sitting back down. August brought over a candle and wax and in a few more minutes, the documents were official.

"Now you may take your leave," Captain Sharp said.

He walked the ruffled kerchiefs from the Atherton Trading Company to the gangway and saw them off the ship. When they got down to the dock Astor asked when they could begin delivering and loading cargo for the return trip to England.

"I am afraid that will be impossible, all my cargo space has been spoken for. Between the cargo I'm purchasing and the cargo space purchased by the Coffee Investment Group, we have no available space left," Captain Sharp said.

Astor was furious, his face grew red. "Why didn't you tell me that before?" he grumbled.

"It must have slipped my mind. Either way it's the ship's business, and none of your concern," Captain Sharp said, and let the wolf out to smile.

57

The next day was practically non-stop with guests and visitors. First thing in the morning, another local restaurant owner arrived and purchased thirty coconuts for ten shillings. His four young daughters accompanied him to help carry the coconuts back to his house. The girls were very excited to see the ship and had all dressed alike. They were absolutely adorable when standing on the deck next to his crew. Captain Sharp figured their ages to be 11, 9, 6 and 4. The girls each carried bags that would hold a few coconuts each. The captain called for volunteers; in the end, each girl carried just two coconuts. Gideon carried the youngest daughter on his shoulders back to their house. The line of volunteers returned less than ten minutes later looking happy and laughing. The captain thanked each of them as they came back on board.

Benjamin Braxton from the warehouse showed up with stacks of papers and congratulated Captain Sharp on being hired on as captain, officially this time.

"I don't know how ya did it, but ya changed their minds in just a few short days," Benjamin said.

"I had a lot of help from my new friends. One of the people I have met since arriving in New Zealand is a controlling investor of the Atherton Trading Company. I explained to him I was not being retained as captain and that the crew had refused to sail on without me. He realized the Tawny Mane would be stuck here and stop making them money. In fact, the investors would start to lose money with the ship out of circulation. It would not make future trips, so they would lose out on the buying and selling of those future goods. They would also have to continue to pay for a berth for the ship. That didn't even include the ongoing maintenance, and hiring people to make sure the ship didn't get stolen. In the end, I think the investors ordered Astor to hire me back no matter what because they were desperate. That allowed me to negotiate a pretty good deal . . . with the help of my friends, of course."

"That was some tight maneuvering, I must say," Benji said. "Now that ya have cleared all the obstacles, let's discuss the cargo that's taking up space in ma warehouse. How much do ya want, how much can ya hold, and how much can ya pay?"

Captain Sharp invited Benji to his quarters for tea and snacks, which he gratefully accepted. He also sent for Arlo, Hickory and Jim-Jim. Maurice got them started with tea and a sweet pastry covered in roasted coconut sprinkles. They discussed what the ship could hold, and how much space it would take up. Benji had paperwork on all three materials regarding how much was available, the cost per pound, and the size and dimensions of the container. He sent Benji, Hickory and Jim-Jim below to start figuring out the space for the cargo, while he and Arlo stayed and looked at the prices.

Arlo looked at numbers, his eyes darting back and forth between several documents. He made notes on a side paper and after a few minutes, he looked up at Captain Sharp. "I think we should make some changes."

"This is your area of expertise, but I want to know why. Sell me," Captain Sharp said.

Arlo explained that the cost of sugar was very low, due to the proximity of the sugarcane fields on the island. The cost of rice was average; better deals could be had elsewhere. He recommended they not take any of the rice and double the sugar order. The tobacco was also a good deal. They should load up on as much as they could. Benji had a limited supply. They should definitely buy all he had. If they could acquire any more tobacco, it would probably bring the best profit. Captain Sharp agreed with everything, and thanked Arlo for figuring out the best deal for the ship and crew. They would go with his plan.

When Benji and Hickory returned and sat back down, Captain Sharp and Arlo explained the changes in the order. Benji said it was no problem, and with the measurements they had just taken, they could now figure out how much product they could carry and thus how much it would cost.

"I have a question for you that may seem out of place, but it could be a huge help in our transactions going forward. Do you happen to owe Mama Ruby any money or favors?" Captain Sharp asked.

Benji closed his eyes and started rubbing the bridge of his nose. "Of course, Mama Ruby got her hands in this." he said. Eventually, he looked up at Captain Sharp and asked what the deal was. Captain Sharp explained that they were selling Mama Ruby and her investors all the coconut cargo. He would rather trade goods for goods than goods for money. If Benji owed Mama Ruby anything, they could do a three-way swap for cargo with no money changing hands.

"I betta go talk ta Mama Ruby and see what she has planned, because she always has a plan," Benji said, gathering his papers.

Captain Sharp turned to Arlo. "Why don't you go with him? It will probably save us some time. Find out how much credit we are going to have after the sale of the coconuts. Ask her about tobacco while you're there." Arlo nodded, and gathered his paperwork.

Next to show up were Jarom and an older man named Mr. Holladay. Jarom happily announced that he was supposed to 'vouch' for the man. Mr. Holladay owned a sugarcane farm on the island. He needed to see how much room the ship had for storage in the hold, and wanted to check the conditions. Captain Sharp hooked him up with Hickory and sent the men below.

Not long after, a horse drawn carriage came out onto the dock and got as close to the ship as possible. When the driver got down and opened the cab door, a very beautiful woman in her late forties got out, deployed a parasol, and walked confidently towards the ship. She had some authority to her.

Men got out of her way and tipped hats to her as she walked past. One of the crewmen had the good sense to duck into the captain's quarters and suggest that he should get on deck right quick.

Captain Sharp made it to the gangway just as the woman started up the ramp. Perkins was on duty and was indeed going to stop her before Captain Sharp tapped him on the shoulder and motioned it was okay. He stepped aside as the woman came up.

Captain Sharp was ready to receive her at the top of the ramp. "Welcome to the Tawny Mane. I am Captain Sharp; how may I be of service?"

The woman stepped onto the deck and now stopped to look at him. "You're the Captain of this ship?" She asked, looking surprised.

"Yes I am miss . . .?" Captain waited for her to identify herself.

"Agatha Willoughby." She held out her gloved hand. Captain Sharp kissed her hand, as was expected.

"I thought that man over there would be the captain," she said pointing to where Hans Michael was working. "He looks like an old captain."

"That is Hans, one of my crewmen," Captain Sharp said.

She turned to look at Captain Sharp with a critical eye now. "You look too young to be a ship's captain," she challenged.

"I have adequate leadership experience," Captain Sharp said flatly. "Now what can I do for you, Agatha Willoughby?"

"It has been brought to my attention that you have a master jeweler on board. I wish for an appointment to view his works," Miss Willoughby said.

"Of course," the captain said, "August!"

August was at the far end of the ship talking to another crewman. He hurried over to the gangway and came to attention.

"Will you please notify Mr. Fetu that Agatha Willoughby is here to view his jewelry collection in my quarters? Also, let him know that a shipment of weliweli wahine just arrived for him." August snapped a salute and headed below to find Fetu.

"Allow me to show you to my quarters, Miss Willoughby. Can I interest you in some tea?" Captain Sharp extended his elbow to escort her.

"Yes, that would be lovely, thank you," she said, tucking her arm in his.

August found Fetu working on his jewelry at a small table in the galley. He was doing very delicate work; August almost hated to interrupt him. He stood close, waiting for Fetu to finish the part he was working on and then looked up.

"There is a very fancy woman here to look at your jewelry," August said.

"Okay." Fetu gathered up his shells and tools. August followed him back to his bunk. Fetu put the work in progress in his trunk and pulled out two rolls of black fabric tied with leather ties. August remembered the second part and told Fetu that Captain Sharp also said a shipment of 'weliweli wahine' came in for him.

Fetu stopped what he was doing and looked up at August. "He said that?"

"Yes, what are they?" August asked.

"'Weliweli' is dangerous, and 'wahine' is a woman. He says this is a dangerous woman. How fancy was she?" Fetu asked.

"Very. Men ran to get out of her way," August said.

"Well, shit," Fetu said.

Captain Sharp and Miss Willoughby had already been served tea by Maurice. She showed interest in the bell, so Captain Sharp let Maurice tell her about it. She mentioned she could use something like this at her home for summoning her own staff.

When Fetu came into the room, Captain Sharp almost didn't recognize him. His hair was unbraided and flowed down his back in waves. He wore a red velvet shirt that used to hang on these very walls as curtains. The red shirt had been made for Pasco. The captain wondered what was going on.

Fetu started speaking in Maru. It took Captain Sharp a second to catch up. "I have no idea what to charge her, so you will translate for me and help me out. If you do not help me, I will tell the whole crew that you slept with three couples in one night. Please tell her that I am Fetu, the exotic foreign jewelry maker."

"Miss Willoughby, may I present to you Mr. Fetu, our exotic foreign jewelry maker," Captain Sharp said.

August looked back and forth between the two like they had lost their minds. Fortunately, he had been through enough craziness that he just went with it. Fetu swept forward and grasped her gloved hand, kissing it as he had seen other men do. "Tell her she is as beautiful as the waterfalls of Vinta Vatina," Fetu said.

"Where is Vinta Vatina?" Captain Sharp asked.

"I just made it up. Now tell her nice stuff and try and keep up with me!" Fetu said sharply.

"Mr. Fetu says you are as beautiful as the waterfalls of Vinta Vatina, and that his jewelry cannot add where such beauty already exists," Captain Sharp said with a straight face.

"Oh Mr. Fetu, you are quite a charmer," Miss Willoughby said, blushing.

Captain Sharp turned back to Fetu and spoke in Maru again. "She says you look like the backside of a wild boar."

Fetu smiled and replied, "Tell her I was supposed to leave for a very important meeting, but I will cancel it because of her beauty, and because you bark like a dog when left alone with women." He laid the felt rolls on the table and waited for the translation.

"Mr. Fetu had a very important appointment, but he will cancel it because of your beauty and your eye for great art such as his," Captain Sharp said.

"Oh thank you Mr. Fetu. I knew you would understand," she replied, directing her comments to the translator.

"She says you smell like a turtle she owned named Mr. Poops," Captain Sharp said back to Fetu.

Fetu made a small bow to her, then invited her over to stand next to him while he untied the wraps. He took his time untying the leather cords, letting anticipation build. He slowly unrolled the black fabric until the bright conch shell pieces were revealed. There were two necklaces and two bracelets on this blanket. Gone was the first one he had made for his future wife, but these two were no less magnificent. The colors burned against the black background and seemed to be alive with color.

Agatha Willoughby gasped when they came into view. Her eyes dilated, and she reached for the necklace immediately. "Heaven on earth they are beautiful," she said. She carefully picked up one of the necklaces and ran her fingers over the edge of the shells. "It's so smooth and colorful."

"Yes, my fingers are covered with cuts from all the sharp pieces," Fetu said in Maru.

She looked at the captain for the translation. "It takes many weeks and many hours to smooth out the shells. They must not harm the beautiful necks they lay upon," Captain Sharp said.

"I have never seen anything like it: the craftsmanship, the detail, the colors . . . I simply must have them," she said. "How much does this one cost?"

"Do you have any idea how much you want to charge for these?" Captain Sharp asked in Maru.

"No. I should have asked Mama Ruby," Fetu answered in Maru.

"I think they should be expensive, but I don't know what expensive is for her," Captain Sharp said.

"What don't you just pick a number, like four," Fetu said.

"Four of what though? Pennies, shillings, Guineas?" Captain Sharp asked.

"What did he say?" Agatha Willoughby asked.

"He said it is hard to put a price on his art. They are like children to him. So much love goes into each creation," Captain Sharp said.

"Tell him I will give him 200 ducats for the necklace," Miss Willoughby said.

"Is that a lot?" Fetu asked.

Captain Sharp shrugged his shoulders. "I don't know. What's a ducat? We should have brought Arlo in here."

Switching to English, he asked August to go see if Arlo was back from his meeting with Mama Ruby. If he was, they needed him in here right quick. August stepped out and pulled the door shut behind him.

Agatha Willoughby watched the men talking and could tell they were both frustrated. She wanted the jewelry badly, and didn't want to insult the jewelry maker by lowballing him. She did enjoy some early morning bartering, however.

"Fine, I will go 250 ducats on the necklace, but no more. I am not some bobolyne from the markets," Miss Willoughby said.

Just then August returned with Arlo. Captain Sharp introduced him to Agatha Willoughby as the ship's banker.

"How can I be of service?" Arlo asked.

"Miss Willoughby has made an offer on one of Mr. Fetu's necklaces in the amount of 250 ducats and we were wondering . . ." Captain Sharp started.

Arlo cut him off and started talking directly to Miss Willoughby. "That is a bargain, I must say. How soon can those funds be transferred? I presume that the jewelry is ready to be given to Miss Willoughby immediately?"

He asked Fetu and Captain Sharp who both nodded.

"Excellent," Arlo said.

"If you can have one of your men fetch my driver and my money chest, I brought it with me, just in case."

Arlo wheeled on August and told him to go fetch the driver immediately.

August hurried off looking as confused as ever.

Fetu was also confused by the speed that Arlo was moving, but decided to trust his shipmate and go with the flow. He spoke in Maru to Captain Sharp. Miss Willoughby turned to watch them and waited for the translation.

"Mr. Fetu says he has yet to show you the earrings and hair brooch," Captain Sharp said.

"Oh my goodness, there is more?" Miss Willoughby said, clapping her hands in front of her. "Show them to me. Show them to me right now!"

Miss Willoughby bought one necklace, one set of earrings, and a hair brooch for the bargain basement price of 285 ducats. Captain Sharp, Fetu, and August walked Agatha Willoughby and her driver down to her coach and helped her inside. They waved her off and walked back to the ship.

"How much is a ducat worth?" August asked once they were alone.

"No idea," Captain Sharp said. "Arlo was quick to accept the offer, so I guess it was a good one. Hopefully ducats are close to shillings, but even if they're like pennies it's still a good deal."

When they came back into the captain's quarters, they found Arlo sitting behind the captain's desk. He told them to close the door and pull up some chairs for the lecture. Captain Sharp, Fetu, and August sat down, waiting to be scolded.

"Do not start any future negotiation with foreign money you know nothing about. You could have been robbed blind! There are some denominations in the world where a suitcase full of money will buy you a banana. You hired me as your banker and accountant. Let me do my job. Next time don't wait so long before you come get me," Arlo said.

The men nodded.

"You have no idea how much a ducat is worth, do you?" Arlo asked.

The three men shook their heads.

"One ducat is worth nine shillings and four pence," Arlo said calmly.

Captain Sharp did some quick math in his head. "Holy shit!"

"Is that good then?" Fetu asked.

"We are currently selling coconuts for four pennies each," Arlo said. "Agatha Willoughby just paid you nearly 32,000 pennies."

"Wow," Fetu said, looking dizzy. "I was going to ask for four."

"Four what?" Arlo asked.

"I don't know much about money. I just wanted four of whatever coins she had," Fetu said.

Arlo let his head sink slowly to the desk. Then he lifted it an inch and let it fall to the table with a thump. Thump. Thump. Thump.

Just after Agatha Willoughby left, a small one sail cargo sloop pulled up next to the Tawny Mane and tied off to the bow on the bay side of the ship. A man asked for permission to come aboard. One of the deckhands on the Mane lowered a rope ladder off the stern and the man climbed up onto the deck. Captain Sharp was ready and waiting for the visitor when he made it all the way up. His name was Arturo; he owned a restaurant down in Christchurch, on the southern island of New Zealand. He had been authorized to buy two hundred and fifty coconuts by Mama Ruby.

Captain Sharp shook his hands with Arturo and welcomed him aboard the Tawny Mane. The captain invited Arturo to come into his quarter for some tea, but Arturo shook his head. He was way behind schedule and needed to get loaded and turned around before the tide was ripping through the straight. He asked Captain Sharp how quickly they could help him load and the captain said 'minutes'. He ordered August to pipe for all hands and get some bodies up here. Arturo had a bag of coins on rope around his neck. He took it off and handed it over to Captain Sharp, who accepted it with a handshake.

August piped the bosun's whistle and everyone ran up on deck. Captain Sharp told them he needed a fast cargo line from the hold down into the sloop. They needed two hundred fifty coconuts loaded five minutes ago. He waved Arlo over and handed him the bag of coins. "Shares for the crew, if you please."

"You are not going to count it?" Arturo asked.

"Is the bag short?" Captain Sharp asked.

"No, no. I counted twice. Eighty-three shillings and four pennies."

"Then there is no need for me to check it now. Let's just watch and see how fast my crew can move," Captain Sharp said. The crew was fast; just under eight minutes.

Arturo gave another quick handshake and climbed down the ladder. Two of the Tawny Mane crew members had climbed down into the boat to help load and now they climbed back up. Arturo and his crew pushed off from the ship and his two men started rowing the sloop towards the bay while he worked to get the canvas pulled up. The loaded barge moved slowly towards the mouth of the bay.

Captain Sharp went into his office where Arlo was still updating his accounts.

"Another few shillings in everyone's accounts. Starting to get really exciting for the crew," Arlo said without looking up.

"Thank you, Arlo. If you can update the notice in the galley, I would appreciate it," Captain Sharp said.

"Will do, Captain. I left plenty of room below the first announcement since I knew the cargo would be sold to several different buyers," Arlo said.

While he was talking to Arlo, Jarom came back with another man he was supposed to vouch for. Mr. Miller owned a tobacco plantation and needed to see how much room they had for how much product. Again, he was paired up with Hickory. The men went below to measure the holds.

Captain Sharp had an idea, and grabbed Jarom before he took off. He explained that he had a new crew member that needed some new duds: shirt, pants, shoes and gloves. He asked Jarom if he and Mama Ruby could help the new crewman get some good quality clothing. Jarom said 'of course,' they could go do it right now. Captain Sharp sent a crewman below to find Dart and Kolohe.

Captain Sharp went into his pocket and pulled out a handful of shillings that he passed to Jarom. "That should cover the cost of any clothing Dart should need. If not, let me know. You should probably stop on the way home and get something to eat too. I want you to keep any leftover money . . . for your troubles," Captain Sharp said.

Jarom looked unsure as Kolohe and Dart appeared.

"Dart, I need you to get some good clothing for the voyage ahead. Jarom knows the right place to go, so get what you need. Buy at least one good shirt, pants and shoes."

Dart looked hesitant, so Captain Sharp spoke again.

"I don't know if you have seen the notice in the galley but that applies to you as well. You are a member of my crew. You have a bank account on the Tawny Mane. There are already several shillings in it. However, the clothing is something I am buying for you today. You helped save a member of my crew from harm, Dart. For that I am grateful. Kolohe, go with them. Try to stay out of trouble!"

The three kids were already running before he finished speaking. They were down the gangway, across the dock, and out of sight in seconds.

58

A captain from another ship in the harbor showed up at the ramp and asked to come aboard. He was escorted by Hudson to the captain's quarters where Captain Sharp was making notes for the log book. Hudson knocked on the doorway and announced Captain Claude Huxley of the ship Guinevere. Captain Sharp rose to greet the other captain, inviting him to have a seat.

Captain Sharp did a quick detour to the ring and pulled it twice before sitting down at the maps table.

Maurice appeared quickly and Captain Sharp simply asked for refreshments. After Maurice left, the captain told his well-practiced story of the bell and his cook. Maurice returned shortly with a full tray and served them both before and back out.

"I thought you'd be older," Captain Huxley said.

"I have adequate leadership experience," Captain Sharp said and sighed.

"Heard that before?" Captain Huxley asked.

"A time or two."

"How did you get to be captain, anyway?"

"It's a long story, Captain Huxley."

"That is what captains do best, me lad: spin tales and weave yarns. I would love to hear yours from you, my young captain, and please call me Claude."

So Captain Sharp told his tale starting with his voyage from England on the St. George with Captain Anthony de la Roche. He covered the shipwreck, the lifeboat, and landing on Pukapuka. He spent a little time talking about his years on the island and becoming part of the village. He talked about the landing of the Tawny Mane, the pirates, the raid, and the taking of the ship. He didn't give all the details but he gave enough. He finished with him finding the documents, taking command, and sailing to New Zealand.

"Astonishing," Claude said. "How many pirates were on board the ship when it reached your island?"

Captain Sharp knew what he was really asking, but appreciated his indirect approach, so he answered him honestly. "Twenty-seven."

"Neptune's bones," Claude said. "You have had some experience; I'll give you that. Captain Roche will be delighted to hear you're alive and well."

"Captain Anthony de la Roche is alive?" Captain Sharp almost yelled.

"He was the last time I saw him. That would be two years ago in Naples, picking up some oil and wine. He mentioned that he'd lost a ship and crew, but did not go into details."

"That is extraordinary! If you see him before I do, tell him Gerard and three of his crewmen are alive and well."

"I will do that, my young captain," Claude said. "Now I hear you are headed back to England for the ATC?"

"As soon as our cargo is loaded, we are headed for England, but not exactly for the ATC. We came to an agreement where they still own the ship, but I own the cargo," Captain Sharp said.

"Be careful there my friend, many people say the ATC is the snake that eats its own tail. They take everything they can today with no thought of tomorrow," Claude said, shaking his head.

"Thank you, my friend, I will keep your warning in mind in all my dealings with the ATC," Gerard said. "Where are you headed next?"

"I have double trouble ahead with the horn and hope. We head south to pick up the forties and then east to skirt Cape Horn and then across the Atlantic and around Cape Hope. Then we float up her backside to Madagascar. It's not a route I have done before, but it's essentially a straight line," Claude said.

They talked sailing for a while before Claude got to the reason for his visit. "After Madagascar, we'll push east into the Orient, which brings me to my question. I heard you might have some conch shells for sale. The place we are headed puts much value on the shells for their beauty, but also for their supposed healing powers. I don't believe it myself, but I don't have to. Do you still have any for sale? Do you know the bigger they are, the more healing power they are supposed to have?" Claude said.

"Hold a moment," Captain Sharp said and leaned out the door, yelling at the first person he saw. "Pierre! Find Vaheana and send her to my quarters." Sharp sat back down. He wanted to know more about the shells and asked Claude to continue. Claude said he once found a shell nearly as big as two fists and sold it for a ridiculous price of four pistole! Captain Sharp thought most of their shells were bigger than that.

Vaheana entered and Captain Sharp made the proper introductions. He explained that Captain Huxley was shopping for some conch shells to trade in the Far East. He nodded for Captain Huxley to continue; the man repeated what he said earlier about selling conch shells in the Orient for outrageous rates, including four pistole for one large shell. Captain Sharp said Vaheana was their conch expert and in charge of the sale of the shells. Claude asked her if she had any left to sell or trade and promised to give her top price if she did.

Vaheana looked at Captain Sharp, who nodded. She walked over to the shelf next to them and picked one of the biggest shells they had, wrapped in leaves. She placed it on the table and unwrapped it. The color was just as dazzling as it was the first time Captain Sharp saw it. It was probably as big as four fists

Claude gasped when he saw it. He stared for several seconds before looking back at the shelf where it came from. He saw the other wrapped bundles lining the shelves around the room. Huxley leaned back and smiled. "I should have brought more money." He reached forward and ran his hand along the topside of the shell where the ridge of spiked crowns stood up. "I will pay two escudo per shell, a ridiculous offer on my part I can assure you."

"It's time to go get Arlo," Captain Sharp said.

"You're absolutely right, that's a ridiculous offer," Arlo said. "Two escudos is only about sixteen shillings. It's insulting."

Captain Huxley tried to give Arlo the stink eye, but Arlo seemed impervious to it. Claude rolled up his sleeves and scooted forward in his chair for some serious negotiating. "Four escudos per shell then. That is a fine and generous offer to take these shells off your hands for you."

"Five pistoles each," Arlo said calmly.

Claude jumped out of his chair. "Five pistoles? Are you mad? That's a fortune!"

"We already have a buyer who is offering around four guineas apiece. That buyer is trying to find more money so she can buy all of our stock." Arlo said, reaching out and softly petting the shell on the table in front of him. "It would be a shame if she bought all the shells tonight and left you with nothing."

Captain Sharp looked at Arlo with a new sense of respect. He was good at this. Arlo continued to pet the shell and even pulled it closer to him and further away from Claude. He was actually very good at this.

"Three pistoles and a peso then! You rob me blind and would have me dressed in rags sir!" Claude said, waving his hands in the air and twirling.

"Four pistoles and one escudo per shell," Arlo countered confidently.

"Blasphemy!" Claude yelled. He clutched his heart like he might be having physical chest pain. "You steal food from my children's bellies. They will grow up thin and weak and curse the name Arlo. Four pistoles and one peso, and my ancestors will roll in their graves at this injustice."

Vaheana watched the negotiations between the men with open astonishment. She had seen bartering before, but nothing like this. Their styles could not have been more different. Claude yelled, jumped up and down and waved his arms with animation. Arlo sat still, calm, and had lowered his voice where she had to lean forward to hear it. Both styles had advantages. Both seemed to be working for each man. She didn't understand the money they were talking about, but it seemed like they were moving closer with each volley.

After his last offer Claude collapsed back into his chair as if he had just run a long race. His body was limp, he looked like he was in physical pain. His face showed strain and exhaustion.

Arlo thought about the last offer in a very deliberate way. He stared at the ceiling and stroked his chin, making "hmm" sounds. Claude covered his face with his hands, almost as though he was afraid of what might come next, but he was sneaking peeks between his fingers.

Arlo looked at Vaheana, suggesting that it was her decision to accept or deny the offer. She looked to Captain Sharp, who just made a motion that it was indeed her decision to accept or decline. She took one last look at Claude, who had taken out a crucifix on a chain around his neck. He rubbed the cross and appeared to be praying for mercy. She didn't understand how much money they were talking about, but she knew Captain Sharp trusted Arlo. He was the ship's banker, and would be looking out for all of them. She felt she could trust him too. As much as she didn't want the show to end, she gave a tentative nod to Arlo.

Arlo exploded out of the chair and jumped to his feet, yelling, "Sold! For four pistoles and one peso per shell!"

Claude also jumped out of the chair and embraced Arlo in a hug, on the verge of tears. "Thank you, my friend, thank you, thank you." The men hugged for a few seconds while Claude got himself under control. When they separated, now it was Arlo on the edge of his seat ready to move forward.

"Now then, how many of these huge incredible once-in-a-lifetime conch shells will you be purchasing today?" Arlo asked.

"Every single one I can afford," Claude said, pulling out a bag of money and turning it upside down on the table. The two men counted together like old friends, making stacks of pistoles and pesos.

The pistole was a gold doubloon coin equivalent to sixteen shillings, and the peso was worth four shillings. The agreed upon price of four pistoles and one peso translated to 68 shillings per shell. In the bag, Claude had 49 pistole's and 32 pesos. The pistole converted to 16 shillings each, for a total of 784 shillings. The peso converted to four shillings each, for a total of 128 shillings. All together he had 912 shillings to invest in the conch shells.

Thirteen shells would cost him 884 shillings, and fourteen shells would have cost him 952 shillings. The men talked about this and agreed that 13 was unlucky for both of them. With Vaheana's approval they agreed on 14 magnificent conch shells for the 49 pistoles and 32 pesos. There was much hugging and eye wiping by Claude after the deal was struck and shook on.

Claude invited everyone back to his ship for a tour, but only Captain Sharp and Vaheana agreed. Captain Sharp went onto the deck and rounded up four men to help carry the shells. In short order, the group of seven walked off the Tawny Mane headed for the Guinevere, each person carrying two shells under their arms.

The Guinevere was a large two masted ship called a brigantine. She was 100 feet long and over 200 tons. Captain Huxley explained that her sails could be rigged with either square sails for quartering in wind, or fore and aft round sails for sailing windward. She had twenty cannons plus six swivel guns on the deck rails. Her long sleek design made for easier ocean crossings and less rocking.

Once the shells were dropped off, also in the captain's quarters, Vaheana and the rest of the crew headed back for the Mane. Vaheana received a few strange looks on the Guinevere, but the crew said nothing outright. The captain's quarters were over the top lavish and reminded Sharp of the way Captain Dominic had decorated his own previously. A large four poster bed, heavy multi color drapes, and enough throw pillows to cover the deck if needed.

The men sat down at what appeared to be a meeting and dining table with large ornate chairs with fabric backing. Captain Huxley stomped on the floor three times and then shrugged his shoulders at Captain Sharp and they both laughed. His cook arrived shortly and he ordered wine.

For Captain Sharp, it was nice to talk to and compare notes with another ship's captain, his first chance to do so since working with Captain Roche nearly five years ago. He made sure to drink less wine than Claude, and ask more questions than he answered.

When Captain Sharp got back to the Tawny Mane, there was a note on his desk from Arlo. He went below and found Arlo playing banker in the galley. He had set up a small table off to the side under the shares announcements and there were three men lined up in front of him waiting to make withdrawals. Arlo had a small bag of coins, the ledger, and quill and ink in front of him. Captain Sharp sat down at a nearby table and waited for the men to finish. When the last man had departed, he asked Arlo how everything was going.

"Everything is going well. I was using your office so often that I decided to set up shop out here. I have established the ship's formal banking hours. I am open for one hour at breakfast, one hour at lunch, and one hour at dinner. Otherwise, I would be sitting here all day getting nothing done." Arlo paused, changing subjects. "I wanted to ask you about the shares for the conch sales. When you left to carry the shells over to the other ship, Hans Michael caught up with me and asked what the breakdown was in shares for the conch shells. I told him it was the same as everything else as far as I knew. He recommended that Vaheana get a larger share for this cargo, as it was her sharp eye and her idea that got us this sale. I told him I would talk to you before dividing it up into the crew accounts."

"That sounds reasonable to me. She did think of it herself. I don't know what her shares should be, though. What do you think?" Captain Sharp asked.

"I think a double share is perfectly reasonable for something like this, or you could be very generous and make it tripp's. I think it sends a positive message and motivates the crew to look out for opportunities like this."

"Let's be very generous and give Vaheana tripp's on the conch shells, and Hans Michael double. Everyone else stays the same," Captain Sharp decided.

Arlo made notes in the ledger, working on the breakdown. He talked to himself under his breath, "getting real interesting now."

59

That evening, Benji Braxton returned from his meeting with Mama Ruby. He didn't look as depressed as he had earlier, and the captain hoped he brought good news. Sharp invited him into his quarters and sent August to find Arlo and Hickory. They made small talk until Arlo, Hickory, and August returned and everyone sat at the maps table.

"So where are we, Benji? I was doing some rough numbers earlier and figured we should have close to a 5,000-shilling credit from the coconut trade to Mama Ruby," Captain Sharp said.

Benji looked through his paperwork. "4,983 shillings ta be exact," he replied. "At last count."

"So what does that get us so far?" Captain Sharp asked.

Benji spread the paperwork on the table and pulled out the list he was looking for.

"Hickory and I have estimated the Tawny Mane to have an incoming storage capacity of 96 barrels in the six designated storage areas. Hickory has also mentioned that ya would be willing to use tha brig as additional storage for tha return trip ?" Benji asked, looking up at Captain Sharp, who nodded. "The brig will hold an additional 12 barrels, for a ship wide total of 108 barrels.

"Your original order called for 22 hogsheads of sugar which we have doubled ta 44 barrels. Sugar is trading on tha island for 2 pence a pound. Hogsheads hold 63 gallons of volume, and sugar weighs 7.05 pounds per gallon. So a hogshead of sugar is 444 pounds, 888 pennies, or 74 shillings a barrel. Your 44 barrels of sugar will cost ya 3,256 shillings," Benji said looking up at Captain Sharp.

"Sounds great so far, please continue," Captain Sharp said while making notes. He noticed all of his crew were taking notes also.

Benji went back to his list. "Tobacco is also shipped in tha 63-gallon barrels. Tobacco is trading on the island 3 pence a pound. The hogshead barrels are packed with 1,000 pounds of pressed tobacco each. So a hogshead of tobacco is 1,000 pounds, 3,000 pennies, or 250 shillings a barrel. I have 22 barrels of tobacco available for the price of 5,500 shillings," Benji said looking up again.

Captain Sharp made a keep going motion.

"Your order for 44 barrels of sugar and 22 barrels of tobacco come to a total cost of 8,756 shillings. Now, Mama Ruby an I worked out a deal to apply your credit of 4,983 'coconut' shillings to tha final cost, which brings tha total price down to 3,773 shillings. As your luck would have it, I owed Mama Ruby some cargo that was lost and had an outstanding debt ta her of 121 shillings. She has agreed to waive this debt if I took the 121 shillings off your total cost. So now, ya total for the goods is 3,652 shillings, or 166 guineas." Benji put his papers down and looked up at Captain Sharp.

"I know ya still selling those conches of yours, but I don't think you're going to make up the difference in shells. Do ya want me to fill the order as far as your credit will go with sugar first and then tobacco?" Benji said.

"No, I want the full order," Captain Sharp said. "I'll have the 166 guineas for you the moment you start loading my cargo. Our ship should be empty by midday tomorrow, you can start delivery anytime after that."

Everyone was quiet and looking at Captain Sharp. He looked back down at his notes. "We still have room for another 30 barrels of cargo if I can find them and buy them?" He asked, looking at Hickory.

"Well yes captain, but aren't we out of money?" Hickory asked.

"Firstly, I am not done persuading people just yet. Secondly, I have saved a few coins of my own to invest at the right moment."

Captain Sharp stood up and approached Benji. "Benjamin Braxton, we have a deal. When can I expect you to start delivering my cargo?" He held out his hand and Benji stood and shook it.

"Day after tomorrow?" Benji said.

"Excellent. I will see you then, and I'll have your money ready."

Later that night Gerard went below to find Fetu. When he walked in the galley, he was more than a little surprised by the noise. Gerard stopped at the doorway to watch what was happening. The galley had turned into a miniature city, bustling with activity. Arlo had the bank open. People lined up to make deposits and withdrawals. Jim-Jim, Stephan, and Edmund had collected used coconuts from the kitchen and were braiding coconut fibers into cordage. They already had a pile of finished rolls marked as 100-foot lengths.

Fetu sat at a table, sanding down shell pieces with the help of Kolohe and Dart. Dart wore his new open neck shirt and deck pants made of a good quality material. He was also wearing a new pair of calf high leather boots made out of a soft calfskin. Occasionally, Fetu would stop one of them and correct the technique or check the progress.

At another table Bothari, Vaheana, and Blaed flint-knapped pieces of obsidian into arrowheads and spear tips. Captain Sharp didn't even know that somebody had brought obsidian pieces with them.

Ambrose and Pascoe were crafting some kind of cage with bamboo strips and coconut fibers. It was at least two feet by four feet already. Captain Sharp thought about asking what it was for, but then decided he probably didn't want to know.

Maurice moved from table to table, talking to the crew, topping off drinks and offering suggestions here and there. In the corner, Pierre played a mandolin while Tanner stood next to him with a harmonica.

Captain Sharp stopped at the table with Fetu and asked if he could have a few words. Fetu put his work down, made sure the boys were on track, and then followed Captain Sharp away from the galley. They found a quiet spot and Fetu asked what was on his mind.

"I have a question for you, Fetu. As your brother, not as captain. Keep that in the front of your mind," Captain Sharp said.

Fetu nodded to proceed. "Ask me anything, my brother."

"What are you going to do with your 285 ducats?" Captain Sharp asked.

"Nothing," Fetu said. "I put the bag of coins in my foot locker because I couldn't think of anything to buy."

"I would like to borrow some of your money and invest it in the ship's cargo," Captain Sharp said.

"Okay," Fetu said.

"We will buy some cargo here, sell it in England, and turn your money into even more money," Captain Sharp said.

"Okay," Fetu repeated.

"Any questions?" Captain Sharp asked.

"No," Fetu said. After a few moments he did think of something. "Actually, would you take the whole bag? August said it makes him nervous having it just sitting there."

"No problem, my brother. Let me know if you think of something you would like to buy," Captain Sharp said.

"Will do," Fetu replied, and headed back to his shells.

60

The next morning, Captain Sharp was up early and went down to start waking up the crew. Today was offload day. All hands would be needed on the deck. Maurice was up before everyone. Already, incredible smells wafted from the galley. Sharp ordered his crew to get up, get fed, and get ready to work. The sun would be up in less than thirty minutes. He wanted his crew on deck and ready when the carts and wagons showed up.

Not fifteen minutes after sunbreak, a line of workers and wagons approached the dock. Mama Ruby sat atop the first wagon, bouncing up and down on the bench seat as Tawhiri tried to keep her from bouncing off. There were two large wagons in the first and third spots, with two smaller wagons in the second and fourth spots. One horse pulled each wagon, with one attending it.

While the workers got the first wagon pulled alongside the ship, Hickory organized the crew into supply lines stretching down both staircases. Tawhiri lifted Mama Ruby down and she made her way over to the ship and up the ramp. Captain Sharp welcomed her at the top with a hug and thanked her for working out the trade with Benji. He also told her it wasn't necessary for her to cash in her favor and drop the price even further. He had plenty of money.

"I kno dat child, but it ain't fer nuttin. I plan on sendin sum cargo of ma own wid ya," she said and laughed. "Cargo space on da ship is worth mor den dat favor he owd meh."

"Let's get out of the way and let the crew work." They headed for his quarters. The cargo line was already tossing up coconut heads from both bow and stern.

Arlo paired up with the accountant on Mama Ruby's team. The two men counted the coconuts being loaded into the carts. The first large cart was filled soon enough and sent it on its way. The second smaller cart filled up quickly and also sent up the road. Arlo asked why the different sized carts. The worker explained they only had two of the larger ones. The nearby warehouse had a doublewide dock that could unload two wagons at the same time. Another group of six men at the warehouse were unloading the carts as fast as possible.

They loaded 500 coconut heads into the first large wagon and stopped there, for convenience's sake. The loaders wanted to make sure they didn't have any heads bouncing out on the bumpy road to the warehouse. It took them eighteen minutes to load the first cart while everyone got warmed up. They tried to get 250 in the smaller cart, but had to stop at 225 as they were starting to fall out near the 240 mark. The second cart took only nine minutes to load up and move out of the way. Pierre came out of the galley with his fiddle, sat on a barrel and started playing an up-tempo song. Some of the crew sang lyrics, some just stomped and clapped. Everyone worked faster.

The second large cart filled in sixteen minutes and the small cart after that filled in six. The first large wagon was just pulling back up after being emptied at the warehouse. Arlo ran on the deck and yelled, "That's round one: 1,450 coconuts loaded in forty-nine minutes. Let's go crew!"

Pierre picked up the pace and so did the crew; the large cart filled and turned in fifteen minutes, the small cart in just over six. The second large cart got filled in fourteen minutes and the smaller cart in six. Arlo ran up and yelled to the crew. "Round two: 1,450 more coconuts counted, 2,900 loaded so far, forty-one minutes. Great job, crew!" A small cheer went up, but most of the crew were busy working. The carts were not being unloaded and turned around fast enough. Coconuts were stacking up on the deck. Mama Ruby whispered to Jarom, who took off running down the road.

"Round three: 1,450 counted, 4,350 loaded, thirty-nine minutes. Fantastic job, crew!" Arlo yelled. The carts returned faster now. Captain Sharp asked Mama Ruby what she did. She had sent Jarom to grab a few of his young friends and offered them cash for a few hours of tossing and catching coconuts back at the warehouse. Captain Sharp went and found Maurice in the kitchen and sent him on an errand of his own.

Rounds four and five took thirty-eight minutes and thirty nine minutes respectively. They had worn out Pierre and the fiddle, now Tanner played his drums for the crew and set a good pace.

Hans Michael cut on his hand in the middle of the fourth round. Captain Sharp was nearby and jumped in his place. He had wanted to help earlier, but he was busy entertaining Mama Ruby. She left a bit before; that freed him up to jump in. As round five started, Captain Sharp yelled to the crew of the Tawny Mane: "We are taking a break after round six, everyone keep going and finish strong."

Just after round six started Maurice, Omar, and one of his cooks came down the road with a cart full of lunch supplies. They set up in a shady spot on the docks next to the Tawny Mane. Pierre went out to help them and ran between the cart and ship's galley for additional supplies.

"Round six: 1,450 counted, 8,700 loaded, thirty-eight minutes. Great work, everyone. Lunch break! Everyone out of the hold and onto the docks!" Arlo yelled.

They were more than halfway done and had been going at it for four hours. The tired, dirty crew made their way to the docks, where the cooks served lunch and refreshments for the Tawny Mane crew and Mama Ruby's workers. They cut up roasted lamb and grilled vegetables, covering these with cheese and spices. These were rolled into a flat bread that was easy to eat and portable. Omar brought a huge container full of ice, fruit juice, and sweet wine. Captain Sharp told the crew everyone could have two full mugs, but not a third. He didn't want anyone getting knocked out by drunkenly thrown coconuts.

Everyone finished eating and there was some food left. Captain Sharp saw a group of five street kids fishing at the far end of the dock. He pulled Dart aside and sent him to fetch them. He then thanked Omar and his assistant for helping with lunch. He palmed Omar a few more coins over and above what Maurice had already given him. Omar tried to refuse the extra money, but Captain Sharp said he wasn't done working just yet. Dart returned with five skinny street kids in tow: Four boys and one girl, none older than thirteen. Captain Sharp said they were to get two lamb rolls each, but were only allowed one mug of the fruit wine.

The break was long enough for everyone to get fed and hydrated, but not long enough for them to stiffen up. The crew reformed their lines and the workers returned to their carts. The crew on deck had four carts lined up and waiting and could push as fast as they wanted to start. A refreshed Pierre got them going with some fast fiddling and they started tossing heads.

Round seven was a slow forty-six minutes due to full bellies and fruit wine, but they got into a rhythm after that. Round eight was thirty-nine minutes and round nine was thirty eight minutes, their fastest time yet. Tanner again replaced Pierre, playing the drums. The lower holds were empty. The crew was working on the upper deck so there were crewmen to spare. Men traded out for others who needed a break or a drink of water.

"Round ten! 1,450 counted, 14,500 loaded. Forty minutes! That was our last full round! Nothing but the leftovers now. Let's wrap this up fast, me boys!" Arlo yelled.

The last big wagon took 383 coconuts, but they were finally done and the ship was empty. It took just over eight hours to offload. Everyone was covered in sand and fibers, but nobody took a coconut to the head. Arlo was on the dock talking numbers and money with Mama Ruby's accountant. Captain Sharp got everyone together on the deck for a talk. He thanked them for their hard work so far, but told them they had a little more work to do. New cargo was arriving first thing tomorrow morning, so the storage areas and holds needed to be cleaned and swept out. He wanted this done now, while they were still dirty and everybody was available to help. There were eight cargo areas including the brig, so he told Jim-Jim to divide up the crew and send three people to each area. He would post information about the coconuts as soon as it was available. He told them to get the work finished, then they could collapse until tomorrow. There was some grumbling in the group, but everyone knew it needed to be done. The crew headed below moving much slower than they were this morning.

Arlo eventually came up to give Captain Sharp the numbers. The official count was 14,883 coconut heads. At 4 pennies per head that was 59,532 pennies or 4,961 shillings. Their projected credit with Mama Ruby and Benji was 22 shillings less than they had estimated. Captain Sharp assured him this was no problem and thanked Arlo for the hard work. Maurice had been using some coconuts for cooking, so he knew the count from weeks ago would be off.

Jim-Jim came up on deck twenty minutes later and reported that the ship was clean and the crew was filthy, but they were done and done. Captain Sharp thanked him and told Jim-Jim he wanted to get the crew together for a five-minute meeting, but not until everyone had cleaned up, been fed, and got some down time.

Captain Sharp walked down the docks to the pier at the far end. Two of the kids he had fed earlier were still there fishing. The floating pier was only a foot above the waterline and the two boys had their feet in the water. He said hello to the boys but stayed on the far side of the pier to not disturb their fishing. Captain Sharp pulled his boots off and laid them off to the side. Then he took off his shirt and shook it out before washing it in the cool water. Once it was clean or clean-ish, he wrung it out and laid it on top of his shoes to keep it off the pier. Next, he took off his pants but left his undershorts on. The pants were also washed thoroughly and then wrung out, and carefully laid on top of his other clothes. Captain Sharp stood on the edge of the pier and started stretching his arms over his head. He was getting ready to jump when one of the kids spoke up.
"Ya can't jump in der mister, dar sharks in de bey," said the younger of the two kids.

"I know. The sharks are my friends, we tell each other jokes." With that, he dove off the pier and into the water. It was cold but refreshing. He swam underwater and tried to rub all the sand out of his hair and off his body. While he was underwater, he kept his eyes open. Yes, the sharks were his friends, but maybe these sharks didn't speak Maru.

Stephan and Edmund came walking down the docks towards the pier with the same idea. They got close to the end of the pier and saw a man out in the water diving below the surface and splashing around.

"Is that Captain Sharp out there?" Edmund asked out loud. "What's he doing?"

"He's talkin to sharks," said one of the boys fishing nearby.

"There sharks out there?" Stephan asked.

"O ya, da bey is rotten with dem," the boy reported.

"Maybe we should go further around to the beach side where it's shallow and clear," Stephan said. Edmund agreed and they walked off.

A few minutes later, Captain Sharp swam up to the dock and pulled himself up. He wiped as much water off him as he could and picked up his clothing. He was about to walk away when the younger boy asked if a shark had told him a joke.

"As a matter of fact, one did. Why do sharks swim in salt water?" Captain Sharp asked. Both boys said they didn't know the answer.

"Because pepper water makes them sneeze," he said, and walked away to their laughter.

Later that night, Captain Sharp got most of the crew stuffed in the galley for a short meeting. He had spent the last few minutes talking to Arlo and got what he needed to hear.

"I have a question for the whole crew that each of you need to think about. We sold the bulk of the coconuts today for a decent profit, about 137 shillings per man." Lots of hooting and cheering from the crew. "What I want to know is, what you want done with those shares. I can put it in your accounts and let it sit until we reach England. There is no risk, and all your money will be waiting for you when we get there," Captain Sharp said.

"There is another option available to you that is both unique and risky. As you know, the Tawny Mane was short on funds when we arrived in New Zealand. I have enough money to cover the cargo being delivered tomorrow morning, but our ship is still only two thirds full. We need this ship full when we return to England for maximum profit for everyone. There is a group of investors who want to buy every available inch of cargo space on this ship to send their own goods to England. I am going to sell them that space, but first I wanted to give my crew a chance to use some of that space for their own, for free. Arlo has done a great job so far making us money and keeping our accounts. I trust him completely, and so should you. He recommends that we pool our money and buy all the tobacco we can, take it back to England, and sell it ourselves, and split the profit ourselves."

There were lots of conversations and murmurs starting up.

Captain Sharp held up his hand for quiet. "You don't have to decide right now. Take some time to think about it. You all know how volatile the price of tobacco is. It could be up or down when we return. We could end up losing some money, but we could also end up making money. Arlo is projecting a double or triple return on investments, based on the price when the Tawny Mane left. The choice is yours, and nobody will be forced into it. I am simply sharing an opportunity to make more money."

Hickory asked out loud what the captain was going to do, and everyone quieted down to hear.

"I am going to invest all the free money I have on barrels of tobacco. If anyone is going to make money on this voyage, it should be us, not the Atherton Trading Company."

61

The next morning came way too early for most of the Crew of the Tawny Mane. Lots of groans and sore muscles could be found in the bunkroom. Captain Sharp didn't get up early today; he put August in charge of it. He ordered August to have the night watch wake him up twenty minutes before sunup and then pipe the crew awake about fifteen minutes before sunup. He figured they had more time today since the carts needed to load up at Benji's warehouse before making their way to the Tawny Mane. Unless they loaded up last night, that is. He needed all of the sail-men awake and alert today. They needed to go into the yards and rig some ropes and pulleys to lift and lower barrels into the hull. The sugar barrels were only about five hundred pounds each, but the tobacco barrels had been compressed by weights and screws until a full thousand pounds of leaves were inside: not the kind of thing you could carry down three flights of stairs.

Captain Sharp got up, cleaned up and dressed for the day. He moved August's ring to awake and opened his quarters door. He counted out ducats on his desk when August walked in.

"Everyone is up and moving, Captain, just not fast," he said, smiling.

"Good. It's going to be another long day, maybe a couple of long days depending on how fast we load these barrels."

Captain Sharp finished counting, and put the ducats in a small red bag. He asked August to close the door, then took what was left of the original bag of ducats and put them under the floorboards in the corner of his room. He told August he could reopen the door again, but August hesitated.

"Are those Fetu's ducats?" he asked.

"Yes. I asked if I could borrow them and invest them and he said 'yes'. Said they were just lying in his footlocker anyway," Captain Sharp said.

"Oh good, I was getting worried about that money just sitting in there. I mean, I trust the crew, but still, that's a lot of money," August said.

"A lot of money to everyone but Fetu," the captain said.

"Can I ask why you're not using the gold coins we found hidden in your quarters?" August asked. "I thought that money was supposed to be used to buy the cargo?"

"That's a good question, August, and I don't know the full answer. Your last captain left me a note begging me to keep the money hidden from the Atherton Trading Company. I think keeping it hidden for now is the right thing to do but I'm not even sure why," Captain Sharp said.

"Is the Purple Tiki whispering in your ear?" August asked. August had been asking more questions about the Purple Tiki lately. Captain Sharp tried to explain everything he knew. There were things he knew and understood, but just as many things he didn't know and didn't understand. He kept coming back to the part about the Purple Tiki helping those who listen, but the Purple Tiki never tells you everything he knows.

"He might be whispering, but I can't hear it. This is more like a feeling, and I don't know where it's coming from. Anyway, I don't want to touch that money until we have to, or there is a very good reason to. Once that cat is out of the bag, everyone will be lining up to take it away from us. The longer Tawny Mane hides her secrets, the better for her," Captain Sharp said.

"I agree on that," August said, and opened the door.

Everyone had some coffee in them by the time Benjamin Braxton showed up with his two wagons. These wagons were bigger and stronger than the ones they used yesterday, pulled by two oxen each. Each wagon carried only six barrels, sitting upright and tied down to keep from tipping. They also moved much slower and more cautiously than yesterday's carts. A group from the Mane went down onto the docks to meet Benji and his men.

Captain Sharp, Bothari, Arlo, Hickory, Jim-Jim and August stood on the dock next to the ship when Benji's first wagon came to a stop in front of them. Benji had a worried look on his face and was looking over his shoulder. He climbed down and shook Captain Sharp's hand and started speaking in a low voice.

"I didn't have a choice in this, and I hope there are no hard feelings. I am really caught in da middle here," Benji said.

"Caught in the middle of what?" Captain Sharp asked.

Just then a large group of men came rushing around the corner of the ship. The Atherton Trading Company was well represented by Samual Astor, Head of South Pacific operations. Caleb Mason, representing the English Branch. Lawyer Tobin Wayne, and banker Harvey Lockland. There were six constables armed with flintlocks running with them and they came up on the captain and crew quickly. There were shouts from the ship but Captain Sharp didn't look that way, he kept his cool and tried to keep his wits.

The constables surrounded Sharp and his men with guns leveled while Samual Astor walked up, smiling. "I bet I am the last person you wanted to see right now," Mr. Astor said smugly.

The constable immediately in front of Sharp read from an official parchment document he was holding. "Captain Sharp, you are under arrest for grand theft from the Atherton Trading Company. You will be taken to a holding facility until time that you are seen before the magistrate to answer for your charges."

"What evidence do you have of this theft?" Captain Sharp asked.

"You're holding it," said a smiling Harvey Lockland. "In each bag of coins sent from England there are a few with special marks on them to identify them as belonging to the ship."

Samuel Astor started talking now. "We knew when you had to pay for your cargo that you would use the gold guineas you stole and hid on the ship. This will prove that you stole from the Tawny Mane, the Atherton Trading Company, and England itself," he finished smugly.

"I see," Captain Sharp said. "Constable, what is the penalty for grand theft from ship, company, and England?"

The man in front of him was at least educated. "The penalty for any theft over 99 shillings is at least five years in prison."

"I see," Captain Sharp said. "Constable, what is the penalty for simple assault?"

The constable looked amused, but answered the question. "Seven days in jail or a ten pound fine."

"I see," Captain Sharp said. "Constable, what is the charge for false accusations . . ."

"I have heard enough!" Samuel Astor yelled. "Let's get on with this." He pushed his way in front of the constable and got into the captain's face. "I want that money, and I want it right now!"

"I will gladly hand over the money, but first let my crew out of this ridiculous circle of death. Your constables are pointing loaded guns at innocent men and risking a murder by carelessness," Captain Sharp said.

The constable thought about this for a moment, then waved the rest of the Tawny Mane crew sideways with the muzzle of his gun. "The rest of you men move over there." Three of the constables moved the group off to the side and had the good sense to lower their weapons.

"Why don't you have one of your men bring over a table so I can dump out the coins. Then Mr. Astor and Mr. Lockland can look for the specially marked coins. I would also like Benjamin Buxton to observe as a neutral third party," Captain Sharp said. "I would appreciate it if you lowered your guns as well. I am not going anywhere, and you have six armed men here."

"Don't trust him!" Mr. Astor yelled. "He is a liar and a thief!"

"Neither of which has been proved as of yet," Captain Sharp said calmly.

The head constable looked back and forth between the two men. He lowered his gun and tucked it into his holster. The other guards followed suit and he told one of his men to bring over a table. The guard found a small table and carried it over to the captain.

"Can I ask what this mark looks like before we begin? I don't want Mr. Astor and Mr. Lockland to claim that every random scratch or nick on my coins were put there on purpose. These coins probably have hundreds of different marks on them."

"Of course," said Harvey Lockland. "It is listed right there on the arrest document. Our sister bank in England marks a few gold guinea coins with three parallel lines on the face near the date in every bag of coins."

The guard had the table placed in front of the group. Benji walked over to join them. Everyone on the dock was listening and staring at the group around the table. Captain Sharp reached into his shirt and withdrew the bag with coins inside. Mr. Astor practically drooled with anticipation. Captain Sharp slowly untied the top of the bag, loosened the strings, and lowered it to the table to dump it out low and slow. The 188 gold ducats spilled onto the table in a neat pile.

As the ducats first came into view, Mr. Astor's eyes lit up and he smiled. After a few seconds, he realized the size and the color were wrong. He reached forward for a coin, but Captain Sharp was ready for it and knocked his hand aside instead.

Captain Sharp directed his comments to the constable. "Do you see any gold guineas with three parallel marks on the face near the date?

The constable leaned forward and pushed the pile around with the end of his billy club. He made a harumph sound and put the billy club back in its holster opposite the pistol. "No, I do not," he said and turned to look at Mr. Astor. "What do you have to say for yourself sir?"

"They were supposed to be here! He was supposed to have them!" Mr. Astor shouted. "We need to search the whole ship. He has the money hidden on his ship. I just know it!" Mr. Astor said.

"I think not," the constable said. He looked at Captain Sharp. "I am sorry to have wasted your time, captain."

"It's not a complete waste," Captain Sharp said, and then punched Mr. Astor in the face as hard as he could. Astor fell backwards and landed on his butt hard. His nose bloomed and the blood got all over his ruffled collar.

"Arlo!" Captain Sharp yelled. "I need ten pounds to pay a simple assault fine!" He turned to look at the constable, who had put his hand back on his billy club. He forced his eyes back to normal and spoke calm and clearly. "I wish to file false accusations charges against Samual Astor, Caleb Mason, Tobin Wayne, Harvey Lockland, and the Atherton Trading Company. My lawyer is Joshua Stevedore, Solicitor of the court. He can have the charges drawn up and presented to your office by the end of today," Captain Sharp said.

"Very good, sir. I think we can forget about the assault fine for now. I didn't see anything, and it's his word against yours," the constable said with a grin.

"Thank your sir, that is very kind of you," Captain Sharp said and the men shook hands, "can I interest you in some breakfast?"

Benji and Arlo supervised counting out the ducats and loaded them back in the bag. Benji tied a leather cord around the bag, hung it around his neck, and tucked it into his shirt. He ordered his crew to start unloading barrels onto the dock next to the ship. Benji walked over to Captain Sharp and apologized again. Captain Sharp waved it off and said he understood that he was stuck in the middle.

Captain Sharp found Dart and Kolohe and sent them on a mission. He gave them directions and a description of Usain's house. Once there they were supposed to ask where Joshua Stevedore lived and go there. They were to ask Joshua if he was available to stop by the Tawny Mane at his leisure today.

The barrels loaded at much slower speed than the coconuts. The crew had two different lifts working fore and aft. The barrels were picked up off the dock, raised over the railing, and then lowered through the open hatches and down into the hull. Each barrel took about ten minutes from pickup to being untied below. Once untied below, a group of men wrestled them into position and braced them so they would not move or break open during travel and storms. The wagons left to get the second load after stacking all their barrels on the deck. When the two wagons returned, one had six barrels and the other had four. All twenty-two barrels of tobacco were loaded in less than three hours. Dart and Kolohe returned after forty minutes and reported that Joshua was tied up for most of the day, but said he would stop by later in the afternoon.

Benji asked Captain Sharp how much more they wanted to load today. The two men decided on two more trips, which meant twenty-four barrels of sugar. The two carts left and came back less than thirty minutes later each loaded up with six barrels of sugar. This part went just a little faster with the reduced weight of the sugar. The first twelve barrels were loaded into the ship in just over an hour and the carts had just made it back with the last twelve barrels of the day. These took another hour to load and Captain Sharp was able to tell everyone they were done for the day. Benji and Captain Sharp shook hands one more time and said they would see each other tomorrow morning for the remaining twenty barrels of sugar. Captain Sharp requested no more surprise visitors tomorrow and Benji laughed and said he would do his best.

A short time later, Captain Claude Huxley showed up with six of his crewmen in tow. They were welcomed onto the deck and Captain Sharp came out of his quarters to greet them.

"Captain Huxley, so good to see you again. What can I do for you?" Captain Sharp asked.

"I was talking to my crew about selling the conch shells for profit once we get to the Orient. After talking about my last trip, some of the men with money decided they also wanted to invest in the shells, so they pooled their money together. These men have come up with 51 pistole together which should buy them another twelve conch shells, if you still have some for sale that is?" Captain Sharp smiled and told Claude this was his lucky day. He sent two men to find Arlo and Vaheana.

Usain, Marcus, and Joshua showed up together and were welcomed aboard the Tawny Mane. Captain Sharp had warned the Koa on the ramp that their investors would be stopping by and to be nice and helpful. Hudson showed them into the captain's quarters where Captain Sharp greeted them and invited them to sit. He rang for Maurice. The cook walked in less than a minute later with a tray already full of tea, four cups, snacks, sweetbread, and pastries. His cook, as usual, was well-informed. Maurice got to hear Captain Sharp tell his bell story again and added his own comments here and there. After pouring tea, he asked the group to ring if they needed anything else and backed out of the room, shutting the door.

Captain Sharp told the men he appreciated them stopping by to talk as he had updated news about the available cargo space on the ship.

Usain held up a hand for him to stop talking, so he did. Usain leaned forward and looked serious. "First, you need to tell us about breaking Astor's nose. Every. Single. Detail."

The three friends started laughing.

Captain Sharp was embarrassed but took them through the story with enough detail to make Fetu proud. When he told about yelling for his banker to come pay the fine Marcus slapped his thigh and said, "I told you so!" and roared with laughter. He leaned so far back in his chair Captain Sharp thought he would fall over.

Usain explained that one of Marcus's brothers was a constable and had stopped by and told him the story already, but it was good enough to hear a second time. Captain Sharp was embarrassed by the whole event but explained the punch was based on the culmination of all the abuse and harassment he had been given by Astor since arriving in New Zealand.

Captain Sharp asked Joshua about pressing charges against the men and company for making false accusations. He wanted to know what his options were, if it would be worth the effort.

Joshua said, "probably not" and he would not likely get any money out of it, but there might be some legal advantages to doing it anyway. Joshua said he would do some research tonight and get back to him tomorrow.

The men asked a few more questions about the event, including the look on Astor's face when he realized the coins were ducats and not guineas. Captain Sharp said the look on his face was worth the delay and hassle all by itself. The punch however, paid for all.

Once they got back to business, Captain Sharp told them the ship should have all of her cargo onboard by tomorrow afternoon. When that was completed, a total of 66 of the 108 available barrels spaces would be filled.

Next, he told the investors that he had invited his crew to pool their own money and invest in some additional barrels of tobacco if they could find some. The ship's banker Arlo said this had the highest profit potential and recommended it to the captain. He estimated that the crew could buy twelve additional barrels for themselves.

This left space for thirty more barrels to be bought and loaded on the Tawny Mane. The captain reported that Mama Ruby expressed interest in buying some of the space, but he didn't know how much. He would check with her tomorrow, after the cargo was loaded.

Captain Sharp, Arlo and Hickory had not yet decided how much to charge for the space, transportation, and sale of extra barrels in England. However, if the three men could help the crew locate some good quality tobacco at a reasonable price, it would significantly reduce the cost of the barrel space for them. Marcus said he might know somebody, and would get back to them soon.

Usain told Captain Sharp to check in with Mama Ruby about the remaining barrel space available and then let them know. The group of friends moved onto other subjects and talked and drank late into the evening.

Captain Sharp found Maurice reading in his bunk as the galley was closed for the night. The captain asked to have a word in private with the cook and led him back up to the galley with a lantern. Once there he told Maurice he needed the two bags of coins for about ten minutes. Maurice led him into the storage area behind the galley and over to a coffee barrel. The bags were pushed down into the soft coffee flakes well below the surface level. He pulled them out, shook the coffee off, and handed them over to Captain Sharp.

"Thank you, Maurice," Captain Sharp said. "I will bring these shortly. I'll want them returned to this hiding spot."

"It makes no difference to me Captain Sharp, it's your money," Maurice replied. He headed back to his bunk.

Captain Sharp headed up to his quarters. Once inside with the door locked, he dumped the first bag of coins out on the map table and went through each coin one by one. He found five of the marked gold guineas from the bank and set those aside. He put five of his own gold guineas back into the pile to replace the missing ones, and refilled the bag. Next he dumped out the second bag and went through the search process again. He found five marked coins in this bag as well. He set these aside and put five more of his own gold guineas back in the second bag, to keep the count even. He took the ten specially marked bank guinea and put them in the hidden wall compartment near the door. Then he took the two bank bags and headed back to the galley and the coffee barrel. Maurice's hiding place was as good as any.

62

Rain started falling lightly during the night and came down steadily by morning. The sun was hidden by clouds, but when the sky started to lighten up in the east, the night watch came by the captain's quarters and knocked three times fast. It was the wake up notice he had requested before going to bed. Captain Sharp got up and dressed for the weather. One of the jackets he had kept from Captain Dominic's closet was heavy and waterproof. He wore that one today. He went onto the deck to check the sky, the condition of the road, and his men stuck out in the rain.

They kept two men on watch at night while in port. One was posted at or near the top of the gangway. The second man could be anywhere on the deck, as long as he could see and keep watch of the first man. Perkins stood at the top of the ramp wearing a good rain coat and foul weather hat. Pascoe leaned in the covered doorway, between the captain's quarters and the armory door. He was out of the weather for the most part but looked cold. Captain Sharp bid him good morning and asked if his shift was just ending or beginning.

"Just ending sir, as soon as its light and the day watch comes up, Perkins and I are done," Pascoe said.

Captain Sharp went back inside his cabin and searched around for a rain cap. As it turned out, he didn't have one. He went back onto the deck and told Pascoe he was relieved and to head down and get warm. He also asked him to start pushing the morning crew out of their bunks. They probably had half an hour before Benji and his carts showed up. Pascoe thanked him and headed down the stairs. Captain Sharp went over to Perkins and told him he was relieved and could go below. The captain also asked where he could find a rain hat like that. Perkins offered his own to use while the captain was on deck, but the captain refused. A hat was a very personal thing. When Perkins headed below, Captain Sharp was alone on the deck in the morning quiet. Water dripping off the yards was the only sound in the quiet morning.

Hickory came up dressed for the rain and also had a good rain hat on his head. The two men talked about being extra careful today with the wet ropes and potentially slippery barrels. They only had twenty barrels of sugar to load, so only two trips for Benji and his carts. Captain Sharp told Hickory to keep most of the crew below and dry if they could, no sense in all of them getting soaked. Hickory headed back down as more of the crew came up holding cups of coffee and tea.

Benji and his crew came into view, working their way slowly towards the docks. They only had four barrels on each wagon instead of the six they hauled yesterday. The oxen were sure-footed in the rain and mud and were in no hurry. Captain Sharp, August, and Hickory met them on the side of the ship and Captain Sharp acted like he was looking around for more constables. Benji and his driver laughed and assured the crew that it was only them today . . . as far as he knew. Captain Sharp commented on the lighter load today.

"Can't go much over two thousand pounds in tha rain and mud. Tha wheels sink an even an ox has trouble pulling them forward. This will mean one extra trip today but it was a light day anyway. Five wagons, twenty barrels, and we should have you buttoned up in a few hours."

"All right, let's get to it," Hickory said.

Benji's crew carefully took the barrels off the carts and placed them on the wood dock next to the ship. The ship's crew roped onto them and hoisted the barrels into the air. The men were careful to keep the barrels low over the rail. They worked slow and steadily and had the first eight barrels loaded in forty-five minutes. The warehouse workers came back with the second load just as the last two barrels from the first load were being lowered down into the hatches.

The second shipment was delivered and loaded without incident. The rain had not let up. By this time the crewmen working outside were as wet as they could get. The last cart got mired in some soft mud right where the road butted up to the dock. Six men from the Tawny Mane walked out and helped lift the cart as the oxen pulled it forward onto the wood planks. Once that was done, it only took another twenty minutes for them to load up the last four barrels.

Hands were shaken and the two groups parted ways. Captain Sharp thanked Benji for his help and flexibility throughout the process. Benji thanked him back and apologized for all the hassles they encountered along the way. Captain Sharp headed back inside to dry off and warm up. His ship was over half full now. They were that much closer to sailing for England, and home.

Later that afternoon Captain Sharp, Arlo, and August slogged through town and up to Mama Ruby's house. She sat in a rocker on her front porch, watching the rain. She invited the men up under the covering and they all sat down on the steps.

Captain Sharp started to bring her up to date on the cargo deliveries, but she stopped him and wanted to hear about the fight with Astor first. He told her it wasn't much of a fight, but told her about it anyway. He gave her the same version he had given his three friends last night and she howled with laughter.

"Ida given anythin to hav seen dat. Lordy," Mama Ruby said, wiping her eyes.

Once that was out of the way, he asked her about the remaining cargo space on the Tawny Mane. She explained that she was putting the finishing touches on her deal with her contacts, but said most likely she would be shipping six barrels of sugar and four barrels of tobacco. She hoped to know for sure by the end of the day today, and have the cargo delivered in the next two days.

Sharp told her he was going to sell the remaining cargo space on the Maine to Usain, Marcus, and Joshua. She thought this was a fine idea and told him so. Then Sharp thanked her for her help and asked if there was anything he could do for her in return. She said not right now, but she might need a favor from him in the future. Gerard said he would do what he could to help her out. He told Arlo and August they could head back to the ship as he was going to make more stops on his way back through town. The two crewmen waved goodbye and walked away while Gerard and Mama Ruby rocked in their chairs on the porch.

"So exactly how much of the black market do you control Mama Ruby," Gerard asked casually.

The old woman chuckled to herself before speaking.

"Does it matter?" she asked.

"Not really, I was just wondering," Captain Sharp said. "I think you're a good person and fundamentally honest, or I would not have done business with you."

"Thank ya child," she said, "tis a knife edge I walk evera day."

"I guess what I was really wondering is how you get started in something like that?" Gerard said.

"Thinkin of a career change ar ya?" Mama Ruby said and cackled.

"No, nothing like that. I'm just trying to learn all I can about the world, and especially the hidden parts and secret rules," Gerard said.

Mama Ruby thought about this before answering. "Ya still young lil lamb, and hav not seen much of de world, but it's a complicated mess. Tis hard being good an fair when ya be the only one playin by de rules. Ya have to carve out a nich for yaself to survive. Ya hav to make rules for yaself dat ya ken live with, and ken sleep with. I neva planned dis path for maself, but I didnt get here by choice. I got pushed here ya see, cheated, robbed and pushed til I had no choice. Ya dont kno what ya capable of till ya pushed into a corner wid no way out. Only den will you kno what ya ken do. What wud ya do to keep ya crew alive child?"

"Almost anything," Gerard replied.

"It's da word almost that gets ya. Der was a time I wud do almost anythin to protect ma family. Den came a day when it wasnt enuf, an I had to do more. Tis a hard life wid hard choices, but when ya family life is on de line, tis an easy choice. Ya do it, and ya move forward. Ya protect what is important, and ya try an stay on de side of de knife widout blood on it," Mama Ruby said.

"That sounds like good advice Mama Ruby, thank you," he said, "I guess nobody knows for sure what they will do when backed into a corner like that."

"Dat is where ya wrong ma lil lamb, I think ya would do anythin to save ya men. Ya mey not want to think about it yet, but de truth is da truth. Everybody got some darkness in dem, your darkness will keep ya crew safe," she said.

They rocked in silence on the porch awhile while Gerard thought about what she said. She was right of course; he would do anything to keep his crew safe. He could also choose to be as fair and honest as he could as long as he could. There was just one more thing he wanted to know. He asked Mama Ruby where he could go to get a really good rain hat.

Captain Sharp walked back to the ship proudly wearing his new felt rain cap. He had sent Arlo and August ahead and told them he wanted to stop off at the hat store. The haberdashery Mama Ruby recommended was overflowing with hats of all styles and sizes. The proprietor, Miss Charlotte Hallewell fussed over Captain Sharp, as he was the only customer on this rainy day. Once he told her exactly what he wanted, she led him over to some functional rain hats designed for outdoor work. He found a sturdy gray felt cavalier hat with a wide brim and buttons on both sides of the hat. The brim could be left down for maximum rain protection, or buttoned up on the sides to channel the rain well away from his face and neck. It also had an adjustable chin strap to keep it from flying away. He paid full price despite her hints that she was willing to negotiate. He got the impression that bartering was her entertainment for the day, and she was sad to see him leave so soon.

When Sharp boarded the ship, the guard told him Joshua was waiting for him in his quarters. Captain Sharp asked how long he had been waiting and was relieved to hear it was only about fifteen minutes. He headed for his quarters, hoping Joshua was not left alone or upset about the delay.

Walking into his quarters he found August, Dart, and Kolohe sitting at the table with Joshua. All of them were laughing. They had tea and snacks laid out in front of them and August was wrapping up his story.

"We didn't know Bothari threw him a cork float until later, but you could have heard a pin drop on that deck," August said. "Then Captain Sharp said to Jim-Jim, 'man overboard,' and walked away just as casual as you please. The crew didn't know whether to spit or go blind."

"That is fantastic," Joshua said, standing to greet Captain Sharp. "I took the chance you would be here and stopped by, Captain. I should have sent a runner."

"Not at all. I am happy I was not further delayed. I trust my men have kept you entertained?"

August, Kolohe, and Dart started giggling and nodded as a group. Joshua also smiled and nodded the affirmative. "You have some terrific stories on this ship, Captain Sharp. Your crew does you credit. I was unaware that Dart had joined your crew. I have used him myself in the past as a runner and courier. He is a good lad. I am happy for his new beginning," Joshua said.

"Thank you, Mr. Stevedore," Dart said, as he and Kolohe got up to leave.

"You're an employed crew member of a well-respected ship now Dart, please call me Joshua," he said. He shook hands with Dart, who looked amazed by his change in status.

August asked if he was needed for notes, or could he take his leave. Captain Sharp got the impression he wanted to go, so he excused him. August took one of the trays with empty cups and plates and shut the door behind him on the way out.

"You should be proud of your young crewmen, Captain Sharp. They hold you in high regard and their loyalty is evident. Whatever else you have done, you have earned their respect."

"Thank you, Joshua, that was one of my goals. Hearing it from a neutral third party is gratifying. What can I help you with?" Captain Sharp asked.

"Tis I who shall be helping you today. I did some research last night into false accusations and found what I was looking for. With your approval, we shall move forward with legal proceedings against the four men and the Atherton Trading Company. We will seek to recover damages in the amount of five pounds from each individual, and five pounds from the Atherton Trading Company. Our lawsuit for slander and libel will be to repair the harm done to your reputation while in New Zealand. They have a choice of admitting guilt and settling to our demands, or we move forward in court and seek damages in the amount of five hundred pounds each. With the written warrant they signed and the testimony of the constable, they will lose without a doubt," Joshua said.

"Twenty-five pounds is hardly worth the hassle. It probably won't even pay for your time. Why even bother to proceed?"

"You're right; it won't even pay for my time. After this you will still need to pay me another twenty pounds on top of their money, which I am keeping by the way," Joshua said. "The reason you are doing it is because they will take the easy way out and pay you five pounds each rather than risk losing more money. The case will be decided in your favor and closed. They will leave the court thinking they got lucky, and in a way they did. You will leave the court with signed documents by the Atherton Trading Company admitting that they lied, made false allegations, and tried to get you wrongfully arrested and terminated. These documents will also show that they were found guilty of these crimes in a court of law, and were forced to pay you compensation for their illegal activities. Do you think having this paperwork would be to your benefit when you return to England? Do you think this paperwork would give you a certain level of protection in England? Do you think this paperwork will help when the Atherton Trading Group tries to slip out of the contract they already signed with you?" Joshua asked.

"Let me get you your twenty pounds," Captain Sharp said.

Just after dark, a man on a horse galloped through town, riding it out onto the docks and down the slip next to the Tawny Mane. Hooves clapped noisily on the deck, drawing the crew's attention. The rider stopped at the bottom of the gangway and tied the horse off away from the edge. Captain Sharp walked out to see the horse and saw it was Marcus hurrying up the ramp for a visit. He went to greet Marcus and asked if he would like to come in for some dinner and drinks.

"Another time perhaps. I am in a hurry and so are you. I found twelve barrels of tobacco that needed to be moved immediately. They are being sold at a discount because the barn they are being stored in is flooding. The owner is letting them go for 220 shillings a barrel if I buy them tonight. I have two carts headed for the barn already. What I need from you is money, specifically 2,640 shillings, right now," Marcus said.

"Give me a few minutes, I'll be right back," Captain Sharp went into his quarters and did some quick math. 2,640 shillings was roughly 126 guineas. He went to his personal stash and pulled out 126 gold coins and put them in a bag. He tied off the top and put the bag on a leather cord to go around Marcus's neck. It needed to be secure if he was riding horseback. All kinds of things could be shaken loose from a man riding a horse. He came back out on the deck a few minutes later and handed the bag to Marcus. "126 guineas, or about 2,646 shillings," Captain Sharp said.

"Fantastic, if all goes well your cargo should be here in about an hour," Marcus said, walking down the ramp where he untied his horse.

"And if all doesn't go well?" Captain Sharp asked.

Marcus vaulted up into the saddle. "Then it could be anytime during the night. Who needs sleep anyway?" Marcus trotted the horse to the end of the dock. Once they hit the stone road, he kicked its sides and they shot off into the darkness. He sent a crewman on deck to find Jim-Jim. It would be a long night for everyone.

The two wagons made their way down to the docks about two hours later. The driver stopped at the end of the road, as he had no idea where he was supposed to go. Captain Sharp sent Hickory and Jim-Jim out to meet them and directed them to the side of the ship. He told the ropers to get ready and sent word down into the hull they had cargo coming in. After some hand waving and shouting the first cart was backed up and they started to load the ship.

The rain had stopped earlier, which gave them a break to work in. The crew took advantage and worked fast to get the barrels on board. The twelve barrels were loaded in just over an hour. The carts were sent on their way, and the hatches were resecured. The crew was excused for the night and everyone went below.

In the middle of the loading, the captain found Arlo and told him they had bought the twelve barrels for 220 shillings each. The accountant was very excited and said they were already on their way to turning profit back in England.

63

Captain Sharp was just getting dressed the next morning when a crewman knocked on the door. "Carts coming down the hill, captain, probably headed for us. Just giving you a heads up."

"Thank you, I'll be out in a minute. You better get Hickory and Jim-Jim up and moving. Tell them the day started without us," Captain Sharp said and dressed faster.

In less than five minutes, the carts were making their way out onto the dock. The crew of the Tawny Mane rallied and was opening hatches, rigging ropes, and running all over the place. The one thing they all had in common was hair going in every direction.

Jarom sat in the front wagon, so Captain Sharp figured this was Mama Ruby's cargo. He went out to talk with the driver and confirmed they had six barrels of sugar and four barrels of tobacco. The men on the carts were able to lift and set down the sugar barrels on the side of the ship, but the tobacco barrels would have to wait for the ropes. Hickory was making up time, yelling orders left and right. The crew was scrambling but getting it done fast. They had ropes on barrels within minutes of them hitting the dock. In less than an hour the last barrels were going down into the hold.

Captain Sharp spotted Marcus riding his horse back down the hill at a very leisurely pace. He sent his crew off to wake up with some coffee and breakfast. He walked out to meet his investor on the docks and see what was up. Marcus rode all the way out to the ship again and tied it off in the same place. He shook hands with the captain and asked if last night's cargo made it. Captain Sharp said it did, thanking him for finding the tobacco and the deal for his crew.

"Speaking of deals, I happened upon another deal last night for Usain, Joshua, and myself. How soon can you be ready for our twenty barrels of cargo?" Marcus asked with a silly grin on his face.

"Anytime, actually. We just finished loading Mama Ruby's ten barrels. Your twenty barrels is all we have left to load," Captain Sharp said.

"I'm glad to hear you say that," Marcus said and glanced back at the road.

Captain Sharp looked that way too and didn't see anything, yet. "How long?"

"About twenty minutes, maybe less," Marcus replied. "It was too good of a deal, I couldn't pass it up."

"Hudson!" Captain Sharp yelled up onto the watchman on deck. "Get me Hickory and Jim-Jim. Move it!"

Hudson saluted and headed below.

"Now, let's talk about shipping fees and commissions. How about we talk over breakfast from that amazing cook of yours?" Marcus suggested.

They walked up the gangway just as Hickory and Jim-Jim came topside.

"You tell them," Captain Sharp said.

"Um, good morning gentleman. I was fortunate enough to buy some cargo last night at about three in the morning, in the dark, for a discounted price. It's on its way now and should be here in fifteen to twenty minutes," Marcus said, trying to sound happy about it.

Jim-Jim and Hickory groaned. Captain Sharp smiled.

"Twenty barrels total: twelve of tobacco, eight of sugar," Marcus said.

"Let's get it done. After this we are full up and can sail for home," Captain Sharp said.

That left the crewmen with a smile as they headed down to the galley to start shaking out the crew for another load up. Captain Sharp asked them to send up Arlo and August to his quarters. He led Marcus that way and started thinking about how soon they could sail.

Arlo had some books open and was laying out standard shipping costs for cargo transportation across an ocean. Everyone else took notes and tried to figure out what the best deal was for their side.

The industry standard for most trading companies was 80 shillings per ton, which is 2,000 pounds of weight. So a 1,000 pound barrel of tobacco would be 40 shillings, and a 500 pound barrel of sugar would be 20 shillings.

Some companies were going with a flat 15% fee based on the price of the cargo. The trading company got 10%, and the ship earned 5%. Under this system, the fee for a barrel of tobacco at 250 shillings was 37 shillings and 6 pence. The fee for a barrel of sugar at 74 shillings was 11 shillings and 2 pence.

In the end, Captain Sharp wanted to show his appreciation to Marcus for finding them tobacco at a great deal. They agreed on a 10% fee based on the price of the goods. This went a long way toward thanking Marcus for finding them the cargo at such a good deal.

The twelve barrels of tobacco were purchased by Marcus at 220 shillings per barrel. The shipping cost was 22 shillings a barrel, or 264 shillings total. The eight barrels of sugar were purchased at 70 shillings per barrel. The shipping cost was 7 shillings per barrel, or 56 shillings total. The total shipping cost for Marcus and his partners was 320 shillings.

"I would rather make a friend than a shilling, but that sounds fair to me," Captain Sharp said.

"I agree, it is more than fair," Marcus said. The two men shook on it. Marcus pulled out a coin bag and started counting out money. Arlo was already figuring out what each person got in their crew accounts.

On the deck, the crew was already loading the barrels onto the ship. Marcus's people arrived with four carts loaded down with barrels. They lined up next to the ship and there was a flurry of activity. The lighter barrels were lifted down onto the dock, while the heavier barrels waited for the ropes to pull them off the carts. As soon as each cart was emptied, it would head off and disappear into town. In two hours', time, the Tawny Mane was full of barrels.

Marcus left once business was completed, but said he would see them before they sailed. The last of the carts cleared the docks and headed down the road. The hatches were secured for sailing. Captain Sharp called for a meeting of all crew onboard to meet in the galley in five minutes.

The galley was packed with all seats taken and crew standing around the perimeter. Captain Sharp moved to the front, where he could be seen by most and raised his hand for quiet. "We are fully loaded and ready to sail for England. Does anyone have unfinished business in New Zealand that we need to delay?" Captain Sharp asked.

Nobody said anything.

"Cornelius, Vaheana, any issues we need to know about?" the captain asked.

"No sir," Cornelius said. "We are well ahead of bad weather. It should be good sailing with a good push from the forties. I think 92 days will put us in England."

"Cornelius says the screaming forties will throw us around pretty good. We need to brace the barrels better to keep them from moving around and maybe breaking open on the walls," Vaheana said.

"Okay, figure it out. Let's get something in place now and figure out a backup plan if that doesn't work. Any cargo that breaks is money we lose," Captain Sharp said.

"Hickory, anything we still need before sailing?" Captain Sharp asked.

"I wouldn't mind one more rundlet barrel of powder for target practice, but we have enough, unless we go to war with France." Hickory said to the laughter of the crew.

"Go buy us another barrel. Arlo will get you the money. Maurice, do we have enough food and water?" Captain Sharp asked.

"Oui Oui we do, full to the gills. I would like to get some fresh fruit and vegetables right before we leave, though," Maurice said.

"Good, make that happen. Arlo will give you the money. Does anyone else have anything else?" Captain Sharp asked.

Nobody spoke.

"Alright, then. Today is Tuesday. We sail for England Thursday morning. That's less than two days away. Get your shopping done today and tomorrow. Be back on board by tomorrow night. It's time to head home," Captain Sharp said and the crew cheered.

"There is one more thing, Captain Sharp," Jim-Jim said as everyone quieted back down. "The crew has decided unanimously to trust you and Mr. Arlo regarding the investment of our monies in the ship's cargo. You've done right by us so far, and we reckon that will continue. Plus you're the luckiest son-of-a-gun we have ever known."

64

Captain Sharp was up early and ready to hit the town. He woke August, Kolohe and Dart and told them they were coming with him. They had a quick breakfast, then walked through town towards Mama Ruby's house. There was no answer at the door, so apparently she was already up and gone somewhere.

Captain Sharp asked Dart to lead them to Joshua's house. Joshua lived in a modest house at the edge of town. Much smaller than Usain's house, but bigger than his neighbors. Joshua was home and welcomed them in with a smile. He picked up a fine leather folder and handed it to Captain Gerard.

"The court documents we talked about, all signed, sealed and delivered. I have also included a bill of lading for the goods we are shipping with you. There is also legal authorization for you to sell our cargo on our behalf. You should find everything you need in there," Joshua said.

"Thank you for all your help, you have been a good friend to us. I will get your money back to you as soon as possible," Captain Sharp said.

"That is one of the few things I am not worried about Captain Sharp. I bid you fair winds and a following sea," Joshua said. They all shook hands and headed back towards town.

About fifty feet away from Joshua's house Captain Sharp stopped them at an intersection for a talk. "Dart, I have a question for you. As your Captain, I want an honest answer. Is there anyone you should be telling that you're leaving tomorrow on a ship for England? You could be gone for months, years, or forever. If you are important in somebody else's life, you need to tell them, and you need to do it now," Captain Sharp said.

Dart looked at the ground for a while, and then looked back up. "I should probably tell my Granny. She is the only one who cares."

"We will come with you as far as you want. We can stand beside you or wait outside. Whatever you want. Let's go," Captain Sharp said.

Dart led the way into town and past the docks. They walked past the warehouses, into an area of huts and shanties clubbed together and leaning with the wind. He walked up to one in the middle and knocked on the doorframe.

An older woman came to the door and grabbed him in a hug. "There you are my sweetie! I haven't seen you in days. Where you been? And where 'd you get them fancy clothes?" She said, Then noticed the rest of them standing nearby. "He didn't do it, whatever you say, he was here with me all the time."

"It's not like that, Granny. These are friends and that's my . . . captain." Dart said.

"What are you saying boy?" Granny asked.

"I joined on a ship Granny, I'm gonna be a sailor," Dart said with some pride.

"Is dat true?" Granny asked Captain Sharp.

"Yes, ma'am. I'm Captain Gerard Sharp of the Tawny Mane. We sail for England in the morning, and Dart wanted to say goodbye."

She hugged Dart again, rocking him back and forth. "I knew you would make it out Dart, I just knew it."

"You're not mad?" Dart asked, wiping his eyes.

"No, sugar! You need to get away and find your place in the world, cuz it sure ain't here. But I will love you wherever you are, you rememba that." She looked at Captain Sharp again. "You sure you old enough to be Captain of a ship, you look awful young?"

Captain Sharp just rubbed his forehead.

"You take care of dis boy, he is something special just waiting to bloom."

"I know; that's why I hired him," Captain Sharp said. He reached into his pocket and pulled out a few gold coins and handed them over to Granny. "This was part of his bonus for signing with my crew. He wanted you to have half of it."

She looked at the coins in her hand and made them disappear into her pockets. She hugged Dart again and whispered, "You always took care of me boy. Shoulda been the other way around."

Gerard let them go for a little bit longer and noticed August and Kolohe had turned away to give them some privacy.

"It was nice to meet you Granny. I'll stop in and check on you the next time I'm in New Zealand," Captain Sharp said.

Captain Sharp moved away and August and Kolohe walked with him. They stopped fifty feet away, and after another minute Dart joined them.

They were almost to the ship when Jarom came running up from behind them. "Captain Sharp, Mama Ruby needs to talk to you."

"I know. We have been looking for her," Captain Sharp said.

"I'll take you to her, she is at the fluff warehouse," Jarom said.

"Fluff?"

"You know, da fluff," Jarom said and told them to follow him.

The warehouse was in falling down condition on a good day and this was not a good day. They walked inside and it was almost as light inside as outside from all the holes in the roof. Mama Ruby was talking to another man, but walked over to them as soon as she saw them.

"Der ya are, been lookin for ya," Mama Ruby said. "Ya got any room left on dat ship o yours?"

"Nope, all the barrels are loaded," Captain Sharp said.

"What bout the between spaces?"

"What do you mean?"

"Between stuff, on top o' stuff, yu kno, stuffed in da cracks," she said.

The warehouse loft was full of fleece sheets. Fleece sheets were packages of 20 shorn lamb's wool pelts pressed together and tied with jute. They were big and fluffy and weighed 132 pounds per sheet. This made them easy to transport to the factory or for shipping. Captain Sharp looked at the piles of fleece when August started talking next to him.

"Do you think we could squish those sheets between the barrels and the walls of the ship?" August said out loud.

"We just might," Captain Sharp said.

The warehouse was collapsing and the fleece needed to be moved somewhere dry right away. Captain Sharp asked Mama Ruby what the price was and how much she wanted for them and she waved him off.

"Dey about to be ruind in de mud. You take dem, sell dem, and we figur it out later. Hows dat?" Mama Ruby said.

"Then get them to my ship as fast as you can, as many as you want," Captain Sharp said. "We are leaving in the morning, so it's got to be now."

"So soon?" she asked.

He nodded.

Mama Ruby turned to the warehouse guy. "Ya heard em, move yer tail fethers."

"Dart, Kolohe, run back to the ship. Tell Hickory and Jim-Jim we got buffers on the way."

The boys took off.

Captain Sharp walked back outside with Mama Ruby on his arm. "I'll get you a fair trade for the wool when we get to England," Captain Sharp said and she just nodded. "I'll get the money back to New Zealand as soon as possible," he added and she just nodded again. "You have been very kind to us. Thank you, Mama Ruby." He pulled her into a hug and she just chuckled.

"Just lik ya hav been good to ma island. I kno bout you helpin people, given away money, feedin kids. Ya a good man Captin Sharp. I be keepin ya in ma prayers," she said and kissed him on the cheek.

The warehouse man yelled over and asked Captain Sharp if he had ever driven a horse wagon before. Captain Sharp nodded.

"Then drive this one back to your ship. I'll save you a walk, and you'll save me a trip," the man yelled.

Captain Sharp approached the ship driving the first wagon full of wool sheets. His crew came out onto the deck to stare at him. He thought they were past the whole 'open mouth stare thing,' but apparently not. He drove out onto the dock and got close enough to the ship where two men could throw the sheets up onto the deck. He jumped down off the cart and set the handbrake.

"Ok, I need two strong men down here to start tossing wool up onto the deck. The rest of you start carrying it down and bracing the barrels. Let's move it, men. We've got more carts coming and we're burning daylight," Captain Sharp said.

Jim-Jim came down the ramp and asked where he got the wool bundles.

"I guess you could say I found them," Captain Sharp said.

"Found them, huh? How much did you pay for these?" Jim-Jim asked.

"There was no charge for the wool, I didn't pay a single penny," Captain Sharp said.

"How exactly does that happen? This is valuable wool! Why would somebody just give it to you?" Jim-Jim asked.

Captain Sharp showed him the wolf smile. "I persuaded them."

While the crew loaded the wool, Ambrose, Pascoe, and Pierre came back to the ship, each carrying two large bags that were moving and making noise on their own. They walked up the ramp and headed for the stairs. Captain Sharp stopped Ambrose with his bundle and asked what was in the bags.

"Hens, sir. We got fourteen hens and two roosters. Should give us around a dozen eggs a day. We can get baby chicks if we want, or just fresh eggs. If any of them die, we eat them. There's no downside. Lots of the crew have asked to take turns taking care of them. Seems like most of the crew had chickens as kids," Ambrose said.

"Carry on," Captain Sharp said. Ambrose smiled and hefted his bags which made clucking sounds, and then walked below.

The ship had a few last visitors that morning. The first one was a friend of Mama Ruby's who owned a collectables store in town. She had been told of some amazing conch shells for sale and wanted to look at them. Captain Sharp had her escorted to his quarters and sent for Vaheana and Arlo. He let them handle the transaction and went below to check on the chickens.

The crew had set up the pens in one of the lower storage compartments that still had some room to move. The two pens were side by side with a few inches in between them. Each side had seven hens and one rooster. The two roosters could see each other, but not peck each other.
    The crew built night boxes the roosters would be put into each night to hopefully keep the crowing from going off too early. They purchased some grains to feed the birds, along with any table scraps from the kitchen. Hens would eat just about anything put in front of them. There were several crewmen crowded around the cages talking about building nests and perches for the 'ladies'.

Back up on deck Captain Sharp found a line of crewmen walking off the ship carrying conch shells, following the store owner back to her shop. Vaheana sold another fourteen shells, but for less money than they had charged Captain Claude. The shop owner agreed to keep the price of the conch shells high until the Guinevere left port. That way there would be no hard feelings. Vaheana walked with the store owner, who had invited her back to her store to shop before they sailed away tomorrow.

The other visit was from Usain and a 'lady' friend of his. They arrived in a very fine carriage complete with a driver. Usain helped her down and escorted her up the ramp. Captain Sharp had been warned and was at the top of the ramp ready to greet them.
    There were introductions, bowing, hand kissing, and flattery exchanged all around. Duchess Venetia was interested in a necklace from the famed master jeweler Fetu. Captain Sharp sent a crewman to find August. When August returned, he sent August to find Fetu and reminded him about the weliweli wahine order. He then escorted Duchess Venetia and Usain to his quarters for some tea and refreshments.
    Captain Sharp, Usain, and Duchess Venetia sat at the table, talking to Maurice about his amazing desserts when Fetu the Magnificent rushed in the door. The hair was down, the red shirt was back, opened to the chest. He spoke fast in Maru, but came up to Duchess Venetia and kissed her gloved hand.
    "Mr. Fetu welcomes you, but says you have wasted a trip, for surely none of his jewelry could compare to your beauty," Captain Sharp said by way of translation.

Duchess Venetia fanned herself with a folding fan and said he was obviously a very intelligent man.

"Obviously," Captain Sharp said, and then called Fetu a bad name in Maru.

"I don't understand," said Maurice.

Captain Sharp nodded to August, who went over and led Maurice out of the room by the arm with some questions about dinner that night. Once the door was shut, Fetu asked Gerard if he should wear a dress next time and say it's the height of fashion in the big cities.

Usain and the Duchess snapped their heads to Captain Sharp the moment Fetu was done speaking.

"Mr. Fetu says your eyes are like the coral reefs of Uka-Nuka, and he just may have something that would go perfectly with them," Captain Sharp said.

Fetu waved them over and laid down his two black felt rolls. He took his time untying and unrolling, just like last time. He stopped just before unveiling the necklaces and told Gerard to say something nice.

"Only a neck like yours could do this masterpiece justice," Captain Sharp said, and Fetu unrolled the flet. On this roll, he revealed one necklace and one bracelet. As always, the colors came alive against the black background.

Duchess Venetia gasped and clutched her hands to her chest. "Exquisite," She breathed. "I'll take them both."

"You don't even know what they cost yet," Usain whined beside her.

"I don't care," She said and Usain palmed his face and started rubbing his forehead like he was in pain.

Fetu asked in Maru which one was paying the bill. Captain Sharp said that judging by the look of despair, it was their friend Usain. Fetu asked if they could make him suffer just a little bit, it had been a slow day. Captain Sharp shook his head and said, "no."

"What did he say?" asked the Duchess who had already put on the bracelet.

"He did not think he could part with his jewelry for just anyone, but Usain is a great man and a great friend, so he will help you."

Fetu picked up the necklace and motioned for the Duchess to turn around so he could help put it on. Captain Sharp grabbed Usain and pulled him off to the side.

"How much are you going to pay for the necklace, bracelet, and probably some earrings? You get to decide. Make it expensive, but not painful. The lady must think she is worth it," Captain Sharp said.

"That's not the way this works," Usain said. "You set the price, then I start crying, and eventually I pay it."

"You have been a friend to the Tawny Mane. Today she pays you back. Pick a price, but make sure you do not insult your lady friend. It would be a shame to lose the jewelry and the Duchess all in one day." Captain Sharp then told Fetu to show her what's in the other roll before Usain passed out.

Fetu unrolled the second blanket and revealed earrings, a broach, and a newly-made bone hairbrush with shells inlaid in the handle. Duchess Venetia made a sound like 'sqeeeeeeeeeeeeeeeeeeee' and somewhere in the distance dogs started barking. Usain started rubbing his forehead again. Fetu just laughed like he was some crazy exotic jewelry maker from a distant tropical island.

There was some mock haggling, before the men agreed on 125 guineas for the necklace, bracelet, earrings, broch, and hairbrush. The Duchess hung on Usain's arm like he hung the moon, which seemed to take the sting out of the cost. Captain Sharp walked them out to the carriage after kissing her hand, and helped her up into the buggy. Usain hugged him and both men thanked each other for the business they shared. Usain climbed up in the carriage and leaned out the window. "I hope to see you again, Captain Sharp."

"I hope to see you again as well. Good luck with your acquisitions," Captain Sharp said and tipped his hat.

Walking back into his quarters, Fetu was braiding his hair back up. He had a huge smile on his face and a pile of gold coins in front of him. "This is great, I think we should open a jewelry store when we get to England."

"Do you know how much we made today?" Captain Sharp asked.

"Yes, 125 of the yellow ones. Although I must say, I like the gray ones better," Fetu said.

"The good news is I don't think Arlo is going to yell at us this time. Do you need any money?" Captain Sharp asked.

Fetu waved it off. "Nah, you hold onto it. Although I was thinking, I want to give some of my money to the ship's crew. Like those shares Arlo was talking about. Everyone on board has helped me in one way or another and I think it's the right thing to do." He stopped and thought for a minute. "Those chickens sure are neat, though. That was a great idea, getting pets that would make food for us. I wouldn't mind a pet one day." Fetu stood up and shook Gerard's hand. "This was fun, let's do it again sometime." Then he walked out the door.

65

Just after dark, Captain Sharp assembled his raiding party for the secret mission. Bothari, Dart, August and Kolohe were selected and briefed in the captain's quarters with the door closed. He gave August a handful of money after giving all the instructions he could think of.

"Bothari, try not to kill anyone," the captain said. "Dart, you know a guy right?"

"Yes, of course," Dart said.

"Whatever else you need, just get it. I don't care what it costs. Don't forget: we will be at sea for a hundred days," Captain Sharp said.

"Captain, we've got this," August said and they headed off into the darkness.

Two hours later, the secret mission was completed. The team returned under cover of darkness and snuck onto the ship with light feet. They were loaded down with gear, bags and bushels. He herded them quickly into his quarters and asked Bothari how the mission went.

"No problems at all. When are you going to bring him up?" Bothari asked.

"Right now. Just try to keep her quiet until I get back."

Captain Sharp found Fetu in the galley, working on some shells. He had spent considerable time on them lately and probably needed a break. Even if he didn't know it.

"Fetu, I need to speak with you for a bit, can you wrap that up for the night?" Captain Sharp said.

"You need to speak with me for the whole rest of the night?" Fetu asked with a confused face.

"Um, yes," the captain said.

"Okay, let me put this back in my trunk," Fetu said. He gathered up his shells, tools, files, and sanding blocks into bags and felt blankets, then carried them back to his foot locker. Captain Sharp trailed along and then led him back up the steps to the deck.

As they walked towards the captain's quarters, Captain Sharp said he wanted to thank Fetu for all he had done for the crew and ship. He was a big part of the crew now and was making money for all of them. Everyone appreciated his work and his talent.

"You could have told me that in the galley," Fetu said as they reached the door and went inside.

"True, but I wanted the first time you met Daisy to be special," Captain Sharp said and stepped aside.

Bothari, Dart, August and Kolohe were on the far side of the room. In front of them on a leash was the cutest, most adorable goat Captain Sharp had ever seen. She looked at Fetu and said, "Baa." Daisy was mostly white with black socks and a black mask on her face. She had a pot belly and a short stubby white tail that was wiggling back and forth.

Fetu stopped inside the door and just stared at her. He got down on one knee and held out his hands. Daisy walked forward towards him, with Dart following her holding the leash. Fetu leaned down to see her better. Daisy headbutted him with enough force to put him on his butt. After that, Daisy climbed into his lap, sat down, and bleated again. "Baa."

"She is so precious," Fetu said, rubbing his own head and Daisy's head at the same time.

"She is a dairy goat, so she will give us milk. Probably one to two pints per day," Dart said.

Fetu looked up. "I have never had a goat before. I don't know the first thing about them."

"I used to help my grandpa with his goats. I can help teach you," Dart said, looking very happy about the job.

"What will she eat?" Fetu asked like a concerned parent.

"Got you covered, brother," Bothari said, pointing out the hay, grain and greens. "We need to be careful though, her owner said she will eat everything at once if you let her."

"You also need to keep her from eating a hole in my ship. Especially below the water line," Captain Sharp said.

"Daisy would never do that! She's a sweet girl," Fetu said, scratching under her chin.

Daisy looked at Captain Sharp and bleated. "Baaaa."

66

As it turns out, there is a downside to roosters, and that is the crowing. The two roosters started early and with enthusiasm. Fortunately, everyone needed to be up earlier today for the cast off. Captain Sharp dressed for the day in full captain's gear with hat, jacket, belt and sword.

The day started dry, but the sky was gray and overcast with the promise of rain later. Captain Sharp had August go around and do a face-to-face head count of the crew to make sure everyone was on board. He sent Jim-Jim down to the harbor master's office to let Oliver Roe know they were pulling out. Jim-Jim came back with Oliver and two deck hands in tow to help with the lines. Oliver took a moment to come on deck and wish good travels to the ship and crew. He said their visit started out rocky but they seemed to have made out okay in the end. Captain Sharp thanked him and said they would probably see him again.

Once Oliver walked off the ship, the two deckhands pulled the gangway back onto the dock and his crew replaced the safety railing. When that was done, Hickory gave the thumbs up and Captain Sharp took his last deep breath of Wellington, New Zealand.

"All hands-on deck! Pull in the lines and secure the ropes. Vaheana, back us out and get us flipped around. Stephan, get ready to drop some canvas. We got a ship full of cargo, and a pile of money waiting for us in England. Let's go get it!"

The crew cheered.

The lines were loosened, unwrapped, and then thrown back onto the ship to be coiled and stored. There was just enough breeze to push them backwards out of the slip and into the bay where the Tawny Mane made a long, slow turn before pointing south towards the mouth of the bay. The wind was sideways now, so they tacked across it towards the straight and the open sea. The wind picked up as they moved. Once they had cleared the northern island, Stephan dropped more sails and the Tawny Mane leaned into her course. Cornelius and Vaheana turned east by southeast to run with the wind and the current. They were only about the 43rd parallel south. Cornelius wanted them to tack south and east until they hit the 45th before straightening out and going due east. "Better winds and a faster trip," he said.

Jim-Jim was close enough to overhear Cornelius. "Sure, but you all know what the old sailors say:

Below 40 degrees south, there is no law.
Below 50 degrees south, there is no god.
Below 60 degrees south, there is no hope."

With the current pushing them and the wind running at an angle, they lost sight of New Zealand in just over an hour. The dry weather held as they were pushed ahead of any rain. The wind was steady at a good fifteen to twenty knots. The ship sat much lower in the water with her belly full. This was a stark improvement over their last voyage, as this made her steadier and more stable. The ship leaned its shoulder into the waves and broke through them with ease. It felt like the Tawny Mane wanted to get home as much as the crew did.

67

Damn roosters. They woke up Captain Sharp and probably the rest of the crew well before the knock on his door and the 'ohe hana' made him get out of bed. He dressed for some morning exercise and headed out onto the deck. They could only do bamboo work twice while in port, so he was looking forward to getting back into the routine of workouts and training.

The morning group grew bigger every time and now took up most of the deck. Bothari, Fetu, Vaheana, Blaed, Stephan, Kolohe, August, and Dart made up today's group. They didn't have enough of the long staffs for everyone to use at once, so half the group practiced with short swords, while the other half used long staffs. The crack of the swords and the thrum of the staff's were both familiar and comforting in the cool morning air.

After finishing the regular workout today with bamboo, Bothari brought out some real swords from the ship and--after spacing everyone out for safety--had them run through a series of strikes on the eight angles of attack. These strikes were the same patterns they practiced with bamboo so everyone picked it up quickly. Then they went over the five main counter blocks as he called out each number. Bothari, Fetu Vaheana and Captain Sharp rotated through the group doing slow simulated attacks that corresponded with the blocks the group was practicing. They got a little faster each time until the group was comfortable with the moments. Dart picked up most of the drills quickly, even though he had never held anything bigger than a fish knife before. As the group broke up, Bothari told them next practice would also cover throwing knives. They had two hay bales for Daisy and he wanted to take advantage of the throwing targets before Daisy ate them too much.

The group gathered around the maps table in the captain's quarters looking over their two new maps: Captain Sharp, Cornelius, Vaheana, Stephan, Jim-Jim, and August. The Tawny Mane had been loaned two maps by Usain that had details on the 'Strait of All Saints' in southern Chile. Using the strait would cut time and distance off their route, but more importantly, it would be considerably safer. The inland route saved them from having to navigate the 'Mar de Hoces', the body of water between Cape Horn and the South Shetland Islands of antarctica. This passage was notoriously dangerous for strong winds, fast currents, and forty-foot waves.

The first map outlined their current eastbound passage with depths, distance, and landmarks. The second map was for a westbound passage with more landmarks and distances. The west bound map was the real prize since it bypassed the most dangerous passage in the world. Trying to go 'right around the Horn' is where most ships were lost, as you had to battle the wind, waves, and currents. Cornelius leaned his face down to the map as he measured some of the channels and inlets. Captain Sharp had asked Cornelius if he could make a copy of both maps for their own personal library. Cornelius said 'absolutely,' he wanted one for himself also. They all agreed that not only could it be done, but it was a wise move. Every sailor knew of ships that didn't make it back from the Hope and the Horn.

Cornelius had been teaching Vaheana to calculate sailing times and distances for weeks now. He left it to her to plot out this first leg of the voyage from New Zealand to Cape Horn. Vaheana complained out loud that she didn't understand all the variables enough to do it as accurately as he did. Cornelius simply replied that technically nobody did it as accurately as he did. He followed this up by saying Vaheana knew more and learned faster than any student he had ever had, and that she was ready.

Vaheana calculated the sailing distance at approximately 4,300 miles, to which Cornelius said nothing. The charts listed average wind speeds for the 45th parallel south for this time of year at 17 knots. Since most of the wind was pushing from behind the ship, her plan was to jib back and forth to catch the wind and push them at an angle between 45 degrees and 60 degrees. With the current weight of the Tawny Mane, she figured they could catch a maximum of eighty percent of the wind speed. According to her calculations, that put them at Cape Horn in thirteen days, mid-morning between breakfast and lunch. She said this last part with a grin to show how confident she was in her numbers.

Cornelius leaned back like a proud parent, but still said nothing. This first leg of their sail home was approximately one third the total distance, but would be by far the fastest part of the journey thanks to the roaring forties.

68

Six days out of Wellington, they caught some big wind. The cargo weight of the ship kept it from rocking side-to-side, but they tipped and topped over large waves as the ship ran. Captain Sharp lay awake in his bed getting rolled back and forth with the waves when he heard raised voices from below. It wasn't light out yet, but he was done sleeping. He dressed quickly and headed below to see what was going on. A half-dressed Jim-Jim helped Stephan move some cargo around. One of the sugar barrels had gotten loose and had started banging against the side of the ship as it pitched over waves. The men were trying to get the barrel wedged into a tighter spot and had moved some of the fleece sheets out of the way to work. Captain Sharp moved in to help. Together, the three of them were able to wedge the barrel into a better spot. The sheepskins were jammed around it, then the whole package was secured with ropes to keep it from moving.

"What happened, just worked its way loose?" Captain Sharp asked.

"Not exactly," said Stephan, holding up a piece of cut rope. It had been eaten through in the middle. Nobody ventured a guess as to the culprit. "It's a good thing I found it on my rounds. It would have broken open eventually and made a mess of the hold."

"I'll talk to him about it. Anything else?" Captain Sharp asked.

"There also seems to be some suspicious damage occurring to the edges of a few of the bunks, the stair handrail on the second deck, and one of Tanner's new leather boots," Jim-Jim said.

"Ouch. Those boots were brand new," Captain Sharp said.

"Yeah, Fetu said he would buy him a new pair as soon as he could, but that could be three months from now in England. In the meantime, Tanner has one new boot, and one old boot with a hole in it." Stephan said.

"Any suggestions?" Captain Sharp asked. "Could we use some of the extra bamboo from the chickens and make a pen for her?"

"Already did that," Jim-Jim said and then sighed. "She ate it."

"Well shit. What kind of plonker brings a goat onto a ship," Captain Sharp said to himself.

Captain Sharp went upstairs to find Fetu, who was asleep in his bunk. Daisy was curled up by his feet like a dog, but watching Captain Sharp with a suspicious eye. Fetu had a leash tied around one of his ankles with the other end tied to Daisy's neck. It looked good until Captain Sharp noticed it had been chewed threw in the middle, and Daisy was essentially free to roam.

The captain gently nudged his friend awake and told him it was time to get up.

"What for? Nothing is happening today," Fetu said, wiping the sleep out of his eyes.

"Daisy got loose last night and ate through the ropes securing the barrels in the hold. We almost lost one," said the captain.

"Not my Daisy! She has been tied up here with me all night, like a good girl," Fetu said and lifted up the leash, only to see it had been eaten in half while he slept. "Opala."

"Get together with Cuthbert this morning and figure something out. She can't keep roaming the ship at night, eating whatever she fancies. She is going to get us in trouble or dead or both. She is too cute to cook. I think even Maurice would fight me on that one," Captain Sharp said.

Fetu grabbed Daisy and held her close, though he knew Captain Sharp was kidding and his brother would never do such a horrendous thing.

"We will come up with something, sir," Fetu said.

"Good. Get to it."

69

The next morning, Cuthbert came to find him and asked if he wanted to see something funny. Captain Sharp said sure, put away his log books and then followed his carpenter down the stairs into the crew quarters. He could hear the men laughing before they even got to the gun deck. Down in the crew quarters he found the men gathered around Fetu and Daisy and had to push his way to the front of the circle. Daisy had been sewn a leather harness or a jacket, depending on how you looked at it. It went around her neck, down her chest and strapped around her waist with two buckles with soft padding on the inside. It looked like it was lined with wool. The harness was made in a way that she could not reach any part of it to chew on it. On the top of the harness, there was a metal ring sewn into the jacket that stood straight up with a braided cord tied into it. That cord was looped over a beam above them and tied off. Daisy could stand, or lie down, but not walk more than three feet in any direction. If she tried, she would be lifted up into the air and would swing back to the center area, which was making everyone laugh. Daisy looked confused, but not upset. Fetu looked happy, sitting on his bunk, watching Daisy swing back and forth.

Cuthbert showed Captain Sharp their back up plan too. Cuthbert had a spare length of wire he cut and bent into chain links. Next, he fashioned Fetu a chain leash that was three feet long. On one end was a loop that Fetu slipped over his foot at night. The other end was attached to Daisy's harness. This would keep her in the bunk at night, since the only thing she didn't chew on was metal. Daisy made a run for it and was lifted into the air, where she swung around like a pendulum. The crew laughed, Fetu smiled, and Daisy complained, "Baa."

The ohe hana group gathered in the long, straight hallway of the lower hold alongside the brig. Two hay bales had been set up against a dividing wall and covered with an old torn scrap of canvas. It looked alot like the canvas they had been shooting at, as it was full of holes. The black rectangle of the torso was two feet off the ground, and the red oval of the head was sitting on top of it. Today, the head had two dots for eyes and an unhappy frown where its mouth would be.

Bothari put three marks on the floor to mark throwing distances: seven feet, thirteen feet, and nineteen feet. These represented the throwing distances for the pahi (knife) throw with a half rotation, a handle throw with a full rotation, and a blade throw with one and a half rotations respectively. He spent some time with the new students going over grip, mechanics, and arm motion while Captain Sharp, Fetu, Vaheana, and Blaed got in some early practice. They had a handful of throwing pahi between them, so they could throw a few without stopping to pull them out. Captain Sharp was good, Fetu was good, Vaheana was okay, but Blaed was terrific. He put knife after knife into the same spot in the neck, between the head and torso. August, Kolohe, Dart and Stephan took turns now giving the group from the island a break. After everyone warmed up and were getting good strikes from each of the distances, Bothari called for a halt and had them pull the pahi from the target.

Bothari went over to the hay bale and reached above him to lower down a coconut on a string. The coconut had been split open, used, and then tied back together. It was on a string and hung down in front of the oval head covering about two thirds of it. You could still see one eye and a part of the frown. Bothari walked back to the group standing behind the thirteen-foot line. "Hostage," he said by way of explanation.

Bothari let the new group go first. Their knives went all over the place. Some way off, some missed the hay bales, some hit the coconut. Those throwers were booed by the group. Blaed threw a great pahi that went right into the eye of the head on the canvas. Captain Sharp tried to get between it and the coconut, but ended up hitting the hostage himself, much to the delight of the throwers. Bothari was in the pahi throwing rotation now and put one into the cheek just below Blaed's knife. Everyone had a few turns. The new throwers were showing improvement already.

Bothari called a halt to the throwing and said they had one more drill today. He had everyone move back so a single thrower had room to turn and throw. This time, they all started with their backs to the target. Each person went through the routine three times and again, and the pahi were all over the place. Captain Sharp missed wide with his first throw. The second throw he got the rotation off; it bounced off the canvas without piercing. He stood ready for his third throw when Bothari called for him to stop and walked up and got into his face.

"Are you going to let Pua die Captain Sharp, or are you going to get your shit together?" Bothari whispered to his student. He watched the anger come forward and saw the eyes go cold. Bothari took a step back and then yelled. "Throw!"

Captain Sharp turned and threw all in one motion. He didn't plan on yelling, but the roar came out anyway. 'Too hard and too close,' he thought as it left his hand. The knife rotated once in the air, then buried itself in the canvas head, right inside the eye next to the coconut. The coconut rotated just slightly after being kissed . . . kissed, but not cut. Nobody said anything for a moment as the echo of the roar was still ringing in their ears.

"Don't forget that place," the instructor said. "It's where you need to be when the pahi matters."

"Thank you brother. I had forgotten," Captain Sharp said before walking away and up the stairs.

"What did you say to him to make him so angry?" August asked Bothari.

"Part of being a teacher is knowing what will bring out the best in your students. When it comes to throwing pahi, some do better being calm and having it quiet. Some need to be a little angry, and some need to be furious. Captain Sharp is good with the pahi, but when his rage is called forward, the huhu, there is no one better. Like all things, this too needs practice."

Bothari nodded for August to take his place on the throwing line. The instructor walked up to him and got nose-to-nose with the student. He looked angry, but August was learning this was a tool he used just like everything else. "Who is important to you August? Who would you kill for? Put a face on that coconut and tell me what would scare you and draw your huhu to the surface?" Bothari growled.

August thought of his sister April back home, being held and threatened in front of some unknown enemy. He thought of April, crying and calling for August to help her. He could feel it welling up inside him.

"Now focus on that, channel that, but don't let it overwhelm you. You need the best throw of your life right this second. Everything you have learned, coming together right here right now. You have one chance to save them August, one throw." Bothari stepped back out of the way.

"Throw!" Bothari yelled.

August turned, roared, and threw.

70

The Tawny Mane was twelve days out front Wellington and it was getting late in the afternoon. Vaheana was restless. When she was not at the helm, she was on the rail at the front of the ship looking forward. She had climbed into the crow's nest twice already to get a better look. They knew they were getting close when they saw birds overhead, the first ones in eleven days. Before the sun got too low and they lost the light, Captain Sharp climbed up into the crow's nest himself for a look around. From the deck, you could see about five miles, but from the nest you could see twelve to fifteen miles, depending on the haze. There was nothing to see yet, but it felt close.

Captain Sharp stayed on deck late into the evening with Vaheana, looking for the coastline. He asked his night crew politely to not crash his ship into South America. They had a quarter moon waxing, so at least there was some light available. He told Stephan to wake him for anything and headed into his quarters. He caught up the log book and laid down for some restless sleep.

This nightmare was different this time in that Sophie was taken away instead of dying right in front of him. He had walked away to use the bathroom as usual and walked farther than normal. Gerard heard Sophie yell for help and ran back as fast as he could, but he was too late. The men who grabbed Sophie were on horses and he caught sight of the last one disappearing down the trail. Sophie was laid over the saddle and their eyes met before she disappeared around the bend. Her eyes were wide with fright and pleading with Gerard to do something. He would never catch the horses on foot, never see Sophie again. The pain of this nightmare was different, and worse. Dead was dead and horrible, but alive at the mercy of another was unthinkable. He lay awake and listened to the spunds of his ship.

The knock on the door came just as the sky was starting to lighten in the east. "Coast in sight, Captain," somebody said and walked away. Captain Sharp got up and dressed for the day. He moved August's peg to 'awake' while he worked and walked out on the deck as soon as he was ready. August came up the steps with two mugs of tea and handed one over.

"Thank you, August, perfect timing," the captain said.

The coast was not just visible, it was close. They were three miles offshore, running parallel northward looking for their inlet. Cornelius and Vaheana were already at the helm, going over the map from Usain. They were looking for a rock formation called 'Missing Finger'. This rock formation looked like a hand sticking up out of a rocky hillside less than 1/8th of a mile inland from the beach. The index, middle and pinky finger spires were still intact, but the ring finger spire had collapsed some time ago. From this formation, they needed to pass two dead end inlets before taking the third inlet, which was the western entrance to the Strait of All Saints. From there they would sail SSE along the mainland side and turn due east at the dogleg where the inlet runs into Tierra Del Fuego. A small port called Puerto del Hambre was nestled in the middle of the strait. Here the waterway was wider and it was a straight shot east to Monte Dinero Bay and the Atlantic Ocean.

They spotted the rock formation easy enough; it was aptly named. The formation was parallel with the coastline with the rocks sticking up seventy feet above the gently sloping hillside below. Vaheana drifted the Mane closer to the coastline as they moved north toward the inlet they were looking for. After passing the two dead ends, they turned into the third inlet and swung around south to follow the channel. It was wide enough for them to maneuver back and forth if needed and they had a crosswind which made the wind perfect. Cornelius had ordered half the canvas taken in to reduce speed, since this was their first time through the strait. Cornelius had Vaheana at the wheel, while he took his own notes of the passage. It was only twenty miles to the turn and then another forty miles to Puerto del Hambre.

Puerto del Hambre was more like a cluster of buildings than a town. There was no dock or port, but plenty of room in the bay to anchor a ship. Captain Sharp told them to drop anchor in the middle of the channel and they would stop in and check out the town. Captain Sharp had a shopping list from Maurice for fruits and vegetables, but aside from that, they were just fine on supplies. After dropping anchor, the men set about getting the longboats over the side. Captain Sharp saw movement on the hillside across the bay and stared for a few seconds before going into his quarters for one of his collapsible monocular. When he came back out he swept the hillside with the spyglass. A herd of deer was moving along the hillside above the bank, a couple hundred of them, and some big ones. He sent a runner for Ambrose, Pascal, Gideon and Perkins. Pascal was the first one up on the deck. Captain Sharp handed him the spyglass and pointed him at the hillside.

"Oh, beautiful beast," Pascal said.

Ambrose walked up right then. Pascal passed the spyglass over and pointed where he should look. Ambrose took a quick look at the bank and blew out a breath and then looked over at Captain Sharp.

"I want the four of you to take one of the boats and get ahead of the herd. Shoot as a group, try and drop four of them with one volley. You can clean them on land, but I want the meat, hides, sinew and usable parts brought back here. You don't have much time, you'll probably only get one shot before they scatter. Make it count." Gerard took the keys from around his neck and handed them to Ambrose.

Pascal grabbed Gideon and some crewmen to lower another boat, while Ambrose went to open up the armory.

Captain Sharp, August, Bothari, Hickory, and Pierre climbed down into the longboat already lowered into the water and paddled for the north side of the strait. Pierre was the only person on the ship fluent in Spanish, so it seemed like a good idea to take him. Conversely, if the people of the tiny village only spoke French, Pierre could help with that too. They reached the north bank in ten minutes and pulled up to a flat sandy beach with several fishing boats lined up on the sand, above the high-water line. Six people from the town walked to the beach to meet them. The longboat hit the beach and Bothari and Captain Sharp jumped out to pull it onto the sand. The rest of the crew got out and they faced the villages with smiles all around. There were four adult men in the group, one younger man, and a middle-aged woman who was probably somebody's wife.

"English?" Captain Sharp said hopefully.

Much head shaking in the negative.

"Hablan español mis amigos?" Pierre said.

"Hola!" the group said, and one of the men came forward to hug Pierre. The group started talking a mile a minute. Captain Sharp stepped back and let Pierre run the show. It appeared that hand gestures were a requirement for their particular dialect, so everyone was waving, pointing and flapping arms like birds. Eventually the group started to move up the beach towards one of the buildings. They motioned for the rest of the crew to follow Pierre.

Inside one of the larger buildings there were six tables set up with a few locals sitting and talking. Captain Sharp's group was invited to sit at one of the bigger tables so they could wave their hands more effectively. The rest of the building looked like a warehouse, with shelves and bins of assorted goods. This was a port town, so most of the items were for fishing or for fishermen. Captain Sharp asked if he could look around, and Pierre translated the request. Judging by the smiles and waving, he got the message and walked towards the rows of supplies. He was looking for anything unusual, or something the Tawny Mane might need. He found cane poles, fishing nets, landing nets, rope, paddles, dried fish skins, seal skins, fur hides and leather hides. There was some handmade clothing, but nothing he needed at the moment.

One of the fishing nets caught his eye, as he had not seen one like it before. He asked Pierre to ask them how it worked. One of the fishermen walked over explaining how it was used. Pierre followed him, translating as he went. It was called a 'cast net'. This one was twelve feet in diameter. The netting was half an inch and small weights were tied around the perimeter of the round net. It could be thrown from a boat, the beach, or a river bank. When it was tossed correctly, the net spread out and sank quickly over the target. One hand throws it, while the other hand puts an easy rotation on the net to make it spread out like a dancing lady's dress. The man picked up one of the smaller nets and motioned for Captain Sharp to follow him.

The two of them went outside and over to a grassy area next to the building. The man moved slowly, counting out each step with numbers. He held the net, motioned to be looking for fish, and then seeing fish. He gave the net a soft toss. It spread out in a perfect circle in the grass. Then he pulled it back to himself with the lead line. He showed captain Sharp how to fold the net for the next throw, then stepped aside and let Captain Sharp have a try. The first toss didn't have enough rotation to spread out the net fully. His second throw had too much rotation and the weights went all the way out and then snapped back, shrinking the net before it settled in the grass. His third throw felt good and the net settled in a neat circle on the grass. He looked at his new teacher and the man smiled.

"Buen trabajo!" the man said.

When they got back inside, Captain Sharp grabbed the twelve foot cast net and laid it on the table next to his cook. Pierre had been talking about the shopping list, because some produce was being assembled on the table. Captain Sharp handed over a bag of coins to Pierre and told him they needed to buy the cast net also.

"Don't get ripped off, but don't barter too hard either. It's well made," Captain Sharp said.

Pierre opened up the coin bag and laid a few of them on the table. The woman was pointing at the gold coins but Pierre was shaking it off and pushing several silver coins towards the middle instead. There was some back and forth haggling but the total price of the casting net and fresh vegetables was three guinea, two shillings, and fifteen pennies.

More trips were made and more vegetables were stacked on the table. One of the villagers brought a discarded section of netting that they could roll up the assorted items in. Their purchases were rolled up and tied off. August and Hickory carried the food supplies out to the boat, while Captain Sharp transported the new net.

On the way to the beach, there was a spirited discussion with lots of pointing towards the Atlantic side of the strait. Pierre had a concerned look on his face and asked questions as often as the group would let him. Captain Sharp let Pierre ask away, using the time to scan the far side of the strait for movement. He couldn't see any movement, and didn't see the other longboat either. He hoped his crew would have good luck. It would be great to have fresh meat and some hides to work on. Finding something to do on long voyages got harder the further you got from your last port.

When Pierre and the group finished their talk, there was much hugging and handshakes all around. Pierre made his way down to the boat and climbed aboard. Captain Sharp and Bothari got it sliding down into the water and jumped inside. Both sides waved as the longboat was turned and headed back out to the Tawny Mane.

"Good people," Pierre said. "Farmers and fishermen."

"I agree, they picked a rocky port to call home, but they seem happy and not starving to death," Captain Sharp said.

"Speaking of which, I need to tell you about the crew that may be starving to death," Pierre said.

Captain Sharp looked at the ship up ahead. "Why don't you save it until we are aboard the Mane? That way you will only need to tell the story once."

71

His shooting team was still away on the island of Tierra del Fuego, but Captain Sharp was not worried. They needed time to hunt and they were not in a rush at the moment. He assembled the senior crew in the galley and asked Pierre to tell his tale.

From what Pierre had learned on the beach, the fisherman from Puerto del Hambre talked and traded with fishermen along the strait, all the way to the Atlantic Ocean, one hundred miles east. Word came down from other boats that a foreign ship had been trying for three weeks to get around the Horn from east to west. They had been pushed back four times by changing winds, strong ocean currents, and some really bad luck. It was thought they had lost some men to the sea already, but communication was difficult as the men on the ship spoke a language that none of the fishermen did. Pierre was told that one of the local fishermen had gone out to the ship and tried to convince the ship's captain to come north through the strait, but the captain did not understand them and became angry, insisting that they needed to go south in order to go around the horn before they could proceed west. The fishermen didn't understand most of their interaction, but did understand the ship was running out of food and fresh water.

"They don't know about the Strait of All Saint's then," Captain Sharp said.

"Obviously not," said Cornelius. "Hell, we didn't learn about it until two weeks ago."

Everyone was quiet for a few seconds while they thought about the other ship and the other crew.

"Can we help them?" Pierre asked.

Captain Sharp had already thought about it. "We can try. If we turn south out of Monte Dinero Bay, we should bump into them before we reach the Horn. If we find them--and if we can communicate with them--I see no reason not to offer help. We could always use some good luck before heading into the doldrums."

The sound of a sharp crack reached the ship, then echoed off the land on both sides of the strait. A few of the men looked up sharply, not knowing the source of the noise.

"What was that?" Arlo asked.

"With any luck, that was the sound of dinner," Captain Sharp said, and then told them about the deer.

Gideon and Perkins rowed hard to get ahead of the herd while Ambrose and Pascal loaded the guns. They didn't talk while they passed the deer on the hillside, saving their whispers until they were around the bend and well in front of the game. Ambrose was the team leader, and whispered instructions.

"Once we pass that next ridge, we can beach the boat and head up the hillside. Everyone be quick, but quiet; one crack and the herd is going to turn. We should have some time to pick out a good firing position before they walk up on us. I want the four of us lined up close together so I can use hand signals when the deer get close. I will let you know what animal I am going to take, and the three of you should take the next three to the right, in order. Make sure we don't double up. We shoot at the same time, just like we've practiced on the ship. You know they are going to scatter when it cracks, so make sure you're on time and holding on target. Let's show the crew that our practice has been worth the headache."

The boat touched the beach and was pulled softly and quietly up onto a sandbar. The loaded muskets were handed out. Perkins carried an extra bag with backup shot, powder, and balls, just in case. The four men ghosted up the hillside and onto the plain at the top. There were rolling hills between the deer and them, but they stayed low and silent anyway. Pascal pointed to a long thin mound covered with tall grass a short distance away. Ambrose nodded, and the men moved towards it, then got settled behind it. They spaced about five feet apart, laying down and using the top of the mound as a rest.

Each man checked his musket and cocked the pan, making ready for the herd's approach. The wind blew in their faces, coming from behind the herd. That was good. They watched and waited for their prey to come to them.

As the herd got closer, Ambrose realized just how many deer there actually were: not hundreds, but thousands. For the first time, he thought about a stampede, but they were committed now. The sound should send them in the opposite direction. He couldn't see through the herd because they were so densely packed together. This wouldn't help if any of their shots were off target. A wounded deer can run for miles before it drops. The crew didn't have the time or gear to track and pack a deer back to the boat.

The leading edge of the herd was less than one hundred feet away when Ambrose signaled ready. A buck approached his lane of fire with a considerable rack. Ambrose signaled that he would take that one. Each man made a fist signaling they understood, then counted over to find their corresponding target. Then Ambrose showed twenty with his fingers. His team signaled they understood again.

Below the hillside and out of sight, Ambrose's fingers started a countdown from twenty seconds. The important part for him was to be consistent and measured so they all arrived at zero at the same time. Just like they did every time they practiced, when the countdown passed 11, 10, 9, he put both hands on his musket and sighted on his target. The three other men also turned their eyes back on target and kept the countdown going in their own heads. As his mind counted down the last few seconds, Ambrose pulled the musket tight to his shoulder, aimed right where he needed to, let out a slow breath, and pulled the trigger in a smooth easy squeeze.

The four shots went off almost simultaneously. The report was loud on the open plain, as the four muskets belched out their powder like a dragon's puff. Two of the deer dropped immediately after perfect killing shots. Ambrose's buck looked up at him and took two steps before falling and went down. The fourth deer turned to bolt with the herd that was already scattering. It took two huge leaping bounds before it crumbled and went to the ground and didn't move again.

Perkins sat up first and said, "Holy shit, would you look at that? Four shots and four deer." He stood and began to move forward.

"Stop. Reload right now, before going forward," Ambrose said, already reloading.

"What for?" Perkins replied. "The rest of 'em have scattered and they won't be coming back."

"The reload is for the bears, wolves, and big cats who will be attracted to the smell of the meat. You need to be ready when they show up and want to kill you for the food. You are not the only hunter out here," Ambrose said calmly.

Clearly Perkins had never thought of this. His head started whipping around, hunting for something that might be hunting them. After assuring himself that nothing was stalking them at the moment, he got to work reloading his own.

Two men dragged the deer that had run furthest back to the main group. Then Pascal started his class on how to dress a deer for Gideon and Perkins. Ambrose was already working on his own. He didn't need the refresher course. The four men all brought knives with them and went to work. After the cavities were emptied, some of the larger bones were cut out and removed. Once the animals were down to mostly meat weight, they were carried down to the boats as they were with the hides still on. The hunters made multiple trips as each deer required two men to carry it down the slope and load it into the boat. Once they had the four deer, the guns, and the four men back in the boat, they pushed off and started the slow paddle back to the ship. The longboat sat low in the water and that was a good thing.

It had been close to two hours since the ship heard the shots. Captain Sharp considered sending a second boat after the first to see if they needed any help. The crow's nest yelled down, 'Longboat!' and the crew on deck went to the rail for a look. Captain Sharp pulled his spyglass out of his pocket and looked at the boat. He could see all four men, and deer piled up in the middle.

"Hickory, Jim-Jim, get some ropes or rigging set up. We got some heavy supplies coming on board," Captain Sharp said.

Both men snapped to and started pulling ropes for the pulleys.

By the time the longboat reached the side of the ship, the crew had ropes and pulleys set up, with the leading edges of the ropes over the side of the ship where the longboat would tie up. Two crewmen went down the rope ladders to help the men in the boat tie off the cargo.

They hauled the first deer up by the ropes, over the railing. It was a good-sized female, probably 120 pounds field dressed. The crew made approval noises as it came into view and was lowered down onto the deck, where it was untied and the ropes sent back over the side. The second deer pulled up was also a female and a bit thicker, maybe 135 pounds dressed. This was also met with approval as it was lowered onto the deck.

The third animal lifted up was a buck with a respectable rack on him. He probably weighed 160 pounds. His raising and lowering was met with a smattering of clapping by the crew on deck. The fourth animal was the big buck. He got some clapping and whistles from the crew. The buck was easily 180 pounds and thick in the chest. This brought more clapping from the crew as he was put onto the deck next to the other three. As the four hunters climbed up the rope ladder and over the rail, they were also met with some clapping and back slapping. It was an impressive showing for their first group hunt together. They would be well fed over the next few weeks. Captain Sharp told them they did a great job and wanted to hear about the hunt.

"How about we tell you all about it later in the galley? Right now, we need to get to work on this meat and these hides," Ambrose said.

"Of course," Captain Sharp said. "Do you need some more volunteers?"

"Many hands make light work," Gideon said.

"You got it," Captain Sharp said. He sent August below to round up anyone with experience with meat cutting, skinning fur, or tanning hides. In ten minutes, they had a dozen men on deck working on the deer meat and hides. The meat was transported down to Maurice and Pierre in the galley. Some of it was being cooked, and some of it was being salted for later. They already had a stew pot going with some of the fresh vegetables in it. Some of the meat was being loaded into barrels to be preserved with brine.

As one group worked on the deer, other crewmen pulled up the longboats and secured them back on the deck. Captain Sharp checked the sky. They still had plenty of daylight left to work with. He ordered the anchor up and told Cornelius to get them moving east in the strait at their best speed. Pierre got the crew singing a shanty about green peas and mutton pies that had the crew either laughing, toe tapping, or both.

The wind in the strait was about half of what it was out on the open sea because of the hills and mountains breaking it up. They were averaging about six knots per hour now and sailed east another thirty miles before Captain Sharp and Cornelius agreed it was too dark to continue. If they had been through the channel before they might've sailed all night with the help of the moonlight, but since this was their first time through, they wanted to make sure they did not discover any submerged rocks. In addition, Cornelius had been making notes of visual landmarks for his own personal notes and future maps. He didn't want to miss anything in the dark. They found a calm wide spot and dropped anchor off to one side, just in case there was any night traffic going down the middle.

Dinner that night was an amazing stew, with fresh meat and vegetables for everyone. Even Daisy and the chickens got fresh vegetables. The crew went to bed that night stuffed and happy. They were already a third of the way home.

72

Captain Sharp left word with the night shift that he wanted to be up at first light, along with the navigators and sail team. He wanted to get an early start to use as much daylight as they could. The knock on his door pulled him out of a deep restful sleep. It was the first time in nearly two weeks that he slept in a bed that wasn't pitching back and forth. He got dressed and went out onto the deck to make sure the crew was being woken up below. There was about an hour between first light and the actual sunrise, but they could start sailing as soon as they had enough light to navigate by. This is referred to as 'nautical dawn', and occurs twenty to thirty minutes after first light. The ship would be well underway by actual sunrise.

As soon as they had enough men on deck, they pulled the anchor, with Captain Sharp's help on the capstan. The sail-men climbed up in the yards, dropping and securing the sheets. The ship started moving slowly, picking up speed as more canvas was dropped. Vaheana was at the helm this morning. Cornelius sat at a small table down on the main deck. From here he made notes, drawing pictures of landmarks, and charting distances. The bag between his feet was full of parchment, quills, ink, charcoal and some new lead pencils.

Just before lunch they entered Monte Dinero Bay, and within an hour turned south in the Atlantic Ocean. The ship was running down the eastern shore of Tierra Del Fuego, a few miles off the coast. The crosswind was better here and the ship made good time. The navigators agreed it was roughly two hundred miles down the eastern bank that was shaped like a crescent moon. If they had not found the other ship by the time they reached the tip, they would turn around and head back north towards England.

The Tawny Mane ran south for five hours before the light gave out and they dropped anchor for the evening. The ocean was surprisingly calm on this side of Chile, protected from the strong polar ocean currents. Pascoe asked the captain to get close to the shore for tonight, as he had an idea he wanted to try. Vaheana got the ship within two hundred feet before the crew dropped the hook and the ship came to a stop. Sails were secured as darkness settled around the ship.

Pascoe, Maurice, Gideon and Edmund came up onto the deck with the latter two struggling to carry a large heavy barrel. They put the barrel down on the deck next to one of the longboats and started to untie it. Pascoe came up to Captain Sharp and explained his plan.

Back home, when the hunters brought back too much meat too fast, they had been taught to smoke it over a fire in small hand built smokers of wood, leaves, and mud. Pascoe and the other men were going ashore to build some fires to dry out some of the deer meat. The plan was to cut the meat thin, and then dry it all night by keeping the fires burning. A second round of volunteers would come out in a few hours to take over and keep gathering and cutting wood to burn.

"I figured if we were going to start six or eight different fires to dry the meat, you would prefer them on the beach and not on the deck of the Tawny Mane," Pascoe said, smiling.

"You are correct. We used a smoking shack back home to hang meat to dry and be smoked, but I have never tried it on a smaller scale," Captain Sharp said. "Will one night be enough time?"

"There was some discussion on that, that's why we are bringing the cook with us. He will let us know if it is ready or not. We also thought if we needed more time, the ship could sail south without us and pick us up on the way back north," Pascoe said.

"Take two muskets with you, just in case," Captain Sharp said, handing him the keys from around his neck.

"Yes sir," Pascoe said and headed off to join his group. Before long, word of the 'great beach adventure' spread throughout the crew and they had more volunteers than they needed. A second jolly boat was untied and lowered over the side to escort them to the shore. As a sendoff, Captain Sharp told the group that Pascoe was in charge and to follow his orders, and to not catch the island itself on fire. Some of the men looked offended, and the others just laughed. They were already singing before the boats were halfway to shore.

Captain Sharp had a meeting in his quarters later with Pierre, Jim-Jim, Hickory and Bothari. He wanted to know in advance what they thought about the other ship's predicament, and what the Tawny Mane could spare in the way of food if they decided to help the other crew. They also made a short list of the different languages spoken by the crew, and it wasn't much:

English, French, German, Maru, Norwegian, and Spanish. Anything else and they would have to rely on maps and hand waving.

When the meeting was over, Captain Sharp walked on deck and leaned on the rail to see how things were going on the beach. It looked like they had built a total of ten smoking huts about four feet tall. You could just make out the light from the fires under the edges of the huts. Some of the men moved from hut to hut adding wood and plugging holes with grass or mud. Two men on the beach chopped wood into smaller pieces. Another group had moved down the beach with torches to find and collect more wood. The remaining members of the group sat around a large campfire, singing songs and drinking from a bottle that somehow found its way ashore. Captain Sharp headed to bed after requesting to be woken up at first light.

73

The first thing Captain Sharp noticed upon waking up was the smell of smoke. He had a moment of panic before he remembered the smokers on the beach nearby. He got up and dressed in what he considered his formal captain attire, since there was a chance he would be meeting another captain today. Once dressed he signaled August that he was awake and headed onto the deck in the predawn dark. The wind was light this morning, so the smoke sat heavy on the beach and around the ship. He counted four men still on the beach. Three of them sat around the campfire and one of them was stuffing wood into one of the huts. The longboat was still on the beach but the jolly was now tied to the side of the ship near the rope ladder. He thought he recognized Maurice as one of the men around the fire, but wasn't sure. He would apologize later for waking everyone up. "Maurice!" He yelled across the water. The man stood up and walked closer to the ocean. He answered back, but didn't have to yell. The sound carried well over the beach.

"Good morning, Captain Sharp, I hear you quite well. We experimented last night and found that you only need to raise your voice a little above normal and it will be heard across the water," Maurice said.

Captain Sharp lowered his volume way down. "How is the smoking process coming along?"

"It is working very well, great in fact. We unpacked the last of the meat from the barrel a few hours ago. We dried that barrel out and then turned it upside down over a fire to heat it up and finish drying the wood completely. Then we started packing it full of the meat that had already finished drying and smoking. Four of the huts are finished and empty but we still have six of the huts smoking away," Maurice said.

"How much more time do you think it will need?" Captain Sharp asked.

"Two of the huts will be done in two hours, the next two huts need four hours to finish, and the last two huts need another six hours. It was working so well, we brought the rest of the deer meat from the ship that I couldn't fit in the barrel last night. Your crew will be well fed and strong all the way to England, Captain Sharp," the happy cook said.

"Do you need anything before we sail south? Do you need food or drinks? Do you still have the muskets with you?" Captain Sharp asked.

"We have everything we need, thank you. Gideon opted to stay on the beach all night as a guard, so I'm letting him sleep with the other two. I told him I would wake him if he was needed. We have food, water, and a warm breakfast. Just dont forget about us when you turn and sail north," Maurice said.

"Leave without you Maurice? I think my crew would mutiny first," Captain Sharp said. "We'll be back by sundown at the latest. Don't wander off."

They waved in parting, and Maurice went back to tending his fires. Captain Sharp told the crew to get the ship moving south and went looking for August. A few minutes later, Captain Sharp learned that August and Perkins were the other two men sleeping around the fire back on the beach.

74

Two hours later the man in the crow's nest yelled, "ship in view!" down to the crew, but it was another forty minutes before they could see it from the deck. The frigate was bigger and wider than the Mane, with twenty-four guns showing on the side facing them. It had three masts and wide yards. It looked slow and heavy. It flew the French flag, but it was hung sideways with a white flag flying above it. He sent one of the crewmen below to get Pierre, then got his own spyglass to see the ship better. Captain Sharp used his spyglass and saw a crewman on the deck of the other ship using a spyglass to look back at him. Pierre walked up next to the captain and looked at the ship getting closer. Captain Sharp handed him the spyglass and Pierre spent some time looking through it.

"What does the white flag over the country flag mean, and why is it hung sideways? I think I know what it means, but I would like your opinion," Captain Sharp said.

"They are asking for help in two different ways, Captain Sharp. The French flag hung sideways indicates they are in trouble and need help. The white flag above the country flag is meant as a plea, 'we are begging for help.' It would appear we have found the ship in trouble the fishermen were talking about," Maurice said.

Captain Sharp yelled up to Cornelius, who was at the helm this morning. "Bring us up behind her in the cannon's blind spot. Stop and anchor about two hundred feet away. I don't want any of those guns pointed at us, just in case they have gone past asking for help and drifted into desperate need to survive."

It took another half an hour for the Tawny Mane to reach the other ship and get into the position Captain Sharp requested. At two hundred feet, they were right next to the other ship and could see and hear all the people who had come out onto the deck talking and pointing at them. By the time the anchor was set, the deck was jammed with people. Captain Sharp put Pierre on the rail closest to the ship and asked him to listen to what he could hear, but not say a word, or identify himself as understanding French. He asked his crew to put one of the longboats over the side closest to the French ship so the other crew would know they would be rowing over shortly.

Captain Sharp had asked Bothari, Arlo, and Pierre to accompany him in the longboat over to the other ship. Captain Sharp and Bothari had swords and knives on them as part of their standard gear. Arlo brought along a quill and some paper. Pierre brought a large shoulder bag full of treats and goodies as a peace offering, and a bottle of wine from the galley's stores. The four men climbed down the rope ladder into the longboat. Captain Sharp and Bothari paddled them the short distance to the other ship and stopped on the side of the boat where the crew was pointing. Captain Sharp tied off the longboat and climbed up the side of the French ship first. He was helped over the rail by a crewman, who then stepped back and allowed his three companions to climb up also. Arlo was the last up, helping Pierre with his large bag.

Nobody was talking at all now. A man in his forties stepped forward with a big hat with a plume of feathers on the side. He was dressed formally with a velour jacket and rapier sword on his hip. He did a short half bow to Captain Sharp and his men and then started talking in French.

"Je suis Capitaine François Luxembourg du navire Saint Basile," he said by way of introduction.

Captain Sharp stepped forward and held out his hand. "I am Captain Gerard Sharp of the Tawny Mane," and the two men shook hands.

"Pierre, tell them we are here to help," Captain Sharp without looking at his cook.

"Nous sommes là pour vous aider," Pierre said in perfect French.

A cheer went up from the crew and now he was hugged and kissed on the cheeks by Captain Francois. In fact, all four of them were mobbed, hugged, and kissed by just about everyone on the deck. They were all talking to Pierre and he was mostly repeating, "Je vous en prie," which means 'you're welcome.' Eventually the captain shooed his crew away and indicated they could join him in his quarters and motioned for them to follow.

Captain Luxembourg's quarters were huge, with the back half of the room separated by several folding screens of silks. Captain Sharp did see a large canopy bed and desk in the back half. The front half of the room had a library off to the right with two comfortable chairs, and a dining room on the left with seating for ten. The French captain indicated they could sit at the dining table. Captain Sharp put Pierre at the very end of the table. Captain Sharp took the first seat on the right side of the table and let Captain Luxembourg take the first seat on the left side of the table.

Three other men followed their captain inside. Two of them sat at the table while the last man, who was bigger than the rest, took up a protective posture a few steps behind the captain. Pierre had placed the bag on the table in front of him. Captain Sharp pulled the bag closer to himself.

"Pierre, why don't you start with introductions? Make sure you get everyone's name and positions on the ship. Arlo, I want you to take notes so I don't have to. Bothari, watch the big guy and keep smiling. Try to make it the nice smile, not the scary one. I'll start laying out the food now and we can get around to the problems later."

Pierre launched into French and introduced himself, and then Captain Sharp one more time. Then he pointed to Bohari and talked about him some, and then indicated Arlo and gave his introduction. Captain Sharp noticed that the guard moved a little closer to his captain when Bothari was introduced but didn't do anything else.

Captain Sharp pulled two long wood bowls out of his bag and laid them on the table. He took out two canvas bags full of food and transferred small pastries from the bag into the bowls set between the two groups. One bag was full of sugar-iced tarts. The other bag was filled with bite-sized sweet bread. Lastly, he pulled out the bottle of wine and set it on the table in front of them. At this, the captain smiled and clapped. He directed one of his men to a wall cabinet who opened it up and then came back to the table with glasses for everyone.

The French captain spoke, pointing to himself and his other men. Pierre was translating softly while he talked. Francois had been captain of the Saint Basile for three years. Next to him was chief mate Andre Vingneault, and his second mate JeanPaul Lyon. The third man was the ship's doctor, Rene Dupont. The man standing behind them was midshipman Matthias Boucher. He started talking to Pierre and the translation slowed down, but Pierre kept relaying the important parts.

The Saint Basile was bound for Pape'ete and then Australia. They were delivering plant starts. The ship had hundreds of dirt pots in her belly. They had made four attempts to go around the cursed Horn, but were turned back each time. On their first attempt, the head wind and ripping current would not let them gain ground. After hours of pounding, they retreated to the lee side. On the second attempt, they got a split in one of the main sails and had to turn back for repairs. The third attempt was the worst: they were making headway and had just about cleared the alley and were preparing to turn north when a rogue wave hit them from on the port side and washed the deck. Three men went over the side. Captain Franncois yelled for a figure eight and the navigator turned the ship around and cut across their own path looking for the crewmen. They rescued one man, but never saw the other two, and they searched for a long time. The ship returned to the protected side of the island to regroup and mourn their loss. The last attempt was six days ago. They had nearly made it. The ship was making good progress into the breach when they hit a partially submerged tree being pushed by the current. The impact was severe and loosened some boards on the port side near the bow. They were taking on water and were forced to turn around and protect the vulnerable spot.

The captain was worried about his ship, his crew, and his dwindling food and water supply. The plants he carried required fresh water. They had left port with plenty, but the delays were costing them dearly. The captain and senior officers were discussing options, including turning around and sailing east towards Africa and then Australia. They probably didn't have enough food or water for a trip in that direction, but they were starting to think the Horn was going to kill them if they tried again.

Captain Sharp asked through Pierre if his crew had ventured on land to look for food or water supplies. He mentioned seeing a herd of deer on Tierra del Fuego. The French captain said yes, they had searched for streams or rivers, but had found none nearby. As for the deer, his ship only had cannons and swords, and no small arms. They had yet to find any edible plants they were familiar enough with to chance eating.

Captain Sharp asked Pierre to translate as accurately as possible. He looked at Captain Luxembourg and said, "there is a newly discovered ship passage two hundred miles north. It bypasses the Horn and would connect them to Pacific."

Captain Luxembourg had a quick conversation with the man on his right, then asked through Pierre if they were sure this passage actually existed. Captain Sharp said they were very confident, since they had just traveled its length over the last two days.

As this information was relayed, the French captain leaned back in his chair and blew out a breath. The French crew talked among themselves but they were smiling. It looked like a huge weight had been lifted from them. The French captain picked up his wine glass and toasted the men across the table from him. He was speaking in French but Captain Sharp picked out two words he had learned from his cooks. 'Ami et sauveur,' friends and saviors.

They talked for another fifteen minutes. Captain Francois asked about the Mane and her destination. Pierre told them they were traveling from New Zealand back to England with a full cargo. The French Captain thought about this and then asked why they were so far south if the passage was two hundred miles north of them. Pierre translated his question and let Captain Sharp answer it.

"We learned from local fishermen that your ship was in trouble. We are men of honor, and sailed south to offer aid and assistance if we could. All sailors at sea are family, and we help each other," Captain Sharp said.

When Pierre was finished translating, Captain Francois stood and came around the end of the table. Captain Sharp stood just in time to be embraced by Captain Luxembourg.

"Famille," he said.

Captain Sharp invited Captain Luxembourg, his senior staff, and his navigator to come back to the Tawny Mane for directions. Pierre relayed this invitation. Captain Francois said he would be happy to, but first he wanted to talk to his worried crew. They would follow in their own boat in a few minutes.

They walked back on deck and found that everyone was still there, waiting for news. At the rail Captain Luxembourg hugged him again and kissed both cheeks before letting him go. The crew of the Tawny Mane climbed down, untied and pushed off for home. About half way back to their own ship they could hear the cheering from the Saint Basile. It sounded a lot like hope.

Captain Luxembourg showed up fifteen minutes later with Andre Vingneault, who was also his lead navigator, and a new man who was their apprentice navigator. Captain Sharp had Cornelius and Vaheana waiting in his quarters and introductions were made all around. The French crew were stunned to learn that Vaheana was one of their navigators. The crew of the Tawny Mane pretended not to notice. Vaheana asked Pierre to translate for her and Cornelius. She had one of their new maps laid out and rattled off instructions to the two French navigators. They stopped staring and started taking notes fast. Cornelius and Vaheana took turns explaining everything they could about the 'Strait of All Saints' until the Frenchmen ran out of questions. In the end Cornelius rolled up the map, tied it with a strap, and handed it over to Andre from the Saint Basile.

The French navigator was shocked they would give up a map so important and valuable and voiced this to Pierre. It was explained that Cornelius had made a copy of the original and they would be happy to share this with their new family. They asked to see the original and the four navigators compared the two maps. The one they'd given the Saint Basile had Cornelius's new notes, drawings, and firsthand accounts drawn on the back. The French navigators used phrases like 'magnifique' to describe his work.

While the navigators poured over the maps and compared them side-by-side, Captain Luxembourg motioned for Captain Sharp and Pierre to speak with him separately. The French Captain removed his hat and spoke to Pierre before he turned and started speaking directly to Captain Sharp.

Pierre said he wanted all of his words translated as best he could, as they were spoken.

"Captain Sharp of the Tawny Mane, you have saved us today as surely as the sailor we pulled from the sea last week. Our debt to you is immeasurable and weighs heavy on my heart. I would grant you a boon if I could. Is there any way we could repay your kindness?" Captain Luxembourg said.

"No, there is not. I am happy to have made new friends and family. Another ship and captain would have done the same thing," Captain Sharp said and was relayed by Pierre.

Captain Luxembourg shook his head as he replied. "I do not think you have met as many captains as I have. It has been my experience that they look out for themselves only. What of your home port of New Zealand? Could we offer them some of our plants to help them grow food?" Captain Francois tried again.

"New Zealand is not my home port," Captain Sharp said, and then paused. He appeared to be thinking about something, or maybe listening to something.

"Could your home port use some fruit trees? We have bananas, oranges, and even some pineapple starts," the French Captain asked. "I would happily share these with my new family."

Captain Sharp smiled and put his hand on Captain Luxembourg's shoulder. "Do you have time to make a stop between Pape'ete and Australia? It's right along your route."

Captain Luxembourg smiled when he heard this and answered back quickly. "Anything for family."

It took another forty minutes for his navigators to give the directions and coordinates of Pukapuka to the French navigators. In the meantime, Captain Sharp told Captain Luxembourg a brief history of his adventures and his time on Pukapuka. He skimmed over some of the pirate details, but figured Mano and Mr. Kim would fill him in on the rest if asked. He tried to explain that his island was home to him: blood, family, Koko.

In the end Captain Luxembourg said he understood, and would honor and protect Captain Sharp's family like his own. This made Captain Sharp hug him back and thank him.

"This means more to me than you can understand," Captain Sharp said.

The Saint Basile followed the Tawny Mane up the coast and they reached the smoking huts by late afternoon. They quickly stopped to pick up Maurice and the shore party before moving on. The barrel was full of smoked meat and would last as long as they needed. The fires had all been put out, but they left the smoking huts standing in case others might need to use them.

The two ships continued their trip north with the remaining daylight. They were still south of Monte Dinero Bay when they started running out of daylight. Captain Sharp ordered the Tawny Mane moved into the shallows to drop anchor while they still had some good light. He had organized his shooting team before the ship stopped and had sent them ashore as soon as the ship was anchored. They had their regular shooting supplies along with a few the captain had added at the last minute.

They waved the Saint Basile up alongside them and then tied the two ships together with netted hay bales between them as buffers. The Basile was much bigger than the Mane and her main deck was ten feet higher. The crews offset the ships just enough to run a makeshift walkway between the main deck of the Saint Basile and the poop deck of the Tawny Mane. This allowed the crewmen to pass back and forth between the two ships.

Captain Luxembourg was the first over and asked why they had stopped with so much daylight left for sailing. Captain Sharp explained that his hunting team went ashore as soon as they dropped anchor. With a little bit of luck, they would find some dinner they could share. If they heard a shot, they would watch the shore for a flaming arrow. It would mean the shore crew needed help carrying the game back to the ships.

In the meantime, Maurice, Pierre and some volunteers carried trays of meat over to share with the French crew. Captain Luxembourg brought over several bottles of wine to share. The crews moved between the ships, sharing food and wine.

An hour later, it was nearly full dark and Captain Sharp was in his quarters showing Captain Luxembourg the conch shells when they heard the muskets. The captains rushed onto the deck. Captain Sharp told his crew to lower a boat and get ready to go ashore to help carry the game. This was echoed by Captain Luxembourg and his crew got ready to help.

A few minutes later, a flaming arrow was shot straight up into the air from a hillside a mile inland and to their right. Both crews saw it and marked the spot for the responding crew to walk towards. Captain Sharp sent another group of men to the beach to start chopping wood, building a roasting fire, and making more smoking huts. He thought they would groan with the orders, but they were happy to do it. They quickly gathered supplies and headed for the beach.

One hour after that, the first group of men walked back with a deer slung between them. A large canvas sail had been staked out on the ground as the butchering area. Both ships sent tables ashore with their cooks and crew. Pascoe came back with the first deer and immediately began cutting meat, handing it over to the cook's table for slicing. Very quickly the mixed crew from both ships had a series of processing stations working efficiently.

Smoking huts were still being built by a mixed team, but they already had a few burning and smoking. They were just finishing the first deer when the next two groups showed up, each carrying another deer. Crewmen cheered and hooted from both ships. Two other butchers from the French ship jumped in and started cutting up the deer.

The main fire pit was set up to keep everyone warm, and also had a roasting spit installed for cooking fresh meat for dinner. Some of the first meat cut up was put on wood skewers and turned over the fire. The French ship had musicians playing music on the ship and on the beach.

Ambrose came back with the last group. Captain Sharp yelled from the deck of the ship, "Great shooting!" to which Ambrose took a bow.

By the time the last deer was cut up, the crew had fourteen smoking huts working, all in a line. Eventually everyone was either eating, drinking, or dancing. Many of the sailors tried to do all three at once.

Pascoe and Perkins came back to the ship carrying bundles of deer hides to be stretched out and dried. Pasco said they had come across a small stream while looking for the deer. If the Frenchmen had a way to transport water, they could probably fill up their stores overnight. Both Maurice and Pierre were on the beach so it took a while and much hand waving for Captain Sharp to convey this information to Captain Luxembourg.

Pascoe went over to the French ship with Captain Luxembourg, where he organized a group of men who loaded up some skins and barrels and followed Pascoe in jolly boats back to the beach. They made a quick row to the beach, then walked off towards the hillside carrying torches and empty barrels.

The beach party lasted all night long. Throughout the night, an endless stream of volunteers from the Saint Basile carried barrels of fresh water back to the ship, where it was hoisted aboard with ropes. The cooks from both ships worked the smokers, turned the meat, and served people from the spit over the fire. Crewmen from both ships cut wood and keep the smokers and the main campfire supplied. The musicians rotated instruments and songs and kept everyone awake and entertained.

At one point, Captain Sharp sought out Cornelius and found him talking to the French navigators over a map without a translator. He told Cornelius to make sure he got some sleep, since he might be the only one awake and sober tomorrow morning. Cornelius said not to worry and went back to the map with his new friends.

Captain Sharp and Captain Luxembourg put away two bottles of wine between them. For a while, Captain Sharp thought he could speak French. He was apparently very funny, because everything he said was met with laughter from the French crew. The two captains caught one of the boats to shore so either Pierre or Maurice could translate stories back and forth between them. A large group of the French crewmen broke out in song that sounded familiar, but not quite. Captain Luxembourg guided Captain Sharp over to the group where they both sang along, even though Captain Sharp was not sure of the words. This was incredibly funny to the French crew who were laughing and falling over in the sand. After the singalong, Captain Sharp decided he better switch to water instead of wine before he fell off the beach.

Sometime before dawn empty barrels were brought out from each ship and dried before the cooks loaded them with meat that had finished smoking. Two barrels were loaded for the Saint Basile and another half barrel was loaded up for the Tawny Mane. This was completed just as the sun came up. The two groups began moving supplies back to the ships.

It took another hour to clear the beach of crew and equipment. Some men had to be helped up the rope ladder, but most made it on their first try. The longboats were hoisted and secured to the deck by weary eye crewmen. Captain Sharp ordered August to do a face count to ensure they did not leave anyone on the beach. It was a good thing they did. August found one of the French sailors sleeping in an empty bunk on the crew deck. He was helped back up and over to the correct ship.

Captain Luxembourg came over the plank one more time and crushed Captain Sharp in a hug. Maurice happened to be nearby and translated for the French captain this time.

"Never before have I had such a night. My crew will be telling stories of this to their grandchildren when they are old. Thank you, Captain Sharp, for everything: your help, the maps, the food, the water, and the friendship. You have turned our miserable voyage into a joyous one. I look forward to meeting your family on Pukapuka, and I look forward to seeing you again, my friend."

"I thank you for your friendship, Captain Luxembourg, and I look forward to seeing you again. Fair winds and following seas."

"Until we meet again my friend, 'Qui vivra verra'. Only he who lives, shall see."

They hugged one more time complete with 'la bise' on both cheeks. Captain Luxembourg went back over to his ship and his crew removed the boards between the ships. Ropes were untied and the Saint Basile moved a ways off. The Tawny Mane pulled anchor and pointed herself north.

The ships moved up the coastline together all morning and into the early afternoon before Monte Dinero Bay opened up on their port side. The Tawny Mane continued north as the Saint Basile turned west into the Strait of All Saints.

The French crew on the deck yellowed 'thank you!' and 'safe travels!' in English while Captain Sharp's crew yelled back 'au revoir!' and 'a la prochaine!' in French. (good bye and until we meet again respectively) All too soon, the other ship was out of sight and the Tawny Mane headed out into the Atlantic Ocean.

75

There are multiple routes to England from Cape Horn. Each has its advantages and disadvantages. The first route takes them north from the Strait of All Saints, which sits on the 53rd parallel. The route hugs the coast of Argentina and uses the Malvinas Current to push them northward until they reach the 40th parallel. Here the South Atlantic Current and the Circumpolar Current join. Both of them push east. Following this would take them directly east to Cape Hope and the southern tip of Africa. At this point, they would turn north and ride on the Benguela Current that runs north along the west coast of Africa. This would take them to the equator and the doldrums. From here they'd be mostly fighting currents the rest of the way, but should have ample wind once they clear the doldrums. This route was longer but considered more dependable because of the winds coming off the African Coast.

The second route started out the same and had them following the Argentina coast northward. They would sail past the 40th parallel and push against the South Atlantic Current all the way up to the eastern tip of Brazil and the equator. Once they got past the doldrums, they could pick up the north side of the Equatorial Counter Current and be pushed east across the Atlantic to the North African Hump. From here it joined into the first route and they would be fighting currents most of the way home but it was tried and true.

The third option followed the second route all the way up past Brazil and the equator. From here they could swing out into the middle of the Atlantic and ride the trade winds towards Spain and then England. This route went across several currents, but not against any of the major ones. The wind was steady for most of this trip and should allow them to tack in the right direction. No matter what route they took, they would have to deal with the doldrums.

Captain Sharp, Cornelius, Vaheana, Jim-Jim, and Hickory had studied the maps and talked about what was fastest, what was safest, and what was recommended. They decided as a group to go with Cornelius's recommendation that they sail up the coast of Argentina and Brazil and deal with the equator on the west side of the Atlantic. Once past the doldrums they would swing into the Atlantic and sail towards England and home. The wind speeds would drop as they approached the equator and sailing would get slower. Cornelius believed by hugging the coast of Brazil they should be able to capture some on-shore and off-shore breezes each day.

The Tawny Mane had dropped all the canvas she owned, trying to catch all the wind she could. The ship did great for the first six days out of Monte Dinero, averaging six knots and over 165 miles per day. Then they passed out of the Northern Malvinas and ran into the Southern Brazilian Current. Now their speed dropped to four knots and they struggled to get 100 miles a day. They pushed and tacked and fought their way north for eleven days straight without doing better than four knots on any one day.

The ohe hana group worked out every three days. The shooting team practiced one day a week. There were deer hides stretched out and drying in numerous locations on the ship, and several people asked about getting hats, gloves, and pillows made. Even Captain Sharp asked for some pieces of hide to work with to pass the time while they sailed.

One morning they woke and out of the blue, the wind started blowing. The ship was blessed with twenty glorious hours of gusting winds that the crew milked for everything it had before it blew itself out like a candle. They even sailed hard through the night, making sure they were well out to sea when they couldn't see the land anymore. Even though it dropped off sharply at the end, they still finished the day with a seven-knot average.

The next four days were frustrating with just enough wind to keep them from being pushed backwards. They averaged two knots, two knots, one knot, and two knots respectively. They were about to pass the 15th parallel near Rio de Janeiro. That was great news. According to Cornelius, the currents above the 15th were broken and inconsistent. They should be able to make better time right up until five degrees south of the equator. Everyone was looking forward to tomorrow, since it couldn't get much worse than today.

The next day was worse. There was no wind. They dropped anchor to keep from being pushed south with the anemic one knot current. They were less than a mile from shore, near a small island covered with rocks and low bushes. They waited for most of the day for a wind that never came. A few of the crew asked to take the longboat over to the rocky island to have a look around. Captain Sharp denied the request. They needed to be ready to go if the wind picked up.

When they got up the next day, the air was as calm as a wine cellar. Captain Sharp told them to go play on the island. Several boats made the trip. The crew reported nothing much to see, but the sand was a nice change under their feet. One of the groups did manage to find some greens and rooted plants they thought the chickens and Daisy would be interested in. It seemed reasonable since Daisy ate everything. Captain Sharp waited all day on deck looking at the sails. They never moved.

The knock woke Captain Sharp. He could see no light outside his windows.

"Yes?" he called out.

"Light breeze starting up sir. Thought you would want to know," Stephan said from outside his door.

"Thank you, I'll be right out. Does Cornelius know?" Captain Sharp said, swinging out of bed.

"Woke him up just before you, sir. He is on his way up," Stephan said and walked away from the door.

The captain dressed quickly in the dark and went on deck. There was definitely a wind starting up, he could feel it on his face and see the water ripple. He stood next to Stephan, who held a small lantern, the only light on deck. Cornelius joined them. They talked briefly about sailing in the dark.

"This is not my area of expertise, Captain Sharp. you need Vaheana for this."

"Alright then, why don't you head back down and wake her up before you turn in? Send her topside for me."

"Will do. Good night," Cornelius said and headed below.

While they waited, the captain and Stephan talked about the things they'd seen in the days leading up to the stall: rocks and islands off the coastline. There were not that many obstacles, but there were some. With almost no current, there were no waves. With no waves there was no noise or foam. With no noise and no foam, you couldn't hear or see rocks. It was risky at best.

Vaheana walked up a few minutes later and turned to face the wind. She held her hair out and let it fall a few times into the breeze. She looked at the water, the sky, the moon, and then finally at the captain.

"What's the plan?" she asked.

"What are our options for night sailing off the coast? How big of a risk is it?" Captain Sharp asked.

"It's a small risk, but one I think we should take to get out of this wind hole we fell into," Vaheana said.

"I agree. Let's do it. What do you need from me?" Captain Sharp asked.

"I'll need six men in the sails dropping canvas, and a spotter in the nest is a good idea. I'd like Blaed on the bow, he has good ears and eyes. Other than that, I'm ready when you are," she said.

"I'll go get the sail crew moving," Stephan said. "Do you want the lantern?" He asked Vaheana.

"No," she said.

"I meant when you're at the helm for the compass," Stephan said.

"No," she repeated.

Stephan shrugged and headed for the stairs.

"I'll go get Blaed for you," Captain Sharp said.

Fifteen minutes later, they had enough men on the deck to pull up anchor before sending the sail crew up onto the yards. Blaed stood on the tip of the bow with his eyes closed for now. As soon as the first sail was unrolled and tied off, Vaheana brought the ship into a slow turn before getting them oriented and facing north by northeast. When the men started up the ratlines, Captain Sharp quickly lost sight of them against the night sky. He hoped nobody would pick tonight to fall into the deep blue.

The offshore breeze came at them from the land mass on their port side. Once the sheets were tied off at the correct angle, it moved them forward in the near dead quiet. This was a new experience for Captain Sharp; he could feel the wind, feel the movement of the ship, hear the water passing down the side of the ship, but had nothing visually to orient himself with. His stomach did a turnover and he decided he needed a distraction and quick.

He climbed onto the poop deck and stood off to the side from his navigator. He thought she might have her eyes closed, but was not sure in the darkness. He put one hand against the mizzenmast to steady himself.

"Can you talk and sail at the same time?" Captain Sharp asked.

"That's kind of a silly question. Of course, I can talk and sail," Vaheana said with a smile in her voice. "I have been doing it on your ship for weeks now."

"I meant at night," he said.

"Yes, Captain Sharp. I can talk and sail at night," she said. It sounded like she was trying not to laugh.

Captain Sharp took a calming breath and tried not to get frustrated. He was asking the question wrong. He thought about what he was asking and tried a different approach. "Vaheana, I would like you to teach me about sailing a ship at night, as long as it is not distracting you or compromise the safety of the ship to do so," Captain Sharp said.

"Ah, I understand now. Yes, I can talk to you while I sail. Edmund in the nest is my eye, and Blaed at the bow is my ear. I look up every so often to check the stars, but other than that, I feel the wind on my face and adjust our heading. What do you want to know?" the navigator asked.

"Everything. Pretend I have no idea what you're doing, and it's my first time voyaging to another island," Captain Sharp said.

"All right then," she said, and started talking. They had several hours to kill before dawn.

76

They got three knots that first day that started in the pre-dawn dark, and three knots the second day as well. This moved them two degrees closer to the equator and further away from the southern current and the wind hole. The next three days the wind slowed to two knots per day, but it never stopped. That was progress. Captain Sharp now employed Cornelius as day navigator and Vaheana at night. He volunteered to relieve her and Blaed at night for breaks and rest spells. He was learning what he could and asked all the questions he could think of.

Blaed and Vaheana had overlapping areas of knowledge. The captain asked each one to explain the nuances of night navigation to help him better understand it. Their methods differed slightly; he wanted to try both methods to see which worked best for him.

Captain Sharp found he enjoyed sailing at night almost as much as sailing in the daytime. Vaheana encouraged him to take his shoes off at the helm in order to feel the ship better; strangely enough he could. He could feel the slaps of water on the bow, and measure the speed of the ship by their cadence. He was more aware of the wind on his face, its direction and speed. With his eyes closed, he could feel the pressure of the water passing the rudder, and the rudder on the wheel. He felt more connected to the whole process.

His first night at the wheel passed without incident; it was calm, relaxing and peaceful. His second night started out just as well. He was barefoot and relaxed at the helm with both hands on the wheel, listening to the waves and enjoying the wind in his face. He was starting to think he belonged to a secret club of nocturnal sailors who were entrusted to guard the secrets of the dark. He thought of writing this in his log book when Vaheana yelled from the bow, "Hazard! Hard to starboard!"

Captain Sharp looked straight up and got his fix on the stars as he spun the wheel hard and turned them ninety degrees before allowing her to straighten back out.

From the crow's nest a man yelled down. "Sea Stack!"

"Are we clear forward?" Captain Sharp yelled, still pointing the ship due east and further away from the distant shoreline.

"Forward is clear," the nest yelled down. "Two or three spires off the portside now, we should be clear of them in another minute or two. Keep us east."

Captain Sharp opened his eyes for the first time and looked over the port side rail. He could just make out one of the rock columns sliding by, about eighty feet off the side rail. Tall and jagged: ship eaters. His heart pounded in his chest, but he closed his eyes again and tried to breathe easy. He heard and felt the feet coming up the ladder but still didn't open his eyes.

"That was a good turn, fast and sharp. Were you watching the stars while you did it?" Vaheana asked.

"Yes, teacher. I marked my star-map, then spun it ninety degrees, and then came out of the turn neat and clean," Captain Sharp said.

"Good work," she said and then was quiet for a few seconds. "Is Cuthbert building something below or is that your heart pounding?"

"Gonna be really cold when you hit that water, Vaheana," Captain Sharp said, trying to sound calm and relaxed.

In the dark, the donkey just laughed and laughed.

The Mane had two good days of sailing with an average speed of just over three knots, then two great days of sailing with a four-knot day and a five knot day. They sailed along the eastern hump of Brazil, approaching the hip where the land turned sharply to the west just four degrees south of the equator. Just north of the tiny city of Natal, the Tawny Mane broke away from shore for the last time and sailed north by northeast into the Atlantic Ocean and the doldrums.

They caught two more days of nice three knot winds, getting them 82 miles a day, and then four straight days of only two knot winds worth about 55 miles each day. The next two days only puffed out one knot per day as the southern hemisphere ran out of breath and the Tawny Mane stalled on the equator. They went to bed that night with the sails hanging limp, and the ocean as flat as glass.

77

Captain Sharp woke with a start when he heard the yelling and pots banging together. Moments later his door burst open with Bothari, Cornelius, and Maurice all rushing in and telling him to get out of bed and get out on the deck quickly, which he did in just his underclothing. They pushed him out onto the deck just as more crewmen were being pushed up the stairs by a rowdy bunch from below all yelling and banging pots with spoons and shouting.

Captain Sharp, Fetu, Blaed, Vaheana, Kolohe, Pascoe and Dart were all roughly moved to the center of the deck near the port rail while the group howled and banged on pots. Everyone being herded was in their sleeping clothes. Fortunately, nobody was naked this morning. Captain Sharp was about to ask what the hell was going on when Bothari put a hand on his shoulder and shook his head. He leaned over and whispered in Gerard's ear. "This is one of those times where you trust your men. Captain Roche was serious and boring, but Captain Sharp is fun and spontaneous; at least that's what I told the crew. You came to the sea to learn its secrets and this is one of them. Now be quiet," Bothari said.

The crew chanted "Pollywog! Pollywog! Pollywog!" getting louder and faster with each round. When they were all yelling and stomping their feet and could go no faster, a booming voice from the back yelled, "Silence!"

Everyone got quiet. The group parted in the middle. Jim-Jim walked forward wearing an outfit made of grass and seaweed, complete with a headdress. A fake white beard had been stuck to his face. He carried a trident that Captain Gerard had never seen before.

Next to him was Hickory, dressed as a pirate in rags with black paint around his eyes, making him look like a dead man back from the deep. He carried a bag with him and dragged his leg like it didn't work.

Bothari surprised everyone by yelling, "All kneel for King Neptune and Davy Jones!" He pushed Captain Sharp down to his knees with the rest of the pollywogs.

King Neptune and Davy Jones walked up to the group and stopped in front of them. King Neptune thumped his trident on the floor three times. Everyone stood up, but the pollywogs were told to keep kneeling. Davy Jones reached into the bag and pulled out a scroll, handing it to King Neptune who unrolled it for reading.

"Hear ye, hear ye, by order of King Neptune, Lord of the Seas, protector of the water realms and defender of the depths, you are here by charged and must answer to these charges."

"Let it be known that all pollywogs wishing to cross the great line that divides North from South must first present a sacrifice to the Great Sea God. Be ye of strong heart and honest mind, a sacrifice of that which you hold dear in your heart must be made to the creatures of the sea.

"You must first prepare yourself for meeting King Neptune by donning the garb of these sea creatures; the scallywags who plunder at the surface or the sirens who traverse its depths," King Neptune said.

Several sailors came forward and pulled the group to their feet and placed hats, necklaces and skirts on the pollywogs before pushing them back to their knees.

When they stepped back out of the way King Neptune continued. "Only those who have proven themselves worthy with sacrifice and endured the Trials of the Argonauts will be permitted to cross. Davy Jones, the tribute if you please."

Davy Jones reached into the bag and came out with a straight razor and a small cup of grease. He came forward to Captain Sharp and told him to turn his head to expose his neck to Davy Jones, warden of the Land of the Dead.

Captain Sharp turned his head and tried to hold still. Davy Jones rubbed some of the grease into his hair behind his ear, then used the razor to cut off a circle of hair about the size of a pocket watch.

"May King Neptune find this sacrifice worthy." He flung the hair over the rail and into the sea.

All the men on deck yelled, "Worthy!"

Davy Jones went to the next person, repeating the process and when he flung the hair over the rail the crew yelled, "Worthy!" This was repeated for all seven of them including Vaheana who looked a little worried about losing the hair. All seven were deemed worthy. When Davy Jones stepped back King Neptune began reading from the scroll again.

"The pollywogs must now drink the royal tonic out of the Thunder Mug to show their bravery," King Neptune said.

Maurice came forward, wearing a seagrass head-dress he had donned at some point, and handed the large Thunder Mug to Dart at the far end this time. Dart took a drink and immediately started coughing, but managed to hold it in. The Thunder Mug was passed down to each person in turn; each pollywog who drank from it coughed or choked on it. When it was Captain Sharp's turn, he took a mouthful and prepared for the worst. It tasted like whale oil with some hot peppers crushed in it. It was probably the worst thing he had ever tasted. He gagged, but didn't throw up, thank Neptune.

"Pollywogs must be steadfast and endure all trials and tribulations," King Neptune read from the scrolls.

Seven crewmen stepped forward and promptly smashed seven eggs on the heads of the seven pollywogs. This was met with much laughter and hooting from the crew.

"Lastly, the pollywogs must prove their worthiness with a show of strength. Pollywogs will stand on the rail and wait for the proper signal. Once the proper signal is given, the pollywogs will jump into the water and can either swim under the boat to the other side, or must swim around the boat two times before being allowed back on board. Though you enter the sea as slimy pollywogs, you shall emerge from the sea as trusted shellbacks, and Sons and Daughters of Neptune. Pollywogs to the rails!" King Neptune shouted.

The seven pollywogs were helped up onto the rail facing out into the sea. Each wog had a crewman on each side holding their hands for balance so they didn't fall early. All the crew gathered close now yelling and cheering for the wogs to get ready.

"Give the signal!" King Neptune yelled. Each pollywog was slapped on the butt hard enough to propel them forward, into the air. The helpers let go and the seven pollywogs tumbled into the sea together.

The group surfaced to the riotous laughter of the crew up on deck. They looked down at them, yelling "swim pollywogs, swim!" Pascal and Dart were not great swimmers and decided to swim around the ship twice.

"Stay together," Captain Sharp said before they paddled off together.

Vaheana checked the bald spot on the side of her head as the five bobbed in the water alongside the ship. Kolohe looked like he was having a great time. Fetu was smiling, but Blaed looked like he was ready to get this over with.

"Did you know they were going to do this?" Fetu asked Captain Sharp.

"No. I heard rumors about the ceremony before, but had never been part of one. On my first sail south with Captain Roche he didn't encourage that sort of thing, so we didn't do anything. I can't believe August didn't tip me off," Captain Sharp said.

"And risk the fury of King Neptune?" Blaed said with a straight face that made Vaheana honk once.

"All right pollywogs, let's get this over with so we can be treated like normal crewmen again," Captain Sharp said.

"And Sons of Neptune!" Kolohe said and then looked at Vaheana, "and Daughters of Neptune too."

"Ok, let's do this together. Three, two, one!" and they all took a breath and swam down for the keel.

They met up with Pascal and Dart on the other side and decided to keep swimming with them as they went around the boat twice. This gave them more time to wash the egg and grease out of their hair. When they climbed up the rope later after the two laps, they were met with hugs and back slaps from everyone. Everyone was eager to share stories of the first time they 'Crossed the Line' and what they had to endure. After hearing a few stories, Captain Sharp decided they probably got off lucky. Maurice said they were all invited to come down into the galley for Neptune's Feast and there was much cheering and hooting.

78

Captain Sharp updated his log book to record that he and several others had been inducted into the royal order of 'Imperium Neptuni Regis'. He kept reaching up and touching the bald spot on the side of his head. On the bright side, they probably had six weeks before they'd make landfall in England; his hair would be grown out by then. Still, it felt odd and just a little bit cold.

It was late afternoon on the same day as the crossing the line ceremony. Still no wind, but Cornelius said he had a good feeling about the clouds building to the east on the horizon. Cornelius, Vaheana and Captain Sharp spent time double checking their position. They agreed they were between the equator and one degree north. They needed another four degrees or 280 miles to get out of the doldrums.

The clouds built on the horizon for most of the day, but never appeared to get any closer or produce any noticeable wind for them. The sails didn't move; the water didn't ripple. Lots of the crew sunbathed on the deck. It looked like a seal colony in the late afternoon, with bodies stretched out all over.

The next morning was more of the same: hot, dry, breathless, though the clouds to the east did look a little bit closer. Captain Sharp found Jim-Jim, asked him a few questions, then told him what he wanted. Jim-Jim said he could figure something out in about thirty minutes and he would be ready.

Captain Sharp went back onto the deck and asked crew members to move equipment or secure ropes out of the way. He then stopped by his quarters and moved the peg to call for August, who reported shortly thereafter. Captain Sharp told him he needed his whistle and to put it on a lanyard around his neck. August headed down to make it happen.

A short time later, Jim-Jim came on deck with Stephan, who had sewn a canvas ball about the size of a head stuffed with extra material. It was soft enough to grab but full enough to keep its roundish shape. When August joined them, they spent some time going over rules and thought they had a workable plan. Captain Sharp told August to pipe for all hands and he did. The crew made their way up onto the deck and crowded around Captain Sharp and Jim-Jim.

They laid out the game for the crew on deck. Two teams: fore and aft. The object of the game was to touch the ball to the other team's mast. Once you got the ball, you were only allowed to take one step before throwing it to another teammate. If the ball hit the ground, it was the other team's ball. Blocking, body checking, and knocking the ball out of each other's hands was absolutely allowed, but no injuring your fellow crewmate. Captain Sharp pointed to crewmen, counting off fore and aft, separating them into two groups. When that was done, he told the team without Vaheana to take off their shirts to help differentiate the two teams. August handed Jim-Jim the whistle, as he would officiate the first game. The shirtless team was one man short, so Captain Sharp took off his shirt and joined in. They spread out around the deck, talking strategy and tactics. Jim-Jim blew the whistle and threw the ball into the middle of the desk and the insanity began.

Perhaps in retrospect they should have spent more time talking about not injuring your fellow shipmate. Maybe there was some frustration about them not getting any wind in the sails. Maybe they had been at sea too long. Regardless, it turned into a bloody free-for-all in no time. The very first time the ball was passed to Captain Sharp, he was tackled from the side by Bothari before he had a chance to throw it. It knocked the wind out of him, but also got him fired up. Shortly thereafter, Fetu got the ball on the other team. Captain Sharp bodychecked him, knocking the ball free. Jim-Jim was blowing the whistle every few seconds with a foul or violation.

Originally, the game was to last until one team scored ten points, but after about ten minutes, the score was only two to one, and everyone was gasping, bleeding, and hunched over. Captain Sharp tried to rally his side, but they were unable to keep the ball and the shirt team was advancing. Bothari got the ball and Gerard hit him with a flying tackle, but not before Bothari passed and advanced the ball. They scored the third and final point shortly thereafter. Everyone on both sides cheered for the good game.

This was followed by hugging and comparing wounds. It looked like everyone on the deck was bleeding from somewhere: fat lips, black eyes, elbows and knees all skinned up. Elyas might have separated his shoulder, but they were already working on putting it back where it belonged. Captain Sharp thought this might be a one-time only kind of game, considering the damage and injuries his crew sustained, but most of the crew told him they loved it and couldn't wait to play again. Vaheana had a split lip and was bleeding from one knee and one elbow. She said it was the most fun she had ever had. Maybe they could do it once or twice a month, he didn't know how much of a beating they could take and still be fit to sail.

The clouds to the east snuck up on them throughout the day, but took their time about it. It was evening--just past sundown--before they felt the first puff of wind. It came from their side, which set them up perfectly for a starboard tack or a broad reach. Either way, they would get maximum speed and efficiency out of the sails once the wind started.

Three hours after dark, the wind machine turned on and the Tawny Mane jumped forward. They had covered virtually no distance for more than two straight days, but in the next few hours of this day they moved at three knots, then four knots, and then five.

After an early evening nap, Captain Gerard limped out to the poop deck to spell Vaheana. The wind felt warm and heavy and filled their sails like bags of wool. His navigator smiled at the wheel with her fat lip and bare feet.

The captain wanted to check the ship's speed before taking over the helm, so he took out the chip log and spool. He tossed the log over the back and began counting. The chip log was a triangular piece of wood about five inches per side with a string attached. The wood held its position in the water as the ship moved away from it and played out line. The line had knots tied every 8 fathoms, or every 48 feet that roughly counted as one knot of speed per hour. Captain Sharp reached thirty seconds and just afterwards the fifth knot passed through his hands and out into the water. Just under 5 knots. Captain Sharp flipped the lock on the spool to stop the line from playing out, and then started to reel the chip log back in. "Just under 5 knots, that's fantastic."

"Yes. It's been building all evening. It smells like rain's coming too. I think we can squeeze another one to two knots out of the clouds before it peaks though," Vaheana said.

"You got anyone up front tonight?" The moon was three quarters waxing and giving off plenty of light, but the clouds were coming in and about to cover it up.

"Not up front, just eyes in the sky, if they can stay awake," she said smiling. Most of the crew took naps, or went to bed early after the ferocious game of mast-ball this morning. Everyone moved a lot slower, too.

"Do you want a break now or later? I'm afraid if I lay down again, I might be out until noon," Captain Sharp said.

"I'll take it now if you don't mind. I am going to lay down for a few hours. Why don't you have somebody come bump me in about three hours? I should be refreshed and ready to go by then," Vaheana said.

Captain Sharp stepped up and put his hand on the wheel. "Sounds good, have a good rest."

Vaheana headed for the stairs and then said casually back over her shoulder. "That flying tackle you did on Bothari today was crazy. When you both hit the deck, I swear the whole ship moved."

"I hope he is half as sore as I am, that would make it worth it," Captain Sharp said as she climbed down and out of sight. He closed his eyes and kicked off his boots. He let his ears open up and turned his head to better feel the wind on his face. Two days of wind like this and they would be out of the doldrums and reaching for England. England, and home.

The wind held for the next three days before dropping off, but even then it only dropped to three knots instead of disappearing. The three knots' winds held for the next five straight days of smooth easy sailing. Because the wind started out from the east but now blew south to north, it allowed the Tawny Main to cut across the Atlantic faster than they had planned. This cuts time and distance off their original route, but as Cornelius said, you have to take advantage of what the ocean gives you. This morning the wind blew almost due north. Cornelius told Captain Sharp they had options. They were within a day or two of Cape Verde if they wanted to stop for food and water.

Cape Verde is a series of ten volcanic islands laid out in an archipelago 420 miles north and west of Senegal, Africa. Sao Vicente was one of the westernmost islands sticking out into the Atlantic, and it made an ideal stopover and resupplying location for passing ships. The city of Mindelo was one giant harbor, and it was booming with commerce and opportunities.

Captain Sharp called a quick meeting with his staff including Jim-Jim, Hickory, Vaheana, Maurice, Pierre, Arlo, Bothari, Ambrose, and Cuthbert. He wanted to know if they were running short on any supplies, needed anything, or if they thought they could sell some cargo in Mindelo for a better price then they could get in England. Jim-Jim, Pierre, and Bothari had stopped at Mindelo before.

They could always use more fresh water, and they needed some fruits and vegetables. The group agreed that it was worth stopping since they knew what the prices were for their cargo in England five months ago, and in New Zealand one month ago. If they could get a better deal selling here, they would.

Captain Sharp ordered Vaheana to have Cornelius make sail for Cape Verde and Mindelo.

79

The first island that came into view at Cape Verde was Santo Antao. Santo Antao is the westernmost island and the second largest in the archipelago. Sao Vicente was tucked just behind Santo Antao, which protected the port of Mindelo from the worst of the wind and waves.

Cornelius brought the Tawny Mane slowly into the harbor. Immediately, they spotted a long boat speeding towards them head on with six people on board: four men wore rags and were rowing, two others in formal attire barked orders. When the ship got within range, the man at the bow stood and yelled over to the Mane in an unfamiliar language, then yelled in Spanish, and then yelled in English. "State your business!"

Captain Sharp watched the boat approach from the rail. He now yelled back to the small boat. "I am Captain Sharp of the Tawny Mane; we are looking to dock and resupply with food and fresh water. We also have cargo to sell or trade if the market is right."

"Any attempt at sacking or robbing will not be tolerated and will result in your immediate execution," the man at the bow said. He tried to give them the stink eye but looking up from a rowboat had its limitations.

"I did not realize you were hard of hearing so I will repeat myself: we are looking to resupply fresh food and water!" Captain Sharp yelled slower and louder even though the rowboat was much closer now.

"I can hear you just fine, are ya daft?" the man in the boat yelled up.

"I was going to ask you the same question," Captain Sharp said.

"Just so ya know we don't put up with any buffoonery." the man yelled.

"I can assure you we have no plan for any buffoonery," Captain Sharp said and took off his hat in a show of capitulation.

"All right, then. The short pier on the north side of the harbor is for short stops. Take the first open berth you find, the closer to the docks the better. Tie her up yerself. If you cause any damage ya have to pay for it," the man said, already pointing the crew towards another ship behind them.

"And thank you sir for the kind and heartfelt welcome," Captain Sharp said as he made an exaggerated bow with his hat in his hand.

The longboat moved off past them, but the man in the bow of the boat continued to give them the evil eye as they passed. The Tawny Mane moved slowly into the harbor and gently into the berth closest to the docks, making sure not to damage anything.

Mindelo was the busiest port Captain Sharp had ever seen. He counted 36 ships in this part of the harbor, loading and unloading cargo. There was a second harbor further north, separated by a peninsula sporting a stone building called Fortim d'El Rei. It looked like it might have been a castle at one time, but had fallen into disrepair.

Once the ship was tied up and secure, they got two Koa set up on the side of the ship near the dock. Next they organized several teams to go ashore and ask about selling cargo. Jim-Jim had been here before and was paired up with Pascoe. Pierre had been here before and was paired with Gideon. He sent Hickory and August in search of fresh water, and Maurice and Fetu in search of fresh vegetables and greens for the animals. Captain Sharp and Bothari went ashore to look around and see if they could find some buffoonery.

The docks were full of people walking both directions, pulling carts and animals. More than once, Captain Sharp got bumped and felt a hand check his belt for a coin purse. It didn't take him long to get into the flow of knocking hands away and pushing people away for space. He noticed that nobody bumped into Bothari.

There was a farmer's market just off the docks, where tents and carts were set up in rows. They wandered through these for a bit, asking questions about sugar, tobacco, and fleece.

Bothari wanted to stop at the local blacksmith to look at some knives, so they headed that way. The blacksmith building was along the south part of the harbor known as the long pier. The long pier was made for ships being built, repaired and upgraded. Set adjacent to the long pier were several support buildings, including a lumber mill, a textile mill, and the blacksmith's shed. The textile mill was huge and could produce large canvases by the rolls for ships and sails. There was also a metal foundry, where iron and other metals were smelted and cast into ship supplies: chains, anchors, and cannons. Being right on the trade route kept this port busy and growing.

Bothari met the blacksmith Dulce Duarte many years ago and had purchased several knives, spear tips, axes and nails from him over the years. He was a skilled knife maker who took the time to do everything right. Duarte did extraordinary work; it was one of the reasons Bothari bought knives from him every time he was in port. They developed a friendship over the years and Bothari looked forward to seeing him again. The captain and his sergeant at arms walked down the pier towards the blacksmith shop. Bothari pointed out the brick and stone building up ahead and mentioned this was the first time he could remember not seeing smoke or steam rising up from the building's roof.

The twin barn style doors had been rolled open to expose the inside of the shop and let the heat out when the furnace was cooking. The furnace was cold today; there were no customers in the shop. A bored looking man sat at a table in front reading a book. He looked up when they stepped inside.

"What can I help you gentleman with?" he asked.

"I was looking for Duarte," Bothari asked.

"Not here today. What do you need? I have some new knives that you gentlemen might be interested in," he said and waved them over to the table. Captain Sharp went up to the table and picked up one of the knives and looked it over. It was roughly made. He handed it over to Bothari who took one look at it and put it back down.

"When will Duarte be back?" Bothari asked.

"He won't be coming back; he was discharged by the Magistrate for not paying his fair share of taxes. The Ministry of Justice took his store and everything in it. I'm Gil. I own the place now, right down to the hand wrought nails. Do you need any nails?" Gil asked.

"I thought he owned this store outright?" Bothari asked.

"He did, but the new Magistrate Luis de Montalvor raised taxes on everyone who was doing too well, if ya know what I mean. Thought old Duarte was hiding some of his money, so he slapped some new taxes on him. Took him for everything he had and then some. Do you need any trivets? I have some new trivets for your hot pots," Gil asked.

"Where is Duarte now?" Bothari asked, looking angry.

"Last I heard he was living in the rookery. That's the run-down parts where the poor peoples live, over south of the harbor. You sure you don't want a new knife? You look like a knife man," Gil asked.

Bothari picked up one of the new knives and looked at it. "Did you even quench them?"

"What's a quench?"

"It hardens the knife and keeps it from breaking," Bothari said and pushed the tip of the new knife against the table and sideways. The end of the knife broke off with hardly any pressure.

"Hey, you're going to pay for that!" Gil said.

Bothari got in his face fast and was growling. "Were you trying to sell me a poorly made knife that would have broken and got me killed?"

"Why no sir, I am sure that was just a weak spot on that one," Gil said, looking nervous.

Bothari picked up another knife and broke the tip off this one in the same manner.

"Hey!" Gil said, "You need to pay for both of those knives now!"

"These aren't knives, these are garbage. You should consider yourself lucky that I don't break the tip off everyone one of them," Bothari said. He turned and walked out of the store, saying 'let's go,' to Captain Sharp as he passed.

Captain Sharp addressed Gil as he backed out of the store. "I hope nobody reports you to the Ministry of Justice for trying to sell inferior goods to travelers. It would be a shame if Mindelo got a reputation for cheap supplies of shoddy craftsmanship." He tipped his hat and turned to follow Bothari out onto the pier.

Bothari walked south at a good clip and people got out of his way in a hurry. Captain Sharp followed in his wake for a short time, until the crowd thinned out some, then got up alongside his first mate. They were headed south away from the docks, towards a collection of small wood shacks and lean-to buildings. Captain Sharp didn't say anything, for all the times Bothari had his back, he had no problem following Bothari into the slums of Mindelo.

The fourth person they asked pointed to a metal roofed shack further back in the rookery. The building was about eight feet square and less than six feet tall. Bothari would not be able to stand up inside. There were only a few feet between each building. Most of that space was filled up with personal belongings that wouldn't fit inside. Bothari went to the door and knocked before stepping back. A small girl of about five opened the door and looked up at Bothari with open curiosity. Bothari went down to one knee and spoke in a soft voice.

"Duarte?"

"Quem?" the little girl said.

"Dulce?" Bothari tried again.

"Um memento," she said and shut the door.

Bothari stood back up. After a few moments, the door opened and a man with ebony skin stepped out and then stood all the way up. He was as tall as Bothari and wide at the shoulders from a life of swinging hammers. He was bald and wore a simple white shirt and loose pants. He looked back and forth at the two men at his doorway without recollection. Bothari smiled for the first time today and spoke in something local. "Ola meu amigo Duarte."

The man's eyes went wide and he slammed Bothari in a hug. "Bothari, nao morto?" Duarte said when they parted.

"No, I am not dead," Bothari said and started laughing.

Duarte hugged him again, also laughing. After a few moments, he remembered there was somebody else and faced Captain Sharp. Bothari handled the introductions.

"Dulce Duarte, this is Captain Sharp. He is my captain, and the reason I am here."

Dulce shook hands with Captain Sharp and spoke in very good English. "It is a pleasure to meet you, Captain Sharp."

"It is nice to meet you also, Mr. Duarte. Bothari spoke highly of you. I am happy to meet a friend of his. I was sorry to hear you had lost your smith shop to another. The quality has suffered tremendously."

For the first time, Duarte looked sad.

"Thank you, and please call me Dulce. That was nice of you to say, I am furious over what was taken from me, but how does the flea fight the dog? Please won't you come in?" Dulce said and opened the door.

"We would be honored," Bothari said, and ducked inside.

Captain Sharp removed his hat and ducked inside behind him.

The room was actually smaller than it looked from the outside. One wall was stacked with crates full of personal items and clothing. There were two sleeping rolls pushed against one wall, and in the corner the small girl played with some handmade wooden toys. There were already two crates set out to be used as chairs and now Dulce pulled down a third one. Bothari and Captain Sharp sat, trying not to take up much space.

Dulce sat with them and motioned all around him. "Welcome to my home. I am sorry I cannot offer you anything right now, but my wife will be home later. She always brings food and water," Dulce said.

"Wife and daughter, huh?" Bothari smiled. "That is new."

"Yes, Jamilia is my sun and Lea my little star. I was not looking for a wife, but Jamilia was looking hard enough for both of us. They have given my life meaning and made me happy. I could not have endured these recent events without them. So what of you, my friend. How is it you are not dead?"

"That is a long tale if you wish to hear it," Bothari said.

"As it happens, I don't have to work today, so please," Dulce motioned.

Bothari told him the story, starting from the last time they had seen each other, which was two trips before the ill-fated trip on the St. George. He talked about the stops they made and some of the things he had seen and done. He spoke of the shipwreck and Captain Sharp helping them make it to Pukapuka. He spent some time talking about his life on the island and how happy he was and the people who became his family. Then he moved onto the pirates showing up on the Tawny Mane. Captain Sharp noticed that Lea had stopped playing and was listening to every word now.

"I am sorry to interrupt, but I was thirsty and was wondering if Lea could show me where I could buy a drink, and perhaps bring back some for everyone?" Captain Sharp asked.

Dulce looked at Bothari, who smiled and nodded. He then asked Lea if she would take Captain Sharp over to 'Colina de Comida'. Lea said 'yes' to her PaPa and then kissed him on the cheek. When Captain Gerard and Lea stepped outside, the captain asked her if she would hold his hand so he didn't get lost. Lea giggled, then took his hand and headed for the food hill. Lea spoke a little English as her dad used to let her help in the blacksmith shop with customers while he worked the forge. She also used to take the money and give change, she said proudly.

Food hill was a collection of vendors and food carts gathered at the crossroads of the three nearby villages, the rookery being one of them. These carts were all business and none of the frills of the dockside market. Gerard asked Lea what was good to eat and she showed him her favorite: grilled chicken and rice. He asked about drinks and was pointed to another vendor who had tea-water sealed in kegs. He asked Lea if she would help him with the prices so he didn't give away all his money, and she said 'of course.' They bought food first, enough for six people according to the man cooking the chicken. He was nice enough to give Lea a canvas sack to carry it in, as long as she promised to bring it back later. Then they stopped at the tea-water cart and brought the biggest keg that Captain Sharp thought he could carry. Loaded down, they made their way back towards Lea's home with Lea sharing a long list of the things she wanted to eat when she grew up and had money. Lea was too thin for her size and obviously spent a lot of time thinking about food. This reminded Gerard of some of his friends back home growing up, and the street kids he had met in New Zealand. Kids should not have to worry about food all the time. It made him angry that it was not something he could easily fix. It kept his mind off the weight of the barrel of water he carried all the way back to Dulce's hut.

When they got back to the home, Lea rushed in and practically jumped on Dulce. She was excited to tell Papa that they had bought all the chickens and rice that Mr. Danner had brought for that whole day and that Captain Sharp carried home a whole barrel of tea. Captain Sharp put the keg down and rolled it inside. Dulce looked a tad bit overwhelmed.

"I was really thirsty," Captain Sharp said, and after carrying that barrel, he actually was.

They ate lunch on the few plates the family had. Dulce and Lea shared a cup as the family only owned three. Bothari had finished his story; Dulce had been able to tell his own without his daughter in the room. Bothari and Captain Sharp both ate light and kept pushing food back at Lea and Dulce. When questioned about this, Bothari admitted they had a big lunch just before coming to visit, but you could see Dulce saw right through it. They left most of the food and tea behind, because they could not possibly carry it all the way back to the ship. Bothari said he would visit tomorrow as he would like to meet Dulce's wife before they sailed for England. Dulce said he would like that. The two old friends hugged outside the door and both visitors got a hug from Lea.

It was late afternoon before they headed back to the Tawny Mane. It was also a quiet walk back, Bothari was always quiet but this time Captain Sharp was quiet too. Both thought about Dulce, his family, and his lost business.

Back on the Tawny Mane, Captain Sharp and Bothari caught up with the other groups in the galley. Hickory and August secured them two full barrels of fresh water, swapping out empty ones. They made the seller tap them and have a drink first and ended up rejecting the first and third ones because they were green and tasted like pond water. Maurice and Fetu made two trips back to the ship, securing some fruits, vegetables, and leafy greens for the chickens and Daisy. They also picked up two more hay bales for pahi practice and Daisy food.

Pierre and Gideon found a man interested in the fleece sheets. The fleece they found in the open markets was coarse and ridiculously expensive, but still there were people buying it. They had not set a price yet for their own fleece; that was something the ship needed to decide today. They promised the fleece buyer that theirs was of a superior quality and could be resold for an even higher price.

Jim-Jim stopped by three places where he had traded in the past. The tobacco price was about the same as England, but the sugar price was higher here. One of his contacts didn't need any, and a second said he would stop by later. His third buyer had actually followed Jim-Jim back to the ship earlier and looked at the barrels stamped from the New Zealand sugar cane farm. He went back to talk to his supply chain and investor to see what they wanted to order. He said it was likely they would take at least some of them.

Captain Sharp talked briefly about their day and the plight of Dulce Duarte. Bothari uncharacteristically jumped in and took over the story in the middle, saying it was a crime what had been done to Dulce.

They got back around to the fleece sheets and discussed what they hoped to get. Captain Sharp revealed the story this time about the storage barn loft collapsing and the sheets were about to be ruined in the mud. He explained that Mama Ruby had told Captain Sharp to take them now, sell them for whatever he could, and get the money back to her at some point. He thought they should charge Mama Ruby the same discounted rate of 10 percent that they charged Usain, Marcus and Joshua. The crew agreed.

A todd of wool was 28 pounds. Wool sold in New Zealand for 14 shillings per todd. Their bundle of sheets weighed 132 pounds apiece, not easily divisible by 28. Arlo recommended they take three pelts out of each stack, lowering the weight from 132 pounds to 112 pounds each. That would make each sheet exactly four todds. This was agreeable to everyone, especially those who were mathematically challenged. So now they had 112 pounds sheets of wool, or four todd bundles. A todd of wool in England was 22 shillings, last they'd heard. A todd of wool in Cape Verde currently sold at 31 shillings, and it was of poor quality at that. If they could unload their wool for anything above 31 shillings per todd, they agreed it would be a great deal.

Pierre, Gideon, and Arlo were left in charge of the sale of the wool and said they would move all they could, as quickly as possible. They were out of the screaming forties and shouldn't need the added padding between the barrels and the sides of the ship between here and England. Captain Sharp said he only wanted to spend another day or two in Cape Verde if possible.

Jim-Jim's contact Corsino showed up that afternoon to check the sugar they had on board for sale. Sugar on Cape Verde was either four pennies per pound, or five pennies per pound, depending on its place of origin. New Zealand sugar was considered superior; that meant their barrels would be sold at five pennies per pound. While they were talking over barrels and catching up, Jim-Jim's other contact showed up and wanted to see the barrels as well. Blaed was on guard duty and asked Arlo to escort Aristides down below to find Jim-Jim.

As Arlo and his guest approached the two men, Corsino looked up and said out loud "what is he doing here?"

On Jim-Jim's last trip to Cape Verde the two men were friends and occasional business partners. Apparently, that was no longer the case. Aristides inspected the barrel and stamp, completely ignoring Corsino.

"How many barrels of sugar do you have for sale altogether?" Aristides asked Jim-Jim.

"Oh, no you don't. I was here first! Me and Jim-Jim go way back," Corsino said. "How many barrels are for sale?"

Jim-Jim felt trapped and didn't know what to do. He didn't want to upset either of his friends, but could see no way out of their current predicament.

He turned to Arlo for help, imploring him with his eyes. Arlo was the fastest thinker that he knew.

"We have 58 barrels of the finest New Zealand sugar money can buy. The plantation where our sugar was harvested is on the western slopes of the northern island, where there is a third more rainfall than the eastern side, making ours sweeter. The ground there is routinely fertilized with ash from a nearby volcano, making our sugar some of the best in the world. I already have a buyer in England who has promised me six pennies a pound and has asked me to save thirty barrels for him. I would feel awful having to give those up to a higher bidder, but these are tough times for all of us. So let me see, that's 58 barrels minus the thirty makes 28 barrels, and then split two ways is 14. I'm afraid I can only sell each of you 14 barrels each at the current Cape Verdeans market price. It's a shame too; you could easily sell these barrels for considerably more down the line. It doesn't seem fair to me that somebody back in England gets rich, when Jim-Jim's friends are right here right now." He was petting the top of the sugar barrel like it was a cat.

"What sort of contract do you have with this buyer in England?" Corsino asked.

"Well, it's more of a gentleman's agreement, really," Arlo said. "We have been doing business for years together and he has always paid. Well, except for this last time. He refused to pay and that put me in a real tight spot for a time."

"Refused to pay you? How awful!" Aristides said. "Why, that man is no gentleman. You should not allow him to take advantage of you."

"Yes, taking advantage of somebody should be discouraged," Arlo said, with his head bowed.

Jim-Jim pinched the bridge of his nose to keep it together and not break the spell. Arlo was a fisherman. Casting the bait, working the line, twitching the lure: waiting.

Corsino bit first. "I would never forgive myself if I let somebody back in England take advantage of a friend of a friend. How about I match that offer of six pennies a pound? That way you have a sure thing right now, instead of an empty promise later."

"Oh, that's very kind of you, sir. Jim-Jim told me you were a fair and honorable man, but I don't know if my principles would let me," Arlo replied.

Aristides was not to be outdone. "I think Corsino is right. What if that buyer leaves you hanging again? The cost of 58 barrels? Why that could ruin a man! I think it would be a huge weight off your chest if you sold all of the barrels right now to your new friends here in Cape Verdes."

"I just don't know," Arlo sighed. "What if he offers to pay me seven pennies per pound to make up for the last time? Then I would feel like a fool. I just wish there was a way I could be sure it was the right decision."

Aristides gave a head jerk to the side and walked a few steps away with Corsino following. The men whispered back and forth a few times with head shakes and nods.

Jim-Jim leaned towards Arlo. "Never have I heard such a tale . . ."

"Shut up, don't jinx it," Arlo whispered.

Aristides and Corsino walked back together smiling.

The unloading of sugar started late that very afternoon: 29 barrels for Corsino and 29 barrels for Aristides. Both of the traders brought a small army of men and wagons to the pier for unloading. While some barrels were being lifted up and off with ropes and pulleys, other barrels were being carried up the stairs and off the boat by warehouse workers. Each time a wagon was loaded up full it was quickly wheeled away only to be replaced by another team and wagon.

Corsino and Arisides were talking and laughing like old friends with Jim-Jim and Arlo on the deck as they counted off and marked the barrels. Both men returned with bags of money to pay for the cargo. Each of the traders had bought 14 barrels of sugar at the market price of five pennies per pound, and 15 additional barrels of sugar at seven pennies per pound. The total cost for each came to 6,475 shillings, or 810 escudos. Arlo went inside the captain's quarters to quickly count the money, just in case the banks had miscounted. Both men said they understood completely.

The sun went down and it got dark, but the line of carts and workers never stopped. Arisides explained that with a port as busy as theirs, working all night was not that uncommon. Eventually, the last barrel was unloaded and the last cart pulled away. Arlo hugged and thanked his new friends for helping him with such a difficult decision. Arlo promised to come find them first next time their ship made port, and even asked if there was anything special Corsino and Arisides were looking for that Arlo might be able to help them locate. The two traders headed back towards town together, and Jim-Jim and Arlo headed back towards the ship together.

80

The next morning, Pierre and Gideon decided to not wait for the buyer to come to them; they decided to go to the buyer. Gideon loaded one of the fleece sheets on his shoulder and they headed into town. They originally had 64 sheets or bundles of fleece from Mama Ruby. Once they pulled three sheepskins out of each bundle, they were able to wrap another 12 additional bundles, for a grand total of 75 sheets of fleece. Arlo waited at the ship; in case anyone came shopping at the Tawny Mane herself.

Bothari left early to visit his friend, saying he would be back before dark. Captain Sharp asked him if he wanted any company today, but Bothari said no. He and Dulce were going to walk around the island and talk some more. Bothari thanked the captain for the offer and was off.

Not long after Bothari left, Gil the blacksmith shop owner showed up with a local Magistrate and the well-dressed harbor guard from the longboat yesterday. They were stopped at the ramp by Fetu. Captain Sharp came out to greet them and walked them back down the ramp onto the dock to talk. He thought it might have been better to have stayed on his ship, but was trying to keep the scene to a minimum. The Magistrate asked the shop owner if this was the man who vandalized his property. Gil said, 'no, it was the other fella.'

Captain Sharp explained that Gil was being untruthful; there was no vandalism and his first mate Bothari had gone ashore to visit a friend and was not on board. Gil repeated that Captain Sharp and the other man came into his booth yesterday, broke two knives, and then left without paying for them. Captain Sharp explained they had actually wanted to buy a knife, but when they picked it up and pressed the tip on the table, it broke. When they did the same with the second knife, it also broke. Captain Sharp said they would never even consider purchasing such poorly made knives and left to shop elsewhere. The man from the harbor warned Captain Sharp that he would not stand for any buffoonery. Captain Sharp slowly explained that there was no intent to cheat anyone. They just wanted a good knife, not some cheap brittle crap. After hearing both sides twice, the Magistrate ruled in favor of the shop owner who looked quite smug.

"You are hereby ordered to pay the proprietor one- and one-half times the value of the items in question, or face arrest," the Magistrate said.

"So you're telling me I must purchase the two broken worthless knives?" Captain Sharp asked.

"That is correct," Gil the blacksmith said.

"How much were the knives?"

Gil gave a sum that was three times what he was asking for yesterday.

Captain Sharp just nodded. He kept his temper in check and yelled for Arlo to come out with some money. Captain Sharp mentioned that when he got back to England, he was going to have to tell Lord Edward that the quality of goods had become questionable at Cape Verdes. This had no effect on the three men on the docks. When Arlo reached the group on the docks, holding his coin purse Captain Sharp played the only wild card he thought he might still have.

"I will gladly pay you now for the two broken knives. Please hand them over," Captain Sharp said, holding out his hand. From the look on Gil's face, it was a winning card.

"I don't have them with me you fusko!" Gil said.

Gerard acted shocked and surprised at this turn of events. "What do you mean you don't have my knives? You came all this way for the money, and you didn't even bring me my knives? I am certainly not going to give you money for nothing!" Captain Sharp said.

The Magistrate did not exactly roll his eyes, but it was close. "How about if you pay for the knives now sir and the proprietor can deliver them to you later?" He asked hopefully.

"Not a chance, this man is a liar, a cheat, a fraud, a criminal, a rapscallion, a charlatan, a . . ."

"Enough!" the harbor guard yelled.

Captain Sharp stopped, relieved because he was running out of names to call him.

"I warned you, sir, we would not tolerate you and of your buffoonery! Now pay the man!" the harbor guard said.

"I will pay on one condition: my assistant here writes out a receipt, and that Gil, and both of you sign it, promising that Gil will bring me the property I paid for," Captain Sharp said.

"Fine!" the harbor guard said.

The Magistrate nodded his head and Gil threw up his hands and said "whatever."

Captain Sharp said they would be right back. He hustled Arlo back into his quarters and quickly had him make out a receipt. He told Arlo to specifically list the knife with the bleached white bone handle and the second knife with the curved antler handle with a black spot on it. These were not the knives Bothari broke, but two other knives laying on the table next to them. He was hoping Gil wouldn't read it and would be distracted by the money. Captain Sharp rushed back out this time wearing his hat, jacket, and sword. He carried the receipt, a quill, and Arlo brought out some ink and a book to write on.

The captain asked for the boat guard's signature first which he scribbled. Next he asked for the Magistrate's signature and got it. Right before he handed the receipt to Gil he started talking. "I do not have exact change, so I am giving you more money than we agreed upon. I hope that is acceptable," Captain Sharp said. He dumped coins in Gil's hand and held the receipt on the book for him to sign.

Gil took the quill, signed it and dumped the coins in his pocket.

Captain Sharp handed the book, the ink and the quill back to Arlo and sent him off to the ship. He folded the receipt up and tucked it inside his shirt.

"Now that we have that concluded, would you accompany me back to Gil's blacksmith hut where I can recover my property. I fear that he will be less than honest once you leave," Captain Sharp asked the Magistrate.

"Let's get this over and done with," the Magistrate said and the four of them walked towards town.

"Those are not the knives he purchased!" Gil screamed.

"I knew he would try and lie his way out of this," Captain Sharp said calmly.

They were inside the blacksmith booth and Captain Sharp had pointed out two knives still laying on the table. He said offhandedly that Mr. Gil must have fixed them. He took the receipt out of his pocket and handed it over to the Magistrate, who read it with the harbor guard looking over his shoulder.

"I already threw away the two broken knives, I don't have them anymore!" Gil shouted.

"You can hardly see the line where Gil forged them back together," Captain Sharp said, holding the knife up and pointing to an imaginary line for the Magistrate to examine.

After reading the receipt again, the Magistrate and the harbor guard whispered a few times back and forth. Finally, the harbor guard turned to Gil and spoke.

"Give him his two knives!"

"Absolutely not!" Gil said and folded his arms.

"That's fine then, since he already repaired them, I'll just take my money back and we can all be fair and square," Captain Sharp said.

"Wait a minute! I'm not giving him a penny," Gil said.

"I knew it! I knew you were a liar, a cheat, a thief, a crook, a criminal, a rapscallion, a . . . "

"Enough!" the harbor guard yelled again. "Gil, either give him his money back or give him his two knives. You can't have both."

Gil was pink going to purple. He started yelling in a different language and was all but hopping up and down. In a fit of rage, he picked up one of the knives and stabbed it into the table, breaking the tip off. Then he picked up the other knife and stabbed it onto the table, breaking off a larger piece of the tip.

Everyone was quiet for a few seconds until Captain Sharp started speaking calmly. "That man just broke the new knives I just paid for. I either want him arrested or I want my money back."

The Magistrate closed his eyes and sighed, while the harbor guard began yelling at Gil.

After getting his money back, the Magistrate and harbor guard escorted Captain Sharp back to his ship to prevent any further incidents. The Magistrate didn't say a word the whole time, but the harbor guard was full of insults, warnings and out-and-out threats. He recommended Captain Sharp stay on his ship for the duration of his stay so he would not cause any more trouble. Captain Sharp was happy with the moral victory and bit his tongue the whole way home. Once they arrived back at the ship, he thanked both men for helping resolve the misunderstanding and even invited them on board for something to drink and eat. Both men declined and the Magistrate walked away at his first opportunity. The harbor guard made a few more threats, using the word 'execution' three times in his final warning before stomping away.

While the captain was out knife shopping, Pierre and Gideon found a fleece buyer who was willing to buy some fleece. He had 1,000 shillings to spend, and they agreed on eight sheets. The trader had paid Arlo, his wool was loaded and he was already gone.

Pierre and Gideon had then headed back into town carrying the fleece sheet to find more buyers. It had worked so well they also sent out Jim-Jim and Pascoe carrying another fleece sheet to cover more ground. They still had 67 sheets to sell.

An hour later, Jim-Jim and Pascoe came back, followed by a woman driving an open cart pulled by a single horse. Suzanna owned a small shop making handmade clothing and immediately wanted the wool to be spun. She had enough money for 16 sheets that were quickly loaded onto her cart. Pascoe helped her tie it down. She mentioned she was not looking forward to unloading all the sheets back at her shop, so Pascoe was quick to volunteer to go with her and help her unload. She said he was a real gentleman and that would be wonderful. She scooted over to make room on the buckboard. Pascoe vaulted up faster than he had moved in some time. She handed him the reins and he snapped the horses forward, waving to the crew as they turned around. The crew gave him a cheer, and a few discreet hand gestures once the lady's back was turned.

Pierre and Gideon didn't make it back until the sun was low in the sky. They had a well-dressed man walking and talking with them. Captain Sharp was alerted and came out of his quarters to meet them as they came up the ramp and onto the ship. Ovidio Viera worked at the textile warehouse on the far side of the harbor. He wanted to see if all the wool was as good as the sample wool that Gideon carried. They walked down together to the upper holding area where the remaining wool had been stacked. Ovidio pushed his hands into the sheets in several places and felt the wool. He asked how many sheets they had left. Pierre looked at Captain Sharp for an update.

"We have 51 sheet bundles left," Captain Sharp said.

"Okay. I'll be back in an hour," he said, shaking Pierre's hand. Pierre walked him up the stairs.

Gideon tossed his sample sheet back onto the pile.

"How did it go?" Captain Sharp asked.

"Great. We covered most of the warehouses before somebody was kind enough to mention the textile mill on the far side of the harbor. We walked over and asked for their buyer. Ovidio came out to talk to us. He looked at the wool and said if they were all that soft, he would take all we had. He asked how much per todd and Pierre asked him what he thought they were worth. The man put his hands on the wool again and closed his eyes. After a few seconds, he said, '33 cents per todd,' and that was that."

"That's brilliant! You two did great work. Let's get some help and move these sheets up onto the deck before Ovidio gets back with his wagons," Captain Sharp said.

They called for everyone on board to pitch in and had the sheets on the deck in about five minutes. While they waited, Gideon and Pierre traded stories with Jim-Jim and he caught them up on his sales. He then told them about Pascoe leaving to help the little lady unload the wool back home. He wondered aloud if Pascoe would make it back to the ship tonight.

It was easy to see when Ovidio was headed their way. Instead of ox, horses, or wagons, he brought a group of 51 men with him. While Pierre, Arlo, and Ovidio went into the captain's quarters to count out money, each one of the men walked on board, grabbed a wool sheet, and then headed back towards the textile mill. The further away they got, the more it looked like an army of ants moving their cargo around the harbor and into the night. Ovidio left with handshakes. He promised to buy more wool the next time they happened by.

Their cargo had been unloaded at a breakneck speed, and now they were ready to sail for England. The only problem was they were still missing two crewmembers: Pascoe and Bothari.

Bothari came back well after dark, while Captain Sharp was on deck talking to Vaheana. He saw his first mate nearing the ship and Bothari made the hand signal for talk. Captain Sharp excused himself and walked down the ramp to meet Bothari on the docks. There was nobody around but still Bothari moved them to a quiet secluded spot, out of habit.

"I would ask a favor my brother," Bothari said nervously.

This was the first time he had ever asked for a favor, but having all day to think about the situation, Captain Sharp was ready for it. It looked like Bothari was struggling with his request and Captain Sharp owed this man more than could be paid.

"Yes, they can come with us, as far as they want," Captain Sharp said.

Bothari looked up and opened his mouth, and then closed it. He opened it again, then closed it again. He dipped his head to collect himself and then looked up.

"Thank you, my brother, you honor me," Bothari said with conviction, and placed his hand on Captain Sharp's shoulder.

Captain Sharp put his free hand on Bothari's other shoulder. "You have sacrificed everything to protect me and keep this ship safe. You honor me."

The two friends did a quick hug.

"What do you need from me?" Captain Sharp asked.

"Um, not much," Bothari said, and then whistled loudly.

Dulce Duarte, Jamilia and Lea walked out of the shadows towards the ship, each carrying a crate full of stuff. Dulce struggled with two crates, one obviously carried most of the way by Bothari. The captain and first mate moved to meet them. Bothari grabbed the extra crate from Dulce as soon as they reached them.

"Welcome to the Tawny Mane my friends. Koo Koo Kushaw," Captain Sharp said.

Dulce put his crate down and hugged Captain Sharp without a word before stepping back. "Captain Sharp, this is my wife Jamilia," Dulce said.

She rushed forward to hug him before he could say nice to meet you. "Thank you, Captain Sharp," she said in broken English.

"I am happy we are able to help," the captain said and turned to the smallest member of the party. "Hello again, Lea! Can I help you carry that onto the ship? It looks much lighter than that tea barrel," he asked.

Lea snickered, then gave him a hug like her parents. "Papa said I had to carry my stuff all the way to the ship if I wanted to keep it," a determined Lea replied.

"That is true, but you made it to the ship. Now, since I am Captain, I get to make the rules, and my rules say I get to help." He scooped her up in one arm and her light crate in the other arm and headed for the ship. "Did Bothari tell you we have a goat on board named Daisy?" Captain Sharp asked, walking up the ramp.

Jamilia, Dulce and Bothari followed.

Pascoe came back an hour later, looking rumpled and slightly worse for wear. He was given plenty of ribbing before being allowed to go below and sleep, because he was exhausted from 'moving all those heavy wool sheets.'

Dulce, Jamilia and Lea were assigned four empty bunks in the crew deck at the end of one of the rows. All their worldly possessions were stacked on one bed, with Lea in the bunk above it. Dulce had the bottom bunk next door with Jamilia above him. Bothari made sure they met all the crew members and that all of the crew were being friendly. Lea was very excited about sleeping in the top bunk since she had never seen one before.

Now that everyone was back aboard Captain Sharp informed the crew they would push out at first light and set sail for England. They had sold all the cargo they planned to, and restocked everything they needed. The crew was excited, because this was the last leg of the journey, and home was close now.

81

Captain Sharp felt like he had just gotten to sleep when there was a knock on his door. He sat up and saw it was still dark outside. "Yes?" he called.

"Need a word with you sir, it's important," Perkins said.

"One minute," Captain Sharp said and threw on something quick and opened the door.

Perkins was standing outside with a lantern; he was on watch duty tonight with Stephan who was standing nearby.

"What is it?" Captain Sharp asked.

"Begging your pardon sir, some crew members just left the ship and headed into town: Bothari, Fetu, Blaed and Kolohe. Bothari asked me not to tell you, but I told him you were the captain and I had to. He asked for five minutes out of respect and I gave it to him, but you needed to know sir," Perkins said.

"Thank you, Perkins. Looks like we are sailing tonight instead of tomorrow. Get everyone up, but keep it quiet. Get Vaheana on the wheel and some sail riggers in the yards. We are going to be leaving in a hurry. No lanterns and no sound, you got that?" Captain Sharp said.

"Yes sir," Perkins said and headed below.

"Well, shit," Captain Sharp said and got dressed fast. He wore his formal gear. In case he was arrested, he wanted to look his best.

Bothari, Fetu, Blaed and Kolohe walked confidently down the docks and towards town. 'Act like you belong there,' Bothari had said, and they did. There were still some dock workers coming and going but most of them were loaders who paid them no mind. The crew members walked on soft feet anyway and kept to the shadows when they could. They reached the blacksmith shop in less than ten minutes and ducked out of sight while Bothari did a quick walk around the building. The two large barn doors in front were locked with an easy lock, but it was way too visible. The small man door in the back was also locked, but the poorly made lock gave up quickly when Bothari leaned on it. The four men ducked inside. Blaed guarded the door and watched outside like they had planned.

Kolohe pulled three bags out of his shirt and handed them out. Slowly and quietly in the near dark the three men loaded up all the blacksmith tools they could carry: hammers, tongs, files, cuppers, pliers, and all kinds of measuring devices. They loaded up two different sized bellows and managed to fit a foot pedaled blower. When the three sacks were full, the inside of the shop was nearly bare. Bothari handed his sack to Blaed and asked if they were ready. Blaed peeked outside and said it was all clear.

Bothari went to the center of the room and looked at the anvil. It was big, probably two or three hundred pounds. 'That should be no problem,' he thought, and picked it up. 'Definitely closer to three hundred pounds,' he decided as he struggled to get the load up onto his shoulder. Once it was there and secure, he nodded, and Blaed opened the door. The four men walked down the side of the building, checked to make sure it was clear, and then walked confidently out onto the docks and turned north towards their ship. "Slow and steady now," Fetu whispered in Maru, and the four of them walked casually towards the Tawny Mane.

Most of the crew was on deck, but nobody said a word. Vaheana stood at the wheel and several men were already up in the rigging, holding sails. The sails they needed to push back were already half down, waiting to be tied off. The large ropes securing the ship to the dock had been pulled and coiled. Only two small ropes kept the ship against the docks. Those were being held by crewmen on the ship.

Captain Sharp waited near the ramp with two deckhands nearby, ready to replace the ship's railing once the ramp was removed. Things were ready to go. They had only been waiting five minutes when the crow's nest made a soft bird call. Captain Sharp made two hand signals now, the first one was quiet, and the second one was fast. He turned and did it both ways so everyone on deck could see it. Then he walked down the ramp and stood off to the side.

The four missing crew members walked down the dock, then over the ramp and onto the Tawny Mane. As the last man crossed, Captain Sharp pulled the ramp off his ship and laid it on the dock quietly. Then he jumped back onto his ship and made the hand signal for 'go.' The dock ropes were pulled free and the sails were cleated off. The ship backed out into the harbor in a slow turn towards the open sea. When they were clear of the pier and other ships, Vaheana whistled softly once. More sails were dropped and they were angled to push the ship out into the Atlantic.

The island of Santo Antao lay directly in front of them, blocking the direct path northward so they veered slightly to the east and passed it on the port side. There was more wind on the open sea. Once they cleared Santo Antao, they picked up even more speed. The Tawny Mane leaned into the sea and pushed forward into the night.

About the time they passed Santo Antao, Bothari came onto the deck and stood next to Captain Sharp. Captain Sharp didn't say anything.

"I owe you an explanation," Bothari said.

"Yes. You owe the whole crew an explanation. You put everyone in danger tonight, not just yourself. I know he is a friend of yours, but the situation could have been handled differently," Captain Sharp said.

"There wasn't time," Bothari said.

The friends were quiet for a few minutes while Captain Sharp thought about it and tried to figure out what they needed to move forward. "I want you to address the crew tomorrow and explain what you did and why. I am sure they will agree with your reasons, but still, they have a right to know. We have spent much time talking about honor and integrity. I don't want them to think we are slipping down the slope of piracy," Captain Sharp said.

"That is fair," Bothari said.

They were quiet together for several minutes.

"I didn't mean to disappoint you my brother," Bothari said.

"You didn't, my friend. I was just surprised. Surprised you didn't take me with you," Captain Sharp said, and smiled.

Bothari smiled back and it felt like everything was all right.

"Now let me tell you what I did to that asshole Gil today," Captain Sharp said.

82

Although the current was not always with them, the wind pushed sideways and that was good. The Tawny Mane ran a steady northern course paralleling the coast of North Africa. After leaving Cape Verde, they caught two days of four knot wind, then two days of five knot winds, pushing them along nicely. The wind died some after that; they had four straight days of three knot winds on average.

Cornelius recommended they stay well clear of the mouth of the Mediterranean Sea, as that was a hotbed of pirates and desperate men. Their plan was to pass by Funchal, a small island settled by Portugal about seven hundred miles off the coast of Morocco.

They had one terrific day of sailing with six knot winds all morning and most of the afternoon. The ship made great time. Everyone came onto the deck to enjoy the speed and the spray. By late evening the wind dropped down to three knots, but they felt like it had been a good day for miles in the bank.

When Captain Sharp saw Cornelius that afternoon, the navigator mentioned that they should be passing Funchal tomorrow and there were some spire rock formations near the island. Some of them might even be mistaken for pirate ships, if you didn't know better. Captain Sharp thanked him for the information and said he definitely wanted to pass close to them, on the starboard side this time. Cornelius said 'no problem,' he would make sure it happened.

It was close to noon the next day and Captain Sharp was in his quarters trying to copy a map when Hudson knocked on the doorway.

"Yes?" Captain Sharp asked without looking up.

"Cornelius told me to tell you 'contact'. Said you would know what it meant," Hudson said.

"Thank you, Hudson. Tell him the message was received," Gerard replied. He finished the tiny detail of the section part he was working on, then dressed in his formal captain attire. He strapped his sword belt around his waist and put on the black and purple captain's jacket. He grabbed a spyglass and his tricorn hat and was out the door. He went on deck and immediately climbed the ladder up to the poop deck. The first rock formations were just coming into view, still way ahead of them. Deserta Grande Island was part of a rocky spine of three islands making up the Madeira Islands Archipelago. The rocky islands were long, thin and uninhabited.

Cornelius was tacking hard to get on the correct side of the rocky islands, but still had plenty of time. Captain Sharp pulled out his spyglass and looked at the rocky spines as they approached. The first thing sticking out of the water was a tall, thin tower of rocks only twenty feet across at the base. The second and third formations were low, not the right shape. The fourth rocky spine looked like a camel's hump. It was 120 feet long and 40 feet tall in the middle. Captain Sharp scanned the rest of the ridge spines up ahead and didn't see a better target.

He told Cornelius which one he wanted. Cornelius nodded, confirming it was a good choice. It had a good shape and it was thin too. They might just punch a hole in it. The two men discussed how much time the cannon crew should be given and decided four minutes was plenty, if they used the time well.

The Mane moved closer to the west side of the rock formation and were now turning north. They would be passing at a range of about 200 feet give or take. It was time. Captain Sharp rang the bell fast and furiously for a few seconds and then took a deep breath. "Enemy ship off the starboard side! Gunners to your stations!"

Most of the men ran straight to the gun deck instead of coming onto the main deck for a look first. Smudge popped his head up the stairwell, looking for the captain.

"The fourth one, the hump. As many shots as you can fire in one pass!" Captain Sharp yelled.

Smudge waved and ducked back down the steps. He shouted instructions again, but not as frantically as last time. Everyone from below not on the cannon team ran onto the deck including Dulce, Jamilia and Lea. Bothari walked beside them explaining what was happening. Vaheana came up the steps and headed for the poop deck. Dart came up the steps to watch. Captain Sharp told him to stand at the top of the steps and yell below everything that Cornelius yells immediately. He nodded and got into position.

Vaheana was at the wheel, while Cornelius stood beside her talking her through the maneuvers. He looked, judged the distance and then yelled, "Axle out!"

Dart yelled down immediately, "Axle out!" and the ship turned away from the target, bringing her guns to bear. The first shot was always a surprise and this was no different. The cannon boomed. The ship pitched away as the shot flew true and hit the hump in low and in the middle. The rocks hadn't even finished falling into the water when the second shot roared. This shot went low and hit the hump just above the water line near the closest side of the hump. Every person on deck cheered them on.

Cornelius yelled, "Coming even!"

"Coming even!" Dart repeated, and the ship turned to parallel the hump.

The next two shots came out almost simultaneously, with a third shot about one second later. Two of the shots hit true and rocks exploded in a huge spray of dust and dirt. One shot missed going wide off the far side of the hump.

Only a few seconds later, two more shots rang out and the cannonballs hit close to the same spot in the middle of the fan. A huge section of the hump collapsed onto itself and crumbled into the sea. Now the rock hump looked like a wing with a missing feather. Another shot rang out, followed closely by another. One slammed into the hump right where the poop deck would be and the second shot skipped off the water and hit the hump right at the waterline near the bow as the Tawny Mane passed the last of the hump. Rocks fell, the sea splashed, and the crew cheered.

"Axle in!" Cornelius barked, and it was repeated by Dart for the crew below.

The ship turned in again and brought her guns back on target one last time. As soon as it straightened out, two cannons fired, belching smoke trails right into the heart of the hump. The third cannon fired; that ball sailed through the new gap in the hump just made a few moments ago. One last shot hit the back corner of the hump right before Cornelius yelled, "coming out!" and the ship turned north again.

Captain Sharp was very happy. Twelve out of thirteen shots were hits, all in under two minutes. The cannon team came on deck to the cheering of the rest of the crew.

Smudge made his way up the captain and then pulled something out of his ears with his black hands. He showed it to the captain. "We got a barrel of beeswax back in New Zealand. I talked to one of the gunners on the Guinevere. He said they stuff it in their ears before shooting the cannons. You can still hear each other, but it doesn't scramble your brain so much when the cannons fire. I have to say it worked pretty well," Smudge said.

"You did terrific Smudge. 12 out of 13 by my count. That is a great improvement. Your team has obviously been practicing. I appreciate the hard work," the captain said.

"Yea, about that miss . . . I would appreciate it if you didn't mention it to Pierre. He is very upset about it. It was his first time ever firing a cannon," Smudge said.

"Pierre is one of the cannon gunners?" a surprised Captain Sharp asked. He had no idea.

"Yeah, surprised me too. He came to me and asked about the position, then said he wanted to do it. When I asked him why, he said nobody wanted food during a battle. Later on, he admitted he didn't want to feel useless if we were fighting for our lives," Smudge said.

"You tell Pierre I am proud of him. I know he'll get it right next time. I have faith in him," Captain Sharp said.

83

The Tawny Mane sailed smoothly between the island of Funchal and the remainder of the Madeira Islands Archipelago. The wind was intermittent with land masses on both sides of the ship, but once they cleared the north end of the island, they fell into a steady four knot wind with light rain.

By early the next morning, the rain came down hard and heavy. It kept everyone off the deck if they could help it. The wind held at four knots. They rotated navigators every few hours, even though they got soaked to the skin after just a few minutes on deck.

Day three of the rain continued, with gusty winds off and on. The pushes helped them get a six-knot average for the day despite the water-logged ship and crew.

The next morning it dawned overcast and cooler, but the rain had stopped and taken half the wind with it. They only got three knots for the day, but the break in rain gave everyone a chance to walk up on the deck to get some fresh air, and dry their clothing. They strung up drying lines all over the ship, on deck and below. The Tawny Mane looked like a floating flea market.

The sky stayed an overcast gray but the rain held off. They had three straight days of four knot sailing that allowed them to push north and east towards the coast of Portugal and Spain. The trade ship route hugged the western tip of Spain and then cut a straight line across the Bay of Biscay to the western tip of France. The bay was 440 miles across and usually had a steady current pushing south, and a wind pushing east to west. From the western tip of France, it was an easy 135 miles across the English Channel to Plymouth and England. Cornelius said they should be seeing the western shore of Portugal either tomorrow or the next day, as long as the wind holds out.

The sky was breaking up the next morning as they sailed north of the rain and clouds. Not three hours after sunrise, the crow's nest yelled down "land to starboard!" Cornelius and Captain Sharp both spy-glassed the shore to figure out where they were. They passed two large inlets in a row. Cornelius confirmed they were off the coast of Spain, passing the Ria de Muros e Noia inlet where the Rio Ulla river empties into the North Atlantic. This meant they had less than thirty miles until they passed Spain and entered the Bay of Biscay. The Ship was moving faster than they had planned for. They attributed it to the lighter draw after unloading the sugar and fleece.

Six hours later, the Mane passed the Virxe da Barca Sanctuary, a church also used as a navigational landmark. The easily identifiable church had two tall steeples and stood close to the beach, so it was easily seen by passing ships. It was also known as the most western point of Spain, and Europe for that matter. The land was starting to fall away on the east side as they approached the opening of the Bay of Biscay. In the very last cove before the bay, the pirate ship sat and waited.

The ship was tucked back into the inlet two hundred feet, mostly hidden until another vessel passed right in front of it. The ship was only flying one flag and it was black; in the center of the flag was a red heart with a spear through it. As the Tawny Mane passed by the mouth of the inlet, the other crew pointed at them and began shouting to each other. It looked like they were already starting to pull up the anchor before the Tawny Mane passed the opening and lost sight of the other ship. Cornelius grabbed the bell and rang it hard and fast.

Captain Sharp ran out of his quarters and onto the deck to look at his navigator.

"Pirate ship in the last cove, coming after us!" Cornelius yelled. Some crew were coming on deck, while the rest headed for the gun deck.

Captain Sharp looked behind them and didn't see anything, but he knew that wouldn't last. He ran to the top of the stairwell and got loud. "Pirate ship coming up! All hands! I want the cannon gunners on the gun deck right now! I want the shooting team armed and ready right now!"

Everyone on the ship was running. Edmund came up the stairs and Captain Sharp was already pointing at the canvas. "I need your best speed, Edmund and I need it five minutes ago." Edmund never stopped and several other members of the sail team got on the rat lines and scampered up. Ambrose came running up and Captain Sharp handed him the keys on the fly. He saw Gideon and Perkins already headed for the armory from the bow steps.

Smudge ran up onto the deck for a face-to-face with Captain Sharp. "No drill?" he asked.

"No drill," Captain Sharp confirmed. "When we turn to attack, what way do you want us to turn?" Smudge took a quick look behind them: still nothing.

"Let's turn to port, that way we can pin them against the shore and they'll have fewer maneuvering options."

"Perfect. Get your men set on the port side guns. I want every cannon loaded and ready for the turn," Captain Sharp said.

Behind them, the other ship emerged from the cove, dropping sails and turning to give chase. It looked smaller and narrower than the Tawny Mane, but had more guns on the sides, at least 18 on the side Captain Sharp could see.

He turned back to Smudge, who was looking at the other ship with some trepidation. Captain Sharp put his hand on Smudge's shoulder to get his attention back. "Every shot counts now, Smudge, just like you have been practicing. I have faith in you, and so does every man on this ship. When you walk down there and show your confidence, you will inspire confidence in your men. Now go down there and kick some ass."

Smudge smiled, nodded, and headed back down the stairs.

Ambrose, Pascoe, Gideon and Perkins walked up carrying rifles, powder, and a bag full of supplies. They had extra ammo, wadding, flints, rods, and everything else they might need.

"Get on the side back rail and wait for my signal. When they get close, we are going to turn hard to port, so be ready on that side of the ship. What is your maximum effective shooting distance?" Captain Sharp asked.

Pascoe answered for the group. "For all four of us I'd say 200 feet, but I can probably hit from 250 if you need it," Pascoe said calmly.

"Make it 200 feet, then. Every shot needs to find a mark. Call your targets so you don't double up. When I say 'fire', you shoot to kill, every shot, every time. Each man you put down saves lives on this ship. Keep that in mind. Go!" Captain Sharp said, and the group moved to the back of the ship to set up on the port side.

The ship behind them looked closer but the Tawny Mane had just got the last of her canvas down and tied off, she was leaning into the sea and giving what she had.

Captain Sharp used his spyglass on the other ship and counted 31 men between the deck and the rigging. He didn't know how many men were below on the cannon deck. The man at the helm had a good sized hat on. Captain Sharp smiled. That would make for an easy target for his shooting team.

Bothari and Vaheana approached, asking what was needed. Captain Sharp told him to arm everyone on the ship who was not already engaged, and have more swords ready if it came to ship-to-ship and hand-to-hand. He wanted everyone from Pukapuka armed with spears, staffs, and knives. He told Vaheana her primary job was to watch Cornelius and be backup if he was injured. Until then, she needed to be ready to kill, and kill fast. "Nothing half way now. When it comes time, lay them down for keeps," Captain Sharp said.

"Done," Bothari said.

"Yes sir," Vaheana said.

"I want Dart at the top of the stairs. Same deal as last time."

Jim-Jim looked at the other ship through another spyglass. Captain Sharp came up next to him. "What do you think?" Captain Sharp asked.

"Well they aren't flying a 'no quarter' flag, which is mildly comforting. The black flag is not one I recognize. I think it's safe to say if we are caught, most of us are going to be killed and the women will probably wish that they had been," Jim-Jim said.

"That's about what I figured," Captain Sharp said. "I am thinking we should turn when the distance closes to about 250 feet. By the time we come out of our turn, they should be moving just inside 200 feet and Smudge can pepper away until they get turned broadside."

"Probably our best option. They don't know what side to make ready until we turn," Jim-Jim said. "I sure am glad you've been making the cannon teams practice."

"So am I," Captain Sharp said. "Keep watching the deck. Let me know if anything happens that we need to know, and let me know when the distance is under 300 feet."

"Yes, sir," Jim-Jim said.

The Tawny Mane was making her best speed now, but the smaller, lighter ship made better speed. It closed the gap little by little, with nothing but open sea ahead of them. Captain Sharp stood midship and yelled up for Jim-Jim on the poop deck for a distance check and a recount of how many men could be seen. The crew of the other ship could be heard now yelling threats and insults from their deck.

Jim-Jim swept the deck of the other ship for half a minute before turning and yelling his answer. "Distance is just over 300 feet. I count 34 dead men in total!" Jim-Jim yelled, and then paused and smiled at Gerard. "They just don't know it yet."

A roar went up from the Tawny Mane and Captain Sharp knew they were ready. Captain Sharp spoke calmly and quietly to Dart at the top of the stairs. "Thirty seconds now, make ready."

Dart relayed instructions below just as calmly, not loud enough to be overhead. Captain Sharp started a countdown in his own head as he walked towards the poop deck and climbed the ladder to the helm. He got alongside Cornelius and said '15 seconds.' He pulled his spyglass out and took one last look at the men chasing them, threatening them, and wanting to kill the crew.

His crew.

"Hard to port," he said quietly to Cornelius.

Cornelius spun the wheel and the Tawny Mane turned smartly to port. As soon as the ship had gone just past 90 degrees Cornelius straightened back out and the Mane settled flat, level, and broadside to her approaching target.

"Fire!" Captain Sharp yelled.

"Fire!" Dart repeated.

The Tawny Mane roared.

Two cannons fired immediately. One shot knocked a hole in the other ship's bow just above the water line, the second shot missing wide left. Two more cannons fired a second later and both struck the ship as she was starting her turn to bring her guns to bear. Another cannon shot and this one punched a hole in the side of the ship right at the waterline.

There was a two second delay before the next cannon fired and this one sounded different from all the rest. It was a 'burp' instead of a 'boom' as a glob of burning black tar was fired into the sails of the other ship. The tar-soaked canvas cannonball wrapped inside the metal frame pierced the mainsail and set it on fire before breaking up and setting the upper and lower mizzen sails on fire. Another burst of cannons from the Tawny Mane below as two shots rang out, followed by two more a second later.

Before those had even reached the target, the pirate ship fired back with three cannons sounding at once. The cannon balls crossed in the air as two of the shots from the Mane hit home: one skipped and punched a hole low near the stern, and one shot missed high just over the center deck. The first pirate shot hit the Tawny Mane at the bow below the main deck, and the second shot hit her midship and low, just above the water line. The third shot missed as it passed behind them. The ships continued to get closer together and were within 200 feet now.

"Shooting team fire!" Captain Sharp yelled and the shots rang out almost as one. He saw men go down on the deck, including the navigator at the ship's helm. The unmanned ship's wheel spun out of control and the boat turned sharply away from them. The next three cannon shots all missed wide right. Most of the rear sails were on fire now and the crew on the deck were working on cutting the sails down instead of fighting back. The only sails not on fire at this point were the foresail and jibs in the front.

Another volley of four cannons blasted from the Tawny Mane as the pirate ship spun in a slow circle with her guns now pointed in the wrong direction. All four shots connected, with one of them blowing a large hole aft right at the water line. The shooting team had reloaded and fired again; more men dropped on the deck, including the one man who had climbed onto the helm to try and get a hold of the wheel. The ship began sinking steadily as sea water poured into the gaping hole now just under the waterline. Another four cannon shots from the Tawny Mane, each shot found a home with one shot shearing off the mizzen mast and dropping its burning sails across the deck.

"Hold fire!" Captain Sharp yelled and was echoed by Dart.

The big hole in the side of the enemy ship was near the stern. The enemy ship was sitting back on her tail and lifting her bow into the air. Captain Sharp jumped up onto the rail and held onto the ratlines so he could see everything better. The few remaining men on deck of the pirate ship jumped overboard before it got too steep, taking their chances in the sea. They were more than two miles from shore now. Some of them might make it, but only if they were very lucky. The ship had not even completed one full turn, and it looked like it never would. The pirate ship slipped into the sea ass first with a groan and then a hiss as the burning sails were pulled under, leaving only steam, debris, and bodies on the surface. A few were swimming, most were not.

"Nobody fucks with my crew!" Captain Sharp screamed, and the crew of the Tawny Mane screamed with him.

Captain Sharp jumped back down and allowed a few quick hugs with those around him before getting back to work, shouting orders. "Jim-Jim, Hickory, sweep the ship and give me a damage report and check for injuries! Cornelius, get us back on course. Bothari, go below and check on our guests. Shooting team, fantastic job! Get those guns secured and report back to me. Vaheana, Dart, get the swords back in the armory," Captain Sharp said.

A few crewmen were still looking over the rail, but most of them were already getting back to work. Captain Sharp climbed down the ladder and headed down the steps to the cannon deck.

It was smoky down there, but with windows opened on both sides it was well-lit and clearing out quickly. Captain Sharp walked up to Smudge and crushed him in a hug. Then he hugged August, then he hugged Pierre, and everyone cheered.

"You men saved us today. All of us!" Captain Sharp yelled. "Each and every one of you saved us. Hard work, training, courage: it all came together today and paid off. Thank you. From the whole crew, thank you." He started hugging again and made sure he got every last one of them.

84

The Tawny Mane had three holes in the ship that were ugly, but not life threatening. The shot that hit her low put a hole in one side of the ship and a matching hole in the other side, clean through an empty hold compartment. Both holes were six feet above the water line, thus not an issue at the moment. Temporary patches were already being placed over the holes. Permanent repairs would have to wait until they reached England.

The shot that hit them high in the bow had punched a hole into the upper forward cargo hold and obliterated a barrel of tobacco. Four other barrels of tobacco had been knocked over like toys, but were otherwise unharmed. The cargo hold now smelled like fine cigars and a cleanup crew was already working on salvaging what they could. The crew had already decided to turn this sacrificial barrel of tobacco into the crew's own supply of cigars for those who enjoyed the occasional luxury.

Nobody on the Mane was injured, except Elyas burnt his hand while trying to light and load the burning tar shot that set the other ships' sails on fire. The crew decided this did not count as an injury and deemed the first cannon battle a complete success with no injuries whatsoever. Elyas may have thought otherwise, but he didn't complain.

The next two days were clear and the Tawny Mane was pushed forward at four knots with a good wind that slowed to three knots over the next two days. Towards that evening they sighted land ahead and confirmed it was the western tip of France.

Cornelius and Vaheana agreed that they should drop anchor off the coast tonight and wait for first light before proceeding. The western tip of France was speckled with islands, shoals, and reefs; they didn't need to take any chances this close to home.

At first light the next day, the crew was up and dropping canvas early as they moved forward and navigated the Ponant Isles. The Ponant Isles are an archipelago of twenty islands laid out in a diagonal gauntlet off the western tip of France. Easy to navigate in the daylight, much less so in the dark. The Tawny Mane sailed just east of the large island of Ushant and made her last turn towards England, just 135 miles away.

The wind didn't want to cooperate for most of the day; they worked to get two knots out of what they had. Everyone repeatedly came on deck to look around before going back below. Cornelius seemed unphased by the delay and just kept repeating 'tomorrow or the next day.' Captain Sharp stayed up for a while with Vaheana, hoping to catch sight of land, but they were still too far away. After giving her a short break, he went below to try and get some sleep.

Dawn the next morning showed up with gray clouds, but more wind. It picked up to two knots in the morning and was getting closer to three knots by the afternoon. Captain Sharp sat at his desk, making sure the log book and paperwork were up to date. He avoided being on the deck because he got the impression his pacing made the crew nervous. He was nervous.

Five years.

It had been nearly five years since he had been in England, or back home in Falstone. He had worked hard during his first year in Pukapuka to stop thinking about England as it always left him feeling down. Now, he was so close it was all he could think about. He thought about his parents, William and Kathleen. He thought about Lord Edward the Black and Lady Joan. He thought about Lady Sophie. He thought about his forest and the places he used to hunt and hide. He thought about his horse Cork, and his old bow, left sitting in a corner of his old room. He thought about Sophie.

The nest called down, "Land in sight!"

Captain Sharp sat at his desk and counted to one hundred. He forced himself to move slowly and dress slowly: Belt and sword, black and purple jacket, tricorn hat. He walked onto the deck and climbed up to the poop deck with Cornelius. He could just make out the coastline in the distance.

The Tawny Mane sailed into the port of Plymouth nice and slow, with Cornelius at the wheel and Captain Sharp standing next to him. Cornelius pointed out the exact berth they had departed from more than six months before. It was empty today, so Captain Sharp told him to go ahead and put her right back where she started.

Nearly everyone was on deck looking at the city open up around them. For the Sand Maru islanders from Pukapuka, it was the biggest city they had ever seen. There were multi-story buildings everywhere they looked, made of stone and bricks. There were bridges that spanned the river, emptying into the bay: cobblestone roads, wagons and carriages everywhere. And the people! There were more people on the docks than the entire population of Pukapuka. Outfits of every color and design, all the men wore hats.

Bothari stood with Fetu and Blaed, pointing out things and explaining them. Vaheana, Kolohe and Dart stood next to Arlo as he did the same on the other side of the ship.

The crew tossed straw bags over the sides for bumpers as they drifted slowly into the opening. Two deckhands jumped off the side of the ship and onto the dock below, then grabbed ropes to be wrapped around the bollard moorings to slow and secure the ship. Their forward progress was slowed and then halted as the rear line went taunt. The front end was also pulled tight against the side of the berth and then the larger more permanent ropes were used to secure the ship to the dock for the duration of their stay.

A section of the Tawny Mane's railing was removed and a nearby gangway, complete with handrails, was lifted into place and tied down with more rope. Double security was assigned at the top of the ramp, until they had the rest of their cargo handled.

Tanner asked for and was granted shore leave immediately so he could go home and see his wife and kids. He took some money from his ship account via Arlo and thanked the captain for everything before he left.

Captain Sharp sent six members of the crew out to ask about selling their remaining barrels of tobacco: Jim-Jim, Hickory, Stephan, Hans Michael, Edmund and Arlo all knew some people in Plymouth. Arlo also had a second task assigned, as Captain Sharp needed the services of a good solicitor or barrister. He wanted somebody Arlo knew or trusted. Arlo said he would find somebody one way or another. Captain Sharp recruited Gideon and Smudge to take Fetu, Vaheana, Blaed, Kolohe, and Dart on a tour of the city and to get some lunch. Pascoe and Ambrose chose to stay behind, in case their arrival turned out like the one they had in New Zealand.

Bothari escorted Dulce, Jamilia and Lea off the ship for a tour of Plymouth. They planned to ask around about the need or possibility of opening a blacksmith shop.

Cornelius knew the location of the Atherton Trading Company office in Plymouth and said he would accompany Captain Sharp and August, so they could report in and bring the company to date on everything.

Captain Sharp intentionally left the log book behind. He didn't want it to be turned over just yet. He wanted to make sure a few people read it before it fell into the hands of the Atherton Trading Company. It was not like he didn't trust them completely. He didn't trust them at all. He told the security detail to protect the ship. Captain Sharp, August, and Cornelius stepped off the ship and onto English soil.

Home.

85

The office of the Atherton Trading Company was two blocks north of the docks and then another five blocks east on third street. The trip was just long enough for Captain Sharp to outline his strategy to his shipmates. They were going to bring the ATC up to date, but not volunteer anything. They would answer the company's questions, but try to leave out any mention of the cargo the ship carried and they were about to sell. Captain Sharp said he didn't want to lie, but there might be some omissions at this first meeting. The ATC had proven itself to be untrustworthy in their last meeting. Captain Sharp was going into this meeting with eyes wide open. Just as they reached the office, a woman walked outside and slammed the door, looking extremely angry. Cornelius pointed her out and said he recognized her as working for the ATC as a copy girl. She copied documents and maps.

Captain Sharp caught up with the woman walking down the street and asked her for a moment of her time. At first she would not stop or make eye contact with him until he said he had business to do with the Atherton Trading Company and would pay her for some advice. At this she stopped and looked at him and the two men standing behind him.

"How much money?" the woman asked.

"How much would you charge me for ten minutes of knowledge and advice," Captain Sharp asked.

The woman looked him over once before making her decision. "Two shillings, up front," she said, holding out her hand.

Captain Sharp pulled some coins out of his pocket.

"How about two shillings now," he said, putting two coins in her hand, "and two more shillings after your expert opinion," he said, showing her two more coins in his hand. She looked around and then pointed to a fountain nearby with a low wall around it perfect for sitting.

"Let's go sit over there and you can ask me your questions," she said and walked away, making him follow behind her.

Tess Saunders had worked for the Atherton Trading Company for three years. She was known as a copy girl, and made copies of documents, contracts, and the occasional map. She had a flat salary which was next to nothing, but was also paid bonuses on a per sheet basis. Some days she copied several things and made reasonable money, and some days there was nothing to copy. She had been told yesterday there was a stack of items to be copied today and she needed to be here early, but when she arrived she learned another girl had stayed late last night and done the work instead, stealing her bonus.

Captain Sharp nodded at all the right times and told her that was completely unfair. He also thought the other woman should be reprimanded for doing something so underhanded.

Once they had established that Tess had every right to be upset, and that life was unfair, Tess asked him what he wanted. Captain Sharp explained that he had just brought in a ship and needed to check in with the ATC. The old captain had been lost, and he was the temporary replacement. He wanted to know who he should ask for, and who he could trust. He also wanted to know who he should not trust.

He asked Tess if this had ever happened before and she said of course, since they had dozens of ships coming and going all the time. Captain Sharp wanted to know what to expect, and what the company was probably going to do. He ventured that since it was her job to copy contracts, she also read and understood them.

"Yes," Tess agreed, "I read them all, and they are going to screw you."

Captain Sharp and Tess talked for nearly half an hour before he felt he had everything he needed. When they stood to part, he passed her four shillings instead of the two they had previously agreed on. He told her the information was invaluable to him and he appreciated her advice. Tess put the coins in her bag and took a hard look at Captain Sharp one last time.

"They will never let you stay on, Gerard. You look much too young to be the captain of a ship," Tess said.

Captain Sharp opened his mouth to reply when August spoke from behind him, "he has adequate leadership experience."

Back at the Atherton Trading Company Captain Sharp, August and Cornelius walked in and asked for Douglas Kerr. The person sitting at the deck in the front room asked about the nature of their business. Captain Sharp said it was personal but important. They were instructed to wait while another person went to see if Mr. Kerr was in and available. They only had to wait a few minutes for a tall man in his forties to walk out and introduce himself as Douglas Kerr. Captain Sharp asked if there was somewhere private they could talk. Mr. Kerr asked them to follow him back to one of their meeting rooms. They followed Mr. Kerr into the back of the building and into a meeting room with a large table surrounded by a dozen chairs. Once inside with the door shut, he first introduced Cornelius and August as members of his crew. Then he introduced himself as Captain Sharp, of the

Tawny Mane. Mr. Kerr shook hands with the captain and absorbed the information for a few seconds.

"Where is Captain Reginald Dominic?" he asked.

"Have a seat. This is going to be a long story," Captain Sharp said.

Captain Sharp, August, and Cornelius talked for the next twenty minutes straight. A few minutes into it, Douglas Kerr took a notebook out of a drawer and started taking notes. Captain Sharp had just finished with the pirate attack and the subsequent sinking of their ship off the north coast of France. He said the Tawny Mane had incurred some damage and would need to be repaired before their next voyage.

"Where is the Tawny Mane now?" Mr. Kerr asked. It was the first thing he had said since their story began.

"In the harbor, berth 17, the same one she sailed from seven months ago," Cornelius said.

"Why did you ask for me specifically when you came in today?" Mr. Kerr asked. He ripped off his notes and folded them into an inside pocket of his jacket.

"Let's just say I heard a rumor that you were one of the only fair and honest men in the ATC," Captain Sharp said.

"Where did you hear such a scandalous rumor?" Mr. Kerr asked with a smile.

"I went for a swim and a shark told me," Captain Sharp said.

"I think I need some fresh air. How about the four of us go for a walk down to the docks?" Mr. Kerr suggested.

"Excellent idea. I hear walking is good for your health," Captain Sharp said.

The four of them walked to the Tawny Mane together, with Mr. Kerr asking most of the questions. Captain Sharp told him about the log book and said he was welcome to read it back in his quarters. They reached the ship and walked aboard, with Captain Sharp formally welcoming Douglas Kerr. "Welcome aboard the Tawny Mane, Mr. Kerr. Koo Koo Kushaw." He gave Mr. Kerr a quick explanation of the phrase and its meaning to him and the islanders of Pukapuka. Mr. Kerr asked to see the damage. Captain Sharp thanked August and Cornelius for their help and dismissed them both. Captain Sharp led Mr. Kerr to the now empty cargo areas with holes in them. The tobacco barrels had been rolled to another part of the ship after the attack. Mr. Kerr checked the walls. Once he was satisfied, Kerr asked to look at the log book. The two men walked back up the steps and then into Captain Sharp's quarters.

"Wow this is quite an improvement I must say," Mr. Kerr said. "I was in here talking to Dominic just before he sailed and those red curtains were hideous."

"I agree, they were the first things to go," Captain Sharp said, pulling out the log book. "I have tried to put a few of my own touches on the room to make it feel more comfortable and functional." He pulled the galley ring twice and invited Mr. Kerr to sit at the maps table. Mr. Kerr had opened his mouth to ask about the ring when Maurice walked in with two full trays.

"Good afternoon, Captain Sharp. I have an assortment of snacks for you and Mr. Kerr, along with your tea. Let me know if you would like lunch or dinner delivered and Pierre and I can facilitate that," Maurice said. Captain Sharp was not the least bit surprised his cook already knew Mr. Kerr's name. Maurice poured tea, set out plates, and was gone out the door in under 90 seconds.

Captain Sharp gave Mr. Kerr the short version of the bell and invited him to have a bite while he read. The captain had opened the log book to the day Captain Dominic picked up the pirates from their sinking ship.

Mr. Kerr read some, skipped around, flipped pages. At one point, he walked over to the bookcase and opened up the not-so-secret compartment, which was empty, of course. Captain Sharp went over to the corner of the room and opened up the floorboard compartment to save time and show him that it was also empty. Mr. Kerr sat back down and skimmed the log book up to the current day.

"Extraordinary work Captain Sharp, I commend you. Might I inquire as to your current plans?" Mr. Kerr asked.

"I would like to continue to be Captain of the Tawny Mane. The crew and I have bonded. I care about this ship and her crew. I think I have demonstrated competence and skill already. That will only improve with time. I was hoping to visit my family for a short time since repairs will be needed before the Mane is ready to sail again."

Mr. Kerr looked thoughtful for a few moments and then frowned. "While I appreciate everything you have done Captain Sharp, I don't think the ATC will keep you on as captain. I think you are a good man, but they have other captains under contract they are more . . . comfortable with. It's all about money with them."

"I understand. I anticipated some difficulties upon our returning to England," Captain Sharp said. He looked at Mr. Kerr and decided to take a chance on him.

"May I ask you something?" the captain said.

Mr. Kerr nodded for him to go ahead.

"What would you put first: the crew or the money?" Captain Sharp asked.

"The crew, always. A good captain will always turn a good profit," Mr. Kerr said.

"In that case, let me tell you a few more details about our trip, to see if there is anything you can do to help me keep this ship and crew, and make the Atherton Trading Company some money at the same time," Captain Sharp said.

He told Mr. Kerr about the coconuts and the conch shells. He told him about the harassment and attempted arrest from the ATC in New Zealand. He told him about punching out Mr. Astor. Mr. Kerr laughed, since he had met the man in the past. He told Kerr about retaining a solicitor and bringing charges against the ATC. He pulled out three pieces of paper and let Mr. Kerr read them. When Mr. Kerr was done, he looked up at Captain Sharp in a completely different way. Captain Sharp then told him about the original contract offered by the ATC, then the contract that was eventually signed and notarized. He slid this document over and let Mr. Kerr read it.

Then he told him about the sugar, tobacco and wool. He said they would be selling the tobacco in the next day or so and the ship would be empty. Unfortunately, those goods were purchased by him and his crew, and the profits would be divided between him and his crew. The ATC had sacrificed a huge profit by not trusting him and trying to cheat him. They would probably be sacrificing huge profits in the future by not trusting him now. He was also undefeated against attacking pirate ships, which was not something most other captains could claim.

When he finished talking Captain Sharp sat back and sipped his tea, letting Kerr digest his argument. After a minute or so he asked his question again.

"So what do you think Mr. Kerr, can you help me keep this ship and let me make you some money?" Captain Sharp asked.

"You better start calling me Douglas, because we are going to be spending a lot of time together."

"In that case, you can call me Gerard. I would appreciate your discretion on these documents. I do not plan on using them unless forced to do so. Because the ATC has already lied, cheated, and made false charges against me, I feel strongly that a magistrate would rule in my favor. All I am asking is that I be allowed to remain captain, and keep making you money."

"You make a strong argument, Gerard. I respect you, and I like your style. I will help you all I can, and get out of the way if I can't," Douglas said. "I am going to report you as arriving tomorrow morning first thing. You should expect a visit from some of the senior staff five minutes after that. Until then, I recommend you move your cargo quickly. They are called ATC for two reasons: people who know them well call them 'Atherton Trading Company'; people who know them very well call them 'Assholes Thieves Criminals'. Just so you know who you're getting into bed with."

"Great! Something to look forward to," Captain Sharp said.

86

Arlo came back with a barrister he introduced as Rory Hughes. He dropped Hughes off in the captain's quarters, said he would be back later and walked right back out. Captain Sharp introduced himself and asked Mr. Hughes to sit down. Mr. Hughes said he could call him Rory and they both sat down at the maps table. Captain Sharp asked if Arlo had explained the problem. Rory replied that he had no idea why he was here. Captain Sharp sighed, then asked if he wanted tea. Rory declined, so Captain Sharp got right to the issue.

Captain Sharp was getting better at explaining the story quickly, cutting out the unnecessary parts: he became captain, sailed to New Zealand, ATC tried to fire him, filed false charges, He sued, he wins, carries signed court documents, and sailed to England. ATC wants to fire him again. Options?

Rory asked to see all the documents from New Zealand. Captain Sharp passed him over the stack, including the captain's employment contract, and the stipulations of his contract being terminated. There was the shipping profit agreement that the ATC missed out on since there was no room for any of their cargo in the end. There were five false allegation judgments against the four individual employees of the Atherton Trading Company, and then the one against the ATC itself.

"Very well prepared," Rory said.

"Thank you, I had some help," Captain Sharp said.

"Can I take these documents with me tonight?" Rory asked.

Captain Sharp hesitated. "I know Arlo trusts you, but I met you just fifteen minutes ago. How exactly do you two know each other?"

"Arlo is my uncle. He helped pay my way at the university and law school."

Captain Sharp pushed the documents across the table to Rory. "Don't lose them, they are the only copies I have."

Captain Sharp told Rory the senior staff from the ATC would be here first thing in the morning. He wanted to know what his rights and options were. Rory said he had to get back to his office and talk with his partners before they left for the night. He said he would be back first thing in the morning, hopefully before the ATC arrived. Captain Sharp told him he would provide breakfast. Rory said that would be great and put the papers in his folder and stood. After a quick handshake, Captain Sharp walked him out and down the ramp.

Three of his crewmen were having an argument just a ways down the dock, and the captain headed that way. Hans Michael, Hickory, and Edmund were all yelling and waving hands when Captain Sharp approached. Each of them found buyers for the tobacco barrels, and two of the buyers were on the way. Each of the men told the other that they should have checked back in before committing to the sale. This would put them all in an awkward spot.

Jim-Jim ran down the dock and yelled to the group when he saw them. "Hey guys, I found a buyer for the tobacco!"

Captain Sharp ordered everyone back to the ship, so they could figure this out, then called Arlo into the circle to help come up with a solution. Arlo got it worked out fairly quickly. He had everyone go intercept their potential buyers and tell them the tobacco had unintentionally been promised to multiple sources due to the need for a rapid offloading. Each potential buyer would need to make a best bid offer; one of those would be accepted immediately. Nobody was thrilled with the solution, but it was the best they could do under the circumstances.

Jim-Jim, Hickory, Edmund and Hans Michael headed out with instructions to be back in thirty minutes with offers. Captain Sharp broke the fortunate news to the two groups who showed up with wagons to unload the cargo. He was as civil as possible, explaining the situation to the workers, but once the insults and threats started, he told them they could either wait or leave, he didn't care, and then walked back onto his ship.

The two groups of dock workers had nobody to yell at except each other, so a fight broke out within minutes. Constables were summoned and arrived in less than five minutes, breaking up the disturbance. The constables separated the two groups and made them stand one hundred feet apart while waiting for the buyer news.

Hans-Michael came back first and reported that his buyer was not interested in a bidding war and would only offer 200 shillings per barrel. Edmund came back next with an offer of 266 shillings per barrel, with a cap at 20 barrels. Jim-Jim's buyer offered 280 shillings per barrel, up to 30 barrels, and Hickory had found a buyer for 270 shillings per barrel with no limit.

Arlo got to work on the math after sending Edmund down to the dock to tell his crew of dock workers they were not needed. Jim-Jim was told to return to his buyer and have them send workers and wagons as soon as possible. Arlo also wrote him out a quick purchase order for 30 barrels of tobacco at 280 shillings per barrel, for a total price of 8,400 shillings.

Hickory told his team of loaders they would be unloading 20 barrels of tobacco as soon as it was paid for. One of the men headed back to his buyer with an order sheet for 20 barrels at 270 shillings per barrel for a price of 5,400 shillings.

The crew on the Tawny Mane got to work rigging the ropes and pulling the barrels up from below. One of the loaders was good friends with Hickory and asked if they could start loading directly onto the wagon since his team had already lost time waiting around. Hickory passed the request onto Captain Sharp who approved it, but said the wagon couldn't leave until the money was here. It turned out to be a non-issue as the buyer with the money showed up before the wagon was even half loaded. The wagons could hold six barrels each but the crew foreman asked for a 7th barrel to be set on top of the load and tied down. This would save them one extra trip. Since it was already paid for, the ship's crew got them loaded up and the first wagon under way shortly. The second wagon was already waiting and moved into position. It went much faster this time and they had another seven barrels loaded up before the first wagon had offloaded and returned. They had about ten minutes of down time until the first driver and his team showed back up for the last load of six barrels. Since they had already been hoisted up onto the deck, it was a quick transition to the wagons.

It took less than 90 minutes to get these first 20 barrels unloaded. Captain Sharp was thrilled with the speed they were moving. If they could not sell and unload the tobacco tonight, he had planned on finding a vacant warehouse nearby and having his crew work all night to move the cargo before the ATC showed up in the morning. He wanted the ship nice, clean and empty when they showed up. First impressions and all.

It was getting dark when Jim-Jim came back riding in the bucket seat alongside the buyer of his tobacco barrels. It was a small wagon, and there was only one of them. He was met by Captain Sharp and Arlo as the crew got to work loading him up. Mr. Thompson only had one wagon and it only held four barrels at a time. He also did not have anyone to help him unload his wagon once it got back to his tobacco store. Mr. Thompson and Jim-Jim planned on asking some of the crew if they wanted to make some side money to follow them back and help unload by hand. This was given the go-ahead and four volunteers were chosen from the crew. Mr. Thompson went into the captain's quarters with Arlo for the money exchange while his first four barrels were loaded up. By the time Mr. Thompson's money was counted, the barrels were loaded and the crew were finishing tying them down. Mr. Thompson headed back with his four volunteers, while Jim-Jim stayed back on the ship. Captain Sharp told Jim-Jim that all the barrels needed to be gone before morning, as the ATC were swooping in like vultures. Jim-Jim said it should be no problem, but he would keep an eye on the situation.

Most of the crew were asking for shore leave. Captain Sharp granted all of them, except the few guards and the men needed to load the remaining barrels. Several crew asked how long they would be in port and if he knew where their next voyage would be. Captain Sharp told them all he should have more answers tomorrow after his first meeting with the Atherton Trading Company.

He gave Maurice and Pierre a heads up that they might have a handful of guests for breakfast tomorrow morning. Maurice asked if they would be friends of foes and Captain Sharp said 'probably a little bit of both.'

He found Hickory and asked him to oversee a ship wide cleanup for an inspection tomorrow morning. Hickory asked who was going to inspect the ship. Captain Sharp told him about the boat's owners and investors. These same people would probably decide if he was hired on as full-time captain.

Hickory said he understood completely and would make the boat shine before morning. Captain Sharp thanked him in advance, and said he appreciated it.

Lastly, he went to find Arlo. They needed to find someplace to put all this money building up on the ship.

87

Gerard and Sophie had just crossed a ridge and stopped for a short break and a drink of water. Gerard excused himself to use the privy and walked a short distance away to a cluster of trees. He heard Sophie give a surprised yell and started running back as fast as he could. When he got back to the clearing where he left her, she was just gone. There was nothing to see and nothing to hear. Her pack was laying on the ground next to the log. It was his fault. He should have . . .

Captain Sharp woke up in a sweaty panic. In his nightmare he had just started screaming her name; he was hoping he didn't yell it out loud on his ship. He kicked off the sheet and waited for the dawn to come.

Captain Sharp was up early and dressed in his best clothing. He figured he would need to look as well as act the part today. He knew this was going to be a challenging and frustrating day. The half night of sleep was not going to help.

Jim-Jim informed him that Mr. Thompson had left with the last load of tobacco about two hours before. They changed volunteers after the third trip to let them get some sleep, and to give the other volunteers a chance to make a few coins. The second group of volunteers were already back and sleeping. Jim-Jim was headed off to bed himself, unless the captain needed him. Captain Sharp told him to go to bed; he would wake Jim-Jim if there was an emergency.

Rory Hughes showed up bright and early with an older man who he introduced as Foster. He did not indicate if this was a first name or last name, and did not elaborate on the man's reason for being here. He handed Captain Sharp back his documents and said he had made copies for himself if they were needed later.

"Something I forgot to mention yesterday; I need a retainer from you to officially be your solicitor. Foster also needs a retainer for this to be official," Rory said.

"Absolutely, I understand. How much do you need?" Captain Sharp said and braced for the worst.

"One gold coin," Foster said, "Apiece."

Captain Sharp just looked at him and waited for the explanation.

"It's an old superstition of the trade. Any man can sell his soul for one gold coin," Foster said.

Captain Sharp went into his pockets and found two gold guineas. He handed one to each man and was given a handshake and thank you in return. Captain Sharp invited them to the galley for breakfast and to wait for the rest of their morning guests. He didn't have to wait long. The shouting at the gangway had him moving before the second crewman could walk down and let him know a group was demanding to be let aboard.

When Captain Sharp got on deck, he found Fetu struggling with two men trying to push their way past him at the top of the gangway. There were four other men lined up behind them, waiting to get onboard, including a smiling Douglas in the back. Captain Sharp easily slipped up next to one of the struggling men and grabbed him. In one quick move he spun the man around to face his friends and put a knife on his neck and pulled it tight. There was a shout of "No!" from one of the men on the ramp and the second man stopped struggling and stepped back.

Captain Sharp allowed a few seconds of quiet before he started talking calmly to the group. "By what authority do you attempt to force your way onto my ship and assault one of my crewmen?" One of the men on the gangway started to speak but Captain Sharp cut him off with a yell. "Shut up! I wasn't talking to you. I was talking to this man who I'm about to kill. This is my ship, and property of the Atherton Trading Company. Any attempt to steal from this ship or harm my crew is punishable by death," Captain Sharp said.

"But he is an employee of the Atherton Trading Company!" one of the men on the ramp yelled.

Captain Sharp waited for a few seconds, then calmly asked, "Then why is he forcing his way onto my ship and assaulting one of my crew?"

"Because your man would not let us onto the ship immediately," said the older man on the ramp.

Captain Sharp lowered the knife a few inches but did not release the man in front of him. He addressed the older man in front of him now who seemed to be the person in charge. "Can you tell me, sir, what happens when a person forces their way into the offices of the Atherton Trading Company building, pushes his way past your security, then assaults one of your employees?" Captain Sharp asked.

"They would be arrested and jailed by the local authorities," the older man said, understanding the issue now.

"On this ship I am the only authority." Captain Sharp said and brought the knife back up to the man's neck who gasped. "The next time you assault one of my crewmen, I will kill you. Do you understand me?"

"Yes sir," the man squeaked out.

"My name is Captain Sharp."

"Yes Captain Sharp, I understand," the man said.

Captain Sharp lowered the knife and pushed him hard into the other man who had been trying to get on board. He waited until that man made eye contact and then held it. "I hope you were paying attention, because that was your only warning also." Now he turned his attention to the older man standing in front of him on the ramp. "Let's start over: I am Captain Sharp of the Tawny Mane, and you are?"

"I am Durbish Clarke of the Atherton Trading Company. May we come aboard?"

"Absolutely, everyone is welcome except those two," Captain Sharp said. "I wouldn't want them getting killed by accident." Captain Sharp stepped aside and waved the four men forward, while the two men who had been refused permission made their way back down the ramp and onto the docks. Captain Sharp introduced his first mate Bothari and his assistant August who stood next to him. He saw Rory and Foster watching from across the deck.

"Would you like to join me in my quarters where we can sit and talk?" Captain Sharp said.

"That would be fine thank you," Mr. Clarke said.

Captain Sharp led them into his quarters, followed by August and Bothari. Bothari just happened to have a sword on his hip and took up his casual lethal stance against a wall. Captain Sharp and August sat at the maps table; Mr. Clarke and his men followed suit. Introductions were made all around, nobody spoke but Mr. Clarke.

"Can I interest you in some tea, or maybe breakfast? My chef is really quite fantastic," Captain Sharp said.

"Tea would be lovely, thank you." Mr. Clarke said looking around the room, he had obviously been in here before and was noticing the changes. Captain Sharp got up and pulled the ring once before sitting back down. Maurice breezed in moments later with his usual flair and set down mugs, pastries, sweets, breads, tea and napkins. He asked if they wanted breakfast and the captain said 'not just yet,' but he would ring if they needed anything. He thanked Maurice for his outstanding work as usual and said he was a credit to the ship. The cook bowed and closed the door behind him.

"Has Mr. Kerr brought you up to speed, or were you looking for the story first hand?" Captain Sharp asked.

"Mr. Kerr informed us just this morning that the Tawny Mane had returned and there had been a change in captains, but not much else," Mr. Clarke said.

"Yes, we got in rather late last night. I think I caught Mr. Kerr just as he was leaving for home," Captain Sharp improvised. "I didn't give him a full report, but promised to do so today."

With that, he asked August to start the story from its beginning. August told his part, and then Captain Sharp told his. He told them about the coconuts, but skipped over the New Zealand cargo. He skipped over helping the French ship Guinevere, but included the pirate battle from a few days ago. As he wrapped up, he went to his desk and pulled out the log book and laid it down in front of Mr. Clarke. He had a ribbon in the place where Captain Dominic met the pirates and opened it there.

Mr. Clarke asked if they could check the hidden compartments, and Captain Sharp said they were welcome to do so. One of the men got up and checked the bookcase door first, then the floorboard hatch second. Both were empty.

Mr. Clarke scanned through the log book when he asked why they didn't take on any cargo when they left New Zealand.

"I couldn't afford the loss. I was willing to buy cargo with my own money, but Samuel Astor is an arsehole." Captain Sharp pulled out the first contract offered to him in New Zealand and handed it over to Mr. Clarke. He read it and frowned several times, sighed twice, then handed it to one of his colleagues to read.

"It became so adversarial that I had to hire my own barrister and draw up a contract so I could remain Captain of the Tawny Mane. Part of that contractual agreement was that any cargo I bought and sold would be 95% mine, with 5 percent going to the Atherton Trading Company," Captain Sharp said.

This was news to all of them. Mr. Clarke sat forward and asked if they could see these contracts. Captain Sharp went over to his desks and pulled out the two documents he had set aside last night. He laid these two on the table in front of Mr. Clarke, then picked up the contract they had finished reading from earlier. This he put back on his desk and under the sand dollar.

"This is most unusual," Mr. Clarke said. "And yet you have no cargo?"

"Actually, after that contract was signed, I did purchase all the cargo I could afford on my own. The crew pooled their money and purchased some cargo as well. The remaining cargo space was sold to a local group of investors I found in New Zealand," Captain Sharp said and sipped his tea.

"Where is this cargo now?" Mr. Clarke asked.

"Already sold; Most of it in Cape Verde, the rest of it last night to a local buyer," Captain Sharp said.

"Exactly how much cargo was sold?" Mr. Clarke asked.

Captain Sharp got up and took the two contracts from them and returned them to his desk. He then pulled out the last document he planned to share with the men from ATC today. It was an invoice for all the sugar and tobacco sold that the ATC had a right to claim a 15 percent profit share. Captain Sharp watched him read the numbers and then arrive at the total at the bottom of the page. Mr. Clarke looked up at him.

Captain Sharp reached into his shirt and took out the leather pouch on a cord around his neck. He leaned forward and placed it in front of Mr. Clarke with a soft 'clink' as the coins hit the desk.

Mr. Clarke had no problem dumping out the coins and making sure the total matched the number on the invoice. It did.

"And this was 15 percent?" Mr. Clarke asked.

"Yes. It would have been much more money for you if Mr. Astor had not lied, cheated, and been such a boil," Captain Sharp said. "Now, how long will it take to repair my ship and where are we sailing too next?" Captain Sharp asked.

Mr. Clarke didn't have an answer for either question. He did send one of his men below with August to check the damage to be able to give a full report on it later. Apparently, the question of Captain Sharp remaining captain was not up to him. Mr. Clarke would need to take it up with the board. Captain Sharp nodded. As for how long until the board was likely to make a decision, that was also unknown. The meeting broke and Captain Sharp escorted the men out onto the deck. Standing near the stairs were Arlo, Rory and Foster.

Captain Sharp apologized for interrupting their breakfast and both men said it was no trouble. They enjoyed catching up with Arlo and hearing some of the stories from their recent voyage.

Mr. Clarke and his men had started to leave when he saw the group and stopped by to join them. "Foster, what brings you here?"

"Captain Sharp has retained my services in the event of any unpleasantness with his new employer," Foster said, his face blank.

"I see," Mr. Clarke said, "Good day, gentlemen." He walked off the ship.

"What was that?" August asked about the exchange.

"A warning shot across his bow," Foster said, and smiled.

Ambrose, Pascoe and Fetu had left the ship together earlier while Gerard was still in his quarters with the ATC. They had been gone for nearly two hours before the three came walking back together. Captain Sharp was on the deck looking at the damage to the side of the ship close up. The temporary patch boards had been removed and the full extent of the damage could now be seen. It looked like a good-sized strip of both outside paneling and inside paneling would need to be peeled back and replaced to make the repairs seamless and sound. His three crewmen walked up and asked how the meeting with the ATC had gone. Gerard said he should have kept the knife to their necks a little longer, it might have worked out better for him. He explained that everything was up in the air, and they probably wouldn't have any answers for weeks. Gerard was going to try hard to forget about it for two months and let Rory and Foster worry about it instead.

Gerard asked the group what they were up to and Ambrose gave a big smile.

"My brother Gilford and his wife have a farm in Brixton just east of Plymouth. We took over all the hens and the two roosters this morning to add to their farm. They have five boys all under nine years old. I told Gilford he could keep them, eat them or sell them. Whatever helped them out the most. We can always get more chickens before our next sail and now we don't have to take care of them for the next two months," Ambrose said.

"I also took Daisy to the farm," Fetu said, looking embarrassed. "I hope you're not mad. She chewed out of her harness the other night and ate one of Vaheana's spears and one of Lea's toys."

"I'm not mad my brother, I'm relieved. Maybe a seafaring trade ship was not the best place for a goat that likes to eat wood," Gerard said with a smile.

"I wanted to make sure it was a good home for Daisy and it was. The boys all fell in love with her the moment they saw her, and Gilford said he had a wire cage so she could sleep in the house at night," Fetu said.

"That was a good decision, Fetu, and perfect timing. I was already thinking of getting you a fire breathing dragon as your next pet," Gerard said with a straight face.

"Wow, you really can buy anything in England," Fetu said.

Douglas Kerr stopped by a few hours later and slapped Captain Sharp on the back first thing. "That was quite a performance earlier today. Durbish didn't know what to make of you, but I think he was impressed. I still don't think it was enough for you to keep the ship. It was a good try though."

"Well I have not played all my cards yet, and I do have a way of persuading people. Do you have any good news, or any usable news?" Captain Sharp asked.

"Actually, yes," Douglas said. "I have two big pieces of news you'll want to hear. The first is that repairs will take 50 days, and they should be getting started the day after tomorrow. The second bit of news is I know the next destination of the Tawny Mane. It's Fiji and Australia," he said with a smile.

88

Captain Sharp called a meeting for all hands on the main deck so the Koa guarding the ship could hear. They waited for a few people to get back from leave, but eventually they had everyone on board except Tanner, who had already gone home. The crew quietly waited for the captain to begin.

"Repairs on the Tawny Mane will get started in the next few days and are expected to take fifty days. You are all officially off duty as of tomorrow. You are welcome to go anywhere. You can travel, and you can visit your families. You are welcome to stay on the Mane and do absolutely nothing for fifty days. However, in fifty days I would be honored if you returned and chose to sail with me again. The next destination of the Tawny Mane is Fiji and Australia. There is a very good chance Cornelius will get lost and we will end up at Pukapuka for a visit." Captain Sharp waited while they laughed and hooted.

"Arlo credited the last of the money into everyone's accounts this morning. You all have choices: you can take all of it, some of it, or none of it. Arlo will be staying at his brother's house here in Plymouth, and has your money with him. You can get more money whenever you want, but only for one hour at breakfast, one hour at lunch, and one hour at dinner," The crew laughed at this since it was the same speech Arlo had given multiple times a day, every day, since being named the ship's accountant.

"As of now the Atherton Trading Company doesn't know if I will be allowed to remain captain of the Tawny Mane. I can tell you that I am not the least bit worried. I have been here before, and I have cards yet to be played. You all know how good I am at persuading people. I have retained the services of the barrister Rory Hughes and Foster to look after my interests while I am away. I have every confidence that when the Tawny Mane sails again, I will be her captain," he finished to some applause.

"In the meantime, I plan to go home and visit my parents. They may be under the false impression that I was lost at sea some five years ago; I intend to prove that to be untrue." More cheering and hooting.

"There is a passenger ship leaving tomorrow for Newcastle. The voyage only takes three days, and from there it's a day's ride to my home. I plan on being home in four days."

Captain Sharp grew emotional but tried hard to keep it together until the end.

"For those of you with nowhere to go, you are welcome to travel with me. My hometown is small, quiet and boring, but the food is good and the company is excellent. There is hunting, fishing, and horseback riding . . . as long as my parents have not sold my horse." Everyone laughed again. "This crew has been a family these last few months, and I am proud of all of you. If you are interested in spending a few weeks in the county, you would be welcomed in my home. It is an honor to call you my family."

89

Pale came to collect Mano from the Kupuna's hut while he was holding court and settling disputes. Pale waited for a break in the stories before telling Mano he was needed elsewhere. Mano let another Kupuna take over and slipped out the side to talk with the head Koa on the island. A ship and sails had been spotted and appeared to be headed for the island. Pale had already requested four of his Koa to meet them at the lagoon as a precaution. The two men walked towards the beach, talking about nothing until they reached the spot where the tree line ended and the beach began.

The other Koas waited just inside the tree line, and out of sight of the approaching ship. Mano and Pale joined them and the group watched the ship work its way around the shoals and head for the opening of the lagoon.

"No boat in five years, and now two boats in half a year. We may need to build a dock to keep up with all our visitors," Mano said, earning a smile from Pale.

"What are your thoughts?" Mano asked.

"Cautions as always," Pale said. "The visit by the pirates is still fresh in the minds of our people."

"Of course," Mano said, "but new friends would be welcome, and could help us all move past that dark spot in our memories."

"Only the sea will see," Pale said.

The ship moved slowly into the lagoon and dropped anchor in the middle. A few crewmen were getting a boat over the side, but most of the crew was along the rail looking towards the beach and tree line.

"Interesting," Mano said. "I wonder what they are looking for."

"Time to make an appearance?" Pale asked.

"Yes, let us welcome our guests and see if they would be our friends," Mano said.

Mano and Pale walked out of the tree line and onto the beach, where they could be seen from the boat. Immediately a cheer went up from the crew on the deck. They waved at the men on the beach. Some sang in a foreign language while others just cheered and waved.

"Well now, that's interesting," Pale said.

"I think it's French," Mano said.

Mano waved back at the ship and the crew went absolutely crazy, jumping up and down, cheering and waving back.

"Have you ever had something like this happen before?" Pale asked.

"No, never," Mano said, and kept waving.

It was the strangest meeting he could ever remember having. The jolly boat was lowered into the lagoon and four men climbed inside. They started the slow row into the beach with two men on the oars and two men sitting near the bow. One of the men held onto his hat so it didn't blow off. It had a huge plume of feathers. When the boat reached the sand, the two men in front jumped out and helped pull the boat higher onto the sand. The rowers got out and the four walked towards the two islanders on the beach.

Mano and Pale had been waiting near the tree line to give them some room, but now walked forward to meet them in the middle. The six men came together on the beach and stopped a few feet apart. The crew on the ship quieted with their approach and now there was no sound at all except the waves lapping on the sand.

Mano was about to speak and offer his usual greeting when the captain of the visiting ship beat him to it. The captain removed his hat and spoke in broken English to the men from the island.

"Are you Mano?" The captain of the ship asked.

"I am Mano," the kupuna said, taking a half-step forward.

The captain of the ship smiled and opened his arms as wide as he could. "Koo Koo Kushaw," he said.

Mano smiled, then he started to laugh. His laughter was loud and contagious. He walked forward and enveloped the ship's captain in a hug.

346

The crew on the ship cheered, the warriors came out of the trees, and the family on the beach met for the very first time.

Made in the USA
Monee, IL
30 December 2021

87481321R00193